SWEET
FRICTION

Other Marcus Van Heller titles available from Carroll & Graf:

Seduced
Unbound
Venus in Lace

SWEET FRICTION

by

MARCUS VAN HELLER

CARROLL & GRAF PUBLISHERS, INC.
NEW YORK

This collection copyright © 1997 by Carroll & Graf Publishers, Inc.

All rights reserved.

First Carroll & Graf edition of *Lusts of the Borgia*s 1992.
Lusts of the Borgia was previously published by Carroll & Graf as *The House of Borgia*.
First Carroll & Graf edition of *Adam & Eve* 1985.

Carroll & Graf Publishers, Inc.
260 Fifth Avenue
New York, NY 10001

ISBN: 0-7867-0451-9

Manufactured in the United States of America

CONTENTS

Lusts of the Borgias   7
Adam & Eve   353

LUSTS OF THE BORGIAS

LUSTS OF THE BORGIAS

VOLUME ONE

CHAPTER 1

When she was only ten years old Cardinal Roderigo had doted on the remarkable physical development of his daughter and now, at the age of eleven, he thought of her as a fresh, young woman with her breasts and buttocks as full as cannonballs.

But it was not only her voluptuous dimensions which produced the burning erection under Roderigo Borgia's robes every time he watched her playing in her little girl's shift which seemed so unsuitable. It was the deep, knowing look in those bright blue eyes, which seemed to look past his apparent paternal smile and see the incestuous desire beyond. And in the look was the hint of a smile, as if she were daring him to translate his desire to action.

Of course, Cardinal Roderigo was aware that his own feelings interfered with his objectivity of vision. It was hardly likely that his daughter, raised in a true God-fearing way, could really have the faintest inkling of the lustful labyrinths of men's minds. And yet there was a definite sexual aura about her which he could not reconcile with his imagination, nor with her youth.

He sat on a log in the grounds of their house near St. Peter's watching her playing now with her brother Cesare. Cesare pushed the swing while she, with her shift above her knees and her legs apart as she urged it to greater heights, sat on the wooden platform as if on a horse.

The paternal smile was fixed on Cardinal Roderigo's face. Any observer would have felt his heart stirred at the sight of the busiest, most important cardinal in Rome, relaxing with his children. But through that smile, the

Cardinal's eyes dwelt on the uplifted breasts as she reached upwards, holding the ropes of the swing. Their outline was forceful; they seemed to spring out towards his eyes. It suddenly occurred to him that she hadn't put on her undergarments today.

"Higher, higher," she urged her brother.

Even the voice, he mused, was that of a woman; it had body and modulation. It had a soft, caressing warmth, the way her flesh would be if it nestled nakedly against one.

The swing was mounting. Back and then forward toward him. His eyes dropped to her well-formed legs. She squirmed her bottom on the swing, exhorting it with passionate fondlings to fly up and up. The Cardinal found the movement exciting. He imagined, tried to imagine, the feel of that bottom against his loins. He stared at her hips. His face colored slightly. He could see right up those delicious, milky thighs to the darkness of their junction. Oh those thighs! He raised his eyes guiltily, with an effort, and saw that hers were on him, lids slightly lowered, suggesting a smile. He started. The little minx. She was positively inviting him. He was convinced of it.

"Lucrezia, my child," he said. "Have you no warm clothes under your shift?"

She squirmed her bottom and kicked her legs forward, urging her mount on.

"No father. It's so warm, today."

"It's not a question of warmth, my sweet one. It's unladylike to be naked under such a thin garment. It shows off too much of your body."

He enjoyed this sort of conversation. It was fatherly because he was, after all, speaking to his little daughter for her own good; it was also rousing because he was speaking to an unknown woman about her raw beauty. It could be indulged in with safety.

"I thought it wouldn't matter," Lucrezia purred. "There is nobody to see me but you and Cesare."

"Paternity and fraternity, my dear, do not turn men into marble statues."

He continued to look at her, suddenly, overwhelmingly aware that he was talking to no child at all. He was talking to some strange, instinctive essence of woman which needed no experience to know about the effect of the apple. She looked back at him, unspeaking, her eyes sphinxlike, her thighs still wide, her arms relaxed a little on the ropes so that her breasts jogged slightly as she jerked forward.

Roderigo glanced past her to Cesare. His son was two years older and as beautiful as his sister. But he was not so aware. Even now, he seemed not to have followed the conversation. He concentrated, grinning, on his job of hurtling Lucrezia up to a horizontal sweep. His secret ambition was to see her swoop right up and over the bar.

"You must always wear underclothes in the Orsini Palace," the Cardinal said, determined to keep the conversation going. "It would be unbecoming to your tutors to treat them like suitors."

She stared at him for a few seconds as the swing flowed forward and back. He knew she was working over his words, but she was clever enough to make it appear that she understood.

"Passion is a poor accompaniment to scholarly disinterest," he pursued, reveling in the train of his thought, the sequence of images—of tutors mixing Greek with French in confusion, while his daughter calmly surveyed their discomfiture with deep eyes and a half-shown bosom.

"Will study make me scholarly and disinterested?"

You precocious little bitch, he thought. I ought to spank you—but I should ejaculate over your flushed buttocks even as my hand lashed them.

"You are too bursting with the good things of life," he answered.

"Cesare," Lucrezia said, "I want to come down."

Reluctantly Cesare caught the swing, moved back and forth with it, slowing it. With the courtesy he'd always been taught, he moved around and lifted his sister down. She slipped down him, still watching her father. Her limbs seemed to cling to her brother's like slowly relaxing rubber. As her feet reached the ground she looked up at his face suddenly and her round mouth parted in a smile to which her brother responded.

Her father saw the smile and sensed the desire behind it. But his son, he saw, was not awakened to his young sister's potentialities.

He looked at Cesare. The boy was already tall and sturdy. He must have had sexual desire, must experience it often, but it did not focus on his sister. A pity, the Cardinal decided. The little witch needed to know what it was like and she had a bit of a crush on her brother —that he had noticed in years gone by.

Cesare would be more or less of a handsome stranger to her of course, away as he was most of the time, studying at Perugia. An idea occurred to him and he smiled at it. He would open Cesare's eyes to the little fruit that his sister was. She would, surely, do the rest without any encouragement. Then, when she had been deflowered by Cesare's growing manhood, the way would be prepared for his own full organ to enjoy an hour or two of passion with her.

"Why don't you go and bathe in the pool," he suggested. "Take off all your clothes and let the sun fill you with goodness."

Lucrezia looked quickly at her brother. Cesare looked at his father. A number of unuttered questions clouded, uncomfortably, in his eyes.

"Oh, don't worry," the Cardinal said paternally. "There will be nobody to see you and you are well sheltered by the pergola."

Cesare continued to look uncomfortable and his sister caught his hand.

"Poor Cesare. I think he's embarrassed," she said innocently. "Why are you embarrassed, my darling brother?"

Cardinal Roderigo heard the innocent-sounding words mincing provocatively from her pretty lips and smiled inwardly. He wondered just how far her mind went, how much of the next hour or two she anticipated.

"Embarrassed," he roared, with mock impatience. "Of course Cesare's not embarrassed. He has too fine and athletic a frame to be embarrassed to let his little sister see it. Give her a spanking Cesare when there's nothing to protect her—and then duck her head in the pool."

Cesare smiled. He was still embarrassed, but now he dared not show it. His father's praise of his body had pleased him.

"I'll make her scream for mercy," he boasted.

"Mind she doesn't make you scream for

mercy," the Cardinal muttered more to himself than to his son.

"Off you go now," he urged. "I have some work to do."

He watched them run off in the direction of the pool, Lucrezia leading, her buttocks straining against the shift as she moved, laughing over her shoulder at Cesare, who followed, smiling, superior in the knowledge that he could overtake her as he wished.

The Cardinal waited for several minutes before he followed them slowly through the grounds, stepping quietly toward the pool.

The pool was surrounded by a covered walk with a single entrance at one end. The Cardinal pushed his way gently through the trees and bushes bolstering the trelliswork. He crouched and peered through the rose-twined woodwork to where the clear, blue pool glittered in the sunlight.

Cesare was immersed in the pool, keeping to its edge, obviously still embarrassed at his sister's presence. She, however, was standing on the marble surround brazenly drawing her shift over her head.

Cardinal Roderigo's eyes became transfixed. She threw the shift down on a wooden seat and stretched, looking down invitingly at Cesare. The curves of her body were generous, her waist tight and slim, breasts opening out like an enormous flower above, hips vying with breasts for roundness and maturity below. The sun, which turned her golden hair almost silver, made her pink flesh shine with an almost luminous whiteness. The large red nipples stood out astonishingly dark against the white background and the down at the solid triangle between her thighs was another quick flash of silver.

If I had been more thoughtful, Cardinal Roderigo told himself, I would have got rid of her nanny and her maids and enjoyed the sight of her womanly body often before.

Lucrezia was walking along the edge of the pool away from Cesare, staring up into the sun, opening her arms to it like a lover. Her buttocks bulged under the slimness of her waist, stretching one against the other as she moved, her legs tautened, hard and slim and then relaxed as each swept forward with her step.

Cardinal Roderigo was hot all over, and sweating between his thighs. His eyes gloated over the fullness of her body, the movement in it as she moved, little eddies of shadow, ripples of half-formed muscle. He watched her parading for Cesare's benefit as if she were an experienced harlot and he was amazed. The little bitch really needed it good and hard and deep enough to make her tremble from her toes to her golden plaits.

Cesare, too, watched her every movement. His own nakedness had suddenly made him aware of hers—as a woman, not as his sister. He clung to the edge of the pool whose water was so clear that if he moved out into the middle she'd be able to see him just as he could now see her.

Lucrezia turned and walked back toward Cesare.

"Isn't it lovely not to have any clothes on?" she called out. "I feel like a nymph."

"Hurry up and come in," Cesare answered gruffly. "The water's warm."

"Why do you sound so cross?" she pouted. And with a quick movement she swept her little foot down into the water beside him and shot a spout of water into his eyes. Cesare gasped, released his hold on the side and plunged out into the center of the pool. The shock of the attack robbed him of his embarrassment.

"I'll get you for that," he called, laughing.

You'll get her anyway, the Cardinal chuckled to himself. He was envying his son the view he must have had of Lucrezia's soft, little vagina as she stretched her foot down to splash him.

"I don't care. I'm not afraid of you," she cried, laughing too. And with that she gave a neat little dive down into the pool, out of sight of both father and son.

Leaning forward, the better to see, Cardinal Roderigo heard his son shout and saw him begin to flail his arms as he disappeared under the water. In another second Lucrezia shot to the surface and broke into peals of laughter at her skill in ducking her brother from underneath.

Cesare came to the surface, furious now at the impudence of the trick. He began to race toward his retreating sister.

"I'm going to spank you as father said," he cried. "And then I may kill you as well."

Shrieking insults, Lucrezia turned her back on him and swam with all her strength to the edge of the pool. She reached up, gripped the edge and hauled herself out, lying along the marble and wriggling herself out of the water.

Cardinal Roderigo could feel the painful pressure of his rigid penis against his clothes as he devoured the back view of her wriggling escape. Her buttocks stretched out, her thighs pushed and flailed in the air. He could see the slim walls of flesh between her legs. She would be the most beautiful, the most voluptuous woman in Italy in a very short time.

Cesare reached the pool's edge and grabbed at one of his sister's feet, but all he succeeded in doing was getting a hearty kick in the shoulder as she swung clear, climbed to her feet and began to run.

Her father's eyes followed lustfully. Her buttocks swayed like helpless jellies as she fled; her breasts sprang up and flopped back within their small range of movement. She laughed as she ran and glanced over her shoulder to where Cesare had quickly pulled himself up to the marble surround and was getting to his feet. Her eyes took in the water-cooled limpness of his organ, the dark hair around it. She wondered fleetingly what it was like to touch that thing which performed the functions of which she'd read vague descriptions in some of the best literature of the times. Then Cesare was on his feet and running dangerously fast after her and she turned her head frontwards again, racing breathlessly around the pool's perimeter.

Cardinal Roderigo drew back a little as her rippling, trembling figure turned the end of the bath and came towards him. He looked back at his son and was proud of him. Slim, strong body. He could have been eighteen or nineteen and his penis was a good specimen, a worthy initiator for Lucrezia.

Cesare was overhauling his sister with ease. She glanced back again and began to laugh with that breathless hysteria of someone in desperation.

She was practically opposite the point where her father was hidden in the mass of foliage when Cesare caught her. She turned away from the pool onto the soft bank of grass next to the inside trelliswork, trying to dodge, to double back. But it was too late, Cesare's muscular young arms had fastened, one around her neck, the other across her breasts, and all she could do was kick and struggle and laugh and pant helplessly.

The battle between their fine young bodies, his lean, muscular, hers ripe, voluptuous, took place about six feet from the unseen Cardinal, who moved forward again, so unlikely were they to see him in the concentration of their struggle.

"Now I shall spank you," Cesare shouted, flinging her down on the grass, falling with her.

"Oh Cesare, how rude and brutish," his sister laughed.

Cardinal Roderigo looked down at her close, fleshful body so near to him and felt a fierce gripping in his rod, so that he longed to burst through the flimsy trellis and the roses and sink himself into the soothing well of relief she promised. He watched their struggle on the ground. Cesare had forced her down on her belly and she had caught one arm and held it firmly gripped under her breasts. He had twined one leg around hers while he raised the other hand and gave her the first sharp-sounding slap across her rearing buttocks.

The Cardinal watched the hand descend, saw her squirm and cry out, half laughing, half startled, saw the pink mark on the white mounds as the hand rose again.

Lucrezia struggled again, desperately, and managed to throw Cesare's leg off her. The Cardinal grinned avidly as he saw that his son's penis had stiffened out, was cleaving the air alongside his daughter's buttock.

Cesare was flushed; he looked a little confused. He noticed, too, that Lucrezia was trembling.

With a sharp movement of his strong arms, Cesare gripped her shoulders, holding her flat on the ground, only her legs kicking wildly in the air. Again he lifted his hand and it lashed down across her behind, and again. His erection had expanded to the limit of its capacity as he half lay, half knelt beside his sister and administered punishment to her darkly blushing bottom.

Watching closely the Cardinal saw Lucrezia's mouth open, was aware that she was pressing her body into the grass as she smarted under her spanking.

"Oh, Cesare!" she gasped out at last.

Her brother eased up, wondering at last if perhaps he hadn't been too harsh. Lucrezia stayed still, her shoulders trembling, her face against the fresh grass.

Cesare lay down alongside her, concerned, and tried to turn her over.

"I didn't hurt you really, did I?" he asked.

Lucrezia turned over at this, edging half under him. She smiled.

"You didn't hurt me at all," she said.

"Well don't be too cocky or I'll give you another," Cesare warned, a little put out.

Lucrezia trembled against him, her soft flesh moving against his. She put an arm over his shoulders.

"Don't spank me any more, Cesare," she begged. "It's made me feel all funny."

Cesare looked down at her. Her flesh against his was an undreamed of torment all of a sudden. His penis felt tight, ready to snap. He knew what went on, but had never seriously considered it. But here was his sister's body all naked and exciting curiosity and a pent-up emotion.

She wriggled under him again, her face close to his and suddenly the other arm had gone around his neck.

"Oh, Cesare!" she said once more. And then she pressed her lips against his.

"Great God," the Cardinal was muttering. "Great God! Eleven years old and with all the wiles of woman born in her! Cesare my son, consider yourself seduced and your father as a serious rival." He was hot as a furnace around his loins and his head was tight with lustful concentration.

Cesare kissed her back. He was flushed in a way he hardly understood. Just the touch of her flesh, her lips, her breasts, the round, nude hips against which his prick was pressed, made him feel almost nauseous with desire.

She took her mouth away from his and looked at him with her deep eyes, half-lidded and deeper looking than he'd ever seen them before. She ran her tongue around her lips and wriggled her body against him.

He bent his head and kissed her lips again and ran his mouth violently over her face. He was afraid at the heat inside him and where it would end.

Get in, Cesare, for the Lord's sake, his father was urging through his will. The little minx wants it so much she'll bite off your prick out of spite if you don't manage it.

He watched her wriggling her hips under her brother's and he wished with a great prayer-like wish that he were lying on her now, poising his hot penis beside that soft little crack ready to pump out his life in love of her.

"Oh, Cesare!" he heard her say more softly. Her arms were hugging him, her hands moving gently over his lean shoulders. Her eyes were closed. The Cardinal could see the slightly crushed globes of her breasts prodding up into Cesare's chest, heaving against him like a sea washing the hull of a ship. Her hips were washing like waves against his loins, too.

"Cesare, dear—do you know how to?" she asked breathlessly after a while in which they pressed against each other and kissed, and he felt afraid.

"Have you read about it in books?" she whispered.

"Yes—yes," he said brokenly.

"Let's do it, Cesare, darling. I feel all tight and it must be the time to do it."

My God, my God, the Cardinal thought. Listen to my daughter. She might be her mother for the way she's talking and acting. Her tutors would be shocked out of their wits.

Lucrezia pushed her hands down Cesare's back, tentatively, letting the palms run over the long, lean curve until she felt the sudden hard jut of his buttocks. She caressed his buttocks and pushed them at her gently with an inspired instinct. She could feel the heavy heat of his penis on her loins and she wanted him, so desperately, to do what it was they did. Deep in her belly, deep in her being she needed it.

Gently she pressed her face against his and bit him on the neck. He uttered a little gasp and his hands tightened on her shoulders, squeezing them until they hurt. His loins pressed against hers with a new pressure. She felt them slither around against her skin.

Perhaps I should really go out and show

them exactly what to do, Cardinal Roderigo was thinking. If he doesn't shove it in and blast her for all he's worth she's likely to turn into a man-hater. He caught his bulging penis through his robes and held it, comforted slightly by the alien pressure.

He watched her hands. What hands, he thought. They moved fluidly, as if in the movements of oft-practiced caresses, over Cesare's back and buttocks. She obviously loved the feel of his skin. He watched her squirming and arching her body upwards. The sexy little bitch'll have an orgasm any minute now, he thought, and then she'll probably be coy and refuse to let him.

But, while his eyes began to bulge at the sight, he saw Cesare slide down on her and, feverishly but inaccurately, push his penis between her legs. At first he was too low. It was as if he intended only to get his knob in, if that. But then Lucrezia, eyes still closed, mouth open, snuggled down against him and brought his knob up against her crotch with a rush.

Cesare prodded uncertainly. Lucrezia in a sudden gust of passion opened her legs wide.

More vague proddings with Cesare breathing so heavily that the Cardinal wondered if his own breathing would reach them.

"That's it! Oh Cesare, Cesare!" The words exploded from her lips and she arched her back, thrusting her breasts up and back with the shock.

Cardinal Roderigo watched Cesare, trembling from head to toes, clamp his little buttocks awkwardly between her thighs as he uncertainly made a bridgehead in her vagina. Lucrezia, too, was trembling and whimpering and holding his shoulders with such force, that the

Cardinal could see the flesh white against the boy's tan, where her fingers were digging.

There, there, at last you little witch. The Cardinal's eyes gleamed with vicarious satisfaction. How does it feel, eh? But you won't really know until you've been screwed by your father's royal rammer.

Lucrezia's body was shaking with continual spasms. She kept her hips still, enduring the certain pain, excited beyond endurance at the thrill of Cesare's entry into her well-cared-for treasure. She moved her face against his, brushing his face with her lips, clasping his lips in hers, wanting to swallow his lips.

The Cardinal watched his son gradually advancing through his bridgehead, wriggling awkwardly up into her, squirming his hips up from their rather distant stance between her lower thighs until he was in the correct position for a full thrust.

After a time, as his hard little buttocks rose and fell above her, Lucrezia began to wriggle under him, too, moaning, kissing him passionately, mouthing his name.

Every so often Lucrezia would throw out her arms on the grass and lie there moaning in abandonment for several seconds before clasping them once more and with renewed passion around Cesare's back.

Cesare was panting furiously. His jerking was getting a smooth, more powerful flow, but the Cardinal could see that he hadn't sunk into her to the full and probably wouldn't before he came.

Lucrezia's thighs began to clasp Cesare's hips, rubbing them as she lifted her knees from the ground and twisted her loins in her passion.

When she lifted her knees and her thighs

rode up with them forming an angle with the grass, Cardinal Roderigo could see Cesare's penis pushing into her hole. It was in about two thirds of its length and her vaginal lips were sucking it voraciously. He noticed that there wasn't any blood. Cesare would enlarge her just enough to make the shock of his prick, when she got it, not too unbearable.

The sun shone down vividly on the bright green grass and the two passionately-fitted bodies writhing out their exquisite pleasure beside the pool. A fine picture of son and daughter with father watching from the bushes, the Cardinal thought with a chuckle.

Lucrezia's plump buttocks were flattening against the ground, oozing and spreading from under Cesare's hips. She was gasping, uttering his name. Her climax was near. Hot little bitch, her father murmured. What a delight you'll be to me.

"Oh Cesare, Cesare, my darling brother...!" Her words tumbled out in the whine of her breath and she sucked his lips again, straining her body at him. Cesare tried to utter something, failed, and gasped instead.

"Oh Cesare, Cesare! Oh, oh, oh!" She pushed against him so hard that she almost lifted him off the ground on top of her, her buttocks hollowing with the strain; her arms clasped him to her as if she wanted to envelop him with flesh. The breath exploded from her open mouth in a great whoosh as if someone had sat on her belly and expelled it as from a cushion. She gave several wild, self-concerned convulsions and then sank back under him.

Cesare had stopped his action, shaken out of his stride by her passion. She put her arms back around his neck, calmer but still loving and he resumed his hard, probing entry into her vagina.

How sweet — sweet minx, the Cardinal thought passionately. Lie there and wait for him to know the climax of pleasure you've just had.

Lucrezia drew up her thighs a little and the Cardinal could see again where Cesare's penis was still only two thirds in. It was too late now for him to learn the art of complete penetration. His head was rolling on his neck, tendons were standing out on that strong young neck of his and a vein pulsed in his forehead.

Lucrezia whispered, but more lazily this time:

"Cesare, darling Cesare!"

Cardinal Roderigo watched his son's body twist up into the culmination of passion as he pressed his sister into the grass. His breath was coming in a series of quick little gasps, he put his arms around her body hugging it to him, he gasped her name at last, the first time it had ever been gasped in passion.

"Lucrezia . . . Lucrezia . . . Aaaaah!"

He convulsed against her, lost control of his movements, actually drew out of her in his excitement and fear at what he was doing and spurted over the grass.

Lucrezia, breathing hard again, stroked his face and shoulders as his hips jerked in the air like a death spasm. She glanced down as he rolled immediately away from her, doubtful and half-ashamed now that it was finished. She saw the thin lines of sperm on the grass, his penis, deflated and small now, with the thin bubble of mucous liquid protruding from the little red nipple at its head.

"Cesare—we've done it," she whispered. She seemed astonished now.

Cesare didn't look at her. He lay on his stomach with his head in his arms. She rolled over to him.

"Cesare, darling, are you cross; do you wish we hadn't?"

He didn't answer and she put her arms around him in an almost motherly way and kissed his head.

"Cesare — don't wish we hadn't . . . because then I should feel terrible that I thought it was so wonderful."

At that Cesare lifted his head and smiled at her.

"That's better," she said softly. "You did like it didn't you?"

He nodded his head and she kissed him gently on the lips. She glanced around them and the Cardinal crouched softly back. His penis was still as hard and hot as a bar of red-hot iron.

"We'd better have another swim," Lucrezia was saying. She looked at her brother with her deep eyes. "We will be able to do it again before you go, won't we Cesare?"

Cesare nodded, jumped to his feet, helped her up and took a running dive into the pool.

Lucrezia followed, smiling. And the Cardinal slowly withdrew through the bushes. "The sexy little bitch," he kept repeating. "The sexy little bitch."

CHAPTER 2

Cardinal Roderigo's mistress, the beautiful Vannozza Cattanei, was sleeping in her room in a wing of the house when he went through to see her later in the day. She was recovering from one of those ridiculous and unexpected summer chills.

He sat on the edge of her bed. She was certainly still beautiful although her youth was past. He still found her delicious in bed. But every so often he felt the need for a fresh body, words and whimpers of passion from a strange voice. He felt the need now. Not an abstract one, but the need for Lucrezia on whom his whole lustful attention had focused.

He leaned over the sleeping woman and kissed her forehead. She awoke and smiled sleepily at him.

"I'll leave you tonight," he said. "You still need rest. Is there anything you need?"

"Nothing, Roderigo, nothing. What have you been doing?"

"Watching the children. They're growing up."

"Yes, indeed," she said sadly. "I wish they could call me mother."

"Hardly becoming, my dear," the Cardinal answered with a chuckle. "The Pope would have the final fit to finish him if such a thing were openly admitted. Think of the disrepute the Church would fall into. Think of the Church, my sweet."

She pressed his hand with a smile.

"The Church is a hypocrite, Roderigo. You are the Church."

"Hush, dear, never let it be said. Now, if there's nothing you need I shall go and read for a while in the library, or perhaps I'll take a stroll in the grounds."

"Yes. I shall be better in the morning," she said.

He bent again and kissed her on the forehead

and she pulled his face down and kissed him on the lips.

"Good-night, my sweet."

"Sweet dreams."

He left her chamber and strolled through the wing of the house, meditating. He didn't head down the stairway toward the library, nor yet to the grounds. He directed his feet instead toward the children's wing.

Candles were burning in Cesare's room when he looked in and Cesare was sitting in bed staring vacantly at the opposite wall.

"Very pensive, my son. You'd better go to sleep now. I want you to be at your best for our little hunting trip tomorrow."

"Oh, yes, father. I was thinking about it."

Liar, thought the Cardinal with an inward chuckle. You'd forgotten it completely. You were dreaming of your little sister's breasts, reliving your first flesh-to-flesh liaison.

He went to Cesare's bedside and kissed him on the forehead.

"Good-night, my son."

"Good-night, father."

Cardinal Roderigo blew out the candles and retired from the room.

His heart beat faster and his penis was already at half-mast as he walked down the corridor to Lucrezia's room at the end. Anticipatory thrills licked down his spine at the thought of what he was going to enjoy. He hadn't decided exactly how to bring it about, but somehow or other he was going to have her tonight.

He opened her door softly, without knocking, and stepped inside.

Candles were burning in her room, too, but she was not in her bed. He glanced around the room and saw her sitting on a stool beside the window, gazing out into the grounds. She was clad in her thin nightdress, but the evening was warm.

She turned, startled.

"Oh, papa. I didn't hear you come in."

He came across to her and peered through the window.

"What are you doing, dearest, dreaming about the stars?"

"Oh, it's such a lovely night, father, and I don't feel a bit sleepy."

She had risen from the stool and stood beside him, looking out with him over the trees. He glanced down at her. Little did she know that he knew what she'd been up to. He found himself breathing nervously. Her breasts swelled out below the square neck of the nightgown, pushing the material out in a twin range of hills with just a slight indentation between them.

In spite of his years, the Cardinal felt quite nervous. Astonishing, he thought, after all my experience, to feel like a schoolboy with my own daughter.

He put his arm around her and she leaned against him affectionately. How often before I've put my arm around her without the slightest tremor, he thought. And now he could hardly keep his fingers from quivering on her soft shoulder. He wondered how she felt, now, with her new awareness. She'd been growing more and more provocative toward him, but, perhaps now, paradoxically, her experience had turned her mind on her brother Cesare; perhaps she could think of nothing and no one else.

"Have you had a pleasant day?" He tried to keep his voice normal.

"Oh, I've had a wonderful day, papa."

"Has Cesare been good to you?"

She looked up at him and he could see those deep eyes in the moonlight! They were not a bit apprehensive, but she was searching his eyes, as if wondering.

"He's always good to me, father. I sometimes think he'd die for me."

"A very romantic notion, my dear young lady. Maybe you mean you'd die for him, eh?"

He squeezed her shoulder and ran his hand down her arm, as if in affection. She moved her other hand onto his and pressed it.

"Perhaps that is what I mean, papa. I never feel I can hide anything from you."

"Ah, you'll learn, my sweet, to have admiration for others than your brother."

"Oh but I have, papa. I love you at least as much as Cesare."

Am I reading into those words what I want to read into them, the Cardinal asked himself? Are they as innocent as they could be — were it not for what I'd witnessed this afternoon? Or is she really being provocative again in a way that only a she-devil could be?

He bent and kissed the top of her golden head, moving his hand from her shoulder, under her armpit so that his fingers lay lightly along the outside bulge of her womanly breast.

"You speak like someone very old in years, my dear."

"I often feel very old in years, father. Much older than Cesare."

He laughed gently. The breast under his fingers was solid and sleek-feeling even through the nightdress. He longed to tear off that flimsy garment and grasp her breast in his hands while he devoured her lips and felt his penis riding up between her thighs.

"Well, you'd better go to bed," he said. "Come, I'll carry you."

And with that he reached down and swung her from her feet, insuring as he did so that his arm rested under her thighs with his hand against the intimate, rounded crevice formed by the tops of her thighs and the beginnings of her buttocks.

He swung her playfully to and fro once or twice, enabling himself thus to let his hand slip, as if accidentally, between her legs where he could actually feel the slim flanges of her sex.

"Oh, papa!" she uttered sharply. And then she added quickly, to hide the real motive for her cry: "I thought you were going to drop me."

"Drop you," he cried jocularly. "As if I'd drop my beautiful daughter."

He swung her again, his hand slipping along her vaginal lips with every movement. She threw back her head over his arm and closed her eyes with a smile on her lips.

Got you now, my beauty, he thought. A little more of this and you're mine.

"Heave ho, heave ho!" he cried in a jolly tone, while his hand pressed and slid along her vagina which he could clearly feel through the thin cloth.

For a minute or two he swung her back and forth, turning in an occasional circle, raising her, lowering her, all the time his hand working on that newly-initiated core of her being. She remained with her head back, laughing nervously every now and then, saying "Oh, papa!" and flushing with ill-concealed excitement for the rest.

Suddenly, his intruding hand felt wetness through her gown. His hand slipped more easily against her vagina. She was getting really excited. The time had come where a facade of fun and games was no longer necessary.

He carried her to the bed and laid her out on it. He stood up then as if to go, eager to see her reaction. She opened her eyes. Her position was one of abandon, with her legs apart under the nightshift.

"Kiss me goodnight, papa," she said. And it seemed to him that even if he made no further move she would embark on an attempt at seduction.

He leaned down over the bed. Her beautiful young face with those full, indefinitely formed lips was very close. She put up her arms and caught his neck to pull his head down. He kissed her on the lips and it was certainly like no father-and-daughter kiss they'd ever had before. He felt those soft lips pushing hard against him, heard her body rustling, knew that she was rubbing her legs together.

Even now, for the last vestige of delicacy, he pretended to lose his balance as she pulled his head. He tumbled down beside her on the bed. She was still kissing him, but now she released him and laughed delightedly. Such a laugh, he thought. It was a mixture of amusement at his fall, of sensuality, of nervous excitement, of triumph — yes, perhaps, even triumph.

"You little minx," he said aloud.

"Why little minx, papa, darling?" she asked.

"I heard you 'darling' Cesare by the pool today," he retorted. "If I were a father like some I'd send you to a convent."

Lucrezia was obviously taken aback, but his attitude reassured her.

"Didn't you mind, papa? Was it very wicked?"

"Very wicked in the eyes of the world, my dear. But, in your father's eyes it was enviable."

"Papa — are you going to kiss me goodnight again?"

Her thighs were working together and the gown rising and falling from her breathing. With an ecstatic sigh he kissed her mouth, hard and then harder, forcing her lips apart so that his teeth grazed hers before he pushed his tongue through and into her mouth.

His hand went away, wandering over her body, trembling over the luscious, still-hidden flesh. He reached right down to the hem of her gown and slid his hand along her leg, up over the knee and up the thigh. He played with the thighs, teasing them with his fingertips, drawing his nails over the glossy, young flesh, right up to her vagina, teasing her without touching her cranny. She moved and slithered on the bed, eyes closed, in a heat of sensuality.

He too was fluttering inside. This was it. This beautiful, precocious daughter of his with her firm, fleshy body was his. His penis was taut with strain. He moved his mouth from hers and ran his lips over her slim, soft face.

"Put your tongue in my mouth," he murmured.

Her lips sought his and then he felt the soft, wet sliver of her tongue edge between his lips and push into his mouth. She flicked it in and out like a cobra; she breathed into his mouth, breathing her passion.

Good God, your mother would never believe it, he thought.

He sucked her tongue, his saliva mingling with hers. He forced it to retreat with his, filling her mouth with his, like a prick in a wide-open female orifice.

Her hands moved around his head and neck the way they had around Cesare's, but occasionally they jerked when his experienced technique gave her more of a shock.

Softly he began to brush her labia with his fingertips. Gently, gently, back and forth, until the moisture began to ooze out and trickle along her smooth, young thighs. Then he moved the lips apart and inserted two fingers, searched for and found the wet, hard little clitoris. This was something Cesare hadn't known. He'd have to tell him.

Gently he massaged it, feeling it thicken, harden in his fingers. Lucrezia began to squeal and jerked her head away from his and then back in little gusts of uncontrollable passion.

He caught the bud of flesh between two fingers and nipped it, drawing his fingers from its base up to the hard little point.

"Oh, papa! Oh, papa!" she squealed and thrust her tongue wildly into his mouth the way he'd instructed her.

The Cardinal, his face hot, perspiration beading on his almost bald pate, worked his fingers along the inside of the lips, easing them apart until he found the little hole nestling between them. He wormed his finger into it, pushing up through the tight, moist flesh which was as wet and smooth as sealskin. Lucrezia jerked and pressed her thighs tightly over his hand, hindering his progress. He felt the warm flesh of her thighs bulging around his hand. Gently he tickled her vagina with his fingers and gradually she relaxed again and opened her legs.

He leaned up from her a little and looked at her. Her face was flushed, she didn't open her eyes, her lips were open, quivering every so often. He looked down at her body. The nightdress was up around her hips, revealing the delicious proportions of her thighs, the soft bulges of skin between her legs, the little area of down at her thigh junction. The top part of her body was still covered. The hillocks of her breasts heaved in shapely unrest beneath the white material. Swiftly he grabbed the shift with his free hand and pulled it right up, exposing first the full roundness of her little belly and her hips, and then the bulbous symmetry of her breasts above with their slim, pointed nipples.

"Oh, you beauty!" he exclaimed aloud. "You beauty!"

He swooped down to her breasts. He kissed them, sucked the nipples, making her squirm with unbearable ecstasy. He ran his lips down over her ribs, her belly which yielded before the pressure. He covered her hips with hot, wet kisses, following the crease of her groin, licking the smooth, warm-tasting skin of her thighs.

"Oh, papa! Oh, papa!" She seemed incapable of saying anything but those two words as she wriggled her shoulders in the air and squirmed her hips and belly under his lips.

He took his fingers out of her vagina and moved his lips tantalizingly along the fleshy tops of her thighs.

"Oh, papa, I can't stand it!"

But she didn't close her legs and he thought —you'll have more than this to stand before I've finished, you lovely little minx.

Gently he pushed his hands under her buttocks. Oh, what delightful buttocks! They were tightened now, tense in his hands as she strained up toward his lips. He grasped a buttock in each hand and felt them, digging in his fingers, feeling them relax onto his palms, flood out in a sudden give of flesh all over his hands.

He gripped them, pushed her thighs wider with his bald head and licked the lips of her vagina.

She made noises of torment, as if she were gargling with water in her throat. He flicked his tongue into the aperture, which seemed to give way on all sides of his tongue. There was a taste of the inside of an oyster shell, soft and salty and indescribable.

The clitoris was there, seeming bigger to his tongue than to his fingers. He licked it, caught it in his lips and sucked it. She began to squirm even more, gripping his face between her thighs in convulsive spasms. Her breath passed through her lips in the form of a continuous groaning whimper. He hoped they would not disturb any of the household.

Her movements became more wild and uncontrolled and at this point he eased off and removed his mouth.

Reaching up he pulled her shift over her head. She stretched out her arms above her head and he slipped it over them and threw it on the floor. He got up from the bed quickly and began to slip out of his clothes. His penis still gave him cause for anxiety. When he came he wanted it to be right up in her.

Naked, with the warm air like a cool hand on his body, he turned back to the bed and saw her wide-open, anguished, desiring eyes.

His penis was sticking out like a pike. He was afraid she might run from the room at the sight of its size, but instead she fixed her fascinated gaze on it as if hypnotized.

He lay down on the bed beside her and kissed her neck.

"Oh, papa I'm frightened — it's so much bigger than Cesare's," she whispered.

"Don't worry, my darling — you'll find that after the first shock you're a match for it."

He ran his lips all around her neck and put his tongue in her ear until she shivered with the sensation and put her arms back around his neck.

For a few seconds he kneaded her clitoris again until she was moaning with pleasure, and then, his penis pounding as if it were a cannon discharging shot every few moments, he slithered onto her body.

Oh, the delight of feeling that warm, soft flesh meet his at so many points at once! It was as if she were gently kissing him all over. Oh, the joy of having that lovely body, that other personality waiting to submit to him, to join with him in an orgy of heart-pounding pleasure!

For several seconds Cardinal Roderigo just lay on his daughter, rubbing his fat penis on her fleshy lower belly, grating his hairy chest against the smooth silk of her breasts, moistening her lips with his tongue, licking her closed eyelids, stroking her golden plaits as he worked his loins into an unendurable state of dynamic tension.

"Lucrezia, my sweet darling," he whispered. "Now I am going to give you real delight."

In answer she gripped him with her slim arms and hugged him tight, murmuring simply, "Oh, papa, papa!"

Cardinal Roderigo slipped his hand down between their bodies, rough hair of his on one side, glossy, white flesh of hers on the other. He felt his penis, swollen and hot as the summer sun; he went beyond it and his hand was engulfed in a shallows of sticky moisture from the vagina. He found the vagina and moved his prick down for the entry.

Lucrezia's arms tightened around him in frightened anticipation, her legs hung limply apart.

"Now, my darling," he muttered.

The hot, wet knob of his cudgel slipped on the moisture of her thighs, encountered — deliciously cool — the soft, giving wetness of her vaginal lips and then, with a gasp from them both, moved into the opening of her aperture.

Inside his breast was a sudden rush of relief as he felt his knob clasped in that soft, soothing embrace. Inside his head, he thought, Oh, at last. Thank God, thank God!

In the liquid clasp he thrust smoothly forward to a tighter region and Lucrezia uttered a stifled scream and jerked her hips backwards. But he followed them with his loins and jogged gently on her, probing in on farther, moving his prick in and out just an inch or so while she became accustomed to the pressure.

Gradually she relaxed and her thighs went limp again on either side of his hips. He put his hands under his chest, between their bodies and squeezed her breasts hard and she drew in her breath with a swoosh, and wriggled invitingly down in the region where his hot organ was waiting to advance.

He flexed his hips in a little more and Lucrezia gasped and drew back again.

"Oh, papa, papa," she moaned. "It hurts, it hurts!"

"We'll go gently, my baby," he breathed. "We have plenty of time. Soon it won't hurt you."

After a second or two she untensed again

and he screwed his loins in little circular motions on hers, pushing his penis no farther into her passage.

He turned her face which was pressing, sideways, into the bed, and kissed her, slipping his tongue into her mouth, licking the corners of her lips until she responded and thrust her own little tongue at his.

He screwed her gently, so gently, moving in a fraction of a centimeter at a time. Every time he moved in she tensed and he moved no farther for a while.

He found it excruciating not to be able to plunge right up her to the very hilt of his power, but it also inflicted on him a fresh innovation, a self-torture which was exquisite.

A considerable heat had been generated between their bodies and he saw that little beads of perspiration were bursting forth passionately on her forehead. No doubt she was sweating between her legs too. He slid his hands up the sides of her body, lingering over the rim of breast which oozed out from under him on either side. He moved his hands under her armpits. Yes, they were sweating, too. She was in a real answering fever heat.

Down at his loins a point of passion was growing, a thin pricking of red-hot sensation amidst the mass of indefinable loveliness which was her wet, excited cunt surrounding and eating at his prick.

The thin pricking of sensation seemed to be a bursting point; it seemed, of its own accord to be bursting up and up into her passage and it was only when she cried out again in anguish that he realized he was thrusting in with greater and greater force. Only this time he couldn't slow down, couldn't stop and mark time with his prick to allow her to recover.

Tightly he held her upper arms while he wriggled his hips in closer.

"It won't hurt, it won't hurt, in a moment it won't hurt," he wheezed through his leaping breath.

"Oh, it hurts, it hurts, oh, oh, oh!" Lucrezia moved her head from side to side, but made no further effort, realizing the futility, to jerk her hips away from her father's.

His great prick was like an elephant somehow got inside her body and barging in still farther. She felt as if her belly, her loins, were being purged in a painful, splitting scourging. And always, always as she thought it eased, the pain broke out afresh and the great object tearing and thundering inside swept up, impossibly, farther and farther.

She closed her eyes, trying to stop the tears oozing from them. She bit her lips and gritted her teeth. She couldn't stand it. She wished it had never begun. It wasn't like with Cesare. It was pain such as she'd never experienced. Was this how women were when they had a child? She would never have a child. Never!

But Cardinal Roderigo was in delirium. He moved his hands under her behind, pushed his fingers right around to feel his own organ crushing into that tightly-grasping pipeline. He squeezed her buttocks in a paroxysm of sensuality, thrust his fingers at her little rosebud anus. And all the time the fire in his prick was growing and growing, drawing oaths and obscenities from his mouth. He had nearly disappeared into her body now. There was little left to go. By the time of the explosion which was twisting his lips with its imminence, he would be crushing right in, stuffing her with the entirety of his penis. He pulled her thighs up to facilitate his last two centimeters.

"Oh, oh. What a delightful little hole," he choked. "Daughter — you're the best — the best — I've ever — had."

Lucrezia heard these oaths and mouthings with a slight chill of fear. This had got beyond expectations. But she was relieved to find that the pain had got no worse and that, apart from a soreness in her vagina, everything seemed to be much easier and she was actually recapturing some of the earlier sensation which had flattened in her as soon as the pain came. Papa had been right after all. It *would* only hurt for a while. In fact, now, as it became easier with every thrust he made and she began to wriggle her loins and thighs against him, it seemed impossible that a few minutes before she'd been ready to die from anguish.

"It's all right, papa," she whispered. "It — it doesn't hurt so much any more."

Her words spurred Cardinal Roderigo on as if she had suddenly bitten the blunt end of his rod. There was a sweetness, a submission about the way she told him that made him feel strangely sadistic.

He pulled her thighs up at an even more acute angle with her belly and pushed home the last length of pulsating flesh. Lucrezia gasped, but a gasp which was three parts pleasure, one part shock.

The Cardinal's loins were aflame. His penis was heavy and prickling inside her. It felt ready to burst along its whole length. His belly was heaving in and out enough to give him a heart attack, his hands rifled her bottom, pinching it, grabbing it in paroxysms, digging at the anus which squirmed on his fingertips.

"Oh, Lucrezia! My darling!" he moaned.

"Papa, papa," she answered tenderly through her regrowing passion.

His lips moved, but no sounds came out except his choking breath. It was coming. He rammed smack into her, burying his staff so deep that his hairy surrounds cracked against her vaginal lips with force and made her squeal. In his belly there was a churning, a churning that was pure essence of sensation. Everything paled, he felt dizzy. The heat and solid pricking fury of the sensation was everything, but for dazed impressions of this beautiful body, this beautiful daughter lying under him, giving him this ecstasy from her lovely passionate flesh.

In the depths of his chest a long-drawn, choking gasp slowly followed the course of the long-drawn, loin-convulsing drawing of his fluid. He called her name through his moaning. He leaned up from her except for his loins. He gripped her waist just above the hips and squeezed it with more and more force as the fluid rushed inside him, fought its way to his penis and with a last rush shattered out and up into her writhing channel, inundating it as he jerked uncontrollably, inundating it until it rolled slowly out of her vagina between her wide-flung legs in the wake of his collapsed penis and he let go of her waist and slipped exhaustedly down onto the warmth of her flesh. Red marks were left on the tender white flesh where his hands had gripped.

Lucrezia had been aware, through her own passion, of the groaning and writhing around her as if a thousand demons were suddenly raping her body from all sides. She felt the hot jets of sperm spurt inside her, with a twinge of pleasure. And then, a few seconds later, she felt fresh twinges of disappointment when her father sank limply onto her and the solidity was withdrawn from her vagina leaving a sudden cool rush of air and the shadow of solidity in its place.

Her vagina was hot and a piquant burning remained. She was sore, but not so sore that she wouldn't have invited further entry to assuage her desire. She sighed and tensed her thighs against the Cardinal's hips.

He seemed to come out of the heavily breathing state of coma he'd fallen into and he stroked her thighs without moving from his position astride her.

"You learn very fast, daughter," he said. "I'm exhausted as a galley slave."

In answer she wound her legs around his and rubbed her cheek against his chin.

He lay on her, inwardly chuckling now, knowing her unquenched desire. It was warm and highly pleasant having her provocative body as a cushion. The wound which had just allowed his sperm to flow from him would soon be cured and then he would be ready for fresh action.

Lucrezia unwound her tightly clamping legs after a few minutes and slithered them in underneath his. He felt her soft little belly squirm against the rotundity of his and then the live pressure of her well-covered hips.

"Did I not hurt you, my sweet?"

"Yes, papa — but it changed halfway and I began to feel that I wanted to die in such happiness."

And she has yet to die in it, he thought, yet

to feel the soporific spread of satisfaction from her father's punishing penetration.

He rolled off her, at last. His prick, hot and tender, had half-risen again. He glanced down at it below the bulge of his belly and then he took Lucrezia's hand and placed it on the hot length of flesh.

Lucrezia looked down at the organ which had began to expand in her hand. She held it gently as if it were a hand, wondering at its great heat.

"Caress it, my love—particularly the knob," the Cardinal said, pressing his thighs one against the other.

His daughter obeyed, drawing her fingers gently, as if afraid, over the smooth, white skin from its hairy base to the fiery red knob at its extremity.

Cardinal Roderigo felt an explosion from him as if passion had broken out from a small cell, shattering the walls, and was now pervading the corridors, the antechambers of his entire body. He flexed his hips against the side of her thigh. He crossed one ankle behind the other, turning his body into an arch with the foremost point his penis. His heart began to gather speed in its pounding once again.

Lucrezia gained courage—or curiosity as the Cardinal became more and more impassioned. She allowed her fingers to slip away from the rigid, fleshy stem to fondle the hairy balls below. They, too, were hot and hairily smooth and she gathered them in her hand, weighing them gently in her palm, wondering at the strange makeup of man. The very feel of his genitals excited her, too, making her wet and exposed-feeling between her legs so that she closed her thighs and grazed them together achingly.

The Cardinal began to undulate his legs, breathing noisily through his hairy nostrils. He leaned his head over onto her, laying it against her breasts, brushing his smooth cheek from one to the other, sucking a nipple, descending the hill into the valley, climbing the opposite hill and kissing that other nipple which shot out like a flag on a mountain top.

Lucrezia felt overcome with a desire to kiss his whole body in return. She swayed over and lay her head on his chest as he relaxed backwards before her gentle pressure. She kissed his hairy chest, loving his breasts with her mouth. He placed his hand on her soft head and pushed her gently downwards. She let herself be pushed, let her head move down him, her lips moistly blazing a trail down his hairy flesh as they passed.

Her hand still held his prick which reached forth for the ceiling, trying to grow like Jack's beanstalk. As her lips crossed his lower belly, his muscles tautened, his prick became a shrieking urge. He wanted to bury it in her—in that soft, learning mouth which was moving toward it. He caught her head by the hair, roughly, so that she gasped and pushed her face down the last few inches which separated it from his prick.

She got the idea immediately and he felt her lips, tantalizingly light and feathery, running up the stem of flesh. He cringed within himself, gritting his teeth.

He held his breath for what seemed an asphyxiating length of time and then he let it out in a long, gasping sigh as the mouth closed softly, like a vagina, over his radiant knob.

From what seemed a great height above him on the bed, he could hear her lips gently sucking. There seemed to be no correspondence between the noise which inflamed his ears and the actual pulling of her lips on his prick which sent chill after chill coursing through his body.

He had released her head as the mouth clamped over his penis, but now, wanting to plunge his rod farther into the tightness of sensation, he reached down again and forced her blonde head down against the rearing pikestaff. He felt his solid heat shoot forward, grazing her teeth. She gave a choking, muffled cry. He undulated his hips with the fury of a whirlpool and heaved them up at her face. He looked down at her slim, flushed face and the distended lips pulling on his prick which had been half swallowed in her mouth. The sight added to the sensation and his eyes narrowed, his lips broke apart, his hand tightened on her soft, fine hair.

In her mouth, his prick seemed to be thickening and thickening every second. His hand moved hard and violently over her head, pulling on those golden plaits, pressing the head with convulsive fingers. He wanted to bury his prick in her throat—but somehow the mouth and throat were not enough; the sensation was not consistent along the length of his rod.

He watched her sucking, her cheeks hollowing, her eyes closing and opening in her passion. Her slim, sleek back, white and without a blemish was presented to him, blooming abruptly into the luxury of her lips and soft, full buttocks that invited caresses, invited the pressure of another body.

He watched her buttocks. They slithered whitely one against the other, an outward sign of her inner excitement. They were smooth, lovely convexes of flesh. He longed to reach out and touch them but he couldn't reach. He longed to press his loins against them, to feel their convexity in all its voluptuousness crushed against the elastic roundness of his own belly and loins.

He pulled her head sharply from his loins. Her mouth came off his raging prick with a sharp sucking noise. She looked up at him with her deep, blue eyes half open. His penis was tingling, the feel of her mouth still around it needing to be replaced.

He slithered down behind her, lying along her back, and put his arms round her to fondle her breasts with their erect nipples. The coolness of her buttocks exaggerated the heat of his penis against them. He pressed his prick against the soft mounds of flesh, biting his lips.

With his hand he reached down and explored her thighs from behind, pushing his fingers between them until he found the long portals of ultra-smooth moisture. He began to caress her vagina once again, kneading the hard, erect clitoris.

Immediately she began to wriggle in the most abandoned way and to moan in a manner which made him impatient to plunge his prick hard in and give her something to moan about.

His prick was down there between her legs, brushing against his searching fingers. He needed only to jerk forward and it would be once again between those milky thighs, breaking in with a strong, skin-rending pressure which would set her atrembling.

He eased her over onto her face. She went just wherever his hands guided. She seemed quite lost to anything but his touch.

Quivering with anticipation he lowered himself onto the provocative pertness of her buttocks, feeling them warm, soft and giving under his loins. His penis waved between her thighs which she had opened. Now he couldn't wait. Every moment was torment.

Swaying back onto his knees, he pulled her up onto her knees in front of him. Her bottom reared up at him, her face was pressed into the bed within the framework of her arms.

There, like a great cleft moon, her behind was juicily presented to him. Her thighs were spread, the lines between her knees forming the base of a triangle, the point at her thigh junction where he could see the red, wet opening of her cunt, its apex. She was kneeling before him like a sacrificial offering. She was his to do with as he wished.

He placed himself behind her. He eased her lips open with his thumbs and ranged his prick against the opening. Then with an all-pervading tremor of sublime pleasure he surged into her.

Lucrezia, her lips working, her mind confused with desire, knelt before the Cardinal, with her bottom right up in the air under his eyes. She felt his thumbs against the lips of her vagina and she squirmed against them, contracting her channel in concentrated passion. She moaned again—and the moan became a cry as, with the force and relentlessness of a battering ram, his great rod which had recently been filling her mouth to the choking point, tore into her channel and raced up with great momentum into the depths of her belly. This time it was easier and less painful, but these thoughts didn't occur to her at the time. She was aware only of the slight pain, the nakedness of her bottom, her whole body and her desire to submit, to be used, raped, hurt even and to enjoy, to wallow in her enjoyment which transcended any other type of enjoyment she'd ever experienced.

She heard her father grunting behind the weight of his hips which pressed at her so hard that they edged her forward on the bed and made her push with her hands to keep her position.

His prick, which seemed enormous — she could still not believe that it could really disappear inside her — bludgeoned in and drew back and then thrust right up again.

On her waist his hands were cruel in the way they gripped her with such force. She felt his knees edging her knees apart. He seemed to want to embed himself deeper and deeper in her. It made the whole of her loins itch and flame. She was aware of the contraction and expansion inside her, the sensation that a regular wave of movement was getting faster and faster, deeper and deeper.

The Cardinal gritted his teeth as the tight sheath of flesh slipped back along his complementary dagger. Her channel was tight around his length, but his knob seemed to want to go farther, to be squeezed so tight that it hurt him.

He thrust in and out, up and up with a regular, strong flow from his hips. His stomach was fluttering, his thighs twitching. At the extremity of his inward stroke he gave an extra flick, feeling her buttocks give and spread under the weight of his loins, hearing her gasps and gulps. Every few strokes he would thrust his own hot organ right in and leave it there, tightly held in her body while he squirmed his hips against her cool buttocks, reveling in the brushing contact of their separate flesh.

He moved his hands from her waist, which,

it seemed, he could almost span, tracing them over her back, the lean, firm flesh. He pressed her shoulders into the bed as he drove his prick into her passage. He saw her shoulders shake and quiver, her bottom sway and rotate against him.

His prick felt like a trail of gunpowder rushing towards its annihilation in explosion. He ran his hands under her belly clasping her to him as he spread her thighs still wider with his knees. He clasped the flesh of her belly in small, elastic handfuls. He lowered his own belly onto her bottom, holding her in a close abdominal embrace as he smashed his loins against her, splitting her vagina with his ever-growing intrusion.

Subject under him, a willing slave, Lucrezia felt his prick filling her whole body. It seemed to surge right in up to her breasts with every thrust. And every thrust brought an involuntary explosion of breath from between her lips. Her hot face twisted in torment against the bed. Her hips waved and squirmed beyond her control. It felt as if his organ was as big as her entire belly and her belly was smarting and tingling and leaping with flame. In the middle of this overall sensation was a central channel of piercing stimulation where he surged into her channel, filling and spreading it as it tried to clasp him firmly.

Lucrezia heard her own groans as if they came from some other throat. She felt as if she were being dredged, all her entrails being dragged down into that channel. With a confusion of wild words in her head, many of them unspoken exhortations to him to fuck her to the last, to destroy her with his prick, she felt a great warmth spreading inside. It was a feeling she hadn't had before, an inexorable advance of nothing which shook her body and made her feel that the end of her life was near. She tried to say something to her father, to ask him something, but when she opened her mouth only muffled exclamations came out.

And the inexorable sensation went on and on and her hips waved as if they had their own delirium and her belly was afire with a burning-like snow. Snow rushing in an avalanche which was lovely and terrible, unbearable and all-desirable, unending yet moving quickly to an end. She groaned and cried out in loud, grating cries. Her whole body was moving downwards to pass out between her legs. She gasped and weaved her hips and pressed back against her father's belly, wanting his prick, loving him, loving the sensation, frightened of it—and now it was there, everywhere, a great bubble which was bursting, bursting and . . . "Oh, my God! Oh-oh-oh-oh-oooooh!" A great flowing through, an escape and a slow ebbing, ebbing slowly, slowly, back to normal which was not normal because it left a wash and a new feeling.

Cardinal Roderigo was inflamed with the sight and sound of Lucrezia's culmination. Her tortured face, pressing into the bed, remained in his mind even when it had calmed and the movement of her lips was nothing more than a muted recognition of the force of his continued penetration.

He felt a great outreaching for her, as if it were not enough to be screwing her here on the bed with all his power, as if he needed to destroy her to ensure a truly positive action.

His penis, hard and with the skin drawn back so tightly that it was often painful, pistoned into her, disappearing up to the very hairs of his belly which became wet and stringy from her liquid outpourings. His penis felt harder and more solid as the moments rushed dizzily past and his mouth opened and closed with furious wheezings. When he gripped her he crushed her tender flesh sadistically, reflecting the force of his grip with a renewed vigor of his thrust. With every forward motion which tightened his buttocks into hard, male globes he crashed against her behind pushing her forward, pulling a little cry from her.

Within him he felt the curling up of the spring which would suddenly snap straight again at the point where it could curl no more. He wanted to push farther and farther into her body to some impossible point. Sensation gripped every hard, fleshy centimeter of his penis. His grip on her waist grew. He fixed his gaze on the little ring of her anus which he noticed now as she pushed her buttocks back at him. It was small and crinkly. He would have to have it someday soon. He watched it, the focal point of those revolving buttocks. He concentrated the whole force of his attention on its hairless contraction. The spring was winding up and up and up. He gritted his teeth. His eyes glazed over the little button. He moved his finger to it, prodded it, felt the cringing reaction. The spring was winding to breaking point. He felt he couldn't stand any more. He couldn't get any farther into her. It must come to an end now. He heard the murmurs of her breath. The anus was like an eye socket looking at him. He gasped, thrust forward in a long, hard stroke and then convulsed in a series of quick tremoring jerks as he spattered his fountain of sperm into the moist sheath which had held him so well.

Lucrezia wriggled a little, at last, from under his dead weight which had become too much for her. Her back ached a little where it had been curved in a concave while the Cardinal satisfied his passion on her.

Feeling her movement, the Cardinal rolled off her and flopped down on his back. He watched her nestle down beside him and wondered how long he had better stay. Then he thought of the sleeping household and decided he had time to show her a few more things yet.

CHAPTER 3

Cardinal Roderigo's thoughts were turned on his future as he sat in his big library which led, by a terrace, into the grounds. When he thought of his future he always thought back, first to Calixtus, who had given the family such a sudden rise to eminence. Don Alonso de Borja, as he had been before ascending the throne of St. Peter, had been a fine old man and Roderigo felt he owed it as much to him as to himself to fully recapture the family's previous office.

And such an aim appeared to be within his grasp. There were many amongst the pontificals who hated him, but he was convinced of his ability to buy them—with money or promises of estate—when the time was ripe.

The only slight stumbling block was the pertinacity with which Innocent VIII clung to his fading life. Already he had violently disappointed the Cardinal—among others—with unexpected recoveries from cataleptic trances after he'd already been taken for dead.

Under his lethargic rule, the Church had

again begun to lose much of the vigor it had possessed under his predecessor, Sixtus IV—a fact which filled Cardinal Roderigo with fury when it occurred to him that he would have the task of rebuilding its strength. What a stupid man he was. He had even openly acknowledged his children for his own, thus enabling his enemies to create open scandal about him. And in fact it often seemed that provision for his seven bastards was the only aim of his pontificate. Truly, Rome would be well rid of such a man.

Cardinal Roderigo idly flicked the pages of a book as he allowed his imagination to flow where his ambition prompted. As Pope he would immediately start a system of alliances which would increase the power of the pontifical troops; he would create fresh cardinals to insure his personal strength and he would force the proud barons to pay the taxes which for so long they'd ignored. That would be but a start. In the process, of course, he would clean up Rome of its lawlessness. It was indeed scandalous and dangerous for the authorities that the present Pope had allowed such lawlessness to scourge the streets. Every morning there were fresh corpses in the streets and it was dangerous to be abroad at night without an escort. Such a step should certainly gain him a certain immediate favor with the common people . . .

But then he realized that he was sitting in his library, that he was simply Cardinal Roderigo Borgia and that the Pope, weak and near-helpless, was still hanging stubbornly onto his life.

However, the possibility of ridding Rome of

the old man seemed rather nearer to the Cardinal today, for an idea had come to him.

He had in the past considered ways and means of doing away with Innocent, but a practicable method had never presented itself to him. There was always some snag either in the form of the Pope's vigilant attendant or the old man's own suspicious nature. Recently, however, he had been turning over in his mind the knowledge that Innocent was the toppling monument to grasping sensualism within himself. The only reason the old man was no longer visited by his courtesans was because his enfeebled state made him fear a fatal stroke if he indulged in the excitement of sexual intercourse. But, the Cardinal smiled to himself, supposing he were forced into it by a seduction he could not resist. In his present state that could well bring about the end of him—and then the way would be clear.

* * *

Several hours later Cardinal Roderigo was ushered into the Pope's chamber in the Vatican. Officially he was paying a duty call, to offer his hope of a quick improvement in the old man's health; in actual fact his thoughts were bent on quite a different path.

The Pope raised a weary hand from his bed. He was thin and pale. He looked worse every day.

"Ah, my dear Cardinal Roderigo, I am happy to be able to tell you I feel considerably better today." His voice belied his words with its thin, scraggy tone. The Cardinal sometimes felt that the old man divined his wishes and enjoyed trying to annoy him with declarations about his improved state of health.

"That is very pleasing news, your Excellency. May it be God's will that you are soon risen from your bed and with us in body as in spirit without delay."

"Ah, you are too kind. But I trust your earnest hopes may be granted."

The Cardinal proceeded to sketch recent events within the Church as well as various communications which had passed through the embassy, notably from the King of France who had his eye on the acquisition of Naples. Finally he discreetly described items of scandal which had come to his ears. These he knew the Pope loved to hear most of all while pretending to be shocked and scandalized. Had he been hale and hearty he would have retained in his memory the names of women involved in doubtful intrigues in the hope of procuring them for his own pleasure at some future date.

"And that seems to be all that I can report at present. I trust that before I come again you will be even farther on the road to recovery."

The Pope made a sign of thanks and settled back in his bed when, as if in afterthought, Cardinal Roderigo added:

"Oh, by the way. I have a niece who has been with me of late—home from her studies—a very beautiful girl. She begged me to crave audience with you for her, saying that just to touch the foot of your bed would be a divine experience for her. For her, your Excellency embodies all that is great and of any consequence in any sphere.

"I told her that in view of your indisposition such an audience was out of the question, but

I promised to beg that you might receive her at such time as you felt able."

The Pope stared up from his bed, his dull eyes alight a little with interest.

"The girl is only a virginal eleven years old, but her mind and body are those of a mature woman," the Cardinal continued. He smiled. "So—if I might use a worldly term in a spiritual sense—infatuated is she with your holiness that she has said to me, 'Did he bid me go to a convent I would go without a thought, did he bid me sink into a slime of carnality, likewise I would obey him.' Truly a remarkable devotion in one so young—and so beautiful that a worldly career would be easily within her grasp. In fact I almost wonder if such passion in things spiritual doesn't go a little too far."

The Pope had sat up again, resting against his pillows. His eyes were sparkling more than they had since his illness had begun.

"Indeed she is a child of God by all accounts," he declared. "And is she really so much a woman at such a tender age?"

"Modesty forbids me to describe how lovely is her form and face," the Cardinal replied. "But Helen of Troy would have recognized her peer."

"Ah, you go too far, you go too far," the Pope chuckled. "But I should like to see her. Her audience is granted whenever she would wish it."

"I will communicate with her," the Cardinal said. "At present she is away from Rome in pursuance of her studies, but within a few days she may be again in the city."

"Excellent," the Pope murmured. "Tell me, what is the child's name?"

"Her name, your Excellency, is Lucrezia."

CHAPTER 4

While Cardinal Roderigo was meditating in his library, Lucrezia and her younger brother, Giuffredo, were on their way back to continue their studies in the Orsini Palace, Monte Giordano.

They rode on horseback, as usual, with their attendants and men at arms—for the highway could be a dangerous spot, particularly toward nightfall—strung out around them. They were both excellent horsemen. Giuffredo, who was almost two years younger than his sister, had shown particular promise almost the first time he was put on a horse some years previously. The horse had, for some reason, suddenly and unexpectedly bolted from under the eyes of the lad's teachers, but he had clung grimly on with his young, sturdy arms and, white as death, but determined, had still been seated when the horse was overtaken at the end of a furious five-minute chase.

Like his brother and sister, he looked older than his years and his body had been strengthened with continual exercise in archery, wrestling and swimming. His character was already taking a determined turn which brought him the respect of those elders who came into close contact with him.

He glanced over at his sister. He was very proud of her and her beauty and he hoped she would soon be tired so that he could take her in front of him on his own horse as was their established custom. Nothing made him feel more male and protective than to know that his sister was tired and dependent on him while he manfully guided their horse forward along the trail.

Lucrezia glanced back at him and smiled. He was rather like Cesare though his nose was slightly retroussé and his hair had faint tints of red in it. She had found, during the journey, that her thoughts, so much centered now on the sexual events of the past few days, wandered to Giuffredo and imagined what it would be like with him. Of course he was younger. But he was always so masculine that she was sure he'd be quite commanding if led. She rubbed her crotch along her saddle. The soreness had almost disappeared, but its traces left the strongly intangible memory of Cesare and her father, both with part of their bodies actually inside her body, crushing wetly, deliciously into her. The memory made her feel suddenly chill in her belly and she pressed down hard on the rough saddle.

It was dusk before she changed over to Giuffredo's horse. It always happened the same way; eventually she felt she couldn't keep her shoulders from sagging forward and her neck began to ache.

The lieutenant of the guard respectfully helped her up in front of her brother and then ordered his men to light the lanterns they carried.

The procession continued, slowly, with the lanterns throwing long, vague shadows on the road and dimly showing up the faces of the riders, glinting on the swords of the men-at-arms.

Lucrezia arranged her long, loose skirt around her. She still wore no underclothes but for her petticoats and she felt the cold leather of the saddle against her genitals with a shock of pleasure. She leaned back against Giuffredo, who put one arm protectively around her waist, guiding the horse with the other. Around them was the clip-clop of the horses, the shadows of the long barrows made weird and stark by the lantern-light. None of the attendants or the guards chatted around them—they were too tired after the day's ride. The procession had a slow, clip-clopping rhythm of its own which seemed to be lulling everyone to the brink of sleep.

Lucrezia's thighs slipped gently against the saddle. The movement of the horse jogged her in a gentle rise and fall. Once again, unconcerned now with the guidance of a horse, she let her thoughts dwell on the events of the past days. In cold blood she could hardly imagine herself prostrated in front of her father while from behind her, unseen, he screwed her with his unbearably big weapon. She wondered what she looked like to him in that position. The thought of herself stretched out with all her openings spread out before his eyes gave her a delicious little thrill of horror. She thought of his prick. How big it had been. How could it have gone in her? All of it! But how wonderful it had finally been!

Her crotch slipped on the saddle, bringing her back to the present. She was getting wet again with the thought. Now that she knew exactly what she longed for, knew the sight and feel of it, she felt she needed it every time her thoughts strayed in a sexy direction.

Up and down she jogged on the saddle. She wriggled her bottom slightly against it on the downward movement. Her breath was a series of small sighs in her throat as she leaned against Giuffredo. His presence and her feelings combined to make him seem the object of her desire. If only they were alone, she'd make him leap down from the horse and fuck her in the field alongside. She wondered if he'd ever done it and came to the conclusion it was out of the question. He was simply too young and they spent most of their time together.

Back and forth, up and down. She squirmed on the hard leather, flattening the slim wedges of her sex against it. There was really very little separating her from Giuffredo, she thought: just her tucked up skirt lying across the horse's back between them and his thin hose. His boyish prick was so close to her. She could actually feel the pressure of his legs against hers where he sat behind her on the same saddle. If only they could do it now.

She pushed her bottom back against his loins. She could feel the pressure of his body down there against the voluminous folds of her skirt; his free hand was still around her waist, her head against his shoulder.

Gently she edged her hips right back along the saddle, straightening her body imperceptibly, so that her bottom was tight against his loins. She held her breath and let the horse's movement jog her behind against his loins. With every pace forward, her buttocks crushed back against the point where his penis was hidden by his tight hose.

The main trouble, she realized, after a few minutes—in which her face became hotter and hotter and her vagina felt as if it were weeping—was that she couldn't feel what effect she was having on Giuffredo; the folds of cloth between them were too many.

She reached behind her, as if simply to arrange her skirt, and deftly drew it up a little above the point where her buttocks rose above the saddle. At the same time, she pushed her hips back again so that her naked flesh was in contact with the thin cloth of her brother's hose.

As she did so—and totally accidentally—her hand brushed against his loins and she knew what the effect had been. She had felt a small, but very definite bulge.

My sweet young brother, she thought. You're beginning to feel how nice it would be to possess your sister.

They jogged for a while and then Giuffredo pushed out his thighs along the horse so that Lucrezia was virtually sitting in his lap, with the point of his bulge pressed against the slit of her buttocks. Her skirt draped over them, falling over his legs quite naturally, so that their point of contact was quite hidden.

Now with every movement of the horse, her buttocks crushed back around the bulge in his hose, rubbing down it with a pressure which sent a spear of delight up Lucrezia's spine.

Giuffredo's hand had tightened on her belly, his arm surrounded her more tightly than it ever had before on their journeys. She felt his chest heaving and pressed hard against her back.

Giuffredo himself wasn't quite sure what was happening. He felt tight and prickly inside, particularly down at his reproductive organ. That was what his tutor called it in his advanced biology lessons. Giuffredo had never quite been able to believe in the process which it was alleged took place. He had never even felt any desire to masturbate, which he understood was a phase some boys got earlier than others. He'd always been rather frightened of the idea—as if something terrible would happen to him if he did.

But now Lucrezia, his beautiful sister of whom he was so proud, was pressing against him in a way which was having a strange and exciting effect on his organ and his whole being. And, what was more, he was certain she was doing it on purpose. She'd deliberately pulled her skirt over his legs and he could feel she had nothing on underneath and her hand had brushed his center of excitement, making it jerk involuntarily against the tight hose he wore and causing him considerable embarrassment.

He felt very strange, almost sick in a pleasant way—if that were possible. And every step the horse made with consequent jog of Lucrezia's bottom against him he felt stranger and sicker.

Guiltily he glanced at the surrounding horsemen. They were dim, unreal figures in the flickering light of the lanterns. They all appeared to be asleep. They could almost have been ghosts, following them, lit up in their own aura of ghostliness.

He closed his eyes. His fingers on the reins were clenched. He closed out everything but the strong rubbing sensation of her bottom on his organ under the skirt as the horse jogged forward. He became aware of his hand on her belly. He could feel the warm, firm arc of her belly under the skirt and the feel of it made him want to explore it with his hands, to feel it naked.

Lucrezia, he noticed, was squirming in a slightly unnatural way on the saddle. She leaned back her head against him so that their faces touched and for the first time in his life the touch excited and embarrassed and delighted him. Her face was warm and her eyes were closed and their bodies were together from the saddle to their heads and the pressure on his loins was making him want to burst through his hose.

Suddenly he felt his sister's hand upon his leg, stroking his thigh—and moving up his thigh, reaching awkwardly under the skirt until her fingers lightly landed on the bulge of his penis. The touch sent a shock right through his body and he drew back his hips involuntarily. But her hand pursued and he let it fondle him there, with an excitement growing in his loins which he couldn't control.

It was at this point that the lieutenant of the guard coughed—and Giuffredo moved sharply, guiltily back from his sister again.

The cough was a preliminary for an announcement.

The lieutenant thought they should ride a little faster to reach the Orsini Palace at a reasonable hour. They had, still, rather farther to go than was wise on a night as dark as this.

Reins were tightened throughout the party and the pace increased to a canter.

The extra attention directed on horses and road and the greater noise of the canter seemed to Giuffredo to act as a cover for his secret activity with Lucrezia and he pressed the bulge of his loins back against the warm nudity of her backside. Her hand, which had momentarily withdrawn, also came back and rose and fell against his protrusion as they cantered forward into the night.

Giuffredo felt hot and almost dizzy with excitement. He kept having to control himself with an effort. Lucrezia, he saw, was breathing very heavily as if in the throes of some strong physical exertion.

Under cover of the noise she half turned to him and whispered something.

Now that she had spoken, reestablished with the sound of her voice, that she was his sister, he felt a new wave of embarrassment.

"What?" he asked leaning forward, blushing.

"I said put it in me," Lucrezia said brazenly.

Giuffredo was horrified and flustered—and then freshly excited. The actual thing! The hand came back and pinched and poked the hot mound of flesh which seemed bent on escaping from his clothing. He pushed his hips forward and pressed them against her flesh with a furious desire.

"It's not possible," he whispered back.

"Yes it is. Nobody'll ever notice with the jogging of the horse—it'll look natural. I can lean forward on the horse's neck as if I'm asleep."

Giuffredo was silent for a moment. He wanted to try it now to the point of desperation. He could never forgive himself if he lost this opportunity.

"But my clothes."

"Slit them with your knife," Lucrezia replied immediately. "You can change them as soon as we arrive and throw them away. "Nobody'll see in the dark."

Giuffredo's heart was pounding with excitement. It was all incredible. He couldn't think it out. There was something which would make it dangerous. It *was* dangerous. Riding through the night on the back of a horse in the midst of a crowd of men-at-arms!

But Lucrezia had suggested it and she sounded as if there was absolutely nothing to worry about. Her confidence was infectious. They were in it together and he was so wild with a frightened excitement now that he couldn't keep his loins still.

"Hurry!" Lucrezia whispered.

Giuffredo glanced around at the dim riding figures. Their lanterns illuminated them in little tents of light. He and his sister were in the central shadow. Besides, everybody was concentrating on the road.

Carefully he took his small, jeweled dagger from his belt. He held it in his hand and glanced around again. Then with a quick movement he inserted the tip in the stitches of the cloth and slid the knife downwards, between him and Lucrezia. He was very careful. He felt the flat of the blade, cold against the heat of his genitals. He withdrew it, shoved it back into his belt. His belly was frozen with nervous tension. Now he couldn't bear to look around him, sure that someone had noticed. But when at last he did, he laughed nervously at his own stupid imagination. It was unlikely that anyone would have been able to see clearly enough to know what he was doing even had they looked.

He sat against Lucrezia, who was still squirming on the saddle. His stomach was so churned up that he felt unable to move. And then she did it for him. He felt her fingers, cool and as foreign and strange as the knife blade, pull apart her skirt.

His organ shot out rigidly at her, short, but stubby in its adolescence. He felt as if he wanted to piss. He couldn't bear her touch. But there was nothing to be done. He couldn't pull back his loins more than a few centimeters and her fingers followed relentlessly.

He gasped aloud and tried to smother the noise in a cough. Her fingers stroked and then her hand closed around the fleshy branch and squeezed gently, and then harder.

Her hand went under his organ and in through the slit and he winced as it caressed his testicles. He felt he would die of the sensation.

"Oh, God—now," Lucrezia murmured. He felt her two bottom cheeks come back against his naked pin of flesh. Flesh against flesh! The thought as much as the sensation nearly made him swoon. His hand tightened on the reins, the other tightened on her stomach.

Lucrezia lay forward on the horse's neck, breathing hard against its mane. This position presented him with a half-full access to her genital region, while her skirt was still sufficiently long to cover them both.

Giuffredo felt suddenly very hopeless and incompetent. He wished the first time didn't have to be on a horse in full canter. But his prick was seething and it seemed that only the unknown thing would give a natural outlet to his feelings.

He pushed his penis against her, felt it nosing on the flesh of her buttocks, felt it rubbing into the rift between them and his chest was thumping all through with excitement.

Gently and then more firmly he pushed against her. He wasn't sure where he was or how to find out. The pressure of his organ against her flesh was enough to make him cough with stifled passion, but he couldn't seem to find the spot.

Lucrezia in her forward position would have made her movement too conspicuous by reaching back to guide him, and their position would have meant a dangerous disarrangement of her skirt, so she lay still, waiting for him to find the place.

Giuffredo edged his prick between the rift right down at its base near the saddle. He had to find the hole. He wanted desperately to find it. He pushed harder. His penis was pricking furiously and it felt suddenly moist. The horse cantered on and the echoes of the others surrounded them in the dimness.

He seemed unable to find the hole. He bit his lips in excitement and frustration. There was no feeling except a great, building pressure —and then suddenly Lucrezia gave a jerk which she controlled immediately and he felt a grip around the tip of his penis which filled him with a fresh wave of sensation. It gripped him like a claw and he tried to push straight in in his mad delight that he was fucking a woman that the unbelieved-in, impossible, was happening—actually happening.

Oh, that claw! Such an excruciating grip! He pushed and Lucrezia jerked and he heard her stifled gasp. Even in his desire he was frightened enough to look guiltily around. The horses cantered on, jogging up and down, gathering speed a little—a bustle of noise.

Giuffredo edged in farther, sliding forward on the saddle, jogging up into Lucrezia as the horse jogged, drawing out a little with the descent.

The hole was very tight. It was pulling back his foreskin with a bruising force which was painful and delightful at the same time. He occasionally heard a murmur from his sister. But she was controlling herself fairly well and pushing her bottom back onto him.

Lucrezia was in an agony of mixed pain and an excited desire to debase herself.

Lying along the horse, with her head so far from her extended bottom where she could feel Giuffredo's finger of flesh stiffly prodding, she had early realized that he was unwittingly probing her anus. She had been about to swing upright and back to tell him when something about the blunt exploration had stopped her. The point screwing there, not yet in the hole, but pushing hard into the cleft of entry made her strain as if she were emptying her bowels. It was a not unpleasant sensation and she suddenly wondered what it would be like to be screwed in her ass. She felt, too, a desire for a completely new sensation and there was something so wicked-seeming about the idea that she quickly resolved to let Giuffredo continue.

She even helped him by stretching back her behind and straining in an attempt to open the tiny posterior slit for him.

His prick was neither as big as his father's nor yet Cesare's, but when the first penetration came it gave her a nauseous shock of pain. She tried not to cry out and hid her face in the horse's thick mane.

From then on it was shock after shock becoming gradually less of a shock but always with the possibility of a relapse into an unexpected pain.

Her return was inflamed with pain which gave way to a sensation of being turned inside out, naked and debased but pervertedly thrilling. She tried not to wiggle and gasp, but she couldn't even be bothered to look up to see if anyone had noticed them.

His penetration, which became easier and easier, began actually to have an erotic effect on her normal sexual organ. She began to get more and more excited. It became more and more difficult to control both movement and sound. She was thankful that the canter of the horse hid her jogging to a considerable extent, making it seem quite natural.

Her anus felt as if it was a wide and deep hole, a gaping chasm into which Giuffredo was plunging his whole body in ravishment. Somehow she wanted more, even though she knew she could take little more. He seemed to be right up in her bowels. She thought of her inner tubes, wondered exactly where he was in them, felt the excitement growing in her vagina, knew she was going to come and pressed her head furiously into the horse's sweating neck and gasped out her fulfillment.

Giuffredo, quite unaware of his mistake, pushed his penis deeper and deeper into the unseen gulf which seemed to hold and suck it in like a whirlpool, refusing to let it withdraw without difficulty.

A million sharp pins seemed to attack his tender organ. It felt sore with the effort of penetration, yet the soreness was an exciting wonderful sensation. He kept his hand on Lucrezia's hip as she lay before him and he dug his fingers into her flesh, intense with his passion.

He no longer looked around him either. He didn't care. His movement was compatible with that of a horse-rider. His main difficulty as he jerked his hips sharply and surreptitiously up at the hole, which was sucking his soul through his body, was to prevent gasps and moans from breaking through his lips. The effort was as excruciating as the crushing of his prick down there under the skirt.

His jerking seemed to get naturally faster. He found that his penis seemed to lead him, working and throbbing with its own life. It was being swallowed in Lucrezia. He could feel the flesh of his loins around his genitals touching the smooth flesh of her bottom which wiggled ever so slightly and secretly against him.

The horse cantered on. Its loud clip-clopping drowning the scarcely controlled noise of Giuffredo's growing passion. Around their horse the men-at-arms scrutinized only the darkness on either side, watching for lawless bands of robbers.

Giuffredo jogged—a natural jogging with the horse. Lucrezia was still, lying along the horse's neck apparently asleep—except for that secretive squirming of her buttocks back against his prick under the sheltering skirt.

Gradually Giuffredo's loins became transformed into a mass of sensation such as he'd never felt before. So this was it! His loins were no longer flesh and blood but some strange, unearthly substance which glowed and burned in its own fire.

He felt himself becoming more and more helpless down in those nether regions. He could hardly disguise his audible passion and every so often a barking gasp broke through his lips and he tried to cover it with a cough. The burning sensation down there was carrying him along with it. He no longer guided, no longer had control. His loins were running away with him. It was excruciating delight and rather frightening as if he were about to have his blood sucked out of his body through his penis.

He felt ridiculously that at this stage he should stop before something terrible happened. But now it was too late; he was no longer able to. The mouth was sucking and sucking,' drawing his blood into his prick, filling it, making it heavy and painful. His prick seemed to have swollen to enormous proportions. He heard Lucrezia give a slight gasp into the horse's mane. He jerked harder, harder. He felt as if his prick were splitting, peeling back in two parts from that small opening at its head, peeling back to let the blood shoot out. He gasped again, trying desperately to cover his noises. The horse jogged and his penis rammed up into the hole. Again, again, he gasped again, finally—and then he bit his lips smothering his groans in the depths of his throat as he felt the sudden release of a wet, sticky substance flowing from him, leaving him after a few moments weak and almost unable to hold the reins.

Now that it was over and Lucrezia sat up as if she'd just awakened from sleep, he felt acutely embarrassed. His embarrassment became wholesale confusion a little later when his sister confided in him what had happened. But she assured him it had been quite pleasant for her and was so open and provocative in her speech that his shame finally left him.

When they reached the Orsini Palace after another hour's ride, he managed to slip into his quarters and change his hose—under the pretext of caring for his horse. On the whole he felt glad, and excited at the new future the day had opened up for him.

CHAPTER FIVE

Innocent VIII lay on his back forming images in his head of his past loves and what he had done with them. That was what he regretted more than anything about his present illness: his doctors had strongly warned him of the danger of any exercise, which had cut out the possibility of having Caterina, his favorite courtesan, brought to satisfy his needs. In spite of his weakness, his sensuality had not left him. In fact, spending all day lying on his back imagining his lovers in all sorts of positions seemed merely to have added to that aspect of his being.

Every so often he thought about the niece that Cardinal Roderigo had told him about. It was so frustrating he could have wept. Now the most he could do was grant her audience and rue the fact that he had not been able to, and would not be able to enjoy her sexually. What a loss! The thought made his stomach turn over. A virgin, beautiful, had said she would do anything for him—even to the extreme of giving herself over to the lusts of the flesh. It needed only a word from him. Innocent felt like weeping, again. Was she as beautiful as Cardinal Roderigo claimed? Could she really have a woman's development at such a youthful age? Anyway he hoped it would not be long before she came to him and then he could truly wallow in self-pity at what he had missed.

For Innocent really doubted his capacity to recover from his present malady—his capacity to recover enough. He saw himself spending the remainder of his life in a continuous convalescence. He would, of course, be waited on hand and foot, and other people would take care of the running of the State although he would hold absolute power still. It was a not unpleasant existence, one that appealed to him. Again the one thing he regretted was his inability to drown himself in the delicious torment of sexual intercourse. But, after all, if he really took great care of himself, perhaps someday . . .

He clapped his hands and an attendant came around from a screen at the far end of the room.

The attendant bowed and withdrew to reappear almost immediately with a large silver salver piled high with fruit.

Innocent began to eat the grapes slowly, spitting the pips out onto the floor. His fingers caressed the taut, cool skin of each morsel. It reminded him of Caterina's breasts—her whole body. If only . . . He cursed suddenly to himself and flung a half eaten grape petulantly across the floor.

* * *

Cardinal Roderigo had lost no time in arranging for Lucrezia to return to Rome. The sooner he found himself in St. Peter's chair the safer he would feel.

He had spent a week or two sounding out his situation. It seemed a good one on the face of it. The Medici, who had long been friendly to the House of Borgia, were for him. Venice, Mantua, Genoa, Siena, the Orsini all were for him. Naples doubted him, rightly fearing the possibility of an alliance between him and Charles VIII of France, whose designs on the Neapolitan kingdom were well known. The French themselves favored Cardinal della Rovere as next Pope, but Roderigo was certain that with judicious gifts they could be won over and withdraw their strong backing of their candidate. Now seemed to be as good a time as any for dealing a death blow to Innocent, who, after all, was serving no good purpose lying sick in his bed with the anarchy of his misrule spread around him.

Lucrezia arrived back in Rome with a small cortege of attendants. The city was still given to the ravages of lawlessness and she made haste to her father's house.

There he had her stay for several days, instructing her in what she must do, explaining the necessity of Innocent's removal if the city and state were to survive—and enjoying Lucrezia's body himself the while.

With Lucrezia clear as to the exact—and fairly simple — nature of her duty, audience was arranged between her and the Pope.

Cardinal Roderigo had her dressed for the occasion in richly embroidered, but simple clothes which would show off the womanliness of her body. He had her plaits let out so that her hair flowed, long and silky to below her shoulders; he placed a string of sapphires set in silver around her neck where they gleamed and threw a blue sheen down onto the visible portion of her bosom, and reflected the bright blue of her eyes.

"My darling daughter—you are already the most beautiful woman in Italy," he declared when she was ready. "The old sensualist will have an orgasm at the very sight of you."

"Oh, papa, I trust all will go well," Lucrezia said anxiously. "I feel a little afraid."

The Cardinal placed a hand on her buttocks and kissed her gently on the neck.

"Don't you worry, my sweet. A beautiful creature such as you can get away with anything she wishes."

* * *

A little later, Lucrezia and her father were ushered into the Pope's chamber. He had propped himself up against his pillows and had his scanty remaining hair brushed and combed. He stared at Lucrezia with unabashed interest, hardly deigning to acknowledge the Cardinal's greeting.

"Truly you did not exaggerate," he said, not taking his eyes from Lucrezia.

Lucrezia curtsied and fixed him with her lovely, deep, knowing eyes.

"It is a great honor for me to be in the presence of your Excellency," she said softly as if in awe. "It is more than such a humble creature as myself could have considered in the realms of possibility."

"Ah, my child — if child you truly be — you are one of the lucky ones who in their natural goodness and humility deserve the highest honors," the Pope replied with an attempt at a winning smile.

"My niece is overcome in the presence of Christ's Vicar," Roderigo cut in. "Such an audience has been her life's object. She did not expect to achieve it so soon."

"I feel unable to speak," Lucrezia said in a hushed tone. "Your Excellency must forgive me."

"My child, come here and give me your hands," Innocent said paternally. "You shall not be afraid of me. Such beauty as you have, particularly if matched by the beauty of soul your uncle gives you, should fear nothing."

He took her hands in his skinny, cold fingers. He was amazed at her loveliness and the warm hands in his filled him with a yearning to be well and active. It had taken him but a fraction of a second to appraise her body as best he could see it under her dress and now he allowed his eyes the delight of fleeting anew and resting on the exposed portion of her bosom and on her neck, so young and smooth.

"I am afraid, your Excellency, that I cannot stay," Cardinal Roderigo said. "I have some important business to see to. I trust you will not find a while with my niece too wearisome. Send her away if she displeases you."

"My dear Cardinal," the Pope answered in sugary tones, "surely you forget yourself. As if such an infant of Christ, reflecting as she does the glorious emblem of early-gained womanhood, could displease me. Pray go your way, Cardinal Roderigo, and much as it grieves me to be deprived so soon of your company, I'm sure I could have no more pleasing visitor than your lovely niece."

Lucrezia wished she knew how to blush at will. But blushes came less easily than tears. She just dropped her head a little, as if overcome at his words. He still held her hands in his.

Cardinal Roderigo bowed and left the chamber. Even as he stepped over the threshold his thoughts were racing with plans for when the Pope was dead.

Innocent watched the exit of his Cardinal. The girl's hands were still warm in his. He didn't speak until Roderigo had left and the door had closed after him. Then he looked back at Lucrezia with eyes which he tried to make kindly.

"But tell me my dear, is it really true that you are only eleven years old?"

"I shall be twelve in a few weeks' time," she replied demurely.

"My child, you have matured far beyond your age. God has seen fit to prepare you for womanhood — who can tell what his wishes for you are."

The Pope's mind gloated over her. He could have given his answer to the question he'd just posed. He looked into her face. Truly those eyes were remarkable. There was . . . what was there? There was . . . yes, there was an aura of the devil about them. His eyes widened as this intuition came to him. But then Lucrezia smiled, as if in flattery at his remarks, a shy, innocent smile and Innocent dismissed the devil from her eyes. What nonsense!

"You are studying, I believe, my child. Tell me, how do you find yourself disposed to the acquisition of knowledge?"

"My studies are simple," she replied. "I find the knowledge of good and evil much more difficult."

In view of his own thoughts, the Pope was quite startled by her words. What precocious thoughts. And what, exactly, did she mean?

"Good and evil, my dear?" he echoed querulously.

Lucrezia suddenly spoke earnestly; she allowed tears to come into her eyes. She hoped she was sounding convincing.

"Your Excellency, I dared not tell my uncle, but I'm beset by problems. That is why I was so anxious for this audience. I knew that in the light of your holiness and wisdom, I should find guidance."

The Pope stared at her. The conversation had taken an unexpected turn which had almost thrown him out of his stride.

"My dear," he said at last, "you are very young and it may well be that the Lord will send you guidance through me. If you would pour out your heart to me, do so."

So far, so good, Lucrezia thought with an inward smile. She allowed a tear to slip over her cheek. The Pope responded to this display of femininity by pressing her hands.

"My child, my child," he said — rather theatrically, she thought —"I had no idea you were so upset."

"Most Holy Father," she blurted, "for most of my life I have known what is good and right — and indeed I still do — but recently things have happened which have made me doubt my strength and courage to continue along the path which I know is that of God."

"Tell me, child, tell me."

Innocent's interest was quickening. This confession from one so young and beautiful and now so obviously upset might prove very entertaining — on the other hand it might be dismally dull. He moved his hands on hers as if comforting her. He wished he could move them on her breasts.

"It is so terrible — I — I don't think I can."

"Now, child," the Pope made his voice slightly stern. He didn't want to miss this now. "You surely would not try to hide anything from God — and I am his representative on this Earth. You can confide in me without fear."

Lucrezia hesitated a minute, cleverly.

"You must forgive me, Holy Father," she whispered pathetically.

"Don't be afraid," he replied majestically. "God is love. All sinners may be forgiven their sins."

"Well, your Excellency, as I began to tell you, until recently my life was blameless. As a child, they tell me I was extremely good and always obeyed. I was brought up to understand the difference between Good and Evil — it all seemed very simple. A saintly life did not seem an impossible idea." She paused, and another tear slipped down her face. She brushed it away and tossed back her hair nervously.

"Until — until a little while ago, I visited a friend's house and the friend put me in charge of her eldest son. I liked him very much . . . and he talked to me. He told me lots of things about men and women until my mind was all confused with what he told me." She stopped and hung her head, letting the tears flow more freely.

The Pope forced himself to fight against impatience. He thought he was beginning to catch on. What a delightful story. What an unexpected enjoyment this afternoon was providing him.

"Go on, dear. God and I are with you."

"And finally," Lucrezia went on brokenly, "he didn't stop with talk. He . . . took me in the grounds and he kissed me and . . . and . . . I believed him . . . it seemed right . . . it seemed right . . . I was all confused . . . until after it was over I knew I had been wicked."

The Pope's thought dwelt on the unmentioned, the undescribed. God, what a lucky fellow this friend was. The thought sent shivers up and down his spine. He felt a ripple in his loins which he knew he should smother or the frustration would be too terrible.

"My dear," he said, after a due interval for consideration, in which Lucrezia broke down and sobbed quietly and he paternally pulled her closer and put an arm around her. "My dear, you had a terrible experience and this man — he should be whipped — took advantage of your innocence in a most unscrupulous way. But, my dear, it often happens that young girls deceive themselves about the seriousness of what has happened. You say that he kissed you and then made advances. That is not too bad, after all."

As he had hoped, his dimness brought a protest from her.

"Oh, but . . . Holy Father . . . he did more than that."

"But he may not have done what I fear, my child. Tell me what he did. Don't be afraid or confused. We are in the presence of the Almighty Lord."

Lucrezia hesitated, as if overcoming a great reluctance.

"I was wearing only a long shift, because it was so hot," she said. "It was modest — it came down to my ankles. But after he had kissed me — it was in a tiny copse in the grounds out of sight of the house — he put his hands on my bottom . . . and — he — he pressed me against him so that I suddenly felt quite faint. And he put his tongue in my mouth and told me to do the same and he felt all over my body with his hands . . ."

She wiped away a tear. The Pope's hand had tightened around her. She had given him an erection. He couldn't wait to hear the rest of the story.

"Go on, my child. Forget nothing. I must know how far it went in order to pray."

"Well, first of all it was over my shift. He felt me all over and everywhere he touched me, particularly when he put his hand between my legs, he made me feel faint. And then I felt so dizzy and helpless that I suggested we sit down. We sat down on the grass beside a tree and, before I really knew what he was doing, he took my shift right off and left me lying there without any clothes on at all. I was . . . I was very frightened, but then . . . then he started feeling me all over again and I only remember the rest as if I were dreaming . . ."

"What do you remember, my dear? If you tell me you will be rid of it. You will have confessed."

"He . . . he kissed me all over — my mouth, my neck, my shoulders, my . . . my breasts and everything. And then he put his finger inside me . . . in between my legs. It made me feel as if I were swooning. I remember thinking that it was wrong, but then it seemed so strong and necessary that I even believed him and thought it might be right after all.

"And then after he'd had his finger in me for some time I began to get terribly excited — even though it was rather painful. I think he put more fingers in me then, because I . . . I felt more pain and I asked him to stop . . . but . . . he wouldn't and I hadn't the strength to push him away. He went on like that for some time until it wasn't painful any more . . . and sometimes he stopped and just kissed me and felt my breasts. And when he did that I wanted him to put his fingers back inside me again because I felt empty and naked as if I needed something . . .

"And then he seemed to leave me for a minute and I just lay there because I was too giddy and too frightened to move. But then he lay down beside me again and pushed me back and I could feel that he was naked, too.

"Then I became very frightened. Because I knew he was going to do something terrible. But . . . but one part of me kept telling me that it wasn't wrong and that I wanted it and that he was right and it would be all right . . .

"He put his fingers back inside me and he

told me to open my thighs wide. I must have done it although I don't remember deciding I would . . . because . . . because — oh Father, it's too terrible!"

The Pope, agog with ill-concealed excitement, had one hand on his erect penis under the sheets. He was inflamed by the story she was telling him about herself in her soft voice, with her head bowing against his shoulder in shame and agony.

"Go on, child," he said, with a great attempt at majestic calm. "You are bound to finish it now."

After a few sobs, Lucrezia continued, as if reluctantly.

"The next thing . . . he was . . . he was lying on top of me and he had my thighs wide open and he . . . he was pushing himself at me . . . pushing his . . . his . . . you know, Father, against mine until suddenly . . . oh . . . suddenly it was in and he was — he was making love to me completely . . . and he went on and on and he got terribly excited and so did I . . . I was almost fainting . . . and there was a little pain . . . and . . . and he began to gasp and groan and then . . . and then he made a great noise . . . and . . . and it was all over . . . it was finished."

"My poor child, my poor child," (oh to have been that young man! the Pope thought) "what a terrible time."

"Of course, afterwards," Lucrezia added, through her tears, "I was terribly sorry and ashamed at what had happened — and terribly embarrassed. But . . . but he laughed at me and tried to — what he called — reason with me. But I knew I'd done wrong."

The Pope was silent for a while, letting her

cry against his shoulder. He appeared to be deliberating. In fact, he was trying to live through what had just been described, trying to imagine every part of her body — the secret, intimate places, trying to imagine that enormous emotional chill that was felt at the moment of entry. Oh, he had been ill and unable for so long. He felt overcome with self-pity and defiance. His penis was hot in his hand, and aching with repressed longing.

"What you did, my child, was wrong in those circumstances," he said at last. "But you have little to reproach yourself for. We all sin — it is inescapable and some sins are greater than others. But you are only a young girl — even though you may have the appearance of a woman — and you were led astray by an older man who, obviously, well knew how to prey upon what, after all, are perfectly natural appetites. The fault is entirely his, my child. God will forgive you, have no fear. His mercy is boundless."

Lucrezia took a deep breath behind her veil of mock tears.

"But, Holy Father, the main trouble has come after the event. I told you I was having difficulty about Good and Evil. Well . . . I find, now, that I'm beset with overwhelming desires to repeat what happened. I do my best to overcome them, but I'm likely to give way at any moment."

"I see — I see."

Innocent's hand moved slightly on his prick. He felt very disturbed. This was better and better, but the thought that he couldn't take advantage of it was killing him.

"Have you seen the young man since?"

"No, your Excellency. I do all in my power to keep away from him. But I feel the desire with any man — oh I know it's terrible. You must think I'm unbelievably wicked."

"Not at all, my child, not at all," Innocent reassured her. That hand in mine is so near, he was thinking. I could just take it and put it on my prick under the sheets. It would take about two seconds in time and mean moving it a distance of thirty centimeters.

"You have had an experience," he said, "which was bound to shake you to your roots. It has opened up a whole new channel of experience . . ." He grinned to himself at his words. "And, naturally given you a desire for sensations and emotional experiences that you hardly realized existed. We all have these desires, my dear. Don't think you are alone."

"But what must I do?" Lucrezia pleaded.

She could see his erection through the sheets and the coverlets. So papa had been right. He would want to. So far, very good. But now she had to take what chances came to her. She rested her head against his shoulder so that her lightly perfumed hair was brushing against his face. Leaning forward toward him, she was able to expose much more of her bosom — showing him more than a third of their rounded fullness.

Innocent's head was in a whirl. Looking down on her, as if with compassion, he could see down the front of her dress. The cleavage of her lovely white breasts was agony to his loins. He could hardly restrain his hands. Her golden hair was against his face. It smelled slightly of lavender. He could see those full, ill-defined lips in the lovely, sad face. If only . . . he thought. If only . . . What did the doctors know about it? Half of them were fools and the other half scoundrels. Supposing he did — what then? His desire for life fought with his desire for her flesh. But the desire for life was weakened because he wasn't sure he'd lose his life if he had her. That could be all eyewash. And her flesh was here, so real and near and unbearably tantalizing.

"It is probable," the Pope said slowly, "that you've built up a myth around this one occasion when you made love. And because it seems so unholy and wicked to you, you therefore, in your deprivation, desire it the more — a very natural reaction.

"In very few cases would I suggest this course of cure. But you know, to overcome a greater, even God will allow a lesser evil. So it may be that if you permitted yourself intercourse just once again — and without any feeling of wrongdoing to add to the excitement — you would get the whole necessity out of your system. At least, you would rid yourself of its full power as you now feel it and would pave the way to a beginning at controlling it. This may seem a very strange recommendation, but reflect, my lamb, that the ways of God are often strange beyond belief — but always with the end in mind. If, by this means, you can help to overcome the acuteness of your desires and thus, eventually, overcome them completely, you will have taken the right and only course. If you go on as you are you will either go mad or give way again and again until you are no better than the lowest whore."

There was a long silence after his words. Lucrezia let her hand slip from his and flop against his thigh, as if accidentally, in weariness. She could feel his skinny thigh under the coverlet — and against the side of her hand she could feel the rising bulge of his erection.

Knowledge of his desire had given her course to be bold.

"I thank you, Holy Father. I'm sure your advice is good. And as it is your advice I'm willing to follow it with a glad heart — even though of my own willing the idea must have seemed wrong to me. I see that it may well be the only way. But there is one thing that frightens me still."

"What is that, my child?"

"Holy Father, it's just something I feel. It hardly makes sense. But I'd know that it was simply lust in the man with whom I made love. I'd know that although I was trying to purge myself, that he was on a different plane simply using me as an object of his passion. Although I could have holy aims and thoughts about what I was doing, it would shame me that the man would feel completely differently."

The Pope turned this over in his mind, gloating, playing cat with the mouse, unaware that he was being outplayed, that his thoughts were being directed along channels which would lead to the inevitable. Amidst his thoughts he was aware of her hand against his erection, the slight pressure making him involuntarily strain the mast up against her hand, trusting that she wouldn't realize what was happening.

"I think I could only do it, now, after what you've said, with someone who knew why I was doing it and sympathized and made love to me with the intention of curing my desires," Lucrezia told him.

"For that you would need the holiest of men," said the Pope innocently.

"Yes," Lucrezia replied from his shoulder, "the holiest of men."

She raised her head and stared into his eyes for several seconds.

The Pope felt her words sinking into his mind like a physical force. They startled and excited him — and her look heightened the effect. He was sure, now, that it would be a simple matter. The girl was very susceptible; she would really imagine she was ridding herself of evil.

Slowly he looked at her breasts again. How lovely they would look swinging free to the air. And her body! What would her body be like? And how would her face look screwed up and lost in passion. His hand clenched over his erection in a fierce surge of emotion. He couldn't pass up such an opportunity — even if it was the last thing he did. The last thing! He wondered. But doctors always exaggerated. It was part of their business to frighten the patient into submission. And surely he wouldn't feel so much like having intercourse with her if it were likely to do him any real harm.

Lucrezia had seen the lust in Innocent's eyes. She had very nearly won. She wondered what it would be like with such an old man, but the thought didn't appall her — in fact she rather liked the idea of being screwed by fatherly old men. The contrast between their balding heads, her golden locks, her young, firm body and their slack flesh added to her excitement, made the whole thing seem less permissible.

Without looking up she raised her hand to her cheek and then allowed it to drop back casually onto the bed — onto his stiff penis. She could feel the bulge under her hand and she felt him tense with her touch.

The Pope felt his breath rise up through his body, as if from his loins, strangling him in a weight of emotion. This was it; this was the moment of choice — but it was already too late to choose. Knowing the inevitable he nonetheless raced through a number of arguments in his mind against having her. But now her fingers were moving gently on his penis, stabbing it with needles of fire and she had raised her eyes to his again, was looking deeply into him as if she knew the depths of his soul.

"You are the holiest of men," she whispered. And her mouth opened gently and her eyes closed as if she were overcome at the awe the thought inspired.

He seized her then and drew her up to him.

"We will drive the evil out of you," he said with a voice he could hardly control. "Together we will prove the strength of the Lord." Inside he burned with excitement and laughed madly at his hypocritical words. He would do it. He would screw her young-girl flesh, fill her young-girl passage with his holy mace — if it was his very last act he would do it.

"I will do anything you think should be done," Lucrezia whispered, with a fine show of youthful, feminine weakness. So saying she pressed her breasts into him and pushed her young body alongside his in a sign of submission.

Innocent's lips trembled with lust. He tried to think clearly for a moment, forcing his thoughts away from a desire to rip her clothes from her with his ebbing strength.

"We are unlikely to be disturbed," he said softly. "My attendants wait in the antechamber when I have visitors, but against emergency perhaps you would go and bolt that door, my dear — and then you can remove your clothes — behind the screen if you wish — and come back here."

Lucrezia ran her hand along his hard tower and then obediently got up from the bed and went to the oak door. She slid the heavy bolt across, looked back to the bed, smiled nervously at the Pope and slipped behind the screen.

She took a fair time about undressing, flinging her garments one by one onto the top of the screen. She peered through one of the cracks at the join of the two panels and saw Innocent's eyes avidly taking in the items of clothing which had intimately draped her body. What a lustful old man he is, she thought—and with all that nonsense about the strength of the Lord. She sniggered to herself. She'd show him her strength and see how he stood up to that.

She pressed her hands down her buttocks. God, what a thrill he was going to have doing that—astonishing that her own body meant so little to her. She smoothed her belly and glanced down at the globes of her breasts. She felt a little nervous about what this was all leading to, but when she glanced for the last time through the crack and saw the Pope playing with himself so obviously under the sheets she took heart and walked around the screen, utterly naked, toward the bed.

Innocent's eyes goggled at her as she came toward him, with head bowed slightly.

"Don't be afraid of your nakedness—you have a rare beauty," he said in an attempt to sound pontifical. But his eagerness seeped into the words making them sound comic.

Lucrezia raised her head and fixed her eyes on him. She had adopted an expression of young and tender helplessness.

Innocent let his gaze rifle her from top to

toe. What beautiful proportions! If he couldn't have had her now he would have been willing to die rather than live with the memory of her body denied him.

Her slender neck ran into slim, sloping shoulders, well-covered with flesh; her breasts were firm and impudent, the sleek ovals begged to be cupped in a hand, to be squeezed. Her waist was very slim, which accentuated the sexy outward curve of her hips and the tapering into firm luscious-fleshed thighs. He could see the slight trace of blonde down on her lower belly and what was little more than a shadow of flesh at the nest between her legs.

Halfway toward him she turned and went back to the door to look at the bolt, as if afraid she hadn't fastened it completely. Her ruse to show off her body was effective.

Innocent strained up in bed, his old penis throbbing at the sight of her oval buttocks which shadowed into gentle hollows as she walked. Seen from the back her waist seemed even slimmer in comparison with her hips, filled out as they were by those incomparable buttocks. What a rump! His fingers itched to hold it in his hands.

Lucrezia came toward the bed once more, quickly this time, and the Pope stretched out his arms toward her.

"We must make it as if we were completely given to the lusts of the flesh," he said hoarsely. "If there is any self-consciousness about our lovemaking it will fail to satisfy and exorcise."

She slipped into his arms and threw back her head as he began, feverishly, to kiss her breasts. He released her and grasped a breast in each hand, sucking the points as if they were trumpets. Lucrezia felt cold shivers slide convulsively down her spine. She abandoned herself to his lips which ran all over the top part of her body, sucking as if he wanted to draw blood from her skin.

She put her arms around his skinny body and pressed his head against her breasts. He was quivering with excitement.

His hands began frantically to explore her body, moving down her back, smoothing her buttocks, gripping them, catching them in voluptuous handfuls of flesh; he ran his fingers along the warm ravine of cleavage between them, pressed the puckered flesh of her anus until she squirmed and whimpered; he stroked her thighs and sought her lips with his. His breath smelled of bad teeth and his tongue was rough. When she poked her fresh, little tongue back through his lips she felt spaces where some of his teeth were missing.

The Pope began to pant with a mixture of excitement and shortness of breath through his efforts. His heart was pounding unhealthily. But his penis was as stiff as a ramrod.

In a very short time his hands, which had savagely ravished her body, lingered over her most intimate parts with a dalliance which betrayed his utter sensuality, became insufficient instruments for his lustful satisfaction.

With each fistful of flesh he clenched—buttucks, breasts, belly, her vaginal lips, his hands showed a wild catholicity—his hips strained up under the sheets and his penis pulsated like barrels of heated gunpowder.

With a shock, sudden and overwhelming as if cold water had been poured on his loins, the Pope felt Lucrezia's cool hands slip under the sheets and enclose the burning heat of his prick in their soothing balm. He shuddered from head to toes.

Her fingers soothed and caressed with what he would have remarked as practiced excellence had he not been so immersed in his own feelings and satisfaction. Then, gently, they began to rub up and down the stiff, brittle-seeming stem of flesh.

The Pope's lips moved the way they did when he prayed.

"For God's sake get into bed!" he managed to utter at last.

Lucrezia quickly slipped under the sheets, with his clawing hands helping her in.

His body was cold against hers—the body of an old bloodless man—an astonishing contrast overall with the heat of his penis, the one part of him truly alive.

She pressed the warm overflow of her flesh against the chilly skinniness, warming him, exciting him so that his hands jumped over her body, unable to keep still on her.

Innocent's lips shivered an accompaniment to his quivering body. He had seldom come across such a completely rounded, filled-out delight of womanliness and his hands could hardly take sufficient fill.

He squirmed as her hand moved off his penis, running down it, skimming over its base and teasing his testicles and the growing nucleus of heat between his old thighs.

Lucrezia, too, was squirming with delight as his fingers brushed her vagina and pierced into its moist outskirts. She rolled over on top of him, infusing his body with her soft warmth. She pressed down on him and rubbed her hips voluptuously against his prick which she felt rolling like a length of doughy bread between them, a length of hot, newly-baked bread.

His skinny old arms encircled her, pulling her at him, his hips pressed up against her, indenting her slight, sensual superfluity of flesh.

Gently, for several minutes they pressed together, with his hands holding her buttocks, his lips sucking her open mouth. And then she wriggled up a little on him until his prick waved wildly between her slightly opened thighs, cleaving up so that she could feel its upper side against her labia and against her buttocks.

She broke from his ardent kissing and levered herself toward an upright position, sitting across his loins, one thigh on either side of his body. She caught his rod in her hand, gave it a last squeeze, knelt up and placed it against the open mouth of her vagina.

The Pope raised his head from its horizontal position and let his eyes augment the pleasure of his bodily senses.

He watched her hold his penis toward her poised aperture, lower herself gently and then flop down on it with a gasp of pent-up breath. Immediately he felt an abandonment of his soul; it rushed down through his body to the head of his penis which was caught in the powerful contractions of her channel. It made the rest of his body, his mind, seem so much putty, so much lifeless clay. It was only down there at that one slim tube of living flesh that there was any reason for existence. The rest of him could have died if only that would go on living forever and ever amen, living and feeling, being squeezed in her slim channel which descended and rose on it, tightly, firmly, wetly, deliciously, forever and ever so that his lips began to mutter feverish, delirious obscenities.

Lucrezia plunged down on that stiff pike, feeling it tear up inside her as if a pikesman had made a fierce homeward thrust. Her breasts jumped with her plunges, her thighs sank lower and lower, her knees slithered farther away from his body on either side until the whole of her crotch was pressed against and around the base of his organ and the staff itself was totally contained inside her juicy tunnel.

From time to time she opened her closed eyes or brushed the hair from her face. Then she would see the Pope lying back, only his hips tensed, moving up at her in slight undulations as she descended. She would see his lips moving and his white strained face. And through her own stimulation which wetly inflamed her trounced passage she had the double satisfaction of knowing that things were going according to plan.

The Pope, too, opened his eyes ever so often and fixed her with his gaze. Then—and it took very little acting on her part—she would screw up her beautiful face in passion, to excite him, mutter obscenities herself and let her hair swing forward over her face in abandonment.

His body began to writhe and twist as his penis sank deeper and deeper into her moist, hot body. It was frail and bony and covered now with a thin film of perspiration.

He could feel the pounding of his heart. It seemed to fill his ears and his whole body. He was panting wildly, but having difficulty in breathing. But these discomforts seemed to add rather than detract from the pure exquisite quality of his sensation. The physical torture of his body whipped up his senses to a fine point of receptivity.

Through half-closed eyes he watched her full breasts leap and sway in their smooth, glossy skin; he felt her thighs warmly press into his loins as she came down, impaling herself on the rod which had impaled so many times before her and which, in spite of the Pope's weakness was still in a state of perfect workability —the only part of him which functioned as always.

He was getting more and more excited. A thrumming in his loins joined with a thrumming in his chest and ears.

Lucrezia pressed harder and harder on him, giving him no respite, drawing herself right up above him, so that only the knob of his organ remained nestled in the warm pink portals of her sex and then crashing down again so that she felt that spear of flesh soar up inside her with a movement which made her stomach turn over. At the end of the downward stroke she ground her crotch and buttocks against him, squirming on him for a few seconds until gasps burst from his lips.

Occasionally his hands twitched out to her and managed to grasp and feebly squeeze her thighs or even reach to her breasts.

So furious was her youthful onslaught that she began to feel the excitement of culmination and forced herself to slow down the pace so as not to lose any ferocity of attack until Innocent was ready to come himself.

The Pope was no longer chill. His whole frame was flushed with a pink heat which was a frame between his legs. His prick felt bloated, aching and growing up to an ecstatic bursting point. His thighs and back ached with the upward pressure he'd continuously exerted at Lucrezia's bobbing crotch. The drumming in his ears was almost unbearable. He was trying desperately to force the explosion at his prick before there was an explosion in his head or in his chest.

His breathing had become a pitiful consumptive whine but Lucrezia showed no mercy at his tortured, pathetic state.

Innocent opened his eyes. In his aching head he suddenly felt a power of great emotion. She was beautiful, so beautiful and innocent and trying to do right. He would keep her after this day; he would keep her and look after her and any future intercourse she had would be with him and then she'd be able to enjoy it because she could tell herself always that it was purifying her, giving her a holy outlet for desires which would, of course, continue to beset her.

In that moment Innocent felt that he loved the child with the woman's body. He wanted to reach out and hold her to him, but he no longer had the strength and he had already closed his eyes and become acutely conscious once again of his prick which seemed to be swelling in her so that it seemed it might never come out again.

He writhed his loins against her. The desire to come was intolerable and yet he couldn't quite seem to manage it. It would happen, but his head felt as if it was splitting and his chest was constricted and he hoped it would hurry.

Feebly he tensed his thighs, felt a twinge of cramp and relaxed them again. He pressed his abdomen against her descending nether parts. He opened his eyes again and fixed her with a gaze which did not take her in clearly.

Lucrezia sensed from his writhing, his agonized expression, his gasps and groans that the end was approaching and she unleashed her body and began to pummel him for all she was worth, letting herself be carried away by her own momentous passion.

She could feel her loins swarming as if a thousand snakes were writhing inside. She released a stream of gasping cries which broke through the blackness in Innocent's head and revived in him a last flush of passion so that he thrust his loins up at her, mumbled painfully through dry lips, groaned agonizingly in an evident warning climax and clenched his fingers into her thighs with a last strength.

Dazedly he opened his eyes again. His loins seemed to be covered with a sticky wetness amidst Lucrezia's moanings. His prick felt grazed, beaten, full of something that must escape. He saw her face mistily, head thrown back—beautiful neck—lips moving. His fingers dug hard into her fleshy thighs in a last paroxysm of life. He felt the climax near . . . on him . . . there! He gasped deliriously, felt his penis explode as if in a thousand pieces, fought for breath, fought for consciousness, felt himself losing both, tried to appeal to her with his eyes and slowly slipped off into a painful darkness.

Lucrezia had echoed his feelings with precision. Her flood of sensation had swamped up in her loins with a dragging delightful pain, swamped up and over just as his prick had seemed to be at its biggest in her so that she felt it would smash right through her and up into her belly.

For some seconds afterwards, still excited and hardly knowing where she was, she had swayed about on his prostrate body and then she had flopped down on top of him.

It took her almost a minute to begin to collect her wits.

The first thing she realized was that Innocent was not just lying still through exhaustion. He had lost consciousness. Lucrezia wasn't dismayed: this was all part of the plan—except that it appeared to be succeeding almost beyond expectations.

Swiftly, methodically, she got up and dressed. With the inside of her dress she wiped away any tell-tale signs of the Pope's incontinence and then she rearranged the bed and his body. After that she collected herself for a moment, checked everything, quietly went to the door and unbolted it. She tiptoed back to Innocent's bed, let out a high-pitched scream and rushed back toward the door.

She hadn't reached it before it was flung open and two attendants rushed in.

Lucrezia pointed to the bed.

"God protect us," she cried. "His Holiness just passed out in the middle of talking."

CHAPTER 6

The news of the Pope's collapse spread like pillage through the city.

His doctors came forthwith and pronounced that the strain of receiving visitors had obviously been too much for his weak heart. There was little hope of his survival beyond a few hours.

His doctors stayed at his bedside and visitors from the Pope's circle were frequent. He got weaker and weaker at a very rapid rate. His physicians were agreed on their helplessness in face of his critical state.

The following day, Innocent, without having regained consciousness, was still clinging weakly to life and a Hebrew physician came to his bedside, claiming to have a prescription which would save the dying prelate's life. For his task, he said, he needed the blood of young boys. The Pope's skeptical physicians eventually found him two young boys, who, for a ducat each, were prepared to give him all the blood he needed.

But so complete was the failure of his remedy that the two boys died and the physician was forced to flee to save his own life from the wrath of those who had doubted him from the beginning.

For just one more day, Innocent lay in his bed breathing very feebly. In the early hours of the following morning he was found to be breathing no more.

* * *

Cardinal Roderigo lost no time in organizing the succession. Even during the prescribed nine days of ceremonies connected with Innocent's death, he was busy arguing, offering, bargaining, encouraging toward his own ends.

On the tenth day the cardinals assembled in St. Peter's to hear the Sacred Mass of the Holy Ghost recited on the tomb of the Prince of the Apostles. They swore upon the gospels to faithfully observe their trust and the Conclave was immured.

A few days later Cardinal Roderigo Borgia was elected Pope Alexander VI. He had bargained well.

Many were the cardinals who benefited from Roderigo's election. To Cardinal Sforza went the vacated vice-chancellorship and the bishopric of Agri; to the Orsini the Church of Carthage and the legation of Marche; to Colonna the Abbey of Subiaco; to Savelli the legation of Perugia; to Raffaele Riario went Spanish benefices worth four thousand ducats yearly. They, too, had bargained well.

Lucrezia, who had played the largest part of all, was rewarded with a beautiful diamond necklace and a passionate night in her father's bed during which he mounted her five times and both were completely satisfied. She was then sent off to continue her studies under the tutors who were shocked at her provocative display of bosom and would have died of horror had they known exactly what had been displayed to the Pope before his death.

CHAPTER 7

Cesare had been brought back to Rome on the news of his father's election. Cardinal Roderigo felt it only fitting that his son, whom he hoped would one day succeed him, should be present at the ceremony.

Ever since his adventure with his sister, Cesare had been in a fever heat to renew his relationship with her, but there had been no opportunity.

Over and over in his mind he had relived those furiously passionate moments by the pool, over and over he had thought of how next time he would be less embarrassed, more expert, more concerned with prolonging the pleasure. His incestuous lovemaking had given him a new awareness of women as well. In Perugia he had watched them walking down the street with their bosoms soaring, had imagined their breasts untrammeled by clothes. He had stared at the occasional traces of a round and protruding buttock under a dress such as the peasant girls wore and had longed to move up behind and place his hand on that undulating mound of firmness. He had longed for lips, for fondling hands, for the aching sensation of that body-grip on his penis—until he walked around with an almost permanent erection and a slight flush always on his face. At night he was haunted by dreams of his sister's passion-wracked body, images of other bodies. He masturbated with a new vigor. He almost wept with desire for a good screw. And on return to Rome he conceived of a daring plan to achieve the aided orgasm he so desperately needed.

The interregnum between the death of one Pope and the election of another was invariably filled with a furious outburst of lawlessness in Rome. Bands of lawbreakers would roam the streets. Murders were committed on an average of several a day, robberies took place on an unprecedented scale and rapes were so numerous that count was lost. It was this savage jungle state within the city that Cesare decided should cover his own fulfillment of his desires.

In the grounds of Cardinal Roderigo's house was a gardener's shed in which Cesare had previously noted some old, cheap clothing such as would be worn by the ordinary citizen. This, he decided, he would don one evening when his father was not at home. He would rub grime into his face, tousle his hair and, with his gold-hilted dagger in his belt under his doublet, sally out into the lawless streets in search of a woman.

It was a wild plan, he realized. It was full of dangers. He, himself, might be attacked; he might be caught in the act of rape; he might be beaten up by the city guard which functioned in a desultory fashion from time to time. But on the first count he hoped his old clothes would make him seem too worthless an object to make it worth anybody's while to assault him—and on the others he'd take a chance, so dearly did he need to plunge his dagger of genital flesh into a female sheath.

For a couple of days, while he awaited his opportunity, Cesare wandered through the city, which was calmer by daytime, watching the women who quickly came and went, or—in large bands for safety—washed their clothes down at the river's edge. He particularly frequented the poorer sections of the city as it was here that he was more likely to succeed in his plan without too many later investigations being made. And it was in one of these quarters that he found the sort of situation he had been seeking.

At dusk, he noted, at a particular spot, three goat-swains—two men and a girl—were in the habit of driving a large herd of goats from the city gates into their pen within the city. They all stayed together until a point near the Bridge of St. Angelo across the river where the girl would bid them good-night and slip across the bridge to her house which was close to the far bank. The two men would continue with the goats under the assumption that their companion was safe with only such a little distance to go alone.

Cesare made a survey of the area. His heart raced in anticipation of the deed. As he marked the spot—dangerously near her home—where he could drag her over the low parapet onto the shrub-covered, shelving bank, his breath came quickly as if he were already lying between her legs.

The girl, herself, was a peasant girl with a saucy, good-looking face and a strong, loose-limbed body with large breasts and a behind that was pert under the thin country dress she wore. She would be no easy conquest. Cesare was well aware. But he thought he could subdue her and the sight of her body, revealed in a way that only peasant clothing would allow, infused him with a nervous excitement that gave him butterflies in his stomach.

The day fixed for the crowning of the new Pope came nearer and Cardinal Roderigo spent more and more time away from his house fixing the details of the ceremony.

Cesare's chance came at last. In a sudden fit of trembling he donned the old clothes in the gardener's shed. The hose he slit between the legs—just enough so that another tug would give his organ free exit. The doublet came down far enough to hide the spot.

He stole out of the house, leaving a door to the grounds unlatched for his re-entry, hoping that no would-be robbers would discover it before he got back.

Along the main streets people were still passing in groups, sometimes singly. He avoided these more frequented places after a time and set out through the growing twilight to the poor quarter.

Narrow, cobbled streets led him down toward the river. Sometimes someone flitted quickly from one doorway to another, sending his heart into his mouth, sometimes a shutter would slam, making him jump and twice he brazened it past a group of men who peered at him in the half-light but made no move to interfere with him.

At the bridge across the river he stopped

and leaned on the parapet for a moment to calm himself and quell the thumping of his heart. He peered through the gloom. He was sure they hadn't yet come. Below, the river was a smooth, dark sheet, behind him odd noises rang out from the Castle of St. Angelo which towered up in ghostly form. In the distance he could still dimly see the outline of St. Peter's. There was nobody about, now. The majority of honest citizens who were able would now be safely locked behind their doors with the shutters barred.

Cesare listened. On the still air he heard the faint bleat of a goat.

Quickly he set off across the broad bridge. His heart was still pounding wildly. The seriousness of what he was doing crept over him and in the middle of his hurrying he wondered, without slowing his place, if he shouldn't just turn back and get home as quickly as possible. But in his head he had an image of the goat-girl with her loose-limbed walk and her body curves embraced in her peasant dress, and he hurried on.

By now the dusk was settling in; in a short time it would be completely dark.

He reached the point where the bridge ran into the far bank. He took a quick look around. He could almost see the girl's house to which he'd followed her twice already. Then he swung himself lightly over the parapet and crouched down out of sight.

The parapet at this point was only three feet high and there was a further six-inch drop on the bankside. From where Cesare crouched, trying to still his heaving breath, the bank, divided into patches of knee-high scrub and dusty sand, stretched gently down to the still edge of the river.

There he waited, not daring to look back over the parapet. He was so nervous that he ripped open the slit in his hose and urinated quickly against the wall of the bridge. He need still do nothing, he told himself. He could just let her go by and then go home. He still hadn't definitely decided he was going through with it when he heard her light footfall on the bridge.

He pulled the dagger from the belt under his doublet. His hand was trembling as he put it over his mouth to try and quiet his breath. In spite of his bladder-emptying, his organ was at half-cock with nervous excitement.

Suppose she was not alone today. Suppose someone came toward the bridge from the opposite direction and saw them. Suppose she broke away from him and screamed for the city guard. What would happen to him? What would his father say? A thousand doubts sprang in on him. But there was her footfall, unsuspecting and so close. He held his breath. There was no other noise at all. She was alone as usual.

Tense as a bowstring he waited. Now she was about ten paces away, now nine, now eight ... now one ... He put his hands on the parapet in the half-darkness, and with a spring he was up and over it just behind her.

The girl half-turned in horror before his hand clapped over her mouth and he flashed the dagger in front of her eyes.

"If you scream or make any sound I'll kill you," he whispered fiercely.

The girl stared at him with wide, horrified dark eyes. It was rather a shock to find himself so near her, touching her, the object of her terrified attention, after watching her from a distance for two nights.

Her body was very warm against him through her thin dress. She held herself taut, but didn't make a sound.

Still holding one hand over her mouth, Cesare, glancing nervously across the bridge, prodded her toward the parapet.

"Climb over and drop down the other side," he ordered. "And don't make a sound. I don't intend to kill you and I shan't unless you scream."

For a moment the girl wouldn't move and he thought she was going to resist. He prodded her side with the point of the dagger and she went in front of him to the parapet and swung over it, dropping down with him to the other side.

Cesare prodded her on down the bank toward the water's edge and away from the bridge. Behind them on the land side, the bank ended some distance up in a high wall. He was safe from that direction.

The girl made no sound as he walked with her, hand still on her mouth in case she tried to shout. It had all been very easy. Through his excitement he looked down sideways at the bulge of her breasts. It was really here at last —and so easy.

At a distance from the bridge they stopped. Cesare glanced quickly back. Nobody on the bridge could see them at that distance. He jabbed the girl with the knife.

"Lie down—and if you try to shout I'll slit your throat."

The girl looked around at him. She had long dark hair which was mussed up now around her dark face. Her eyes had lost some of their startled horror and were gleaming with anger.

"What do you want?" she said fiercely. "I am poor—I have no money."

Cesare was beginning to feel very sure of himself.

"You have something worth its weight in gold," he said softly. "Now lie down and I will show you."

The girl's sudden defense took him unawares. He had come to expect an easy victory. She twisted suddenly from his grasp and took a half step toward the bridge. But Cesare's reaction was quick. He caught her again before she had even the time to cry out. He clamped his hand roughly over her mouth and pushed her to the ground. She fell under him and he dug the knife at her ribs.

"I told you I'll kill you," he hissed.

But this time his warning had no effect. The girl probably thought he would slit her throat anyway when he'd finished with her and she resolved to sell her life dearly.

She twisted over and struggled furiously with him so that Cesare, who'd had no intention of using the knife and adding murder to his crime, was forced to drop the weapon and use both hands in an effort to overcome her.

His prick, which was erect as a raised drawbridge, had flipped out of the slit in his clothing and was crushed and rubbed between them as they struggled.

He managed to stretch her arms out on either side, but her legs continued to writhe and buffet him as he lay along her.

Her face, wrinkled with dark fury, was directly below his. With a little gust of triumph he closed his mouth over hers as she struggled. He could tell he was much stronger than she.

When he took his face away she spat in his face. He released one of her arms and slapped her face with his free hand. She pushed with her released arm, jabbing him with her elbow and he fell off. The girl took full advantage of her gain and slithered out from under him, rolling over on top, clawing at him, reaching for his throat with strong fingers.

Surprised, Cesare decided that the time had come for stronger measures. He was afraid someone might hear their scuffling from the bridge—and apart from that he was almost coming against her wriggling body.

He pulled back his right fist, pushing her wrists away with his left, and punched hard and straight into her belly.

The girl collapsed on him, gasping with pain and he rolled her off and swayed over on top of her again. She was completely winded. She lay there helpless for the moment, with her dress halfway up her strong, naked thighs.

Cesare lost no time, now. He was very scared that somebody might have heard the noise. He ripped her dress up what remained hidden of her thighs, felt between her legs for the love-slit she was in no position to protect and guided his hungry prick at it.

He held the girl's arms with his hands once his knob was against her lower lips—and then he pushed in against her.

For several seconds he couldn't seem to make progress. He released an arm and reached down again, feeling for the opening. He pulled her flopping thighs apart to facilitate his entry and pushed again.

The girl squealed even through her lack of breath when his throbbing knob pierced into her. Automatically she swung her arm up and tried to push him off, gasping with the pain in her belly and the fresh pain down at her treasured vagina.

Cesare caught the arm and forced it down again. He was really in now. And it was tight enough to hurt. He was flooded with a great sense of relief, as if the frustrations of a lifetime had suddenly been put right.

The girl was squirming with pain. But his push had so hurt and winded her that she could hardly groan, let alone put up any serious opposition to his assault on her maidenhood.

Cesare breathed out his relief. At last he was able to quench his desire in a tight, loving, tender body. He thrust in as if he were ramming shot into a cannon and with each thrust he expelled a toe-shaking sigh of relief.

With his body quivering all over he wriggled his loins into her pelvis. He didn't want to take long now that he'd succeeded at last. His prick was heavy and prickling and the girl, her face creased in pain, had almost given up struggling under the fury of his attack.

Cesare lowered his face onto hers and kissed her lips. Her lips were unresponsive, tight together and she forced her face away from him. So he kissed her dark neck as his prick seared up into her clam-gripping vagina. He wriggled in and in until, for the first time, his whole prick from throbbing knob to tingling base was buried in a soft female passage.

He shagged her furiously with quick hard strokes. He couldn't take too much time, but he had to have that final world-shattering explosion; that had to take place in her soft, tight body.

The girl lay under him, still too wounded in her belly to resist. He let go of her arms and put his hands under her buttocks, scraping the backs of his fingers against the sand. Her rump was firm and springy. The feel of it sent a new zest winging through his hot ramrod. He pulled her belly up against him so that it seemed as if he was holding her vagina in a framework for his prick. He looked down at her belly which he could see, dimly white in the darkness. He could also see his weapon, dimly white, moving into the cranny at her thigh-junction.

He held her buttocks tightly. Each stroke now was as if he were bursting into her for the first time. His prick had grown tight, intense with sensation. It was coming. He gritted his teeth and fixed his eyes on her dim face, turned sideways, still creased in pain. She was a stranger, a total stranger. And he was joined with her here in this most complete of intimacies! They were one flesh—united by his bridge of penis!

As he felt the soaring mount in him he never took his eyes from her face. She moved her legs occasionally, but simply because she was uncomfortable. From start to near finish there had been little resistance.

He burst in and in and with each burst he felt the moment edge excruciatingly nearer. He was trying to keep his noises back in his throat. There he was, coughing and growling, trying not to lose control.

He felt the last movement in his loins. It was joy and beauty and savagery all combined in his screwing into this firm and beautiful unknown body. He squeezed the buttocks in his hands as he thrust, and his thrusts slowed to grinding heaves. He was losing control. It was heaven. It was hell. He couldn't keep it back. It was coming, coming, into the body of this strange, prostrate girl whose buttocks were in his hands, whose tight, clinging vagina was around his prick, whose face was there pressed into the sand in the darkness. It was coming, whirling, here, oh God, here . . . "Aaaaaaaah!" . . . the final cry groaned from his throat, forcing his lips apart and he flopped and bit her strained neck as he shot his sperm into her helpless, wide-open passage.

The girl lay as though dead and after a while he pulled his hands out from under her behind and rolled off her. Now that it was over he felt a flatness. It certainly didn't seem worth the extreme and violent measures he'd gone to to get it.

His thoughts, as he tucked his limp penis into the slit in his hose, turned on the difficulty of getting home, of getting away from the girl— it seemed too unnatural just to get up and walk off—of keeping clear of her in future, of avoiding recognition. It was chilly, too, now.

He glanced back at the bridge, wondering if anyone had heard the cry of his climax. As far as he could see nobody was there. But, by now, it was impossible really to see anything at that distance.

A slithering movement beside him brought his glance quickly back to the girl. He recoiled. Having had time, at last, to recover from her winding, she'd reached out and grabbed the dagger which he, so carelessly, had left lying beside them on the sand.

Now she had drawn herself up onto her knees and was glaring at him with eyes whose gleaming fury he could feel even through the gloom.

He drew back, without a word, slithering

back onto his knees, getting warily to his feet as she did.

"Now I shall kill you," she said with a quiet intensity. "Now I have the dagger and I shall kill you."

He didn't answer. He kept his eyes on her and the dagger, whose gold handle gave off a slight luster in the darkness.

Crouching, she came toward him. He faced her, arms bent out toward her like a wrestler, watching intently. There was danger in running. He might fall; she might overtake him on the rough ground and stab him from behind. He waited for her to come at him.

When she did, leaping forward suddenly with the knife upraised, his foot lashed out and caught her in the groin. She fell on one knee and he leapt on her. In spite of her pain, she clung desperately to the dagger. But he was too strong for her. Slowly he forced her arm down until the knife was between them. He brought up his knee under her elbow from his standing position and the knife fell from her momentarily paralyzed fingers.

He pushed her back with his foot and groped quickly for the knife. He was half aware of her body flying at him once more as he rose with the knife. There was a slight moan from her lips and she fell heavily against him.

He twisted and leapt away. But the knife didn't come away in his hand. Behind him the girl slumped heavily to the ground and lay face down without a tremor.

Cesare stayed stock-still where he was. A flush of horror washed over him. He waited for her to move, to groan, but she lay like a corpse.

Cautiously he moved back to where she lay.

He looked around for the knife, but he couldn't find it. He looked back at her still figure, chilled. He stood over her. He could see both her hands and the knife wasn't in either of them. Overcoming a sudden urge just to leave, to rush off into the night, he bent and turned her over. The cold sight of what he had known from her stillness petrified him. The dagger was buried in her breast almost to the gold hilt. Around it her brown, peasant dress was stained a darker brown. Her eyes were open, but unseeing.

Cesare's mind became a confusion of irrelevant, frightened thoughts. It was some minutes before he was able to think with any clarity. Then he forced himself to be calm and work out what to do. The main thing, he told himself tensely, was to be quick. The next, leave nothing to identify himself. He looked down at the hilt of the dagger and shuddered. He stopped his gaze from rising to the girl's face just in time and, closing his eyes, caught the handle of the knife and pulled. It came away with a smooth springy pressure and when he opened his eyes it was wet and dripping in his hand.

Have to wash it. He glanced around at the river a dozen paces away. He started toward it and then stopped and looked back at the body. He went back to it and put his hand on the girl's breast. No, of course she was dead. Steeling himself, he took her under each armpit and dragged her as quietly as he could manage to the edge of the bank. He swilled the knife in the almost still water of the river and wiped it on her dress. Then, very gently and carefully, he rolled her over into the water.

He stood up, breathing quickly. Now the city guard wouldn't see the body immediately if they came down onto the bank. He glanced back at the bridge which was like some great conscious presence, a witness to the drama. Suppose her people were out looking for her there, wondering why she hadn't got home. But surely they'd have come straight down onto the bank. Maybe there were a dozen reasons why she might be late on any particular day. He'd only watched her for three days in all—far from conclusive evidence that she followed an unchanging pattern.

Cesare stuffed the dagger back into his belt. He glanced at his hose and then pulled his doublet down as far as possible, hiding the slit as best he could. He didn't look back at the river.

At the parapet he heard voices. They filled him with a consuming dread. He *knew* they were looking for her. The voices came from people who must be standing on the bridge. There were several voices. He listened. A voice came out distinctly from the others . . .

"She came across the bridge just like everyday . . ."

And then another.

"Never should have left her. It was so near . . ."

Cesare didn't stay to hear any more. With his heart in his mouth, he crept down toward the river and slipped into the darkness of one of the great spans of the bridge. There he waited, quietly, hardly daring to breathe, hoping that the obvious wouldn't occur to them— to come down and scour the river bank.

For half an hour he waited, but nobody came down onto the bank and after a few minutes more he crept slowly back to the parapet higher up. The voices had gone; there was nobody about.

Not much later he let himself into the grounds of Cardinal Roderigo's house. His clothes were still in the garden shed. He changed, rolled the others into an unrecognizable ball and went into the house to his room. He was there, reading, when his father came to see him much later and tell him the news of the morrow—it was to be the crowning day for Christ's Vicar.

CHAPTER 8

Cardinal Roderigo was crowned Pope Alexander VI next day on the steps of the Basilica of St. Peter. The streets of Rome were crowded with citizens, shouting, laughing, applauding.

Their common eyes were dazzled by the colorful beauty of the procession to the Lateran, the Pope's cathedral church.

Alexander, smiling and serene, completely confident and happy in the fulfillment of his aim, rode on a huge white stallion surrounded by banners including the arms of the Borgias —the Bull. The new Pope held his hand high, blessing the populace with the Fisherman's Ring which glittered from his forefinger in the sunshine.

The magnificent cortege included seven hundred priests and prelates, two thousand knights on horseback, three thousand archers and Turkish horsemen and the Palatine Guard with their flashing halberds and shields.

Watching the procession in all its blaze of color, listening to the music, smelling the incense and the flowers which heralded a night of festivity, Cesare could hardly believe in his adventure of the previous night. A desire not to recall the details of its ending denied him the liberty to enjoy remembering the beginning. It was an episode he preferred to forget.

One of Pope Alexander's first acts was to deal with the violence which had been rife in the city. To this end he used an iron fist.

His first decree was that the house of a murderer should be razed to the ground and the ruffian hanged for all to see above the ruins.

CHAPTER 9

Lucrezia was fourteen years old and a woman of great and varied experience before the Pope succeeded in arranging for her a marriage which suited his ambition. Such a marriage as would have been worthy for a daughter of Cardinal Roderigo Borgia was no longer good enough for Pope Alexander VI. He sought for her an alliance among Italy's princely houses.

It was thus that she became bestowed upon the Lord of Pesaro with a dowry of 30,000 ducats.

The Lord of Pesaro, Giovanni Sforza, himself no more than a youth, thus provided the Pope with much desired stronger relations with Milan — albeit Giovanni himself was no more than a bastard of the powerful Milanese house of Sforza.

The nuptials were celebrated with magnificence in the Vatican, and culminated in a supper party given by the Pope to which ten specially picked cardinals and a number of the ladies and gentlemen of Rome were invited.

After a meal of much good food and more good wine, the Pope announced a special attraction and following on his words some fifty courtesans were brought in and set to dance with the servants.

Many among them were of considerable beauty. They were well known to the Pope, the majority of them having already shared his bed.

The dances were stately and well-performed and the guests applauded politely, wondering what was so special about a spectacle which one could see at any Roman ball.

But, just about the time when those present were beginning to get a little bored with the dancing, Alexander clapped his hands. And at his signal, both courtesans and their partners stripped off their clothes and continued the dancing stark-naked.

There was an appreciative buzz of excitement at this unexpected novelty in the holy place. The men felt their pressures rise as they examined the stately sway of some of the most curvaceous bodies in Rome. The ladies, for their part, tried discreetly to hide their enormous interest in the flopping lengths of meat which dangled between the husky servants' legs.

The Pope, well flushed with liquor, stretched back in his chair and appraised the comparative qualities of various breasts and buttocks. To his nearest male neighbors he gave descriptions of the bedworthy qualities of many of the female dancers, while the ladies within earshot sniggered and replied with quips about the men's pricks, wagering on how big they would grow, which would be the longest under titivation.

Already having anticipated this argument,

Alexander clapped his hands once again and, continuing with their dance, the courtesans, each time they came into contact with their partners, gave a quick, expert rub or tickle to their organs until the latter were rising up majestically.

"Now you will have the answer to the problem," the Pope said with a chuckle to the Lady Manfredi who was his nearest neighbor. Her hand stole over to his lap and pressed him playfully at his genital region.

"I'm sure there can be no better than the holiest," she said with a grin.

The Pope leaned toward her with a smile.

"You flatter me," he said, "but modesty prevents me from comment. Perhaps you would like to join me in consideration of the possibility after the spectacle."

"You are very bold, Roderigo," she replied softly. "But a bold man usually gets what he wants."

She gave his penis a squeeze and withdrew her hand, smiling, to turn her attention back to the scene.

All the servants had big erections by this time. The great cudgels soared out from them like artificial fixtures. In spite of what must have been some turmoil in their loins, they contrived to keep poker faces as the Pope had previously ordered.

The eyes of the spectators were goggling. It was the first time most of them had seen such mass nudity and such mass sexual excitement so openly displayed. Many a prick and many a cunt, well hidden by clothes and the festive tables, was hot with desire at the sight.

Another sign from Alexander and more servants appeared with huge baskets of apples with the centers hollowed out so that only an outside husk remained. These were fitted onto the stiff rods of the nude dancers, so that they clung more or less closely to their reddening-to-purple knobs.

There were gusts of uproarious laughter throughout the great hall at the comic sight of the artificially bloated knobs which had changed color to green, yellow and rosy-apple pink.

Still with perfectly serious faces, the servants sank to their knees on the beautiful mosaic floor and remained kneeling while the laughter shook the chandeliers.

As the first wave of hilarity from the guests began to fade into a ripple of private titters, the naked women dancers knelt down on all fours with their backs toward each of their partners. There was a fresh craning of necks, goggling of eyeballs at the fresh views which were presented of juicy crannies and a frequent fuzz of soft, many-colored pubic hair.

Slowly, without looking backwards, the courtesans moved back until the apple-bloated pricks were touching the soft flesh between their thigh-tops. Then began a series of hip and bottom-wrigglings as they tried to work the apples into their vaginas. It became clear that the idea was for them to swallow the fruit in their orifices and then withdraw it if they could from the male organ it surrounded.

Cardinals watched with panting lips as vagina after vagina opened and distended and tried to ooze around a rosy apple as the woman it belonged to pushed gently back.

"It's a race," the Pope confided. "The first woman to get the apple off can choose the biggest penis to delight her in bed tonight."

The fascinating race was on. Some of the

women seemed unable to expand their holes sufficiently to get them around the large husk of apple. They were forced to rub against and around the fruit until their juices began to flow and they were able to slip backwards more easily. Others got halfways impaled but could get no further, while still others soon got the whole of the apple inside them but couldn't pull it off the prick, which had in most cases expanded within the husk.

The male servants were very excited and many of them gripped the hips of the woman kneeling against them, whereupon they were warned that they were not allowed to help her task in any way.

In some cases, careful watchers suspected that a woman was really making little effort to remove the apple, but was, on the contrary, trying to keep it in place while she jogged excitedly back and forth on it and the hilt of prick behind it.

In fact, the race appeared to be something of a put-up job for the benefit of the spectators' lustful instincts, for it certainly wasn't won quickly and soon every woman had swallowed the apple in her crevice. But each continued to push sexily backwards and forwards on her apple-crowned staff.

At last, however, one of the performers contracted her organ tightly and determinedly around the bulging apple which was killing her with its size and pulled it off its stem of prick with a fierce sucking 'plop' which was heard throughout the hall. There was an immediate, raucous round of applause and a number of the spectators stood up to get a clearer view of the winner.

She was a slim, dark girl with top-heavy

breasts, surprisingly slim hips and strong, unusually big thighs. She was kneeling with her head hanging as if in exhaustion, her lips apart, the apple spreading her vagina and presenting it as a large, fruit-filled cavern. Her partner's rod was red and chafed from the friction of the apple during her efforts to remove it. He, too, was panting and had fallen forward onto his hands, his stomach heaving deeply.

The Pope stood up and clapped his hands yet again. There was a gradual slowing down of the tempo in the hall. Reluctantly, the remaining couples recognized that someone had succeeded. There was a cascade of fresh 'plops' as one after another they followed up their achievement. Now they were in a hurry for the last to succeed was to be refused sexual intercourse for two months.

One by one the apples were swallowed in expanding clefts. At last all the apples had been confined in their moist and temporary dwelling-places. The servants stood up, showing off the extended proportions of their stimulated stems.

"Right, honorable gentlemen," the Pope addressed himself to the guests. "I'm sure you'll all agree we've just witnessed a delicious spectacle. What will happen to the apples? Well, gentlemen, it's not often that you can have tasted the finest fruit inundated with the finest love-juice. So the ladies will now pass over their delectable morsels for your gourmet taste."

With that, the courtesans divested themselves of their fruit as if dropping babies from their wombs. Some squatted and ejected the apples with a straining effort into their hands; others opened their slits with their fingers and pulled out the fruit that way; others still allowed their partners to spread their nether lips and pull out the slippery spheres.

Each of the women then carried her issue to the long banqueting table and presented it to a man of her choice—a cardinal, a knight, a baron, whoever took her fancy.

The apples were wet, slightly slimy. Each recipient eagerly took the fruit, raised it to the donor and then bit into it with relish, swallowing great mouthfuls.

The courtesans watched with gleaming eyes, smiling at the avidity with which the orbs from their crying orifices were munched in the mouths of the princes and prelates.

Alexander gave a fresh order and the woman who had first managed to suck the apple from her bloated branch looked around at the specimens of genital rigidity. They were of all lengths and thicknesses—little to choose between them. She walked among them, feeling them for heat and fleshiness and eventually she chose that of a handsome young man whose prick was so shaped that it grew thicker and thicker from knob to base. Thus she would be ensured of fresh delight and surprise through all its length.

At a sign from the Pope, the servant pushed the woman face forwards over the banquet table. He seized a banana from a cluster in a nearby basket and thrust it into her exposed channel from behind. In and in he jogged it while the spread-eagled strumpet wriggled against the heavily draped edge of the table in front of a hundred pairs of high-ranking eyes.

For some minutes the servant shoved the banana into her, holding it by one ripe, yellow end until it had almost disappeared. Then he withdrew it at last and with the first sign of animation he'd shown, rammed his tapering prick into her moist cleft.

The ladies present didn't know which to look at most, his handsome, passion-wracked face or his enormous, penetrating penis. They watched in a thigh-rubbing fascination as he thrust deeper and deeper and the woman, bent under him, her breasts crushed against the table, groaned and pleaded for more.

He had settled down to a steady, moan-drawing rhythm, gripping her table-flattened hips, pulling at the same time as lower down he pushed, before Alexander glanced at where Lady Manfredi was wriggling on her seat, a slight smile on her lips.

"It pleases you to see such a scene?" he whispered with a smile.

"I can think of only one thing to please me better," she whispered back, glancing significantly at the place where his organ was hidden by his robes.

"We needn't wait for the end," he said. "Cardinal Rovere will take over."

"Let's go then," she said. "I can't wait."

CHAPTER 10

Against the disturbing scene of national and international events which saw Charles of France claim Naples and advance with his enormous army down upon Italy, the domestic carnality of the Borgia family continued.

While the Pope was trying to gain time by refusing passage to the French troops, and then giving way when Charles, supported now by the unruly northern barons, made it clear he would brook no refusal, Lucrezia, tiring of her young husband, had reverted to relations with her brothers whom she still found—with her father—the most sexually exciting of men.

Her two favorites were still her brother Cesare and, now, his younger brother Giovanni, the Duke of Gandia. She had seen very little of Giovanni in her youth as he had spent even more time away at his studies than Cesare. During his young manhood, however, he had been brought back to Rome and had been kept in close attendance on the Pontiff, while Charles of France, reveling too early in his victory on Naples, had been cut off from the north by allied States and attacked from the south by the Spanish under Gonzalo de Cordoba.

Charles had escaped from the trap somewhat precipitously by the skin of his teeth leaving King Federigo of Aragon to be crowned in Naples behind him.

Throughout this period, Cesare and—unknown to his brother—Giovanni, had been sharing their beautiful sister during a long holiday she was taking from her husband in Rome.

* * *

It was only two nights before the two brothers were due to leave Rome together to the crowning of Federigo that Cesare arrived, unexpectedly, at the apartment that Lucrezia had been given by her father. He let himself in, discreetly, with the key he'd had made for his own purposes, and walked into the apartment to find Lucrezia spread-eagled on a couch, her knees pulled up almost touching her breasts, urging her sweating brother Giovanni to greater efforts to satisfy her.

They were making such a bustle with their

squirmings and pantings that neither was aware of his presence until he spoke.

"I had no idea that we were all so in love with the family."

His cutting tones broke through their abandonment and brought them both to a standstill. They lay together on the couch, staring at him in confusion. Lucrezia slowly put her legs down from their exaggerated position. Both lay, nude and panting, in a momentary, shocked silence.

Lucrezia gathered her wits first.

"Cesare, darling, you surely didn't think your rights on me were exclusive." She gave a little laugh at the monstrosity of the thought and smoothed her round belly with her hand.

"I didn't expect to find my own brother sticking his prick in you." His tone was hostile, controlled but dangerous. Again it was Lucrezia who spoke.

"You're sounding very moral all of a sudden, dear," she said smoothly. "After all, Giovanni knows all about you and he doesn't mind." She laughed again as if she was thoroughly enjoying the situation. She swung her legs off the couch and came toward Cesare, her big breasts pointing out at him. His eyes flickered. He was furious. It had shocked him to find his brother with her. He didn't analyze his feelings, but his reaction was very simple: he was consumed with a sudden, hating jealousy.

Lucrezia reached him and put her arms around his neck.

"I'm surprised at you, darling," she said. "You sound jealous—anyone would think you were my husband." She laughed a third time.

Cesare caught her arms, holding the flesh so hard that she cried out. He pulled them from his neck and pushed her away from him.

"You're just a whore," he snarled at her.

Lucrezia colored, her eyes pinpointed, but she kept control of herself.

"You're being quite ridiculous, Cesare," she snapped. "I think you'd better go and come back some evening when you've got a sense of proportion and reality."

She looked around at Giovanni, who had slid slowly off the couch in front of them. "Besides," she added spitefully, "Giovanni and I have some business to finish."

For a moment it seemed that Cesare would strike her. His dark eyes raged furiously from her to her brother. Then he turned with a scowl and went out.

Lucrezia turned to Giovanni. Her eyes had assumed a wide, innocent look of wonder.

"Well, well," she said, "would you ever have believed that—from him of all people?"

"Amazing," Giovanni agreed. "I do believe he's really in love with you."

Lucrezia looked thoughtful. Her eyes softened. She had already forgiven Cesare at the thought. Her mind wandered off on one of her now frequent fantasies.

Giovanni came over and stood behind her. He put his arms around her and pressed her breasts. She turned her face sideways toward him as she felt his hips pressing her rump and his trunk growing fat again.

"I wonder which of you I'd choose if I had to," she mused. "Do you think Cesare's really angry?"

"It won't last long."

He drew her back to the couch and pulled her down on it. She seemed to come suddenly back to the present, to become aware again and she opened her legs and put her arms up to him, opening her mouth and beckoning him with the deep, reawakened desire in her eyes.

She closed her eyes with the sharp sensation as he drove into her and she dug her nails into his shoulders. For the moment she had made her choice.

* * *

Cesare was not outwardly hostile to his brother when they met the next night. Their mother, Vannozza—the truth had been admitted to them at last—was giving them a farewell supper in her vineyard at Trastevere.

They dined in the rose-surrounded terrace with a number of other guests—including their younger brother Giuffredo. The conversation was easy and quite gay although a close observer would probably have noticed that neither of the two older brothers addressed each other directly and hardly once so much as glanced at each other.

However, the two left together in the early hours, accompanied by a number of servants, and set out for Rome on horseback.

Within the city, Giovanni reined in his horse and took his leave. He announced to the company in general that he was going elsewhere to amuse himself. With one attendant, he set off toward the Jewish quarter.

Again, a very close observer whose attention was on Cesare rather than his brother would have noticed that a faint smile which contained both vengeance and a shade of triumph, fleeted over the former's face.

After the Duke of Gandia had left, the company continued on their way for a time until Cesare in turn announced that he, too, was going in search of a little relaxation. He set off alone in the opposite direction to that taken by his brother.

* * *

Giovanni trotted his horse gently down the narrow streets toward the river. He had said a passionate farewell to Lucrezia last night. Now there was a little Jewish maid with a body like quicksilver that he wished to take his leave of in an equally passionate manner tonight.

He allowed thoughts of Cesare to interrupt his excited anticipation of the fleshly joys in store for him. He didn't relish the journey with his brother tomorrow. He was aware that he was still culpable in his brother's eyes and the knowledge disquieted him; he knew how ruthless Cesare was capable of being.

With a quiet clatter of hooves, the two horses crossed a little, deserted square.

From it they passed into the gloom of another narrow street with the deeper oblong gloom of courtyard doorways.

They were near the river. Giovanni decided he could soon tell his servant to leave him. He didn't want the man making use of his knowledge of the little Jewess during his absence.

He called to the man, who was riding a little ahead of him.

"You may leave me now."

The servant saluted, glad to be relieved at last of his duty, and cantered back the way they had come. Giovanni continued on his way down the narrow street.

Hardly had the sounds of his retreating servant died before something flew from a dark alley and hit him on the side of the head.

It dazed him, but he remained in his saddle

with an instinctive effort and drew his sword, turning wildly in the direction of the dark alley mouth.

Immediately he was pulled off his horse from behind in a sharp, muffled bustle of grunts and swishings and the sudden rearing of his mount. Flashes of silver flew rapidly in quick arcs and the next moment the body of the Duke of Gandia was being dragged into the alley, while his mount went trotting on without him.

"Is he dead?" a voice asked in the sheltering gloom of the alley.

"Aye, sir, he's dead all right," came rough answering voices in loud whispers.

"Right. Sling him over my horse — and then lead on to the river."

There was a bustling in the darkness, followed by a moment's silence and then three rough-looking men in the garb of sailors crept out of the dark passage and started off in a slanting direction from the path taken by the riderless horse. At the first corner one of them looked back and beckoned.

Another sailor came out of the darkness — and immediately behind him came a horse carrying a richly-cloaked figure with a mask. Behind Cesare on the horse, his brother lay dead with a dozen stabs in his back and chest.

The macabre little party continued cautiously and unchallenged toward the river at the very point near the Bridge of St. Angelo where Cesare had some years earlier disposed of the first of his corpses.

At a point where the narrow streets of the city emptied onto the quayside, Cesare reined in and motioned the men forward. He watched while they crept stealthily out onto the quay and surveyed the surroundings, including a number of timber-laden boats on the river. One of them turned and waved him on.

He rode carefully down to the water's edge, to a point where the scavengers normally tipped their refuse carts into the river.

There, he turned the horse's hindquarters to the river and two of the men seized the prostrate body behind him and flung it as far out as they could into the river.

"Is he well out?" Cesare asked softly.

"Aye — well out, sir."

Cesare strained his eyes through the dimness. The river was calm as usual, disturbed only by the disappearing ripple of widening circles where the body had gone under.

"Good work," he said, and turned his horse into the shadows of the narrow street again.

A little later, when he arrived at Lucrezia's place, he was completely self-possessed. He told her he was sorry for his previous night's behavior and that he had already apologized to Giovanni.

He found Lucrezia was delighted with him and she continued to be that way when his penis was shattering up to her cervix. Little did she realize that in his mind he was taking further delicious revenge on his brother.

CHAPTER 11

Rome had been deeply shocked at the murder of the Duke of Gandia, but not a soul dreamed of attaching the blame to his brother — not even Lucrezia. It was generally assumed he had been done to death by some political enemy of the Borgia House.

Cesare certainly felt no remorse and left Rome with a sense of considerable satisfaction to attend the crowning ceremony in Naples.

Lucrezia, robbed of the attentions of both her brothers, was forced to rely again on her husband for her nightly pleasures. As before she found him so comparatively frigid that, with her passionate nature, his very presence eventually became quite obnoxious to her. Some months later the Pope, on her request, dissolved Lucrezia's marriage to the young lord — on the grounds that he was *impotens et frigidus natura* — an impotence which was admitted by himself, and then became so widely published and lampooned that he became furious and in retaliation publicly accused the Borgias of incest. It was a charge which seemed so obviously designed to draw attention from his own comic state that nobody — not even the most gullible of the public — believed him.

After the dissolvement of the marriage, Lucrezia withdrew to the Convent of San Sisto in the Appian Way — partly to escape the various items of scandal which were rocking Rome, partly to appear to act with the decorum her situation demanded.

She was to spend a period of some six months in her own private quarters, taking part with the nuns in daily prayers, joining with them in much of their work.

For some weeks she lived with them, praying, making baskets, carving small figurines in wood, walking in the quiet grounds, feeding their dozen hens. She was happy for a time to be free of the world in which she always felt a little as if she was living on the summit of a volcano that was likely to erupt unexpectedly.

But, at the end of that time, accustomed as

she was to fierce and frequent intercourse, she began to feel an aching void in her loins, began to consider how to best soothe it.

During her walks in the grounds she had particularly befriended a young nun who had been in the convent only a short time before her. This young girl, whose name was Carlotta, was designated to show Lucrezia how to make the baskets and the little wooden figurines.

They got on very well and it soon became apparent to Lucrezia that the younger and unworldly Carlotta was quite fascinated by her.

Lucrezia managed, cleverly, to discover that the girl, who had never had a lover, was taking ill to her new and voluntary exile. She felt in her a need which she didn't understand, although listening to her confused explanations, Lucrezia was only too well aware of the trouble — the young girl needed a good fuck.

Carlotta was very attractive in her own way. She was dark, with a long face and slightly Jewish nose dominating long, well-defined lips. Her body was completely concealed under the shrouds of her long robes, but the melancholy attraction of her face was quite enough to excite Lucrezia in her present manless state.

Giving way to the girl's hinted-at curiosity, Lucrezia began, during their walks in the grounds, to tell her a few things about her sexual life. But always she exaggerated the brutality of the male, making him sound an utter, unbearable brute.

"I don't think I could stand to have a man using me in such a way," Carlotta said one morning as they sat staring at the water lilies in the little stream which ran sluggishly through the lower reaches of the convent grounds. "I should feel stripped of any sense of dignity I'd ever had."

Lucrezia took the plunge.

"Yes. If the choice was between man and this convent, I would choose a cloistered existence within these walls," she said. "But, fortunately there are other things one can do."

The girl raised her fine, dark eyebrows.

"What — other things in place of a man?"

"A woman, Carlotta. Women are much gentler and more loving than men. And they understand a woman's needs whereas most men are selfish and oafish in their lovemaking."

"But . . ."

"I think," Lucrezia went on quickly, "much as I respect the Mother Superior and the individual right of choice, that any woman who locks herself away in a prison is betraying her function as a woman and displaying a fear of the world which belief in God should not justify."

Carlotta stared at her, shocked. She had never dared to voice such sentiments, but they fitted well with her present mood of boredom and rebellion.

"You only have to look at the majority of the women here," Lucrezia continued, "and you see immediately that they're women who are too ugly or too witless to succeed in a competitive and natural world."

She took Carlotta's hand.

"But you don't belong among them, Carlotta. You are lovely and full of life which won't allow itself to be kept in check forever."

The girl was flattered and moved by the words which were spoken to her in such sincere tones. They sped her own unformed impulses along the channel that Lucrezia intended.

"I feel you are right," she said. She glanced around at the distant figures of the other nuns wandering in the upper part of the grounds among the trees. "I'm beginning to wish I hadn't taken my vows."

"You should make the best of things as they are," Lucrezia said. "We are both in the same cul-de-sac of frustration. We should help each other."

"But what can we . . .?"

"We can take the place of men for each other."

The girl dropped her eyes and gazed down at the lilies. There was a silence for some seconds.

"I — I wouldn't know how . . . and — and I'm not sure that it's . . ."

"We all have deep centers in our beings which others may never reach," Lucrezia cut in, "but unless they do, unless we try to help them to, we all live lonely, unsatisfied lives, lives which wrinkle us up with bitterness, the feeling of having missed what was essential."

Carlotta raised her eyes from the stream and found herself unable again to withdraw them from Lucrezia's deep, compelling gaze.

"Come to my quarters after evensong tonight," Lucrezia went on, "and I will show you what it means to reach that center."

The dull peal of a bell calling them in to prayer cut short any reply the young girl might have made. She stared at Lucrezia, dropped her eyes at last and walked away toward the building. Lucrezia smiled after her for a moment and then slowly followed her.

* * *

That evening, alone in her quarters — two

rooms at the far end of a wing of the convent — Lucrezia, garbed only in a dressing gown, waited for Carlotta to come. She was almost certain she would come although the girl had given her no answer. She knew how the possibility of sexual adventure could play on one's nerves, stimulating, frightening, exciting all at the same time.

For Lucrezia, too, this would be the first lesbian experience and the idea filled her with the same lustful chill of eagerness that her first fuck had — especially as she had been deprived of her conjugal and fraternal rights for some weeks now.

She found herself unable to keep still as the minutes went by following evensong. She rose time and time again and looked out of the sloping window down to the grounds. At last she sat on her bed and tried to concentrate on the pages of Boccaccio's *Il Decamerone* which she had smuggled into the convent with her.

As time passed she became more and more anxious. If Carlotta didn't come now she would die of frustration. She put down the book and stared out of the window again before walking into the next room where she studied herself in a small, silver-backed hand mirror.

Her heart leapt as there came a light tapping on her door. She ran to open it and almost clasped the young girl to her bosom as she drew her into her room.

Carlotta smiled at her briefly and stood uncertainly just inside the door while Lucrezia closed and bolted it.

"Make yourself at home," Lucrezia urged, turning around to her.

Nervously, the girl went to the window and looked out as if to reassure herself that the outside world was there, solid and unchanged. Lucrezia watched her pretending to interest herself in the exploration of the rooms, pretending to examine the few books, flicking pages over with a pointless speed.

"I was afraid to come," she said at last. "Wasn't that ridiculous — we are quite free to visit one another's rooms."

"We are quite free to act as we please," Lucrezia added.

"Yes," the girl said uncertainly.

"I have another gown — why don't you make yourself more comfortable and put it on," Lucrezia suggested.

She handed over the garment and Carlotta took it nervously.

Lucrezia turned away and studied *Il Decamerone,* listening to the rustle of clothes as Carlotta slipped out of them. She kept swallowing with nervous excitement.

At a well-judged moment she glanced around and caught her companion naked. Carlotta gazed at her with wide, embarrassed eyes and Lucrezia glanced back at her book immediately. But not before she'd had a glimpse of the girl's small, firm breasts, high up and dark, with the splodge of dark nipple giving them body, and her slim figure below it with the eye-catching fuzz of dark hair above her thighs. Lucrezia felt almost matronly beside the girl's small proportions.

She did not look up again until the girl came and sat beside her on the bed. Carlotta seemed to have lost some of her uncertainty. It was as if she'd reminded herself that she had, after all, come for a specific purpose and that there was no point in trying to pretend she hadn't.

Lucrezia replaced the book on a shelf over the

bed and lay back on it, looking at her companion. Carlotta looked even more attractive out of her nun's somber garb, and the long V-neck of the gown revealed a smooth stretch of her succulent-looking skin between her breasts. The beginning of their bulge on either side of the valley of flesh was heaving with a nervous emotion.

"You are really very lovely," Lucrezia told her. "It was a great mistake for a girl like you to get such a mad idea in her head that she wanted to pass the rest of her days in a tomb."

The conversation brought a sense of normalcy with it and Carlotta's voice hid a trace of relief as if a spell had been broken.

"If you hadn't come, I might never have realized it," she answered.

"Sooner or later you would have — but I'm glad it's through me that your revolution is to be achieved."

Carlotta had again, as in the afternoon, become lost in Lucrezia's eyes. They seemed to hold her hypnotically. She came, as if Lucrezia had commanded her, and lay down on the bed beside her. Lucrezia touched the girl's cheek, lightly.

"Remember that this is the only way to liberate yourself from the horror and monotony of a death in life," she said softly as her lips followed her hand.

Lucrezia was not very surprised to find that a relationship with a woman gave her as strong an erotic urge as with a man. It was as if it were something she'd always known, even when her conscious thought had included nothing but images of Cesare's, her father's, Giovanni's embraces. Now she felt the soft, smooth skin of the girl's cheek against her lips, a softness and a leafy fragrance which were missing in a man, and she felt her spirit stirred with the upsetting excitement of a new and forbidden experience about to come to fruition.

She slipped her hand into the girl's gown and Carlotta winced. Then her hand was caressing the small, firm breast with the lightest of touches. Her lips moved over the girl's face without losing contact — and found her lips. The lips were still, slightly reluctant and unsure. But as Lucrezia's hand moved from one breast to the other and tweaked the nipple, as her tongue played hide and seek with Carlotta's lips, the mouth opened with a sound which was near to a sigh, the lips relaxed and then kissed back.

Lucrezia's tongue gave up its game and lunged right out to fill the mouth which opened and spread at its assault.

Gently, her hand untied the belt of the gown. The material slipped slowly down to the bed off the glossy flesh of Carlotta's hips and thighs.

Lucrezia's hand rested on the girl's waist for a moment, the index finger playing with her navel. She noticed the girl was trembling faintly, like a leaf in the merest zephyr. She let her hand float away over the glassy expanse of flesh, lingering, unhurried, exploring every part while her tongue continued to caress the moist, heavily-breathing lips.

As her advancing fingers encountered the silky van of pubic hair, she slowed. She let her fingers course through it as through money. Under it she could feel the flesh swollen in a little mound, like a slight rise in the ground covered with a fine grass.

Carlotta wriggled her hips very slightly. She

seemed ashamed of their movement, which was like an effort at escape.

Lucrezia sucked heavily on the lips which were trembling now in unison with the body.

With her free hand, she awkwardly unpulled her own belt and then pushed the plump flesh of her thigh against Carlotta's.

Slowly, as if stroking a timid animal, she allowed her fingers to continue on their downward progress. They moved down the rise and into the hot, little hollow between the oozing flesh of Carlotta's tightly-gripped thighs. Her path was barred for the moment by the instinctive inward pressure of those thighs. She stroked all the flesh she could reach and was rewarded with a sudden seepage of moisture around her fingers.

She moved her lips off Carlotta's and kissed her neck.

"Relax, darling," she whispered. "Open your legs."

"I can't bear it," Carlotta whispered back after a moment. "It makes me jump every time you touch me."

"All right — just let it go naturally. It'll come."

Lucrezia went on with her gentle fondling. The hollow was very warm now and Carlotta was letting out an odd "oh" every so often from deep down in her throat.

Moving her lips down the neck, over the slim shoulders, Lucrezia invaded the breasts which were taut and straining with sensation. She closed her mouth over a nipple and sucked hard and strong, bringing forth gasps of torment from the girl.

Carlotta's thighs relaxed and, awaiting her moment, Lucrezia was able suddenly to advance her fingers so that the texture of flesh changed and she knew she was in the beginning of the wet ravine formed by those nether lips. Carlotta clasped her thighs together again, crushing the tormenting hand, but Lucrezia bore the weight and tickled the wet flesh with her fingertips.

She drew on the nipple again with her lips, sucking in as much of the breast behind it as she could.

Carlotta thrust her breast at the lips which seemed to be drawing milk from her shapely udders. She arched her hips and gave way suddenly, opening her thighs, relaxing them so that the raping hand was suddenly right between her legs, the fingers in at their target.

Lucrezia moved a finger in the suddenly conquered vagina. Carlotta groaned in submission.

Slowly Lucrezia titivated and explored the flood-washed well. She pushed in through the tight ring of flesh, to the accompaniment of a little squeal from Carlotta. She thrust up, and then up again, feeling the hips withdraw instinctively, pull up away from the hand and then ooze back as they became used to the exquisite pressure.

Steadily Lucrezia sucked the breast, gnawed it, remembering all the things she liked a man to do and doing them with that greater finesse which was born of her own intimate, subjective knowledge.

Her fingers could move more loosely, more freely now. The ravine had become a great river, like a dried-up wadi suddenly swollen with the seasonal rains, the channel leading from it had become bigger, more accommodating and the hips were moving and bobbing against hers, brushing her flesh with another's exciting, strange flesh.

Breathing hard herself, Lucrezia moved her finger out of the hole and fastened it on the hard little clitoris which had reared up with its first touch from an alien hand.

Carlotta cried out and then spread her thighs in complete, won-over invitation as the finger bit into that little stem of sensitive flesh. She was wriggling incessantly, her mouth wide open, gasping for air.

"Oh God, oh God!" she exclaimed.

Lucrezia worked furiously and delightedly on the clitoris which expanded at her touch, grew harder, longer. She could feel passion growing in it as her finger and thumb pinched it, tweaked it, stroked it, masturbated it. There was only one thing left to make Carlotta's initiating delight into utter rapture.

Lucrezia slid down her body, reveling in the tight, straining pressure of flesh against hers. Her wet lips followed the swells and hollows of the body in their descent. She withdrew down to Carlotta's thighs with them. She ran her lips down the thighs, kissing tantalizingly on their buttery, yielding insides. The thighs twitched, clasped her head, relaxed. She heard the fury of Carlotta's moans washing down upon her ears like the continual flow of waves against a reef.

Her thighs clasped and unclasped, tensed and untensed continually; her hips wriggled like fish on a hook and she was fastened to the bed with her own overwhelming passion which was no longer timid but demanding.

Sliding her lips up the thighs, Lucrezia met first the slippery ooze of fluid glossing the tops of the legs. She lapped it like a dog. It represented the passion of a lovely girl — nothing unpalatable about that.

Over the swamp and to the very brink of the ravine, a plunge of the tongue and she was kissing and licking in that inundated wadi which squirmed and pressed against her and squashed its side flat against her mouth.

She searched, her tongue leading her blindly in the wadi until she found that steep, stiff monument. She grasped it in her lips and Carlotta's hips went mad, writhing and twisting so that Lucrezia had to hang onto her prize as if she were on a wild horse. But she clung to it, sucking it voraciously while a thin whine of passion, broken often by a deep moan, crashed down on her ears from the tortured face high up above her.

Her hands grasped those slim hips. How slim they were compared to her own. They made Carlotta seem that much more girlish, innocent, helpless.

She slid her hands under the hips and ran them all around the firm, tense balls of bottom. What an excellent little bottom.

She squeezed and worked its pliable bulk as she sucked and licked. The buttocks tightened and relaxed in her hands, swinging wildly in torment. The girl had become a raging form of sexuality. There seemed nothing left of her except a moaning, writhing mass of sensual flesh.

Lucrezia pulled the buttocks apart forcibly. They were hot in the crack between them. There were a few young hairs and then a sweating smoothness. Her fingers slipped over it like little snakes.

The anus nestled there, unprotected now and she rifled it with her fingers they way she'd liked her father to intrude in hers. And Carlotta had no reticence any longer. She didn't even try to press her backside cheeks together. On the contrary she pressed them wide and back so that Lucrezia's finger actually penetrated the anus, the tight little ring of flesh, near to her sucking lips.

She used her tongue on the clitoris which seemed so big as to be unreal. There was a taste of salt and parsley in her mouth; the liquid was running over her face, growing into a torrent.

Above, out of sight, she heard Carlotta's sob.

"Oh, oh, it's here, it's here," she heard her cry, out of control.

She sucked even more furiously, jabbing her finger deeply into the tight, tearing hole. She was terribly excited herself. She got a vicarious pleasure from the girl's helpless passion.

Following on her gasped out words, Carlotta twisted first one way and then the other in a quick, shivering convulsion. Her mouth opened wide and a long, continuous moan of sound exploded from it as she clasped her thighs around Lucrezia's head and squeezed.

The grip on Lucrezia was strong and suffocating, but she bore it until it slowly relaxed and the thighs fell away.

She straightened up, realizing just how hot her loins had become. A little longer and she'd probably have come herself.

She looked at Carlotta. The girl seemed to have collapsed in a coma. She lay with her head thrown back dramatically, her arms wide out beside her head. Her eyes were closed, her breasts heaving in a great swell of emotion.

Lucrezia lay down alongside her and kissed her shoulder. After a while she spoke.

"Wasn't that worth a year in a convent? Isn't it worth anything on earth?"

Carlotta's eyes opened slowly, sleepily. She'd lost all trace of her early embarrassment.

"I feel purged," she said softly. "I feel satisfied and purged of all the frustration and not knowing that I've ever felt."

Lucrezia smiled at her and kissed her bare arm.

"You obviously enjoyed it," she agreed. "Your enjoyment was so infectious that I almost had a climax myself."

Carlotta opened her eyes again and looked at her. Realization had dawned that there were, of course, two of them, that Lucrezia had given her undreamed-of pleasure, that it was now up to her to reciprocate.

"I'm not at all expert," she said. "I shan't know what to do."

Lucrezia began to quiver with anticipation.

"Just do what I did," she said with a break in her voice. "And that will be wonderful."

"I have to get my breath back a moment."

They lay together for a few minutes longer. Lucrezia could hardly wait and she kept pressing her round belly again Carlotta's side and tensing her pelvis against her.

"God, I want it very badly!" she muttered.

At that Carlotta turned over toward her and she fell backwards on the bed. She lay there staring up at the ceiling concentrating on herself, looking inward at the sensation inside her.

She felt the warm face come down on her breasts. To Carlotta her breasts were enormous in comparison with her own. They just asked to be nestled against, to be used as a pillow in which to bury one's face.

The face brushed against the tight, hurting points of her breasts, piquing her with a spear-point of ecstatic pain that rushed straight to her genitals. And then those cool, well-defined lips closed on her nipple in a soft, fondling grip that made her squirm already.

They began to suck, drawing her pear of breast into the mouth, drawing it in, in, swallowing it, sucking it, pulverizing it with sharp, needed pain.

Lucrezia's legs began to jerk in spasms and the unknown fingers slid down her body, the image of her own, and went straight to the spot which played no timid games with them but waited, wide open like a trap, thighs wide apart and squirming.

Lucrezia held her breath waiting for the contact, expecting it, but still jumping with delight when it came. Cool fingers caressed her long, deep cleft which was stinging as the juices were washed into it from her inner regions.

The fingers explored like timid animals—and everywhere they touched and slid they left a burning, a prickling sense of near-destruction.

Lucrezia groaned. She liked to groan. She let the groans escape from her mouth—not that she could really have controlled them—to show her appreciation of what was being done to her.

Then with a sudden jump she felt the fingertips find her little erection. That was too much. She squirmed her hips in a movement that was almost circular, that was wild, exaggerated.

And the fingers were relentless. They pressed there, loved there, pinched there, gave no quarter although her moans became helpless sobs of passion.

Lucrezia felt her hole growing wide. The love-juice was swamping, too, and her belly was in unbearable torment. There couldn't be much more to go.

"Your mouth, your mouth!" she pleaded.

The fingers came out of her sultry cleft giving her a brief respite. But they were replaced immediately by a pair of cool lips which seized on her clitoris, sending a shock through her whole body.

"Oh, wonderful, wonderful!" she gasped. She could hardly utter the words. They tumbled out in a rush of sound which was mostly escaping breath, wheezing out like steam from a hot spring.

The mouth was working hard, giving her no chance to catch her breath. She was out of breath as if she'd been running hard.

And then the hands, remembering, slid around her hips and dug handfuls from her big buttocks, rummaging between them to find the anal orifice.

"Wonderful, wonderful!" she breathed again, lost and helpless.

She felt the heat like a great wood fire down in her passage. It was as hot as a lump of smoldering charcoal, felt ready to splinter into pieces at any moment.

"It's coming ... it's ... coming ... oh!" she gasped, more as an outlet for her feeling than as a warning. She jerked her legs this way and that as if they were puppets and she held the strings. Speech was now impossible. The sounds from her mouth were animal noises, enlarging in abandon with every lick of that tongue on her erect little organ.

She clamped her legs around Carlotta's head and squeezed her loins up at her face, forcing, straining, arching. She felt the burst, the splintering and she cried out, stifling her cries with her fist as the last suck drew her liquid passion through her channel.

A new and regular activity was begun in the quiet haven of the convent.

CHAPTER 12

While Lucrezia was still enjoying her quiet life in the convent, Cesare was pondering his future.

For some time now a marriage between him and Carlotta of Aragon, whom he had never seen, but of whose beauty he had heard, had been in the offing. To achieve this marriage, the Pope had been in contact with the new King of France, Louis XII, trying to enlist his support.

As was usual in these cases nothing was given for nothing, nobody gave his support if he gained nothing in return. So it was with Louis.

He chose this moment to apply to Rome for the dissolution of his marriage with Jeanne de Valois, daughter of Louis XI—an application which the Pope readily conceded to.

In the way that this sort of bargaining gathered momentum, the Pope freshly asked that Louis should confer the duchy of Valentinois on Cesare.

In this way he hoped to settle ownership of a morsel of territory in Dauphiné which had long been disputed between France and the Holy See. The claims of the Church would be given up — but Cesare Borgia would be in power.

Louis granted all this in turn, asking at the same time for a cardinal's hat for an old friend of his and a dispensation to marry the beautiful widow of Charles VIII, Anne of Brittany. So the wrangling, conducted in an aura of politeness and political courtesy, came to an end.

Cesare chose this moment to crave permission to doff the purple. He had long ago been made a cardinal, but Carlotta's father, Federigo of Aragon, would not have his daughter marry a priest. Her dowry, it was known, would be enormous—and Cesare prized money and territory above all at this time.

The only cardinal to stand out against this move was Cardinal Ximenes, the Spanish representative, who saw through the move and the proposed marriage an imminent alliance between France and the Holy See—an alliance which would not be at all in the interests of Spain.

Alexander routed these objections with the unanswerable pronouncement that he could not hinder Cesare's renunciation of the purple, as such a renunciation had clearly become necessary for the salvation of his soul. To appease Spain, however, he bestowed all Cesare's yielded benefices on Spanish churchmen.

Thus it was that Cesare Borgia, Duke of Valentinois, set out for the Court of France where Carlotta of Aragon was being raised.

His suite was enormous, with one hundred attendants, a dozen chariots and a score of mules for his baggage and presents for his future hosts.

In spite of the early hour chosen for departure, Rome was packed with people fighting to catch a glimpse of the newly-created Duke and to cheer him on his journey toward his prospective wife.

Cesare rode at the head of his retinue, following the Tiber along the Trastevere. He was mounted on a large white charger caparisoned in red silk and gold brocade—the colors of France. The Duke's doublet was of white damask laced with gold; a mantle of black velvet covered his shoulders, matched by a black velvet cap, studded with rubies.

Behind him his lackeys also wore the colors of France, as did his Roman gentlemen. The Spaniards in his cortege, however, retained the costumes of their native land.

The procession, hemmed in by cheering crowds, was escorted to the end of the Banchi by four cardinals. The Pope, his heart swollen with pride at the sight of his son so gorgeously arrayed, watched from a window of the Vatican.

At Ostia, the whole retinue boarded a ship, which, with a protective fleet of galleys Louis had sent to fetch the new Duke, set off for the coast of France.

* * *

Over a week later, they dropped anchor at Marseilles, where the Duke was met by the Bishop of Dijon, who had been sent by the King to meet him.

From Marseilles the glorious procession rode on to Avignon, everywhere watched by gaping crowds who broke out into cheers from the very awe of its color and royal appearance.

At Avignon, Cesare was met by Cardinal della Rovere, who was to escort him to the King's court at Chinon.

A month or so after leaving Italy, Cesare was welcomed by Louis in an atmosphere of pomp, ceremony and cordiality—a welcome he was not to receive from the lady he had come to woo.

CHAPTER 13

In spite of Cesare's good looks and strong personality, Carlotta hedged and procrastinated until it became clear to all that she was not going through with the marriage. The background reasons were, of course, political and Carlotta followed the instructions of her father's ambassador. She also displayed a certain hauteur towards the Duke of Valentinois on the few occasions when they came into contact.

The final blow came when Cesare, who was impressed by the beauty and inaccessibility of the princess, sent word telling her in the most courteous of paraphrasing that he could not wait forever in the court of France and that he failed to see what was delaying her decision.

Carlotta sent back a message saying that her family was not in the habit of being pressed—even by Italian blood of noble ancestry. This was an open slight on Cesare's foreign origin and social history which cut him to the quick. He began immediately to plan his revenge, taking into his confidence his closest attendants and companions.

It was common knowledge that almost every day in the afternoon, Carlotta, a few ladies-in-waiting and a handful of male attendants went riding for exercise in the woods near the King's court. They would often be away for two or even three hours, cutting across the hillocks and hollows until the brush and trees became too thick for further progress. Sometimes they would descend from their mounts and continue their promenade on foot a short time—all dependent on Carlotta's whim of the moment.

Cesare had the movements of the little band

watched for a few days while he lingered on in the hospitality of Louis—who was somewhat embarrassed that his end of the bargain had not been fulfilled, through no fault of his own.

During the mornings, Cesare himself would ride discreetly out into the forest with a few of his men to explore, to scout out the ground on which he was going to carry out his plan—the rape of Carlotta.

At the beginning of an afternoon a few days after the princess's curt reply to Cesare's entreaty to make up her mind, the Duke and some twenty of his men rode out into the forest. In a clearing not far from the spot where Carlotta and her company usually began their jaunts, they all changed into a motley collection of clothing such as might well be worn by the bands of outlaws which infested the forests farther to the south. Several of the band then rode back to the forest outskirts and posted themselves to watch the approach of the princess.

Cesare had not long to wait before the first of the lookouts raced back to report the entry of Carlotta into the wood at a certain point.

For the next two hours the Duke and his men silently shadowed the unsuspecting party from the court. They kept well in the wings, only the lookouts keeping the party in sight. The laughs of the women would filter through the leaves and the sunlight every now and again, whetting the appetites of the stalkers who were soon going to enjoy their bodies.

A light breeze rustled through the foliage, conveniently covering the soft swishings of the horses, trampling through the grass and leaves. Nobody in the Duke's band spoke, communication being made simply through signs. The horses had been muzzled.

Deeper into the deserted forest the two bands made their way. Sometimes, from a ridge, they would have a view of the trees stretching out solidly in a great plain before them, at others they were almost enmeshed in a web of leaves and creepers as they advanced.

It was late in the afternoon and the sun was well down in the sky when a lookout came trotting gently back to report that Carlotta and her band had reached a spot near some rocks and had dismounted to pick some flowers.

At a sign from Cesare, his men donned rough masks of sacking which they had made themselves. They dismounted, unhitched bows and arrows from their horses, hobbled the animals and began to creep through the brush toward the spot indicated by the lookout.

They moved slowly, crouching, making use of every available cover, avoiding twigs with mathematical determination. As the sound of voices whispered through, they began to fan out, to surround the unsuspecting flower-pickers.

The wall of foliage became slighter and slighter, until Cesare, slipping slowly from tree to tree, could see the white garments of the women through the spaces in the low-hanging branches. He crouched lower and advanced a step at a time until the whole scene was clear to him. He stopped, a man on either side of him, and listened. There was no sound from his men, invisibly surrounding the small, rocky clearing.

The women, buxom wenches, were laughing and talking as they helped the princess gather

her blooms. The princess, herself, was in a gay mood which, for the moment, chased the haughtiness from her face, leaving only the tilt of her features to suggest her pride, her disdain of lesser mortals who thought themselves as good as herself.

Around the women the male attendants—less than a dozen of them—idled and wandered and exchanged a few words with each other.

Such a blissful, sylvan scene, Cesare thought with a grim inward chuckle. What a shock was in store for them. He watched Carlotta, laughing, unaware, bending to the ground. His lips curled in desire and revenge. He'd soon take that haughtiness from her, he'd soon debase her so that she couldn't lift her head again with that proud tilt. He'd provide the French Court and Society with the scandal of the decade—at Carlotta's expense. He'd have her haughty, inaccessible cunt so filled with prick that she'd never be able to close her legs again.

He straightened his bow in front of him, silently fitted an arrow. The two men at his sides followed suit. He took aim, slowly. He gave a sharp, piercing whistle and let fly. His arrow slashed straight through the neck of one of the men-at-arms. The man uttered a strangled, coughing cry and staggered to his knees before falling flat on his face.

The sunlight of the clearing was suddenly crisscrossed with a hail of arrows. All around the horrified women, their escorts crumpled up and ceased to exist. The attendants had no chance to escape. A few managed, pathetically, to draw their swords and start uncertainly toward the woods at their nearest point. They never got as far as the first thickness of foliage.

In the space of a few minutes the ground was littered with the still bodies of the dead. The women had gathered around Carlotta and were cringing in terror. The forest around them had relapsed into a temporary silence.

Cesare smiled his satisfaction and raised his bow once again. His arrow pierced the clothing of one of the ladies-in-waiting, stabbing through the hem of her dress and pinning it to the ground. There was a guffaw of laughter from his men on all sides at the sign—and then they moved into the clearing, a sinister-looking bunch with their rough masks.

Some of the women screamed as they were seized by the men. Their screams were stifled with rough and ruthless hands. Their clothes were torn from them, their eyes blindfolded with strips from their own undergarments.

Overcome with horror and a helpless indignation, some of the women struggled desperately, others yielded, sobbing and pleading for mercy.

Cesare watched while Carlotta was stripped. She was weeping, but more in rage and shame than fear. During her manhandling she continuously threatened and cursed the men who were denuding her. Her clothes were in rags by the time her captors succeeded in getting them off her and she stood between them, trying to cover breasts and loins at the same time.

Cesare's heart began pumping faster as they blindfolded her. She was small and slim, with a sinuous, perfectly proportioned body. Her breasts were not large, but they were high and firm with a luxurious curve which made him itch to run his hand slowly, gently around it; her hips were well-molded with a thrust of flesh on the peak of the bones; her legs were slim and rounded into light curves of muscle.

A delicate morsel, he thought, as his men began to march her toward the point where he still stood in the shelter of the surrounding bushes. If I can't have her legally, I'm sure I'll lose little by having her against her will. She'll still be warm, juicy flesh and blood. Her hips will still yield under mine, her breasts will still press hard against my flesh, her thighs will still ache from being spread so wide, her passage will still grow wet in spite of herself— and her hauteur. He clacked his tongue in satisfaction at the rape of her dignity, her reputation.

The strange trio had reached him while the thoughts wafted through his head. Close up she was more perfect than ever. He could see the moisture on her skin — the sweat of fear. He could make out the light down on parts of her body, a mole beneath her left breast, the puckered, corrugated skin around the base of her nipple, the slight quiver of her thighs as she approached.

He made a sign to his men and took her by the arms as they released her. Nobody spoke, no voices were to leave traces in her memory. With a wave, Cesare dismissed the men back to the clearing where the rest of his band were drawing lots for the order of ravishing the other women.

Left alone with her, he marched her in front of him, holding a slim bicep in each hand, away from the clearing.

She had a slim, straight back, a firm curve to her spine. The narrow waist rounded out into a fleshy dome of bottom which quivered sinuously as she walked. Her buttocks were like the heads on columns, rounded, well-fitting from the well-shaped, classical thighs. He put one hand down against her buttocks as she walked and the brushing of them, smooth as eggs, made his hand tingle, brought his penis crushing up inside his clothing, giving it that solid, blood-filled ache which only intercourse would relieve.

"Whoever you are I warn you you'll lose your head for this," she snapped suddenly, with a choke in her voice.

For answer he slapped each of her buttocks in turn. She squirmed and tried to break free but his grasp tightened on her arm so strongly that she cried out with pain and stumbled forward.

"If you get my clothes and put me on a horse I'll arrange a pardon for you personally," she urged with a sob. "You're all doomed—but you who are with me can be saved if you help me."

He jabbed his thumb between her quivering buttocks as she finished her desperate speech and she cried out and tried again to squirm away. He pulled her back toward him to control her and felt her buttocks writhing against his erection. He joggled against her, crushing his penis against her flesh, rotating it around the inner banks of the ravine between them.

"You beast, you swine!" She was crying bitterly again. He rubbed his hands over her breasts and sucked her neck as she struggled vainly. He had to get in her quickly.

Flushed and perspiring, he pushed her forward again. He ran his hand down her spine, let it swoop out with the lift of her buttocks. She kicked back at him and he slashed the flat of his hand across her rump anew.

At a distance from the clearing where he could no longer hear the scuffling of activity, he tied her to a tree while he cut four stakes with his dagger. The stakes he shoved deep into the ground in a rough square. He went back to the tree and looked at his victim. Now that she was in his power he tortured himself, gloating over her body, taking his time in the preparation.

He kissed her lips and she started at the unexpected assault. The lips trembled under his and tried to drag away but he pressed on them hard and bit them so that a muffled cry of protest tried to escape from her throat. He moved his mouth off her and nibbled her nipples.

"Oh, you swine, you swine! If you touch me I promise you you'll be tortured to death!"

He sucked the breast, letting it bulge right into his mouth like a perfect rounded fruit. He moved his mouth again and kissed her belly. She tried to fight him off with her legs, but emotion was exhausting her.

Cesare stepped back after a while and slowly began to undress. He stripped gradually, garment by garment, feeling the cool touch of air on his naked flesh. He revealed his loins last and a tremor of excitement ran through his body as his penis shot warmly into the cool atmosphere and soared there, tensed up, in a static thrust against nothing.

He went close to her and untied her from the tree. She felt his naked body as he brushed against her and she began to fight, weeping almost hysterically at the same time. She was no match for him. He held her easily in his arms while he pressed his hot joint against her loins, against her behind as she twisted. His knob was a deep blood-color; it had moistened over.

With a grunt of effort he pulled her to the ground and tied her wrist to one of the stakes.

She jerked against it while he held her other wrist and moved the second stake to a more suitable distance before tying the second wrist.

He smiled with lustful satisfaction at his work and pulled her left leg wide out from her body, as near a right angle with her hips as he could make it. She tried to kick him, gasping with pain and rage. That leg fastened, he caught the other and pulled it wide, moving the last stake over. The angle between her thighs was now an obtuse one. It left wide and unprotected that mass of delight between her white columns. He gazed down at her. The lips of her vagina were pink and fleshy, a muff of hair receded from their surroundings.

Cesare walked in between her legs and pressed her vagina with his big toe. She gave a little scream and tried to recoil.

"You can have anything if you'll get me a horse," she gasped, "pardon, money, jewels—anything you want!"

He inserted his toe slowly in her vagina. He felt it open and yield and he jogged his toe into her. His penis was sticking straight out from his loins like a handle; a drop of moisture dripped from it onto her belly.

He grinned and knelt down between her legs, staring at the opening he was going to fuck. He wanted to make her degradation complete. He lay down between her thighs with his face right up against her mossy opening. He pulled the lips wide apart with his thumbs and pushed his lips against her warm flesh. He kissed and licked and then he poked out his tongue into her hole.

Carlotta strained at her bonds and gasped out exclamations of horror and shock.

"Please, please!" she begged. "No, no!"

Cesare continued to lick. He had found the clitoris which was soft, unresponding and was sucking it hard, intending to hurt her physically as well as mentally.

At the same time he slipped his hands up under her behind, his fingers rustling on the bed of old leaves on which she was pinioned. Her buttocks squirmed tight and cringed at his touch. But so widely were her legs splayed apart that she couldn't hide her dark, little hole and he began to push it and pull it apart, so near to his lips.

"Oh, God, God, no, no!" Carlotta was almost in an hysterical delirium. But that only increased his thirst for revenge.

He released her anus after a while and caught both her wide-spread thighs, pulling her pelvis down at his mouth, pushing his tongue up into her passage as far as it would go. She was small, and obviously a virgin. He wondered if she'd bleed when he had her. He wondered if it would shame her more to bleed. Perhaps he shouldn't finger her too much for fear of making his passage easier.

He brought his tongue out of her and knelt up on both knees, looking at her body. She was a flesh and blood dummy there for him to use. There was nothing she could do or say to stop him from doing anything he wanted to in any way he pleased.

He lay down on her and slithered up her body. She gasped again at the horror of his weight on her and what it meant. Her breasts were firm and springy under him, balancing him up like two rubber cushions. Down at his thighs was a void, just the leaves under him, no thighs of hers, nothing. She was pulled too widely apart; there was just the almost horizontal line of legs and pelvis.

He put his hand down there and felt for her aperture. It was moist, but tight, difficult to open a little. He took his prick in his hand and aimed the knob at the small hole he'd found. She squirmed away, but there was no hope. She began to cry and to mutter a prayer. His knob was against the little orifice. He drew back his hips a little and then lunged forward and up.

A choking cry of pain burst from her lips as he smashed through a tight channel, right in and up, bursting the hole all the way until it was just too tight to take the rest of his thickening stem.

He drew his prick back a little. It was so tight in her passage that he felt a stab of pain in his organ, a pain that was exciting because it seemed to draw the fluid from him with his first thrust. He rammed up again, tearing farther this time so that his teeth gritted with the painful ecstasy of it.

Carlotta uttered a low groan which seemed to expand and contract as if she couldn't get her breath. She seemed to fade into a half-stupor, still crying and very white.

The sight of her pale, agonized face acted as a spur to Cesare penetrating her. He wanted to get up and up, right up into her haughty belly so that he could see that haughty face creased in the painful knowledge that a man was raping her, shagging that guarded treasure of hers so that it was numb with pain.

The pull on his penis was like the hug of a mountain bear. It was almost unbearable, but just bearable because it was so exquisite at the same time.

He flexed his hips at the horizontal bar of her legs and pelvis in sharp, powerful movements. His prick ran solidly up, bringing his loins against the fleshy undersides of her thighs with a bump. He was panting hard. There was such a tight pull on his organ.

He felt warmth and wetness. She had bled. It made it easier. He crammed it in short strokes, flicking up the last with an extra thrust until he could feel his knob right up in her as something separate from the rest of his penis. It seemed to make contact with something in its path in addition to the crunching pressure all around its hot, drawn-back length of skin.

This seemed to be the most pulverizing screw he'd ever had, and the sweet sensation of vengeance made it all the better, all the more sadistically exciting to grit his teeth and curl back his lips in passion as he seared into her squirming channel.

He grasped and squeezed her thighs in a grip that brought her out of her semi-coma and made her groan with a fresh awareness of reality.

He slipped his arms around her, grazing them on the leaves, and hugged her to him, crushing her in his strong arms. She was utterly in his power, crushed in his arms, crushed by his great, in-tearing mast. As a final possession he crushed his lips again on hers, forcing them savagely apart, feeling them yield and slip back on her clenched teeth. He bit her lips and the teeth came apart enabling his tongue to invade her mouth.

His prick and loins were boiling. With each thrust it seemed as if matter were being drawn from his penis with a hot poultice. His loins were churned with chilling, twisting clasps which seemed to be tearing out his very guts.

"Oh, God . . . oh, wonderful!" he breathed—and then half-remembered that he shouldn't speak and fresh words merged into animal sounds of passion.

He leaned his body up from hers, pressing his knees into the leaves. Now he could exert more weight, more of a thrust from his loins. He slipped his hand down holding her buttocks, each oval of smooth flesh in his hands. At each stab he pulled her lower body hard against his loins, letting out a groan of pleasure.

Carlotta, her face wet with tears, could manage no more than a continuous whimper—the proud beauty was reduced to a sniveling, agonized toy. Her lips trembled, the bandage around her eyes was soaked from her weeping.

Cesare felt the end aproaching in a delicious agony. He pushed his prick ruggedly in to its full length and pressed there, trying to push farther than was possible, while he wriggled his hips against her pelvis, brushing her pubic hair with his, flattening the fleshy rims of her vagina.

He reached to her breasts with his hands as he felt the scorching helter-skelter from his stomach to his genitals. He grasped them, twisted them so that she cried out afresh with pain. He pulled her nipples. His face was a mask of lost, bacchanalian sensuality. His hips jerked and jumped, screwed and squirmed as if of their own volition while his hands trounced her breasts and his eyes glazed over.

"Ah, ah, ah!" He couldn't hold back the eruption of his breath. Carlotta cried out in despair, recognizing that she was soon to be filled with the polluting sperm of her tormentor, the final, cruel, inescapable indignity.

A rack seemed to be torturing Cesare's organ, pulling it, distending it, punishing it with a voluptuous, throbbing clench.

His hands moved off her marked, reddened breasts, clamped on her waist, jerked her hips at his prick. He slowed his stroke, surging into her to the very root of his pulsating tube. His head swayed back on his neck, his chest heaved with choking breaths, his buttocks clamped together as he flexed inwards, his hands made fresh marks on her waist. It was here, here, gathered ready to fly, gathered, gathered, couldn't be held. "Uuuuugh!" His head jumped, his teeth gritted and fell apart, gritted again as he pumped the full extent of his lust between her legs, discharging it into the slim, gripping channel.

The princess lay under him, her head turned sideways into the leaves. It was over now, over and done, an eternal, ineradicable shame. The tears dried on her face, her head ached, her vagina ached and throbbed. It felt swollen and inflamed and her breasts hurt. She wished she were dead.

Slowly Cesare climbed off her. He stood up, wiped his penis on one of her garments and looked down on her. There was nothing haughty or inaccessible about her now. Her body was marked in a number of places from the rough usage he'd subjected her to. And her gaping legs were divided by a red, raw-looking area of flesh where his prick had scourged her.

He looked down at his organ as he wiped it. It was red and hot and there were traces of her blood around its limp base. He wiped the blood off and threw the garment down beside her.

He dressed with a feeling of triumph and satisfaction and, leaving her fastened and spread-eagled, walked back through the trees to the clearing.

Most of his men had finished loosing their lust on Carlotta's ladies-in-waiting. Some were dressing, others still naked, yet others still bobbing on the nude bodies of their prey. Many hadn't bothered to seek the privacy of even a small bush in order to indulge their sexual appetites.

Cesare gave a loud whistle and after a few minutes lookouts rode in. They had taken up their posts as a matter of course although it was highly unlikely that there would be any wanderers at this depth of the forest.

The Duke indicated to the newly-arrived that they were to take the places of their companions, a task they fell to with gusto, while those who had worked out their passion moved off through the trees to keep guard.

Beckoning to three of his men, Cesare led them off toward the spot where Carlotta lay.

"Have her one after the other," he told them in low voice on the way, "and make her suffer."

The men grinned lasciviously. They considered themselves lucky to be offered the most noble lady of the group.

For a while Cesare watched his men tormenting the prostrate body of the princess as a preliminary to fresh rape, then he walked off through the trees to make sure the lookouts were well posted.

He felt highly satisfied with the day's events. He had taught Carlotta a lesson she would never forget. It was very probable she'd feel it necessary to leave the French Court. In any case he wouldn't have her now even if she suddenly agreed to his suit. She could keep her dowry.

Cesare had no fear of discovery. The coup had been well planned and executed. He was aware there was a slight possibility that in some quarters suspicion might fix on him. But he was not afraid of suspicion. And for the most part it would not be dreamed that such a dastardly crime could be authored by any but the crudest of brigands.

He and his men, he mused, would ride back —with suitable scouts—along the tracks made by the princess and her cortege on the outcoming journey. Near the fringe of the woods they would have to separate into pairs and ride off in different directions, getting back to their quarters at different times and from different directions. They would leave the women tied to trees with the dead for company. By nightfall the King's men would be scouring the woods in search of them and their cries would soon bring about their rescue. He'd have them left naked so that Louis' men would also have a very astonishing eyeful—an eyeful they would hardly be able to keep to themselves. And so the story would be quickly spread.

Whistling softly, Cesare finished the checking of the lookouts, and strolled back to the spot where Carlotta was finding over and again that her flesh was not inviolate.

The sun was still splaying through the leaves, though from a more acute angle. Perhaps he had time for one more act of revenge. Perhaps if he screwed his prick into her ass that would be the crowning indignity.

He skirted the clearing, avoiding the locked couples from whom gasps and screams emitted at intervals in a more or less regular accompaniment to their rustle of movement.

The last of his men was reaching the climax to which Carlotta's well-gripping passage had brought him and Cesare squatted down with his other two henchmen and watched the man from the back view, his balls dangling, his behind tensing as it swept forward and his rod widened her. Carlotta no longer showed any emotion except for an occasional gasp as an extra-hard thrust took her by surprise.

In a low voice Cesare gave orders to his men.

"When he's finished you can leave me with her for a short time. Go back and help the others lash the women to trees. Make sure that they remain blindfolded—and not a word if there's any chance you'll be heard."

The buttocks of the ravisher were whipping in faster and faster, the backs of his thighs trembling. He gave a staccato series of coughing barks in which his body straightened and jerked convulsively. Then he staggered back from her on his knees and rested, kneeling, with his head dropped forward onto his chest.

Nobody hurried him and after a minute or two he turned, grinned without embarrassment at his companions and began to dress.

Cesare waited until all three were disappearing through the trees and then he stood up and walked over to Carlotta. Her body exuded an air of crushed and beaten animal. She could go no lower—she thought.

He took his knife from his belt and cut through the cords binding her wrists. She lay there, motionless. He pushed her with his foot and she seemed to come to her senses. She moved her hands up to the blindfold but he knocked them down.

Carlotta cringed in terror, completely subdued by the treatment to which she'd been subjected. He watched her, a cruel smile on his lips, until she moved her wrists and began to massage one with the other. She made no further attempt to remove the blindfold.

Watching her, ready for any movement to release her eyes from their confinement, he cut the bonds from her ankles and, painfully, she moved her legs together and wriggled her feet. She gave a little moan as she sat up and her vagina brushed the ground.

For a few minutes he allowed her to move her limbs and then he gathered the pieces of cord and knotted them into lengths again.

When he seized her, she made no effort to struggle. He turned her over so that she was lying face down on the ground. She lay pressed into the leaves, lifeless while he ended her brief freedom by fastening her wrists to the stakes once more.

He stood up and looked at her buttocks. They were like swollen buds preparing to burst into bloom—a little soiled from their contact with the ground—inviting a touch, to be fondled and held.

She had made no attempt to press her buttocks together or even to close her legs. She lay limp, exhausted, legs and arms slack, waiting for whatever was to come. She'll never be the same again, he thought with grim satisfaction; something in her will be broken forever—apart from her maidenhead.

He undressed for the second time that day. Desire was welling up in him again like a dried-up river suddenly growing again with the floods.

His penis when it flipped into view was still pink, with veins standing out on it prominently. It was hot, too, and heavy, needing a fresh release.

It was still warm in the spots where the sun's rays crept through the tangled branches, but the air was cooling. He braced his wiry body. His penis was the hottest part of him.

Carlotta stirred and groaned. He bent toward her to hear.

"No more . . ." she murmured. "No more . . . have pity . . . please."

Her helpless throwing of herself on his mercy produced an opposite effect to the one she desired. It made a nervous throb pulse in his chest, a little crest of sexual excitement, which began to break over his body like the surf on a shoreline.

He kicked her thighs apart with his feet. She let them flop where he kicked them. She had no more strength to resist.

On her thighs he could see the layer of slight, fair down, but her bottom, so smooth as to be almost glossed with a sheen, held his gaze. He gripped his organ in his hand. It felt enormous. He wondered how women could take it all. It moved in his hand involuntarily, a little jerk over which he had no control.

He sank to his knees on the soft bed of leaves and stroked her buttocks with a hand that quivered. He caught each of the glossy hillocks and pulled them apart. She stiffened, tried to close them together and then gave up as he jerked at them rudely again.

Her anus was disclosed like the center of a flower whose petals are pulled apart. He gazed at it. It was hairless, simply a small garden of the same slight, fair down leading up to its crinkled edge. From the crinkled edge, the little pouchy slit curved into itself redly.

Cesare ran his tongue over his lips. He settled down on her back, kissing her spine. He slid his hands between them and drew the buttocks apart like curtains and wriggled his prick between them. Alongside his prick he let his fingers glide, feeling the way. His index finger encountered the sudden rubbery point of her posterior opening and he nosed his knob after it, prodding tentatively.

"No, no . . . please, no!" he heard Carlotta's weak, muffled appeal beneath him.

He pressed down vertically with his stand of rigidity. He felt it come in contact with the spot and took his hands under her loins, gripping her tightly.

For a number of little strokes which were just rebuffed pressures on her anus, he jogged up and down, pushing his loins at the soft cushion of her rump. In, out, in, out, he sawed without any specific feeling but a growing sense of pressure, vague and ill-defined in his genital region.

The princess, who might have been his wife, lay quivering under him, knowing that he was about to sodomize her, not knowing what it would be like, only aware of the intense shame which burned in her like a disease.

Cesare pushed, pushed, levering his whole body on his stiff stem of flesh until it suddenly broke through with a great grip on his knob.

Carlotta uttered an agonized cry which sputtered into a gurgle.

He pushed down, thrusting into her, feeling his prick sliding in, now, the clamping pressure fitting tightly and strongly-defined along his inflated flesh.

Carlotta began to struggle, trying to press her thighs together under his, finding new strength to twist and fight against her bonds.

"No, no! I can't bear it!" she cried.

But Cesare held her in spite of her struggles and plunged more and more thickly into her with a slow swampy advance which seemed to be tearing his rod to shreds.

His victim couldn't keep back fresh tears. The pain forced them out of her eyes. The agony from her anus spread up into her throat and choked her. She felt sick and slightly dizzy. She continued struggling in her mind even when her body was not making movements, was taking no direction from the mind.

Her head was dazed, but through it all she was aware that his thick protrusion was entering her behind, spreading it, opening it up, making it wet and large, splitting it, making it ache, burn and protest with pain and indignity. She bit her lips until they were warm and wet. She didn't know it was blood on them.

The daze in her head was a mixture of pressure from her behind and noises from around her. It was only later that she realized the noises—which seemed impersonal—were those of her own groaning and his gasping on her back.

Eventually the pain meant nothing. It was simply a continuous, overwhelming cutting away of that opening between her buttocks, an enlarging which felt like the whole of her innards being pushed up into her chest and out of the way of the intruding pike.

There was pressure all around her, which

she also recognized later as the weight of his body on her back and backside.

For a long time the tearing, chafing in and out which was a wave of advancing and withdrawing torment, went on, until she was aware of herself performing certain actions which were dictated by his guidance. She was kneeling up with her head left on the leaves. Her thighs were widespread and pushed in under her. Her legs felt stiff and jelly-like at the same time.

She was aware of a greater edge to the continuity of pain, an extra pricking stab which her new position had enabled him to make. Now she was sure that her body was being ripped from that tiny point which now seemed so large, as if the entirety of her behind were just a gaping hole.

She became aware of another pressure on her waist just above the hip bones. That was his hands, pulling her back onto his enormous, indefinable mass of intrusion, pulling her back as his weight pushed forward and surged into her behind with a fresh shattering wave of pain every second.

Cesare skewered and screwed in from all angles, moving his hips at and across her bottom. His prick was burning again. It had never felt so deliciously crushed and pulverized —and yet so huge and swollen because the great pressure made it more acutely sensitive along the entirety of its throbbing length.

As he swept in, his belly smacked against her bottom. The well-fleshed buttocks provided a buffer from which his body recoiled with a spring before flowing in again with a smooth, agonizing fluency.

His penis was undergoing the most voluptuous torture. He wished it could go on forever —but he wanted it to gather momentum as well, to sweep to the inevitable climax which was such sweet torment.

In and in he surged, his prick tearing right in until it was completely swallowed and his hair squashed against the down on the inner crack of her buttocks.

He felt the liquid of climax growing in intensity and his mind reeled with the pleasure of it. His mind took in the groaning of his soft-fleshed victim, the abandon of her posture, her helplessness, the fact that she was crying again through her groans. He gripped her waist like a vise as he felt the thin, fluid movement right up to the base of his rod.

The moment of oblivion, wonderful oblivion was almost on him. He gasped for breath, his chest heaving in great, gasping sighs. His prick was crushed and squeezed beyond endurance. He couldn't keep on at the same pitch. It was too much.

The fluid blocked into a great, pricking weight at the base of his penis. He couldn't hold it. His mouth twisted into a multitude of ungovernable shapes. Her buttocks were there containing his penis, glossy and smooth, lovely and exciting and her prostrate back and her thighs like a tripod under her and her groans and her sobs. He couldn't hold it. It was rushing suddenly along the thick length of his staff, terribly clear and acute like scalding water. And it flowed straight through and burst from his knob with a force which dragged a long, grating cry from his mouth. Twisting his mouth under the cries he smashed his prick home again and again, ridding himself of a great weight of sperm, letting it shoot up into her, hearing her cry out sharply every time he shattered in.

By the time he felt sufficiently recovered to dress and return to the clearing, the sun had gone down and the twilight was on its way.

His men were waiting for him. Their naked victims were already grotesquely attached to the surrounding trees in positions which were at once revealing and comic.

CHAPTER 14

It was close on the following dawn before Carlotta and her women were found by the search party the King sent out a couple of hours after dusk.

The captain who led the party was hard put to stop his men from committing too many indiscretions with their wandering hands as they untied the unfortunate women. And many a lady-in-waiting had her breasts and behind slyly stroked in the process of being set free. But, so relieved were they after a chilly night in the woods at the mercy of any vagabond who might happen upon them, that the women didn't even notice that they were being rather unnecessarily felt as hands fought with their bonds.

Carlotta was too ashamed and exhausted to be indignant about the fate she'd suffered. She mounted a horse with difficulty and conserved all her energy to prevent the physical pain she felt from showing on her face as, surrounded by their fresh escort—bodies of the dead flung over the horses' rumps—they headed back to the court.

By that time, Cesare and his men were sleeping soundly in their beds—a sleep of exhausted passion.

The following day a large band of men-at-arms, including many of Cesare's retinue, set out to scour the woods in search for the villains who had attacked the ladies of the court.

But, although they spent the whole day, they found no trace of any possible aggressors—in fact the forest seemed to be totally deserted and uninhabited for many miles around the spot.

There was much discreet talk about the dastardly fate of the ladies, but nobody seemed even to think of Cesare Borgia as the possible dispenser of the treatment. The King was restrained by Carlotta from offering a large reward for information leading to the capture of the unknown rogues. The less said the better, she decided. As it was she felt unable to leave her chambers for shame.

His Majesty, after a few more days of searching and interrogating, called off the hunt. But not before half his kingdom was aware of the story—often in a grossly exaggerated form. Some even suggested in the countryside's inns that the King himself had already tired of his wife and desired the haughty Carlotta, who had enhanced her desirability in refusing to accept Cesare's suit. Certainly many were the tongues which wagged over the Duke's part in the plot. But they wagged only among the peasants, who loved to talk about things connected with nobility, and the more scandalous the better. In the court itself, Cesare, who had always conducted himself in a manner of the utmost courtesy and delicacy, was considered beyond reproach. Besides, he had never had a definite refusal to his plan for marriage from the princess.

* * *

Such a scandal, however, certainly put Carlotta out of the marriage market for the time being, and Louis, still wishing for a firm alliance between the Pope and himself, presented Cesare with two fresh possibilities for a wife. He was offered either one of the King's nieces or the daughter of the Duc de Guyenne, Charlotte d'Albret.

Charlotte was only seventeen, beautiful and she was a sister of the King of Navarre. It was she that Cesare chose.

For a short time her father appeared to oppose the proposed marriage. But the King of Navarre needed the friendship of France to withstand any possible attack from Castille and pressure was brought to bear on the girl's father so that he eventually consented.

The marriage was politically sound, uniting both sides as it did at the time when Milan was noticeably belligerent over disputed territory.

Cesare was able to spend a few months only, consolidating his reputation in France and enjoying his duchess. For the trumpets of war with Milan were soon sounding forth and the Duke of Valentinois was riding south in Louis' train to chastise the Italian kingdom.

In the Vatican, Alexander breathed a sigh of relief that his son had thus consolidated the alliance with France, and began to prepare celebrations for his homecoming.

Lucrezia, to whom news of her family came once in a while, also began to make preparations—to leave her little love nest in the convent and give herself once again into Cesare's arms.

LUSTS OF THE BORGIAS

VOLUME TWO

CHAPTER 1

Cesare Borgia sat still and straight on his horse smiling wryly. Across the green plains of Romagna which surrounded the river Po, the city of Imola was humped behind its great, protecting wall. A siege would have meant a long delay in his campaign, possibly into winter. But Imola, like all the other towns he had taken since Louis had gone back to France after the fall of Milan, was coming over to him without pressure of arms.

He watched his lieutenant, Ramiro de Lorqua, in earnest conversation with the little delegation from the city. They had met to parley in a little group some several hundred yards in advance of Cesare's army which stretched in an ominously broad arc across the great valley. Away to the south the Etruscan Apennines shimmered and misted in the blue haze of summer. The weather was as satisfying as the campaign.

It was with the psychological cunning which Machiavelli was to take as example for his book, *Il Principe*, that the Duke of Valentinois had contrived to triumph so easily everywhere he went. Romagna was, in fact, noted for its tyrants and it was merely habit and tradition which had brought citizens loyally around their despotic leaders in times of crisis. With the capture of his first city, Cesare had pardoned all the citizens who had fought against him and had forbidden his men to indulge in the usual postcapture assuaging of their lusts. There had been no pillage, no killing, no rape, no disorder. This he had enforced with the severity for which, when occasion demanded it, he was notorious.

The effect had been miraculous. Word had been allowed to spread of the good treatment received by the beaten populaces and, as if Cesare possessed some new and irresistible weapon, the common folk of all the cities in his path had denounced their tyrannical lords and flung open their fortresses to the Pope's son.

In front of the great army, Ramiro de Lorqua and his subordinates reined round their horses and sped back across the intervening space toward their chief. The councillors of Imola remained in a motionless group—a helpless, hopeful band almost surrounded by the mass of Borgian troops.

De Lorqua reined in beside the Duke. A grim smile of triumph flickered across his normally austere visage.

"The gates are open, Sire," he said quietly. "Imola is ours. They will lead us across the moat into the city."

"Good," Cesare replied, briefly but with satisfaction.

He spurred his mount forward and the great army came to slow life behind him, following patiently in his wake.

"If it please God, no soldier of mine shall have to raise his right arm to fight again. He will be received like a visiting monarch and have to find his exercise in the brothels."

De Lorqua laughed, a quick, unbelieving laugh.

"There is yet Forli to come," he reminded.

As the towers and campaniles beyond the tall buff walls of the city became clearer, Cesare reflected on his advance. If all went well he should, in time, succeed to the title of Duke of Romagna, a pleasing thought. His campaign, which had begun as a war to recover the temporal power of the Holy See in these areas where the barons refused to pay their taxes, had developed into a personal triumph, which —intelligence had it—was being talked of throughout Italy and beyond. Already the subjugated people—if one could give that title to a people liberated by an alleged enemy from despotism—were demanding that Cesare be made their permanent master and that they enjoy his protection forevermore. His ambition was fired and seemed likely to be rewarded.

But there was, of course, Forli, with that amazon of a Countess, who would doubtless defend it to the last, crying death to the enemy even as death shattered her heart—or, as was very likely—rapacious lust shattered another part of her anatomy.

Crowds were thronging the streets and the squares to cheer the invading army; flags and kerchiefs fluttered in the air and women of doubtful character hung their half-naked bosoms from the windows of establishments of doubtful reputation in a surge of welcome.

But the battle was not quite over. A councillor of the city joined the vanguard to warn that a captain of the guard with a body of troops had withdrawn to the almost impregnable citadel, swearing to surrender only when death claimed him.

Even as the populace waved and the women flaunted their waiting breasts before the eager arrivals, a cannon boomed out from the citadel and sent the crowds screaming and scurrying for shelter.

Cesare immediately trained a number of his cannons on the stark, scarred walls of the citadel and returned fire until the challenge had petered out for a while and he was able to direct the billeting of his troops and arrange a siege of the inner stronghold which still resisted him.

CHAPTER 2

Cesare stretched himself at ease on the red plush couch which had been put at his disposal. Around him, his principal officers shared with their leader the privilege of being the guest of the Chief Councillor of the city. Outside, the cannon was quiet, the citadel comfortably besieged. Full-scale assault operations could wait until tomorrow. The army needed rest and a little entertainment.

Throughout the city the brothels were doing fine, wine-flushed business. And any woman who showed herself willing was feeling the full pent-up strength following days of abstinence on the part of the visitors between her thighs. But, as usual, Cesare had forbidden violence. Any man reported stealing a citizen's unwilling wife or raping a reluctant maiden would be made an example of for all the town to see.

Within the mansion of the Chief Councillor, gypsy music was playing. A band of well-dressed nomads were strumming their guitars and tambourines. There was controlled passion in the music and in the dark, gypsy faces. There was ill-controlled passion, too, in the loins of Cesare's officers. This man, their host, had promised them, later, the full benefits of the high-class brothel which was virtually his harem. They were anxious to relieve this ache of longing in their lower regions.

Cesare toyed with his glass, sipping the

rich, sweet wine with which his host had bolstered a magnificent meal. He was thinking of Lucrezia, wishing she were here, now, so that they could retire to a quiet nook and enjoy each other with the furious abandon of the days before he had left for the French Court.

"How do you like my gypsy orchestra?" his host asked, leaning across from his neighboring couch.

"Excellent, excellent, but they look a little domesticated."

"You mean they are well dressed, well fed? But of course. They have become quite famous these last few months. Everybody is paying big prices to have them play and dance. Their days of dirt and rags are over."

He swallowed a glass of wine in one long draught.

"But if you talk of domestication, wait until you see Maria. Domestication! I'd like to see the man who could domesticate her. Violence, passion, sensuality! They ripple in her limbs when she dances, they reach to you from her breasts, they writhe in her buttocks. And yet she's not for sale. Oh, they've tried to rape her —many a man in torment. But she carries a stiletto and knows how to use it, they say. She's a proud one. I have to rush to my mistress in excitement after she's danced, and then I try to imagine she's the divine Maria who won't be bought."

Cesare listened, idly swishing the wine in his refilled glass and letting the music flow in him. The old dotard, he was thinking; the thought that he couldn't have her would make him pay groveling homage to the ugliest old whore.

"Well, when does this proud creature deign to appear?" he asked.

"Immediately if you so wish it."

The host clapped his hands and gave orders to a servant, who disappeared, gliding over the rich carpets which covered the tiled floor, into the other rooms which led off from a portico at the far end of the main dining hall.

After a few minutes, he reappeared, gave a few whispered instructions to the leader of the gypsy orchestra and withdrew.

The music changed suddenly to a wild, passionate flamenco in true Spanish style, the notes hurtling and gyrating one after the other in a loud, fiery torrent. There was a sudden strumming of chords and then a lowering of tempo and pitch. The guest officers glanced up from their conversation and wine. There was a foreboding in the music which immediately attracted all attention. While they stared, not knowing quite what to expect, but certain that something was going to happen, a figure danced slowly in from the shadows of the portico, a shadowy movement at first, growing into a flame of red and black, becoming a beautiful girl who swayed sensually in before the gypsy band which accompanied her.

There was an instant tension in the assembly. Men who had been engaged in, at least, the semblance of war for more than a week or two, flushed over with the tightening of desire. Cesare put down the glass with which he had been describing circles in the air.

"You hardly exaggerated," he said quietly and in some surprise.

"Almost worth a stiletto in the ribs if one could be certain of achieving one's fill before the death blow, eh?" chuckled his host.

Cesare Borgia didn't reply. His thoughts were away on the hips that revolved gently, the breasts that were taut from her upstretched, slender brown arms. Her face seemed to spark and blaze with pride and a controlled sensuality; her dark hair swept back, dropping, long onto her shoulders; broad brow over dark, almond eyes, a straight nose which flared lightly at the nostrils, long, full lips which opened often in intense concentration as she danced, a good, clear chin which was round and smooth under her mouth; and then the neck, long and unexpectedly well-developed as she came forward into the light, full and with the slight ridge of a vein; below the black lace frill of the tight-bodiced red dress she wore, the breasts which forced out the yielding stuff in strong, taut lines, the slim waist which moved and writhed inside the dress, the skirt tight over her hips, enclosing her buttocks in a tight embrace and then flaring out loosely around her thighs to permit her freedom of movement.

"Superb, superb," Cesare murmured aloud and his host smiled with a pleasure that conflicted with his mask of almost miserable longing.

The music gathered in crescendo and the girl made a full, twirling tour of the room, skimming the tables of the spectators with her flying skirt. She seemed to see nobody. At times her face was serene and ethereal, at others working with passion as if she were in the throes of sexual intercourse. The men seemed to come to life, out of the still, electric petrification her arrival had induced. They slithered forward on their couches the better to see. There were odd comments of coarse appreciation uttered without a withdrawal of the eyes watching her every movement, every crease and tension of every part of her body under the flaming silk dress.

The Duke of Valentinois watched with the others. He felt his heart pounding and that empty sucking in his stomach. She was as beautiful as Lucrezia, this Maria, the gypsy; as beautiful at the other end of the scale, each of them perfection of their own kind.

His eyes ran over her avidly. As she swayed toward his end of the room, slim arms flowering in the light of the candles around the walls, he watched her breasts, full and alive under the slender covering. They bulged and moved in unison with her movement. The points of her nipples jutted, large and voluptuous from the summits of the warm mounds of flesh behind them. He let his glance fall, taking in the slim waist, so slim that it moved all by itself inside the dress as if it wanted no part of these protecting clothes. And then the tight containment of those hips, the rounded belly, which could be cupped with a hand, the protrusion of hipbones, well-fleshed and bulging against the silk, the lines of the strong, sexual thighs and then the slim, lightly-muscled calves that twirled below the whirl of the skirts.

"Beautiful, beautiful," Cesare whispered.

His host leaned toward him, hotly.

"You must forgive me," he muttered. "I can't bear to stay. It is a mistake for me to be here at all and I must take my leave in a few moments. If there is anything you or your officers require of me, you have only to ask my servants. They will show you to your quarters and to the source of your future enjoyment."

His breath had come with difficulty and when Cesare looked at him he saw that his face was almost crimson and his eyes drawn in anguish.

"My poor Chief Councillor," he whispered sympathetically, "I understand your predicament. To have such a delight within your house and be unable to sip of the ecstasy she promises is hard indeed. But I crave one boon before you leave—that I may be permitted to try my gallantry with the lady."

There was a note of envy in the Chief Councillor's tone as he gazed into Cesare's handsome, commanding face.

"By all means," he said, "and I wish you success. Perhaps a conquest would soften her heart toward others who would give their souls to share her bed. I will see that she joins you alone after the entertainment and that you are not disturbed."

With that the Chief Councillor rose, not waiting even to hear his guest's thanks, and slipped from the banquet hall as if he were afraid he would in some way disgrace himself if he delayed his exit a single second.

Grinning to himself, Cesare turned back to the spectacle. The music was throbbing, drugging the room with its heavy insistence. The girl had her back to him, arms high above her head, hips swaying, heels tapping on the marble floor. The outlines of her buttocks pressed and relaxed in firm ovals against the seat of the dress. Each seemed to move of its own accord, rounded and naked, inviting lustful attack. She whirled and flitted forward with flying, little steps, toward Cesare's table. Her eyes seemed to catch his for an instant. He held them and they bored back at him until slowly he dropped his gaze and stared meaningfully at the triangular crease of her dress between her thighs.

When he glanced up again, her eyes were still on him, but flicked away immediately, her head bowing to the ground in concentration.

A hot glow consumed Cesare, slowly, from his genitals. He had no thought of failure. The meeting of their eyes had established the beginning. He would, as always, win.

For a moment, he took his eyes from the scene to witness its effect. His officers were hypnotized. Some faces were scarlet, others white with desire: a band of civilized men, suddenly naked and primitive in the face of elemental sexual passion. The difference between most of them and himself, Cesare knew, was the difference between himself and the Chief Councillor: that he would not give his soul to possess this woman. It was, also, this very aloof quality which communicated itself even in moments of intimacy, which gave him his extraordinary power of attracting and, if desired, maintaining the interest of the most difficult and independent of women. Cesare had learned from his sister, Lucrezia, the intricacies of intrigue and attitude that women were capable of; he had, perhaps, been fortunate in learning from her the necessity of keeping himself beyond the snares which they set, of keeping himself whole in mind and emotions, of being always the master.

Now, catching again the eyes of the beautiful gypsy girl as she danced toward him, letting his eyes rove insolently over her breasts as if he were stroking them with his eyelashes, he felt certain that she was his. He could hardly wait to hold those buttocks naked in his hands and drive his strength and mastery between her naked thighs into the conquered lips that waited softly to receive him.

CHAPTER 3

It was very warm in the banquet hall — as if all those who had left had jettisoned their heat before departure. Not all the candles still glowed smoothly into the gloom, only a few at odd points around the walls cast deep and slightly moving shadows. There were two red candles flickering on the table and they threw a warm, flattering light on the faces of Cesare and the gypsy girl.

"A little wine," Cesare was saying, as he filled her glass again.

She took her long-stemmed glass and sipped, looking at him over its rim. Her eyes were warm, and so friendly that they would have turned over the Chief Councillor's heart had he been there.

"They say that you will soon be lord of all Romagna—perhaps of all Italy," she said softly.

"Gossip," Cesare said. "But it may be true." He smiled. "My chances would be greater had I your power of reducing men to willing slavery."

"Gossip," she retorted, "if we speak of men. I can think of many I would not put in that category."

"Our poor Chief Councillor is slowly dying of suffocation—suffocation of his desires."

"He is like a cow," she said. "He chews his food and watches me with great, gawking eyes. When he desired me he had to send a servant to try to procure me so afraid was he that I might spit in his face."

Cesare took a long gulp of wine.

"Are all as unlucky as he?"

"Did he not tell you I'm not to be bought?"

"I'm not talking of buying."

She raised an eyebrow at him over her glass and smiled. She gave no answer and Cesare put his hand on hers on the table, gently but firmly.

"You remind me of my sister Lucrezia," he said.

"But isn't she blonde?"

"I mean that you are perfect in your particular beauty as she is in hers. I am told, too, that she is perfect in bed. As for that, I would never be able to compare you."

He watched her closely. But she didn't take his words amiss. Clearly he was not in the same class as the Chief Councillor, nor had she removed her hand from his.

"What happens when you want to give—and not be bought?" he asked.

"These are very personal questions—I had heard you were very direct," she said, still smiling.

"It's the only way to know people," he replied. "Hedging and social protocol are all very well in their place."

"Yes," she said and she turned her hand in his and entwined their fingers gently. "I have given very rarely,'" she went on. "I only give when I'm moved, otherwise it's not worth the pestering which would follow from all those who assume that because a woman gives she is free to all."

She had leaned forward slightly and Cesare could see deep down between the swellings of her breasts. The skin was a tawny flame-color and as smooth looking as parchment. He let his eyes run from her breasts up over her shoulders and that strong, voluptuous neck. When his eyes reached hers she was looking at him without the smile. It had been replaced by a look he recognized—Lucrezia's look of desire. In those few seconds he thought with amazement that she must always have looked like this. That even in rags, running the streets of the slum quarters in her youth before she joined the gypsy band, she looked this same lovely, haughty, sensual woman who might, at that time, have given herself to anyone who was prepared to make her rich, to give her the life of a lady. He wondered that no rich merchant, straying on his horse through the poor quarter, had caught a glimpse of her—probably with half a breast naked through her rags and tatters, or a side view of a straining buttock. She could, by now, have been at the court of kings.

"What are you thinking?" she asked softly, the desire still heavy in her eyes. "Why do you look at me like that?" He looked at the dark shadows below her high, smooth cheekbones, his glance lingered on those full lips which had hardly moved as she spoke.

"I was thinking that you are, perhaps, more beautiful even than Lucrezia," he said quietly.

"She would not be flattered to hear you say that."

"She would probably retort by claiming that she was far superior in the boudoir."

"But even after tonight you would have no way of comparing us—you would never have slept with her."

Cesare stood up, slowly, not taking his eyes off the girl. Mingled with his unexpectedly easy triumph was a sly amusement at her peasant assumption. He was tempted to tell her, but the moment was not to be spoiled and, in any case, her tongue might wag.

He walked around the table toward her and

she stood up with her lips parted, waiting. When he reached her and caught her face in both his hands, her body swept in and wriggled against him. Sparks seemed to fly in his body. God, he thought, it's almost as if she divined and were determined to prove herself the better. The flesh, smoothly, glossily almost, covering the fine bones of her face was hot under his fingers. There was a delicate perfume of roses about her hair. Her lips were moist and gave like a sponge, opening under his. They seemed to swallow his mouth—and then her tongue, smooth as milk was panting into his mouth, exploring it, brushing against his own. Along his whole length he felt the warm slender solidity of her body pressing and moving slightly—the weight of her breasts protruding, the smooth roundness of her thighs brushing and clinging to his, her hips and that excruciating abdominal area which pressed against his confined genitals and slithered against them hotly. He pulled his mouth from hers and she let it go reluctantly. Audible little pantings breathed through her lips, now released, as he moved down her neck, sucking it, biting it, drawing a pattern of little red marks on the velvety skin. He reached her shoulders, the top halves, naked halves, of her breasts, which bulged and wanted to escape and soar forth for him in their entirety. As he bit her breasts gently, her abdomen, that triangular section between her strong thighs, squirmed furiously against the mound of his genitals which she could feel in an erect hump beneath his clothes.

"Let's go through to the private chambers," he whispered.

"No, now—here!" she said passionately.

He pushed her gently back toward the divan from which he'd watched her dancing earlier in the evening. The Chief Councillor had promised they would be alone—and what did it matter if a servant did tumble onto them? Guilt and fear were for the weak and subordinate.

She fell back onto the couch and he lowered himself down with her. She put her hand on the covered heat of his penis and he felt its trembling, demanding pressure with a wild surge of immediate desire. He began, quickly, to slip off her clothes and she helped him, breathing heavily, looking at him with deep, fire-filled eyes, concentrating on ridding herself of the garments that hid her body from him.

In a matter of seconds she was stretched out on the couch, more naked than in the days of flimsy rags and Cesare's mouth was avidly sucking her large, erect nipples, as his hands flared over her body, exploring its firm, beautiful contours while his penis seemed to throb and hum like a hive of bees.

Her breasts were taut and high in spite of their size. The nipples that he sucked crowned them in a dark, hard summit which seemed to epitomize her desire; the hard bosses yielded and flipped back in rubbering resilience and seemed to reach out to him in pleading desire for assuagement. Below her breasts her hard, narrow waist was the pivot for her writhing hips. No bones showed in her hips, the flesh was full and rounded, the little bulge of her abdomen heaving in and out with its crest of fine, dark hair. Her sensual, well-holding thighs pressed and slithered against each other, opening wide from time to time as Cesare's hands moved over her flesh. Between them, dark rose lips, moist and ready, were crushed with her movement.

Cesare's penis felt wet inside his clothes and the throbbing was unbearable. When, without opening her eyes or stopping the convulsions of her lost body, the girl put her hand again on his penis and began to squeeze and caress it, he stood up quickly and began to tear off his clothes.

She lay there, her breath exploding from between her parted lips, her thighs tight together as if to keep the sensation locked tightly in. She opened her eyes after a few seconds and watched Cesare baring his body. Her eyes were in anguish and her hands, which had moved up to the breasts on which the heat and fury of his lips remained, twitched gently.

Feeling the warm air strike his suddenly naked flesh with a cooling draught, Cesare looked back at the girl's body as he stripped. She was beautiful as a Greek statue and burning with sexual life. He could worship a body like that—except that he didn't worship bodies. He had a sudden irreverent thought of the envy the Chief Councillor would feel when he knew. What that man would give to be here now in his shoes—or rather in his skin.

Nude at last, with his penis soaring ruggedly out and up at an acute angle with his belly, Cesare moved toward the couch. She watched him come, her eyes flowing over his face and from it down over his lightly haired and muscular chest to the slim hips dominated by that great boom of penis with its narrowing, fiery tip. As he reached the divan she reached up and grasped it and icy darts shot through his belly and clashed in his genitals.

He lay down beside her and she stroked and

caressed his prick and smothered his lips with hers, flicking her tongue in what seemed an almost involuntary spasm of sensuality.

Cesare pressed her dark head back onto the couch. The rose perfume was all around like an ethereal cushion and her dark hair brushed softly against his face as he sank into her lips and sucked them and her tongue into his mouth. Her flesh was hot and receptive, trembling against his as he slid his hand down over those firm, reaching breasts and the belly with its little indentation and then over the fine hair which was warm and soothing to his fingers, and so between those hot and slightly sweating thighs, right at their topmost point where they merged into the hot arch containing the point of desire.

She gasped as his hand reached the lips of her cunt, gasped into his mouth and was unable to keep her lips against his with the sudden sensation. She dragged her head away and turned it so that her cheek lay along the divan, pressing into it as if she were resisting some torture.

Through the loose, wet flesh, his fingers wandered and into the suddenly tight and opening hole which he found.

"Oh, oh!" she gasped and bit her lips under his passionate, watching eyes as he lay with his cheek against hers. Her hand on his prick redoubled its activity and she began to stroke him gently, moving her fingers lightly on the hot, stiff flesh.

He felt her thighs moving and then opening widely and her crotch rose up slightly toward him, facilitating and demanding the entry of his searching fingers into the moist channel at whose entrance they dawdled. He pressed in, wiping a finger around the elastic rim and plunging on into the depths of the cavern beyond.

"Oh, oh, oh, oh!" Her face on the couch swung back at his and she released his prick and held him tightly with both arms as she kissed him wildly and rubbed her face all over and around his.

Cesare could feel his prick, hot and waiting, pressing up against her hip, the cool, yielding flesh of her hip. He moved in against her, crushing it against that flesh, rubbing his loins against her, moving one of his thighs half over hers.

His finger, now, had penetrated all the way and he could feel the smooth, viscid roof of the cavern. Her thighs alternately clamped his hand in the pressure of a vise and released it, sweeping apart in a wild, passionate gesture. She was panting continuously and punctuating the panting with little moans as he moved his fingertip gently against the roof of the cavern.

Her lovely lips were trembling and her nostrils were slightly flared the way he'd noticed them as she concentrated on her dancing. She had closed her eyes and the long lashes made tremulous shadows on her cheeks. Her long, slim hands ran convulsively over his body, not seeming to be controlled by her at all.

Cesare moved another finger into her vagina and she cringed away and then pushed back on the double prong which filled her. He allowed his fingers to roam all over and through the moist channel of her sex and then slowly withdrew them and searched for the tiny stub of her passion. He found it, hard and erect. It evaded him from time to time as he caressed it, slipping away into the fleshy folds of her lips.

The touch of his fingers on her clitoris had sparked even greater depths of passion reaction from her. She had caught his penis again and squeezed it hard. She ran her fingertips over his balls as far down as she could reach. She brought up her head and bit his neck and lips. She was like a tigress.

Caressing her, tantalizing her, bringing her to a pitch of excitement, with his own thunderous, growing passion as a controlled background, Cesare felt her thigh slipping and digging under his trying to get him to mount her. Her arms pulled his face onto her chest over against her breasts which strained up, digging him with erect, large nipples.

"Now, now," she murmured. "Do it now."

Overcome with a nervous excitement, now that the moment had come, as if afraid of the power of his own passion, Cesare hesitated, drawing his fingertips up her hard, little clitoris for a few seconds longer until she was groaning with ecstasy.

"Please, please, now, now, now," she begged, hardly able to utter the words, squeezing blindly on his rod of flesh.

Cesare slithered over onto her. She made a superb, warm cushion for his body. Her thighs swung wide apart as she felt the knob of his penis tickling against the lips of her vagina. She gripped both his shoulders very tightly with her hands which quivered with emotion.

Cesare wriggled on her, longing to plunge in but enjoying the sight and sound of her passion and desire.

He felt her release a shoulder and then her hand came down under her thigh and felt for and found his penis. She held it gently, seeming to hold her breath, too, at the same time, and guided it at her wide-open cunt.

Right, now, at last, Cesare thought in a sudden, fierce, violent joy. He thrust in with a long, excruciating grind, all the way in one long, agonizing movement. She drew up her thighs with his penetration and her hands bit into his shoulders.

"Aaaaaah!" The ecstatic groan dragged out from between their lips at the same moment. With her it continued on a slightly lower key, a continuous, gentle, lost groaning. With Cesare it broke down into a shunting accompaniment of groans and pantings for breath as he drove in and in, crashing and plundering, right to the soft, giving wall of the cavern's roof.

Her thighs which had opened, giving him wider access, and moved back toward her shoulders giving him depth, came down and clasped his hips, moving and slithering against them as he pistoned in and out. Her breasts flattened and rounded under his varying pressure and her eyes opened to look abandonedly into his as her groaning lips sought to touch, to bite, to kiss his face, any part of his face.

His loins aflame, consumed in the ecstatic relief of her moist, claiming containment, Cesare felt her passage plucking sensation from his prick along its whole length. Her channel fitted him like a glove, smooth and with a gentle pressure which became stronger as the tip of his organ coursed right through to its end.

Already he could feel pressure building up in his pulsating staff. All that preliminary titivating had prepared his prick for a quick release.

Under him, squirming and mouthing noises, the gypsy girl, too, was building up to the intense final pressure. Her arms moved around him, over his shoulder, down his back, to his buttocks which she could just reach. She pressed on them exhorting him into her and her legs swung up suddenly and entwined his thighs and then up further and gripped his waist.

Cesare slipped his hand under her full, soft buttocks which strained down firmly in his hands and then relaxed, soft again. He reached underneath, feeling her thighs from behind and she gasped anew as his fingers entered the long slit of her vagina, pulling the lips gently apart, brushing in with his hard length of penis.

Her head began to move from side to side on the divan. Her legs released his waist and swung down, flattening into the couch and then gripped him again before falling away, almost at right angles to her body.

Her crotch was running with moisture. Cesare's fingers slipped from it and ran up the crease between her buttocks. He pulled the buttocks apart and she gave a start of passion through her moaning. He plunged a finger against the tight, warm, puckering of her anus and felt it give and his fingertip break through to soft, tender flesh.

"Oh, oh, oh!" she gasped again and again.

She began to writhe as if in a paroxysm. It must be now, Cesare was able to think as he drummed into her, pulling back and then thrusting in his whole length in a slow, grinding crush.

She opened her eyes and looked at him desperately. Her eyes seemed to be speaking to him, loving him, wanting him, abandoning herself to him. Her mouth opened and her tongue came out—a long, point-tipped, moist and perfectly smooth tongue. Cesare lowered his lips to hers and bit the tongue gently. He ground in with slow, strong strokes. He could feel his penis swelling in a hot tingling expansion. He couldn't keep his mouth on hers and drew up, his hands under her buttocks, pulling them up off the divan, against his loins.

She wriggled furiously, her shoulders quivered, and her breasts under his eyes. She groaned and looked at his eyes in a last gleam of passion and then her mouth opened in a great circle, her head dropped back, her thighs clasped him and she emitted a loud, aching gasp and another and another, dwindling away into body-racking sighs.

Still holding her buttocks in his hands, fired by the sight of her fulfillment, Cesare, himself, trembled on the brink of release. His penis was chafing against the flesh of her passage and his loins were screwed up in a turmoil of pre-explosion. Her beautiful body, heaving with passionate sighs, was in his hands. He looked down and saw her thighs hanging over his hands as he held her bottom, and saw his prick, inflamed and wet, disappearing into her red, loose lips. Her breasts swayed and heaved below him and that narrow waist was heaving too, above the hips that he held up slightly off the bed.

He thrust savagely in and felt his knob growing and growing as if it would burst into a thousand pieces. He ground slowly, slowly, extracting every iota of sensation from the long, slow stroke. His breath was rising up from his chest, rising up through his throat at the same time that his knob was expanding in unbearable torture. He felt the quick fire dart in his loins and come racing through. His mouth opened wide as the breath finally, suddenly, reached it. He shattered his sperm up, up into her belly as the breath broke from his throat, twisting his mouth out into an agonized explosion. He felt the pressure of her thighs renewed, fleetingly, heard a faint gasp echoing a recognition of his orgasm.

For several seconds he pumped into her, seeming to loose all the juices of his pent up body into that lovely, waiting receptacle. Then, slowly he collapsed on her warm, cushioning flesh and felt her arms encircle him gently and her lips, light and tender on his cheek.

Later, nude still, she preceded him as they walked to the private chamber Cesare had been allotted off the banquet hall. Watching her buttocks swaying and rounding under the slim, taut waist, Cesare wondered if the Chief Councillor meant it when he said it would be worth getting a stiletto in one's ribs if one could be sure of fulfillment first. Looking at her thighs, slenderly moving under the rounded volptuousness of the buttocks, he felt pretty sure he meant it.

CHAPTER 4

It was a very cheerful Cesare Borgia that directed his forces for the storming of the citadel the following day. He was to have the delight of Maria's company for the remainder of his nights at Imola. She had fallen for him and was his to do with as he wished. In his mind he was even turning over plans to establish her near him when he finally settled in a permanent headquarters after the campaign.

So touched and pleased by his success had Cesare been that he'd even refused himself the satisfaction of giving the Chief Councillor an account of his conquest.

"She is, indeed, a fiery one," was the only comment he would make when discreetly pressed by his host.

With a concentration equalling that of his lovemaking of the night before, Cesare set about the quelling of the citadel.

His lieutenants had suggested a storming of the walls immediately a breach appeared. But the Duke, with some acute questioning, was able to establish that munitions in the citadel were not very plentiful and were likely to give out in a very few days.

Content with his host and his companion of the nights, and ever sparing of the lives of his men who would have to cross a deep moat in order to reach a breach in the walls, he settled down to a siege, maintaining a steady bombardment, producing a breach from time to time, which, those inside, panic-stricken at the thought of a resultant assault, rushed rashly to repair, exposing themselves to a deadly fire from the Borgian troops.

The Borgian army, after a week of womenless nights, were very happy, in turn, to remain in a town long enough to win over those maidens who were conserving of their reputation in the first encounters.

For four days the siege continued. The last breaches in the walls were not repaired and it was doubtful whether Dionigio di Naldo, the rebellious captain of the guard, could risk losing any of his dwindling number of men to see to them.

Those days of constant cannon fire from outside, dwindling ammunition and men inside, wore down the defenders with an inescapable psychological inevitability. They had little hope of relief from Forli which was too busy preparing its defense as the next on the Duke of Valentinois' list and they were surrounded by a vast sea of Borgian troops. There was no hope of victory and very little hope of holding out until Cesare tired and moved on leaving just a covering force which might afford some hope, at least, of escape.

At the end of the four days of concentrated pressure, during which he was able to profit from no risks taken by his besiegers, di Naldo begged for a parley.

Within a few hours he had made a formal surrender of the citadel, Cesare having, generously and not without political acumen, granted a safe conduct to his garrison.

Joy at yet another triumph was tempered in the Borgian ranks with a reluctance to leave what had proved to be such a sexual haven. But lusty men will find lusty women no matter where and Forli was likely to prove as welcoming as Imola once the amazon Countess had been removed.

CHAPTER 5

Countess Caterina Sforza-Riario was often described as a virago. She was certainly beautiful, severe and of a fiery independence. Life had hardened her. She had seen her father murdered by patriots in Milan Cathedral and her husband, Girolamo Riario, butchered by a mob in the very city she now defended. Her second husband, too, had been killed by a band of rebels. She had ordered a massacre of all who lived in the quarter from which the rebels came and had ridden, herself, at the head of her men-at-arms, to see that her orders were carried out.

A third husband had died of natural causes. It would be true to say she had, in spite of her terrible revenge for her second husband's death, not been floored by the loss of any of them.

Caterina Sforza-Riario was one of those unfortunate women unable to find her place. She didn't like to be alone, she wanted men, a husband, a lover. But she also wanted independence and was totally unable to make any compromise by which she surrendered any or part of it. She had finished by despising each of the three men she had married. Fascinated by that very independence, their devotion to her had grown in proportion to which hers for them had diminished. They had been unable to lead her as she really needed to be led and consequently she had found herself doing the leading—and that was the way the world saw her, as a severe, often cruel and totally unbending woman.

Like most women in Italy, she had heard of Cesare Borgia. She had, in fact, wondered what manner of man it was who, finally, was coming to attack her city under orders from the Pope. Talk had it that he was handsome and of iron will. She thought of her poor, weak husbands and the thought made her sick. Who knew what Cesare Borgia really was? Certainly she would have little opportunity of discovering now as he ranged his enemy troops in preparation for the assault.

The citadel in which she was ensconced, within the town, was well provisioned. She could and would resist this man of iron will, this "monster" as some preferred to call him. For weeks she had had outworks thrown up all around the city and built in nearly all the gates as a fortification. Now, with the Borgian troops a few hours' march away, she had another trouble: as in Imola, there were rumblings among the townsfolk to whom she had never been overly-generous, rebellious rumblings, which talked of handing over the city, her city, to Cesare Borgia, the upstart son of an upstart cardinal who had bargained his way into the papacy.

Even now, the Countess' brother Alessandro had left the citadel with a strong body of men to exhort the council of the city to stand by their overlord.

The Countess, standing with her guards on the ramparts of the citadel, shielded her eyes to gaze down into Forli. Her ample bosom was heaving slightly. She had heard of the turn of events at Imola and she was well aware of the heavy hand with which she had long ruled her people.

Down in the city, lost in the mass of winding streets and the old, uneven buildings there was noise and shouting. It was impossible to tell whether this was simply excitement and fear at the imminent arrival of the enemy or whether harsh words were flying between her brother and the council.

Below, under the shadow of the citadel's walls, the heavy drawbridge was still down across the moat.

"What's happened to them," she muttered fiercely.

"There, Madam!" a captain of the guard called from a point some distance along the thick crenellated rampart.

She squinted in the direction indicated and her blood boiled with anger. Her brother and his men, surrounding a couple of the leading citizens of Forli, were fighting a retreating action against a rabble of the townsfolk. While she watched, she saw a couple of her hard-pressed men fall under the sword and stave-blows of their attackers.

"Turn the cannon on them," she yelled.

But it was impossible to scatter the townspeople without risking injury to her brother and she ordered a couple of shots to be sent among the houses in the rear of the mob and a body of soldiers to go to the aid of her guards.

The portcullis was raised within seconds and a crowd of soldiers ran across it as the cannon crashed. Seeing the reinforcements and hearing the shot flying over their heads, threatening to cut off their retreat, the mob of townsfolk began to break off, to disappear in ragged, hurrying groups along the cobbled streets in all directions.

Caterina Sforza-Riario climbed down from the ramparts to meet her hard-pressed troops. Her brother was wild-eyed and there was blood from a flesh-wound on his wrist.

"They are handing over the city!" His voice was choked with venom and he motioned to the two city elders who stood, surrounded by his men in the center of the courtyard.

The eyes of the Countess sparked with anger. She was not used to having her authority flouted. She walked up close to the two men. She knew them well, Ascanio Guicciardini and Galeazzo Ferrante.

"Do you dare?" she spat. "Do you dare to assume authority for what is mine?"

Galeazzo Ferrante did not flinch from her blazing eyes. He was known as a fearless man.

"It is a time to see reason, Madam," he said. "There is no hope of survival if we fight; if we lay down our arms the Duke of Valentinois will show the generosity he has shown elsewhere."

"You cur!" She moved closer to him. "Have you no loyalty? Would you thus defy the order of your rightful sovereign?"

Galeazzo Ferrante hesitated for half a second and then in tones which rose loudly on the still air inside the citadel's courtyard, as if he were ringing his death knell, he said:

"When, Madam, a sovereign has lost the confidence of the people and must rule them by oppression, she has forfeited her right to be obeyed by her subjects."

The Countess' hand slashed across his face and a dozen lances pricked at his body as he made an involuntary movement toward her.

For several minutes she stared at him, eyes afire, hardly able to believe that this common vassal had spoken to her in that way.

"When we have chased this brigand back to his churches in the south," she said slowly, "you will know what right I have forfeited. Long before then you will wish you could have forfeited your life rather than face what is meant for traitors of your caliber."

Ferrante made no reply. So hard had been her blow that a ring she wore had cut his lip and blood oozed thickly down his chin.

"Take them down and put them among the instruments," she said after a short silence. "They can have time to consider what is in store for them."

CHAPTER 6

Later on the same day that the two elders of the city council had been taken to the dungeons beneath the citadel, Cesare Borgia rode into Forli at the head of his army, to the vast wave of cheering from the inhabitants which welcomed him as deliverer from the warlike Countess.

He began immediately to make preparations to take her stronghold. This was the time to make an impression of invincibility, against this warrior lady whose reputation of fearlessness and martial ability represented the last hope of most of Italy against the threatening papal army. He wanted quick results to prove that his campaign was not won by diplomacy alone but could equally be carried on force of arms if the occasion arose.

By early the following day his siege guns were in position, trained on the citadel above which the Countess' flag still ruffled bravely in the slight breeze. Her men could be seen from time to time moving along the ramparts, and she herself appeared occasionally as if to inspect the measures that were being taken toward her downfall.

Cesare, well aware of her determination to fight, nonetheless made a cunning gesture to prove beyond all doubt to the people of Forli that he was a fair and generous man from whom they need fear nothing if they stood with him in the future. He rode out from his surrounding troops toward the broad moat of the citadel and offered to parley with the Countess on the terms of her surrender. He did not, he said, enjoy the thought of such a loss of life which her blind obstinacy could only assure.

There was silence behind the ramparts at his offer and, smiling to himself, Cesare reined his horse away to be pulled up short by the shouted intimation that the Countess would descend from the ramparts to talk with him and that he, well covered by his men, should meet her on the broad drawbridge.

There was nothing to be done. She had a nerve this Countess, but, decided Cesare, it would make his gesture all the more spectacular if he met her on her own drawbridge. He turned on his horse and waved to his men, at which a posse of some sixty men rode forward and ranged up a little behind him with swords ready.

Slowly the drawbridge creaked down and the portcullis went up. At its far end Cesare saw, for the first time, the figure of the Countess with an immediate impression of an austere beauty which was there, although she did nothing to enhance it.

She was on foot and Cesare got slowly down from his horse, felt for his sword hilt and walked with measured step to the drawbridge.

He stepped forward, feeling the heavy wood under his feet and then, instinctively, hesitated. There was a sudden creaking of winches and with several times the speed with which it had been lowered, the drawbridge swept up as cannons boomed out from the ramparts.

Cesare's hesitation gave him the seconds to fling himself clear; another step or two and he'd have been too far advanced on the bridge to do anything but be swept forward into the citadel's gate where the Countess and her men were waiting to receive him.

He landed heavily on the side of the moat, grasping at strong plants to prevent himself from slipping into the deep, muddy water. His advance guard were with him immediately under the very walls of the stronghold to help him clear and, under the orders of his lieutenants, the Borgian cannons and falconets were replying, like thunder drowning the roar of a rapids.

"Are you hurt, Sire?"

He pulled himself up and, with heavy vengeance vowed in his heart, waved aside his men's concern.

"She shall be paid for this treachery," he said.

For the rest of that day and well into the next, Cesare's cannons cracked and thundered and the citadel shook and lost pieces of its scarred old stone. The recruited citizens stood eagerly by with great cartloads of faggots, waiting for the order which inevitably grew nearer.

They were firmly for Cesare Borgia, now. Talk had raced through the town of his offer to parley—an offer to parley when he had the strength to crush all resistance almost before it had begun. And hadn't she dealt with that generous offer in just the way one would expect from such a mean-hearted tyrant? And hadn't Cesare Borgia given out the usual order to his troops that no woman of Forli was to be molested under pain of death? And weren't their two most respected councillors languishing in the citadel, probably being tortured even now if they hadn't been killed already? There was hardly a man in Forli who would not have risked his life for Cesare and for revenge on the oppressor of his life's years.

The Borgian cannons, concentrating on forming a breach, soon had dangerous cracks zigzagging down the walls of the citadel and the citizens stroked their bundles of faggots as if they were lovers, waiting and ready for the order.

The obvious approach of the end seemed to fire Caterina Sforza-Riario with madness. As the walls began to crack under the furious onslaught of the attackers' cannons, she had both the elders of the council brought out and hanged from the ramparts before the eyes of their fellow citizens. Their bodies were left swinging over the breach which was rapidly forming in the walls, while cries of hatred and revenge burst from the lips of the townsfolk gathered in a vast mass behind the lines of Cesare's ready troops and the busy cannons.

Cesare watched the gap in the walls with a grim smile. He saw the vain attempt of the defenders to fill it in with earth and stones, watched them scatter or be blown to pieces as his cannons continued a relentless punishment.

"Tell the citizens to move forward with their faggots," he ordered. "Another dead hit and the time is with us."

The carts, swaying and creaking, with the Borgian army advancing slowly just behind, moved slowly, ominously, toward the moat, while the cannons redoubled their fire to keep the defenders at bay.

The bodies of the two hanged councillors had fallen and were lost somewhere under the debris.

"They shall be well revenged," Cesare muttered to one of his lieutenants. "This misguided woman shall learn that it is not for her to meddle in men's affairs and oppose the foremost army in Italy."

The gap in the wall had broadened and the defenders had given up attempts to seal it as more and more sections were swept away under the unceasing bombardment. They could be seen, beyond, forming a wall of falconets ready to hotly receive the invading forces. There was activity too on the ramparts, where the smaller, more wieldy guns were being swiveled in an effort to cover the impending attack.

The citizen army moved like an exodus across the intervening space, slowly covering it, approaching like death, the grim defenders of Forli's suicidal stronghold.

Soon they had reached the broad, murky expanse of the moat and although some carts had been overturned by the guns on the ramparts and some of the citizens floated facedown in the waters, they set quickly and determinedly to work, piling both carts and faggots into the depths.

Cesare had ridden forward to be in the vanguard of his forces, just behind the first spearhead which would take the brunt of the defensive counterattack. The cannons, which had moved nearer, played over the heads of the bridge-builders, aiming with greater and greater accuracy, shot after shot through the gap in the wall beyond which the ranks of the defenders were trying not to break but to organize and reorganize as death took its toll of their lines.

Steadily the rough bridge forged across the moat. The citizens, volunteers to a man, worked with vigor and courage. Cesare's men stood waiting for the word to storm over the light, rocky pathway which was being made and hurl themselves through the waning fire of the defense whose ranks and guns they could clearly see in some confusion through the broadening gap.

Almost before the bridge was completed, Cesare gave the command for which his men had been waiting. The first lines of the attack had to jump the last four feet to the debris of the citadel's wall. They were met with a scattered fire from within and rocks and missiles from above, but forged on and in, pressed forward by those from behind until they were all over the courtyard and spouting up into the ramparts.

The faggot bridge was finished. The army pounded over, the citizens seized the arms of the dead to fight against their Countess, Cesare crossed and joined in the hand-to-hand fighting in which the weight of his men's numbers was a crushing advantage.

So quickly had the invasion of the citadel come that the defenders had had no time to withdraw across the smaller inner moat and into the tower where munitions and provisions were stored. Attack and defense together in a great, struggling mob, swept over that small moat, preceded by a few paces by the Countess and her personal guard.

"The tower, the tower!" Cesare roared, seeing the danger. Locked in there they'd be able to hold out for a week or two.

Behind him came his fresh body of men through the gap. Nobody to engage them. They swept in his wake over the inner moat, through the struggling dogfights and up into the tower.

The fighting was short and bloodcurdling. One by one, giving their lives with a devotion which flamed an aura of death around them, the Countess' guard fell until only she was left, knocked to the stone floor, a point of steel at her throat and one of Cesare's Swiss mercenaries grinning with lustful delight over her prostrate body.

CHAPTER 7

A great wood fire had been made in the dungeons. Its red and sparkling heat was fighting to keep the chill of the thick, stone walls at bay. Along one wall a couch had been placed on which Cesare was lying eating the meat from a leg of chicken. On mats on the floor his four or five principal lieutenants were quaffing wine, filling their glasses from a barrel which had been brought from the stores, and themselves devouring pieces of fowl which they were roasting on spits over the fire.

"When are we going to get up this beauty, Sire," one of them asked with a slight slur to his speech as he rose and crossed the dungeon. Cesare followed him with his eyes and his glance took in the defenseless form of the proud Countess. She was naked, stripped of all her austere covering. She was stretched out on the great wheel of a rack to one side of the gloomy, shadowed room.

"When I've finished with her," he said, swigging a draught of wine and passing his glass to one of the men for a refill.

"Seems such a pity to keep her waiting," the man replied. "She obviously loves us."

A gust of laughter greeted his words.

The eyes of the Countess were still able to give a feeble reflection of their earlier glitter although by now she was hurt and exhausted and thoroughly humiliated.

Cesare looked at her as his strong teeth pulled at the chicken flesh. Would any of her subordinates have expected quite such a physical beauty? When she lashed them with her tongue would they have pictured those glossy, firm breasts, high and perky with their small impudent nipples? When she scowled and barked an order would they have thought of that tight waist with its rather sinewy, muscular stomach? When she ordered men to the dungeons and had them hanged from battlements would they have thought of those soft, feminine buttocks, that bottom which asked for caresses? When she rode through the town to order a massacre of reprisal, supervising its execution, would they have considered those warm thighs and those fleshy hips with the moss of pale hair and the heavy overlap of flesh between those white, tapering columns? She was really a beauty. She could have taken her place in an elegant court as one of its prime beauties at any time, except that her attitude had decided that lines of severity were to be drawn between her brows, that her mouth was to be hardened into grimness and her eyes, which could blaze and spark like any insulted courtesan's, should grow to contain the disgust for her fellow creatures which gleamed constantly in them.

They had watched her writhe on the rack—and it had to be admitted she had borne her punishment like a martyr. They had humiliated her, her eyes wide with horror had revealed just how much, with their mauling of her breasts and the supple contours of her naked body. But Cesare had reserved her principal humiliation for himself. He had yet personally to repay her for the near loss of his life on the drawbridge and also he was impressed with her looks and hauteur.

He grinned as his lieutenant took the leg of

fowl he was munching and with a quick movement thrust it up between her straddled thighs into her cunt. The Countess gasped and swore. The lips of her vagina opened and then closed over the knobby, half-chewed meat.

"You wouldn't think a chicken would have enough guts to do that to a Countess," his lieutenant jested, and there were fresh guffaws from the spectators. The man moved the fleshy bone around in her for a few seconds and then, tiring of the game—or perhaps being made too hot by it—withdrew the leg and flung it across to a corner of the room.

"Well seasoned," called another. "Why didn't you eat it."

"By the look of her Ladyship it might have poisoned me."

Cesare swung himself off the couch and crossed to the rack. He stared at the inert body spread-eagled across it. The Countess glared back at him. All she wanted was a dagger, her eyes seemed to say, and he'd regret these humiliating tortures and liberties to which he'd subjected her.

Cesare lowered his eyes over her body. He could see the small blue veins on her white breasts and on the taut flesh where her thighs ran into her hips. He reached out his hand and stroked it softly over her breast, gently savoring the butteriness of the firm skin beneath his fingers. He could feel his lust rising in confined warmth at his loins. His eyes glittered and he looked up at hers again and saw something like fear in them for the first time.

"Leave us," he commanded.

His men ceased their jesting immediately and began to gather their belongings prior to departure.

"Later, perhaps, we too may pay her out for her treachery to you, Sire," murmured his principal lieutenant as they passed the rack on their way to the steep stone steps that led up the wall to the dungeon exit.

"Did you not know it was an offense to have any kind of intercourse with a corpse?" Cesare asked.

His lieutenant roared with laughter, laughter which was taken up by the others and followed them up the steps and beyond the citadel, leaving only a wan glinting echo of itself in Cesare's ears.

"They tell me, Madam," he said softly, "that you have had three husbands. I wonder were they afraid of you—such a woman as could hang from the battlements two of her most respected citizens in the face of a besieging army."

Her eyes blazed at him and she made no reply.

"Difficult to think those husbands were ever permitted to mount you," he mused on, "but I'm told you have some fine sons safely out of harm's way. Were you afraid I might take them and train them for my army?"

Caterina Sforza-Riario moved her lips in a grimace of fury and loathing. Her voice was soft and a little strained and hoarse.

"Your army," she mocked. "Your rabble, a horde of barbarians like their leader, an upstart drunk with power."

Cesare almost raised his hand to strike her, but instead, with unerring instinct to humiliate her further, he stroked her breast instead and pinched her nipple between his thumb and forefinger.

"Were those husbands of yours allowed to

see the body they entered?" he went on. "Or were they allowed only shamefacedly to slip their pricks up under your skirts and do their best to produce children for their lord and mistress?"

"They were weak and wretched—but each was a better man than you," she spat.

Cesare sighed and let his fingers slide down over her muscular belly to dabble in the hair around her crotch.

"Madam, your desire to be brave seems to have injured your reasoning capacity."

"Take your hands off me you vile beast," she flared.

For answer Cesare bent and kissed a nipple and his fingers slipped into her crotch and penetrated her vagina which he tickled, grinning into her eyes.

She turned her face away from him. He saw a light muscle twitching in her cheek.

"And your body was so meant for spending days and nights in the throbbing heat of bed," he went on, knowing that his words and attitude were making her desperate with fury and humiliation. "You have such a moist and ready cunt. I do believe you'd like to tryst with every man in my army."

"Beast . . . swine . . ."

The words were faded echoes of her recent outburst. She was exhausted, physically and psychologically.

Cesare gloated over her helpless body. Now, he felt just like it. But a mere fuck wouldn't be sufficiently humiliating for her. He could feel his penis, large, hot and pushing to escape. With an image of soft, juicy entry into her and the relief it would bring to his lusting loins, he began to unstrap her legs.

She turned her face back to him, her eyes questioning.

Her legs flapped freely in a few seconds. She seemed to have lost the use of them. He untied her wrists which were stretched out above her head and she slid down over the wheel and crumpled to the floor, her eyes open and alive, but her weakened body refusing to obey her.

On the cold stone floor, she tried to move and stand up, but her ankles were stiff and dead, her arms numb, so she lay there where she'd slid, moving her hands weakly to restore the circulation.

For a few minutes, Cesare allowed her a little respite. He wanted her to recover so that nothing was lost on her. Then, when she was able, rather stiffly, to move her limbs and sit up, he pulled her to her feet, letting her stand a moment to get used to the pressure. She leaned on him, helpless to pull herself away. He breathed heavily with the touch of her flesh along him and moved her over toward the rack again.

She began to struggle weakly and with little gasps of pain as she realized that he was going to attach her once more to that instrument of torture, but, especially in her enfeebled state, she was no match for him and he pressed her face forward against the wheel while he tied her hands to it high above her head once again.

Her body moved fleshily against him as she tried to escape and he felt the spongy warmth of her buttocks squeezing against his organ as he pressed into her to hold her fast.

With her wrists firmly attached, he moved and caught one of her ankles, drawing it up around the side of the great wheel to attach it to the hub. She lost balance with the other foot and sagged down to the floor, held up only by her wrists as the wheel swung around with her weight.

Dexterously, Cesare fastened one ankle to the hub and then moved around to the other side and fastened the other. Then he pulled the wheel back to its original position, fixed it with a prop of wood and stood back.

The Countess was now in more or less a sitting position against and around the rack. Her body was held in against it, her legs spread wide and wrapped around the wheel at an angle of something more than 60 degrees with the floor. Her hanging behind was the lowest part of her.

"Now we'll see what your husbands should have done to teach you a little obedience and your place as a woman, wife and mother," Cesare said.

Her eyes were closed, all the weight of her body on her fastened wrists. She was white and subdued and said nothing.

Quickly, Cesare pulled off his clothes until he was standing naked on the cold floor. His prick was tingling and the foreskin had drawn back to reveal the ardent, almost purpling knob. A little seminal fluid was already moistening its hot expanse in anticipation. He held it with his hand for a moment and he could feel its throbbing desire. Its heat was like an aura of red-hot lust around his genitals.

Around the fire, still blazing merrily, were the carpets and rugs on which his lieutenants had been reclining. He arranged them rapidly near the wheel under the Countess' behind which hovered a couple of feet above the ground.

He knelt down on the thick rugs and ran his hands down the smooth lines of her back until they flared out over the soft cushion of her buttocks. The skin was smooth and sweating slightly with the strain she was undergoing. He ran his fingers between her buttocks where a few fine hairs straggled and the skin was suddenly softer, more tender feeling, like a raw steak. He dug his finger gently against her anus and felt it tight and denying like a pursed, puritanical mouth.

For some minutes he played with her anus while she sagged, seeming almost lifeless, then he felt it give and she gave a repressed squeal as his finger penetrated the tiny hole and moved like an animal in the soft portals of her rectum. She gasped again as he dug farther in up to the first finger joint and then the second. He squeezed in another finger and she cried out and her head fell back from the rack and then swung forward against the wood again.

Cesare moved his fingers around in her bottom, pressing out and up alternately, broadening, preparing the nether hole that was to receive the issue of his lust. The Countess wriggled her ankles against the hub of the wheel, but was unable to escape. Her widely spread legs and widely spread buttocks prevented her totally from escaping that foreign invasion of her private domain.

Easier and yet more easily Cesare's finger slipped and explored in the softening, yielding depths of her anus. His two fingers had easy access now and he thrust them right in to their full extent. In front of him, his prick carved the air like a sword, hard and ready for action. His balls seemed to ache and in his loins there was a ferment of sharp, spiraling coils of sensation. A drop of seminal fluid had dripped to the floor and he felt he could wait no longer.

Carefully he lay down under her and moved into position so that her dark, little hole would descend onto his rearing mast. Then, with his foot he deftly kicked aside the prop, reached up to catch her hips as she swung down toward him and pulled her down onto his prick.

The trembling arm of flesh battered in at first thrust and he felt her buttocks tense and try to close the slit to him. She cried out in pain and struggled with her bonds, but could do nothing.

Cesare pushed her upwards gently and the wheel swung back so that all the weight was on her wrists again. Then she fell slowly back with the turning wheel onto his prick once more.

The breach was made and broadened. Cesare felt her tight, rasping back channel tearing at his penis as he surged into the squeezing depths. He gritted his teeth and flexed his hips upward, sighing with the excruciating sensation. He heard her moan and pushed up again with his hands. Her anus slid off his prick and she swung up a little and then wheeled back again, her bottom meeting his hands and the spread crack between the buttocks enclosing his penis once again.

Her anus was becoming easier. He was already half buried in her and encountering no resistance with the exploring forepart of his rod. Only around the entrance, with the thickening dimension of his sex down to its root, was the pressure still enormous and every further tearing inch thrust into her drawing fresh groans from her open lips.

The great squeezing pressure, the tight contraction of her unused back passage around his long arm of violation began to draw panting gasps from Cesare. He had never felt such overwhelming pressure before. He wriggled as his prick thrust in and pulled her right down so that she yelled out in exhausted pain.

Now he didn't push her up very far each time, but allowed the rocking movement of the wheel to do it for him, simply guiding her gently with his hands.

Every time she came down and her behind rested for a moment on his belly its elastic entrance crushed the base of his penis. His loins were in fiery turmoil and his knob seemed to itch with desire to rid itself of his load. He wanted to get farther and farther into her and he spread her buttocks wide with his hands and screwed in for all he was worth.

The strain on the Countess' wrists when he pushed her up was so great that she was relieved each time she sagged back. She began to resist his efforts to push her up away from him and he let her rest on his loins while he wriggled his prick around inside her and she gasped and moaned and began to feel a strange, unanticipated tingling.

The Countess hated herself for this unexpected reaction on her part, but she couldn't help herself. In her exhausted condition there was little resistance left and it was easier to let herself be carried away on a sexual tide, to allow this creeping in her loins to crawl forward and farther forward, tingling her inside and pulsating in her vagina. His great invasion of her backside no longer seemed so vile nor yet so painful. It was producing these sexual feelings in her which she more normally associated with ordinary sex. She could hardly believe that it could happen, but it was.

She knew that he filled her behind like a spear, not sparing her at all, shagging her pitilessly, but she almost wanted more. It was such a relief on her wrists to be able to rest on his hairy stomach and to feel that fleshy wand digging into her.

She felt his hands clasping the fleshy rotundities of her buttocks, clasping them so hard that his fingers dug into her deeply and must have made deep weals in the soft flesh. His action was becoming more and more rapid; he was virtually pummeling her with thrusts and she could feel his hard belly, rising up, straining up to meet her downward rush so that they met in a clashing embrace and his spear tore in making her shriek with the shattering advance of it.

She heard him grunting and gasping, heavy masculine grunts with a certain savage brutality in them. With the growing desire in her belly she felt an outgoing to him, to Cesare Borgia, who had dared to submit her to this fantastic experience, who respected her not one jot and was not afraid to use her as he wished.

She heard his gasping become a heavy whine of exploding breath, felt his body tense along her buttocks and press there.

Then, with a sense of disappointment and the reality of her captive situation, she felt him relax on the floor under her and she rested, sagging on his stomach as he lay for a moment, motionless, breathing heavily.

When he slipped from under her and got to his feet, she became aware of the ache at her anus. She felt sore all the way up inside her; her back passage seemed to be burning and around its portals she felt wet and open and exposed.

She had slipped down to the rugs and hung there, trying to take the weight off her wrists, with her legs up in the air toward the hub of the rack. She opened her eyes and looked sideways at Cesare Borgia. He had climbed to his feet and was looking at her with a smile of satisfaction. Her eyes dropped to his long, limp, white prick which swung down between his hairy thighs.

"How was that, my proud Countess?" he asked.

She didn't answer. She looked away from him back to the wooden slats of the rack. The desire in her loins was still there, albeit ebbing. She could not remember having felt so sexy before. It was like confession under torture only this was sexiness under torture.

She heard him pad away to a corner of the dungeon and she opened her eyes which she'd closed for a moment in an attempt to clear her head. She saw him, still nude, returning through the flame-stabbed gloom. He was carrying a short-handled whip with a dozen narrow thongs. Her eyes opened wider in fear and her throat felt constricted. She felt as if there was nothing of her left that was real; she was exposed and helpless in a way she'd never been before. She could only hope that this man would eventually spare her.

Cesare replaced the wooden prop and she found herself again hanging in midair with the straps biting into her aching wrists, the muscles of her back aching under the strain. She could hardly move at all, only press her body into the wooden wheel as she prepared for the punishment he had designed for her.

She heard the thongs swishing in the air, but nothing happened. He was tantalizing her. There was silence. She bit her lips and rested her head against the slats which were hard and unfriendly.

Suddenly she cried out and flattened involuntarily into the wood as the first lash of the dozen-thonged whip wrapped around her body, stinging it and leaping away again to leave an unbearable stinging in its wake.

Her chest and stomach cringed under the pain and then she flattened into the wood a second time as the lash flicked all over her back and buttocks. No sound would get past her lips but a deflated "Ouff."

The next lash was around her thighs, curling in a weal-tracing embrace with a pain that sickened and made her bite her tongue.

Tears of pain forced their way from under her lashes, her belly felt like a void and down in her loins was a strange, frightened, tingling, tickling, sick, sexy reaction to the beating. The humiliation of being whipped like a slave was lost in a horror of the pain and her reaction to it. She began to sob softly as the lash rose and fell, stroking her back, buttocks and thighs in flesh-cutting caresses.

When he'd stopped and she slowly became aware of the fact, she felt the individual strands of pain across her body and that unfinished symphony of aching in her loins which craved for fulfillment. In an unreal world of pain and longing and humility she was capable of strange reactions.

"Well, Madam, now you see how it is to be a slave, to be a city councillor who can be tortured and hanged from the ramparts of your citadel."

"Fuck me," she croaked.

There was a brief silence and then Cesare broke into peals of astonished laughter.

"A disguised pain-lover of the first order!" he exclaimed. "Such ardent wishes should never be spurned—even though the spurning would make the torture greater."

The act of flagellation had sparked off erotic feelings deep in his core and his penis had risen once again and was jutting out toward his prey. The proud Caterina was begging him to fuck her!

He walked over to where she sagged with the thin pattern of weals across her back. She looked exhausted. It was difficult to believe she would have the energy to make love. He untied her hands and then her ankles and she fell back onto the rugs to roll over immediately onto her stomach away from the pain of the lashes.

She lay there for some minutes with him standing over her, looking down on her pink-grooved flesh. She moved her hands and feet gently and groaned a couple of times. Then she raised her tear-washed face and looked at him. There was no hostility in her eyes, nothing but desire and her eyes dropped meaningfully to his ramrod of a prick.

"So you desire a good length of male strength inside you, my proud Madam," Cesare mocked.

His taunting brought no reaction but a nod of almost desperate agreement. She climbed painfully to her knees. The ache of anticipation had shifted from her loins and seemed to flame all over her.

Cesare helped her to her feet. If her citizens could see this, he thought, their proud, haughty tyrant begging to be upthrust by the enemy chief!

She pressed hard against him and his prick ran up between them, crushing against the soft flesh of her hips and the sinewy mound of her belly. She joggled against him and he felt the prickling of reciprocation swimming about in his long length of rigidity.

He began to lead her to the couch. Her eyes showed no reaction to him, no feeling, but that of an inturned yearning. It was as if she were drugged.

As they stepped slowly toward the divan, she stroked his penis tenderly as if she adored every inch of it. He made way for her to lie down on the couch, but she intimated that he was to lie down himself. Her back was too sore.

Cesare stretched out, tensed his buttocks and jutted his organ massively up toward the gloomy roof of the dungeon. The fire had begun to diminish and the glow was now a centralized one, surrounded by a half-pierced gloom.

When he tensed his behind, a live desire moved like a solid thing along from his loins to the base of his reaching rod.

For a moment the Countess looked at him. She ran her fingers softly up his hot tube of flesh and then swung herself painfully astride him, poising above his prick, arranging her vagina directly above it. She leaned forward, resting her hands on either side of his face while she positioned herself. Her knees brushed his ribs. And then with a long-drawn moan of deliverance, she sank down onto the prick that seared up into her belly like a jet of oil.

Her head rolled on her neck and she felt giddy and out of control as it raced up inside her and she sank down, until her buttocks met his thighs. Her movement was mechanical, dictated only by the feeling brain in his loins. She rose up and sank again with a broken sob of relief. She began to squirm and skewer her buttocks on his thighs, feeling the point of his prick at its summit pressing and poking at her cervix. She rolled about on his body like a puppet, a puppet crazed with human desire for the orgasm which was so agonizingly slow in coming.

Cesare brought his thighs up from the horizontal and contained her buttock and hips in them. He reached down with his tingling hands and grasped her thighs in which he could feel the light muscles flexing and unflexing with her movement.

My God, he thought, this woman was made for one thing only and all her life by all accounts she's lived a lie.

Her breasts swayed and jumped over her heaving belly and her mouth hung open, under flared nostrils and closed eyes. Her long, fair hair swung across her face each time she descended and with her uprise she shook her head so that it swung away.

Cesare tensed his buttocks and felt sensation tremble and palpitate at the base of his prick. All the way up, his organ was alive with pinpricks and the knob almost hurt with the treatment, the ferocity she was subjecting it to. He knew he wasn't far off and he dug his fingers into her thighs so hard that he brought a murmur of shock from her puppet lips.

As she bobbed on him, the Countess tensed her loins, aching for the sensation to flee. She couldn't stand it much longer, that yearning, bursting ball of flame inside her. She had to have release.

She clasped his hips with her thighs and squirmed her bottom from side to side as she fell. She had forgotten the pain of her thrashing, all sensation was in that long, wet channel in which his prick was like a great, drumming barge-pole. His penis was spreading and battering her belly. It hurt, it was wonderful, it was hateful, it was necessary to be over or she would die.

As if she were drowning, her past life seemed to mist into the sensation that racked her. This moment seemed to be what she had always lived for, this moment when thinking was painful and the only thing that mattered was the prick in her quim and the manflesh consuming her in its embrace. If there were only this moment it was all that she had ever desired, this acuteness of sensation, this beyond-reality that she had never truly experienced with her tired, frightened, fawing, subservient husbands of before.

The name of the man who had subjected her fused with her gasps of pain and love: "Cesare Borgia, Cesare Borgia . . ." It was inevitably this man that everybody had said was just the way he was — and she had thought to feel differently from everybody else.

There were times when she'd wondered what it was that would tie her to a man so that she felt no longer free and strong. It was no physical beauty, it was not intellectual strength— both those had been embodied in various of her husbands. It was—what could one say?—a *je ne sais quoi* which was nothing more than an animal force in a man, an understanding in a man that he would lead, a lack of fright in a man, of doubt, of hesitation in his certainty that he would stand by his acts.

These thoughts moved through her head like a phantom, not clear, felt rather. In a feeling connected like cause and result with the wide, scourging opening of her loins which was beginning to happen now, now, now. In a maze of wild, swimming confusion in head and loins, she heard, like a distant train, his breath growing under her, recognized his climax trembling. With a great giving thrust down in which she contracted her loins and concentrated them on the pole down which she slid, she felt the fire within her burst out into a great conflagration as she moaned in delirium and seemed to die and die and die again . . .

She was aware after some seconds which were like darkness, that he had held her up with his strong arms and that his staccato gasping was flailing the cooling air of the dungeon as his prick jerked quickly into her in its fading heat.

Her last thought before she flopped exhausted along the length of his hot, strong body was that she was his for as long as he wanted her.

CHAPTER 8

It goes without mention that Cesare Borgia, Duke of Valentinois, carried more than military glory back with him to Rome. Maria the gypsy was already established in Imola, well provisioned for his return in a few weeks or months, and in his train, strangely changed to anyone who knew her, the Countess Caterina Sforza-Riario dressed in stark black and white, sat her horse, impressive and emotionless but a willing captive.

All those cities which had refused to pay their fiefs to the Holy See had been subdued and Cesare's fame—as much his personality as his achievements—had spread throughout the whole of Italy.

Small wonder that on his return to Rome, the city was the scene of wild enthusiasm. There is nothing the crowd will take to its heart more than a strong man who has a reputation for magnanimity.

Alexander, himself, overflowed with pride at his son's victories and the glory of his reputation. He dispatched a deputation, which included two cardinals and a number of dignitaries, to meet his son on the road beyond the gates of Rome. A huge reception was prepared for him within with prelates, ambassadors, generals and officials of the city waiting eagerly to receive him.

When he made his entry through the northern gate, wave upon wave of thunderous cheering filled the air above the seven hills; people threw garments and flowers into the air; there was a salute of cannon fire.

His train was splendid enough to inspire awe and devotion. In the van were the baggage carts, splendidly caparisoned, and immediately followed by several thousand foot soldiers in full campaign apparel preceded by trumpet-blasting heralds in the livery of the Duke and the King of France. The Duke, who followed next on horseback, was surrounded by a guard of fifty mounted men simply clad and with the Borgian bull emblazoned on their breasts.

The Duke, plainly dressed in black velvet with a gold chain about his neck, was followed by several thousand cavalry, with halberds and banners. A posse of trumpeters, blowing hard enough to reduce the walls of Jericho, brought up the rear in a fine flourish . . .

With Cesare, within his protecting body of men-at-arms, rode the deputation which had met him, broad smiles on their faces, happy and proud to share in his glory for a brief moment.

And not far behind him rode the Countess, unsmiling, severe, but hiding deep thoughts of unbelievable incidents.

Around this vast cortege, the city was *en fete*. Guns continuously thundered salutes, banners floated from the Castle of St. Angelo.

The Pope, tears of joy in his eyes, watched from the loggia above the portals of the Vatican as his son approached. He remembered that son of his, that athletic, gawky boy who had been initiated in the art of love by his young sister Lucrezia, he remembered that panting embrace, guilty and half-afraid beside the pool in the grounds of his mansion. And he thought: This is my son, Cesare Borgia, riding in triumph through the streets of Rome with the whole world as far as the French Court listening to tales of his exploits and success.

It was only a couple of nights ago that Alexander had, himself, stuck his prick up his daughter's cunt and fucked and fucked her until they had both been paralyzed with inertia —and Cesare had, indirectly, shared in that. It was with him, under the Pope's guidance, that the young girl had lost her virginity and started on that path which made her such a bone-shaking joy to men.

Alexander brought his thoughts back to the present with an effort. Later tonight, Cesare, if he had no other plans—and who could possibly have other plans—would be able to enjoy his sister in a nude-entwining embrace. This would be a fitting reward for his achievement and richly deserved.

He watched as his son dismounted at the steps and his bright army ranged itself behind him. When Cesare began to climb the broad flights with the two cardinals and the ambassadors who accompanied him, the Pope, his heart overwhelmed with pleasure, descended to the comfortable chambers below and arranged himself on his throne.

Cesare, his eyes alight with pleasure at the sight of his father, advanced through the marble-pillared chamber and fell upon his knees before the throne.

As Alexander, tears in his eyes, placed his hands upon his son's head, prior to embracing him, he thought what a fine and imposing figure his son had become even in the months since he'd departed. Every tiniest period of time seemed to add to his stature. Lucrezia would be overjoyed; indeed, the juices would start to run between her legs at the very sight of her brother, whom she still adored.

CHAPTER 9

With the departure of Cesare's army from Romagna, it was not long before the physical absence of troops began once again to cause rebellion. News filtered through that the town of Faenza, which had once enjoyed the protection of Venice, was arming itself to the teeth prior to proclaiming itself independent of the Holy See. Thither, after a period of recuperation, Cesare marched again at the head of his army. With winter fast approaching and the town much stronger than had been expected, he settled down to a blockade, cutting off all entry and exit. He had plenty of time.

In fact, leaving his troops in charge of one of his lieutenants, he repaired with the others to Cesena with the idea of a little light relief.

At this time of year, late autumn, there were many rustic sports held in the villages of the northern part of Italy where the village Hercules and Appolos were able to show off their prowess in such different arts as wrestling, running and archery. It was to one of these villages, dressed as peasants, incognito, that Cesare and his lieutenants laughingly made their way.

Each of these sports days was the great local event of the year. The local dignitary, duke or count, with his ladies and retinue, would have the place of honor in a temporary stand at the edge of the sports field, from which he would present the awards when the day was done. The people, drinking and making merry all day, would explode into a carnival of conviviality as darkness fell. There would be dancing in the streets and fireworks, people would get lost, there would be necking and an occasional robbery or rape. Often, long-bored wives would choose this occasion to get caught up in the crowd away from their half-drunk husbands and join in a furious and desperate copulation with any stranger who caught hold of their long hair and planted a kiss on their longing lips. In the morning, their husbands, who, perhaps, had not been particularly virtuous either, would find their wives sleeping a sleep of the dead in a bed it appeared they'd never left during the festivities. At this time, too, young maids, in sober times so careful of their virginity, would, under the influence of a glass or two of wine, allow themselves to go far enough in their lovemaking for there suddenly to be no return. They would find themselves, startled and helpless, tumbled on their backs in the corner of some field, with their skirts around their waists or perhaps on the nearby hedge and their thighs unbelievably wide as a masculine rigidity brought them pain and then relief from their days of fear and wondering. Many a bastard owed his birth to the abandon of carnival time in the villages, many a maiden found herself the following day, or in the days that followed, wondering which of the many men she passed in the streets had deflowered her while she lay in half-drunk ecstasy beneath him. If it were not that so many were in the same boat and everybody knew it, there would be great embarrassment. And, of course, some of the one-night affairs developed into liaisons of a more permanent nature so that many a wife on a shopping expedition, would take to wandering through the fields and woods on a sunny morning, to return, rather late, with crumpled dress and a guilty expression, to the family bosom.

It was to join in such ribald and licentious gaiety that Cesare and his party left Cesena in high spirits one morning.

CHAPTER 10

"Who is the lady next to the Duke of Alfaro?"

Cesare voiced the question to Rossano Erfredi, one of his followers. His eyes gazed up to the nearby stand where the Duke, a pompous, condescending old fellow, was surrounded by his wife, a band of men and ladies-in-waiting and a very attractive, fair-haired girl with pale, blue eyes which sparkled occasionally like sun-flecks on a shallow, Mediterranean sea.

"I've never seen her before, Sire—but I can find out in no time."

"She appears to be alone—she's a beauty, isn't she?"

"Indeed, Sire, worthy of any gentleman's attention, grinned Erfredi.

"I'm glad our views concur," smiled Cesare. "Go and see what you can find out."

With Erfredi gone, Cesare turned back to where the village champion was in the act of eliminating yet another of his wrestling challengers. The man was stocky and over-muscular, probably the village blacksmith. So far he had won all his contests against his fellow villagers and foreign rustics by sheer brute strength. He was certainly dangerously strong, Cesare reflected, but he'd have to use more than brute strength if he wanted to keep his title this year.

The crowd was excited, as much by its own effervescence as the spectacle and the cheering and encouragement was considerable. It had not escaped their attention that there was a stranger in the field this year who looked a force to be reckoned with, but their money was on their local celebrity.

"A moronic mountain," one of Cesare's lieutenants whispered at his elbow, "but one would have to be careful if one got in close with him."

"I have his measure — I trust."

"If he looks like breaking one of your bones I'll put an arrow through his arm."

"You want us to be lynched from the trees over yonder—no, I have his measure, I say," Cesare replied.

While his bulging adversary had been breaking bones and spirits in dealing with his challengers, Cesare had, himself, come gently through the earlier rounds, with well applied pressures, to a less spectacular but just as efficient entry into the final bout which he was destined to have with the champion.

Already, the ladies had remarked his tall, slim-hipped figure with its supple muscular chest and arms which were in such contrast to the bulky power of the favorite. Many a feminine heart had already felt a twinge of desire and of curiosity as to who this handsome young man might be.

"There should be fun tonight," Cesare said to another of his lieutenants. "The whole place is swarming with pretty women and you can see their eyes gleaming with hope for a bit of freedom."

"Aye, Sire, I've made up my mind to have four in turn tonight—at least four."

"What a gourmand, Enrico, you'd better mind you don't break your neck in the races."

"It's something else I have to mind I don't break."

Cesare chuckled. "Well, Enrico, I'm a gourmet, and I've made my single choice already."

"Indeed, Sire—might one ask . . . ?"

"Over there in the stand. There's only one I could mean."

Enrico gazed discreetly towards the aristocrats' shelter.

"Ah, yes," he sighed. "I'd reluctantly put thoughts of that away. She's much too well chaperoned by the Duke and Duchess—might even be their daughter."

"The better she's chaperoned, the more determined she'll be to escape them once the idea's in her," Cesare said, with a grin.

"Well, good luck, Sire—perhaps the result of the wrestling will be an omen."

"Ah, Rossano, you must have intelligence in every village in the north to be so quick—who is she?"

Rossanno Erfredi was a little out of breath with hurrying to obey his chief's command. He spoke quickly, his words punctuated by little gasps which seemed, somehow, to enshroud the object of his inquiries in an exotic urgency.

"Her name, Sire, is Dorotea Caracciolo. She is the wife of Gianbattista Caracciolo, a captain of foot with the Venetians. She's here as a friend of the Duke and Duchess of Alfaro."

"And her husband—where is he?"

"In Venice, Sire—the lady is quite alone."

"Well done, Rossano—I'll save you a piece of the lady's garter for your pains."

There was a gust of laughter which died away as one of the sports officials came to say that the champion was ready for his final challenger. Across the greensward, his muscles more extended than usual from his limbering efforts with earlier adversaries, the champion strutted in an orgy of self-congratulation from which it was clear he saw no likelihood of losing his crown.

"I wish you'd let me take him, Sire," Rossano Erfredi said quietly. "He's an ugly looking brute and I could more easily afford to break a bone or two than you."

"You don't trust my strength, Rossano?

Come, is that worthy from a lieutenant to his captain?"

"Oh, Sire, forgive me, no!" Erfredi was covered with confusion. "It's simply that . . . if there were any risk—and I don't suppose for a moment there is—I'd sooner it were me than that you should risk a strain . . ." He was embarrassed now that he'd said anything which could be taken ambiguously when it had merely been an automatic statement of his devotion to the Duke of Valentinois.

"Yes, Sire," another lieutenant added. "I wish you'd let any of us take him. He's not worth your trouble."

Cesare laughed.

"It's no trouble, Enrico, I assure you, and it's only reasonable that I should lead our spearhead into the sports. Rossano, I don't forget a man's concern for my skin. It's the highest tribute anyone could ask."

A slight hush, broken with odd shouts, guffaws and other noises of movement and early tipsiness, had clouded over the green. Few doubted that the champion would be champion yet again. But the stranger provided a little more interest than was usually taken in a foregone conclusion. The fact was, that Cesare's victories had been so easy that they had lacked the impressive cock-strutting dazzle of his opponent's.

"Here's to the omen for the fair lady," Cesare said, as he moved out, away from his little band of disguised officers, and walked alertly toward the approaching champion.

Both were dressed in tights. Cesare in shoes and the champion in boots. The muscles in their torsos contained no shadows from the dying sun, but veins stood out on them like marks traced heavily around the highland on a map.

They approached each other slowly, cunningly, surrounded at a distance by a crowd of several thousand villagers and countryfolk above whom the Duke of Alfaro's party looked on from the height of their perch.

Both men reached a point just beyond each other's reach and circled for a moment, sizing each other up. Then the champion, a man of uncomplicated reactions, who wanted a quick and spectacular victory to make him the undisputed wrestler of all time in his village, rushed in. Cesare caught his fist as he came, ignoring the other arm which reached out triumphantly for his neck. As the champion's fingers, all in a second, grazed his skin, he gave a quick twist to the fist he held. With a gasp, the champion jerked over off his balance and landed with a breath-shattering thud on his back. It was not for nothing that Cesare had had a Turkish instructor during his student days.

Quickly, Cesare was in with a full nelson on his opponent. The astonished referee counted according to the village rule, while the champion fumed and strained at the vise-like pressure on his neck, trying to jerk his shoulders from the ground. When Cesare released him at the end of the count, he got up slowly, easing his neck. The cheers of Cesare's lieutenants hailed over the green, followed, rather uncertainly, by cheering encouragement from the crowd.

The champion was furious, his eyes were the sparking color of red-hot coal in his blacksmith's furnace. He had not yet realized his danger. This was an accident. Some insolent, quick-moving stranger had taken him off his guard. Perhaps he'd been just a little too confident. But now he knew what his opponent was up to he'd crush his insolence out of him —but quickly before he lost face in front of his countrymen.

He came in again, caught Cesare's arms which came out to meet him and felt vague astonishment that his progress was completely checked. Those arms were as stiffly strong as the barrel of a cannon. For a second or two they stood there, leaning forward slightly, arms on each other's biceps and then the blacksmith swung Cesare and felt him going, sideways, apparently off-balance. He moved in to get his bear grip around the man's neck and suddenly, Cesare seemed to have righted himself. As the champion came to close quarters a sharp ankle blow knocked his legs together painfully and an even sharper jab under his chin sent him crashing on his back for the second time. There were fresh cheers and sounds of triumphant merriment from Cesare's little band of lieutenants. The rest of the crowd was hushed in something like awe.

Cesare leapt onto the heaving, almost deflated chest of his opponent, bent over him, so that their faces were close together and slipped a stranglehold around his neck with both arms.

The champion flailed for a moment, grabbed at Cesare's shoulders, arms and then his hair, but sudden, sharp tightenings of the asphyxiating grip on his neck made him release his hold each time with squeals of pain.

"Lie still or I'll strangle the life from you," Cesare gritted. Half-conscious only, with tears of strain in his eyes, the champion lay back, hardly knowing what had happened to him. The referee counted, slowly, it seemed, as if he could hardly credit the possibility of the title-holder being out for the second time in such a tiny space and with so little resistance.

When Cesare sprang to his feet, lithe as a gymnast, his opponent lay where he had fallen for a moment. Then he rolled over on his side and looked dazedly at Cesare with something like real fear in his eyes. He didn't move and the crowd began to shout for him, a shouting which slowly turned into a barracking as he turned a white face around the field as if he'd like to run for it.

"Had enough, my friend?" Cesare taunted. "Do you want to hand the title to me on a platter?"

A momentary gleam of hatred chased the fear from the blacksmith's face. All his dominance, all his respect in the village was dissipating. He had held a sure place in the set-up in this part of the world. Everybody knew who he was, what he was, how strong he was, what he could do to a man who questioned his position. And now, this fellow, this devil incarnate had arrived from nowhere to make what should have been a splendid, strength-displaying sports day into a farce in which he couldn't even seem to get near his opponent.

He struggled to his feet. He would make this effort. One more throw and hold and he was finished. The fellow was slippery, but he must be stronger. He *must* be stronger. Nobody could question that. If he could get the fellow before he had any chance to perform one of those dirty conjuring tricks, he'd have him crying out for mercy and then they'd see if they hadn't decided a little too early to flout his authority, to decide that if this fellow could beat him he wasn't so strong and wonderful after all.

On his feet, he moved slowly, carefully. His neck hurt with a searing pain when he moved it, but his eyes had cleared and the breath had come back to fill his big body. This time he'd keep hyper-alert for a nuance of a movement, ready to counter it.

Cesare knew, he knew what was going on in his opponent's mind and in his own the little warning that always came when things seemed to be going almost too much his way, spoke out. "Don't relax for a moment," it said. "Don't assume that you've won just because if you keep your head it's a cakewalk. First you have to keep your head."

So Cesare, too, moved slowly, hyper-alert, rather than dulled into carelessness by his near-victory.

Silence had come on the crowd again. They seemed to sense the desperate plight of the local champion, for whom no love was lost, certainly, but for whom there was a certain feeling of kinsmanship in that he was born and bred in the village in which they all lived and worked and made love.

During several seconds they circled each other, hands taut and moving slightly, arms taut and waiting. The blacksmith was unwilling to rush in this time and waited for Cesare to make the first move.

It came, suddenly. Cesare moved in, catching his opponent's fist again. But this time, the blacksmith flung himself in at the Duke's waist, not quick enough to avoid the knee which caught him a searing blow in the chest as he came in, but quick enough to get his great arms around his adversary's body so that, like a boa constrictor, he could slowly squeeze the life out of him.

There was a gasping rustle of excitement in the crowd. Cesare's men fidgeted, hands on the daggers in their belts.

Cesare was too late to resist. He felt the backbreaking grip around him and let himself go limp, suddenly, reaching behind at the same time with both hands. He found the little fingers as the breath began to heave and choke in his chest, and tugged at them sharply. The blacksmith gave a cry of pain and released his grip, his hands hanging limp as Cesare seized an arm, levered with his hips in the man's groin and threw him heavily again to the ground. There were gasps which resounded all over the field as if every member of the assembled multitude had had the breath knocked out of him by the fall.

Although strained, the blacksmith's fingers had not been broken. Cesare had not applied all the pressure he might have done. After all this was not war to the death. But in the mind of the champion it might have been. Winded, his fingers smarting, he nonetheless managed to seize Cesare's foot as he came in and twisted him off his balance so that he in turn slipped onto his back. He was up in an instant, however, and the blacksmith, slow, cumbersome and opening his mouth to get his breath, was not able to follow up his momentary advantage. The two men faced each other again, circling, chests heaving, muscles sliding in their arms and shoulders as they moved.

Cesare knew he would be wise to exploit the other's temporary exhaustion and injury quickly, but, having felt the strength of those great tree-trunk arms around him, he was cautious. The champion's eyes were afire, but mingled with the fire was a recognition of defeat staring him in the face. When his gaze met the cool, unyielding look of his unknown adversary he felt that he was up against some strange presence against whom he could do little.

Suddenly Cesare moved in and the blacksmith's arms went out in mingled defense and attack. But with a speed which took his still half-winded opponent completely by surprise, Cesare had ducked under his arms, seized his widespread legs with each hand and pulled upwards as he thrust up with his shoulders in the man's crotch. The blacksmith was bewildered by the lightning thrust and unable to do anything but flail his arms in the air as he found himself flung into the air and then crashing on his face. He had not time even to roll over before Cesare was on him from behind and gripping him in a leg hold which brought tears of pain to his eyes. He scratched at the ground with tensed hands and tried to unseat his opponent with his buttocks, but Cesare was unmoveable. He simply applied more pressure until the blacksmith was bellowing in pain and beating on the ground in surrender.

A great roar of appreciation went up from the crowd. Their champion had been well beaten by a man who was immeasurably his superior. There were no hard feelings and it would take the cocky blacksmith down a peg or two.

Among Cesare's officers nobody could understand how they'd ever even considered that he was running a risk in taking on this adversary. Their chief was invincible.

* * *

"Who is that man?" Dorotea Caracciolo's pale blue eyes were sparkling in their depths with admiration.

"Don't know," said the Duke of Alfaro indifferently. "Some lout from one of the villages, I suppose."

"He doesn't look much like a lout, does he?"

Dorotea had caught his tone and she knew what he was thinking. Since the beginning of her stay, the old man had been trying hard to seduce her, a fact that didn't cause her much concern. Except that last night in a flush of desperation he had come into her boudoir in his underclothes, while his wife slept. She had been bathing and had time only to cover herself with a towel before he had seized her and was begging her to yield to him or his life stood for nothing. In half earnest, half bravado he'd actually managed to lay hold of her and pull the towel from her breasts. She'd felt his hand on her buttocks, his panting breath on her neck and his fat body with its hot penis crushing against her before she'd managed to fight him off, threatening to tell his wife if he persisted. Really, such conduct wasn't to be tolerated and she'd informed her hosts that she thought she should leave in two days' time. Although she was more amused than offended. After all, all men were the same at heart and she recognized that he had a genuine heart-aching lust for her which was not unflattering. However it was too boring to have to be subjected to invasions of her boudoir and, who knew, he might take her unawares some time, get her at some disadvantage and actually screw her— rape her. That would disgust her. His hot, fat flesh. Now . . . if it were the young man on the field . . .

"Looks a typical country bumpkin to me," the Duke persisted in a disgruntled tone. "Eh, my dear," he added a little more loudly for the benefit of his wife on his other side.

"I think he's glorious—looks like a prodigal prince," his wife said.

Dorotea laughed to herself. Now he was going to be as jealous as hell if he thought she admired this young man.

"How beautiful he is compared to that ogre of a man he's just beaten so soundly," she went on. "I think he has one of the finest bodies imaginable."

"Well, you can guarantee he'll have no brain," the Duke said, eyeing his guest with annoyance. "A beautiful carcass and nothing whatever in his head — probably can't even read or write."

"Oh, but I thought he used his brain very well during the match," Dorotea teased, "and I'd sooner take a body like that than what passes for brains any day."

She pulled her hand away as the Duke tried to hold it on the bench on which they sat.

"Any woman would be proud and happy to have a man like that," she added, maliciously.

Pangs of envy and frustrated fury skewered through the Duke's breast. He knew how she was tormenting him. But she couldn't be serious —give herself to a common rustic like that when she could have a man of quality. But tomorrow she was leaving. Oh those delicious little white breasts with their pert, pink-rimmed nipples, high, firm, cheeky almost. He had a picture of them ever before his eyes. And the feel of the smooth skin of her buttocks and the animal warmth of her body behind the towel against him. Oh heaven and hell! He would live his life in a dream of what might have been if she didn't yield to him before her departure. Tonight was the only chance. If only he could drug her with wine or something. It wouldn't matter not to feel her responses if it had to be that way. Just to enter in up that moist, warm creek would be salvation. His eyes glanced sideways at her lovely profile, that tremulous, sexy, jutting lower lip, that small nose and firm chin, that high forehead with the sweep of long fair hair back from it—and most of all those pale, mysterious eyes, sphinx-like half the time, dancing with animation the rest. Oh to have that face close to his as her body wriggled—or just lay dead—under his. Better to see those eyes dancing with passion, that jutting lip trembling with emotion and ecstasy as he drove her and himself to fulfillment. Oh, darling Dorotea! A country bumpkin with muscles and straw in his hair! How could she be so ridiculous—or so cruel!

The sports continued, with their closing events. Cesare and his lieutenants had entered separately in only some of the events so as not to attract too much attention. They had won everything they'd undertaken and Cesare closed the day by walking off with the archery contest.

"It was as well, Sire, that we didn't enter for everything or they'd have nothing to show in the village except a mass of long faces tomorrow," Rossano Erfredi said.

"Oh, they'd have had time to recover their good spirits in the dark corners tonight," Cesare said with a laugh. "Nothing like a good orgasm or two for a relaxed view of life."

It was the Duke of Alfaro's privilege and duty to present the awards—hogsheads of wine, great hams and sides of bacon with little silver cups—and the successful competitors, donning jerkins, lined up in the last rays of the sun, with a cool night air beginning to freshen, at the foot of the stand.

Cesare took his place in the queue, smiling at his role of prizewinner in a local fete. And when he looked for Dorotea Caracciolo, he found her eyes were on him.

She was standing next to the Duke of Alfaro, helping him to present the trophies, but her glance had risen from the immediate presentation and traveled along the line of waiting men to Cesare. With a twinge of pleasurable excitement he met her gaze and smiled slowly at her. She pulled her eyes from him and he suddenly remembered that he was a simple rustic. Hardly the thing to be making advances to the wives of captains in the service of Venice. But maybe she liked country pleasures. He chuckled quietly.

The line dwindled and Cesare found himself face to face with the aristocrat of the district and his lovely guest. Now that he saw her close up he felt a flush of eagerness to get on intimate terms with her, to get in intimate postures with her. Her figure, well draped in her dress, was nonetheless visibly exciting and her face was alive with a vivacious fire which sprang out of her eyes in twin points like mischievous children. What an excellent carnival companion she would make.

Solemnly the Duke of Alfaro handed him two cups: one for the wrestling, one for the archery. At his side were a ham and a hogshead of wine, the supplementary, gastronomic prizes.

The Duke had not meant to address this rustic. It seemed quite enough to him that the man had already given rise to some conversation—rather uncalled for. But when confronted by Cesare he was reluctantly impressed by the man's presence—and made hostile by it.

"Tell me, my man—you don't belong to the village?" he asked.

"No your Grace. I'm an infantryman with the Duke of Valentinois' troops—on leave at the moment, so please your Grace."

"You see—he speaks," Dorotea cut in, laughing lightly and looking first at Cesare's muscular, uncovered forearm and then raising her eyes to his handsome, commanding face.

"Did you think me to be a deaf mute, Madame?" he asked.

The Duke of Alfaro began to expostulate, but Dorotea cut him short.

"We were simply wondering whether such a splendid physique could really be crowned by any brain at all," she said, with another little laugh.

"It's not unknown for the two to go together," Cesare said with a smile. "You, Madame, are, I'm sure, a fair example of such."

"Why you . . . " the Duke of Alfaro began to splutter, but Dorotea put a restraining hand on his arm while her eyes continued to smile at Cesare.

"I thank you for a very nice compliment," she said. "I have heard that the Duke of Valentinois is an iron-willed man of great physical strength. If he could out-wrestle and out-shoot you, it would be worth the seeing."

"Madame, I owe all I know to His Grace," Cesare replied. "A finer man never lived."

"Yes, indeed, they say all his men would die for him. Are you visiting all the carnivals and sports you can reach on your leave?"

"No, Madame, I have a feeling that this area has something really delightful to offer. I shall probably stay for a while if I and my friends can find a suitable inn."

"Well, I hope you are able fully to enjoy the delights of which you speak."

During their conversation, the Duke of Alfaro had not hidden his annoyance and his obvious irritation that Dorotea should talk so easily with a mere infantryman. But he had restrained his anger not to appear ridiculous in front of the villagers who had gathered in a great throng around the stand, and some of whom could hear the words which were being spoken. Also he didn't want to offend Dorotea, although he was certain she was doing this just to tease him. He still wanted to fuck Dorotea. Fuck Dorotea! Fuck Dorotea! He repeated the words to himself, fiercely and then blushed with desire at the images and sensations they brought forth in his mind.

He refused to have anything further to say to the lout, however, and simply began to lift the hogshead.

"Your Grace," Cesare said, "if it would not displease you I'd like the village to have the hogshead and the ham—a gesture of friendship from strangers in their midst."

This sign of gentle manners somehow annoyed the Duke even more. There was something disturbing about this stranger. He actually felt a little afraid of the man although he wouldn't admit it to himself in such terms.

"All right," he said curtly, "as you wish."

"Come Benvenuto—a very fine gesture, too," the Duchess chided from his side.

The Duke of Alfaro was about to add a reluctant word in agreement when his voice was drowned out by a great gust of cheering which thundered out through the quietening night air. The word had been passed back that the carnival victuals of the village were to be reinforced through the generosity of this stranger who had fought so well.

Cesare bowed slightly to the Duke and Duchess and then to Dorotea, whose eyes, glinting with what might have been a light amusement, or something else, continued to watch him as he withdrew.

"What a charming fellow," the Duchess whispered to her companions. "He hardly seemed like a peasant. Manners and speech are improving in the country."

"No, he didn't, did he?" Dorotea mused.

"Well, I think he was damned insolent speaking that way to our guest."

"Oh come, Benvenuto, he was just paying a bold compliment. No lady really minds. Yes, he struck me as a bold man—quite strange."

A bold compliment? the Duke was thinking. What could have been bolder than my compliment? God! I nearly had her. Just a towel between us—and not even that between parts of us. His loins cringed at the thought of what had been so near and now seemed so far away.

CHAPTER 11

Night had now fully fallen. The stars were on a high, dark, mellow ceiling and there was a reflection below from a huge fire which had been built in the center of the field. It cast a broad, bright glow over the faces of the nearest rank of the people who were gathered in a great, loose mob around it. It was hot, too, and those who had sat, cross-legged on the ground near it, had, several times, to get up and move back a little.

Over the fire on an enormous spit an ox was slowly roasting. The deflated hogsheads of wine were lying in the small clearing formed by the crowd and illuminated by the fire. The wine was now either smoldering in lustful bellies or swishing in the water-bottles which the villagers had brought with them. Bread had been distributed and bits of it, broken and dusty, lay around the field. The hams, the sides of bacon had already been privately eaten or taken home to fill the larder for a few days. Now everyone was waiting for the distribution of the ox which the Duke of Alfaro ritually provided for this occasion.

The Duke, himself, was basting the animal with ponderous, self-important deliberation, drawing back from the heat of the fire every so often when it became too much. For the moment, concentrating on his official task, he had allowed lustful thoughts of Dorotea to slip into the recesses of his mind. Which was just as well. For Dorotea, standing with the aristocrats' group, a little within and away from the main sprawling mob, was gazing at Cesare, who, from the front ranks of the crowd, was returning her look just as meaningfully.

It was nearing Dorotea's time to conceive and she was feeling the lack of intercourse which her trip had deprived her of. She was full of honest, animal appetites. Her husband would have done, although in truth she was not in love with him. But this athletic rustic who didn't seem to be a rustic had captured her imagination and would do much better. He was the only *man* she could recall having come across since her arrival. What a pity he wasn't one of the Duke's entourage. It would be so much less complicated.

She saw him smile at her and gave a sideways glance with the corners of her eyes before returning his smile quickly, briefly. He was so handsome and he had a sort of fire in him, a controlled fire that was quite obvious. She just knew that he hadn't been the slightest concerned about the Duke of Alfaro's ill-concealed anger. She believed that for two pins he could have snapped his fingers in the Duke's face. There was something very strange somewhere.

"Done, done, I think," the Duke called, red-faced and sweating beside the crackling, delicious-smelling ox.

The distribution began—a hunk of ox for everybody and bread and wine flowing liberally. The power of the grape was, indeed, stalking in the crowds and with the fireworks and main carnival to come, some young couples were already so fired that they were creeping off for a quick, ecstatic embrace before the public displays. Before the night was out there were going to be some very exhausted, very satiated bodies in this corner of Italy.

The Duke of Alfaro had rejoined his party and was now looking once more at the object of his desire as he munched a fat piece of meat. Cesare saw his look and understood. It was very understandable, after all. His own feelings were identical.

Dorotea, unable to go where she felt inclined to, unwilling to put up with the Duke of Alfaro's verbally amorous advances, engaged one of the Duchess' waiting women in conversation. The Duke withdrew, hurt and cross, to watch her curvaceous movements from a slight distance. Cesare took a long swig of wine from a bottle passed by one of his men and settled down to wait.

While the big fire was still blazing there was a fizz of color and noise from the direction of the village and a long-tailed rocket swooped into the air, scattering a confetti of varicolored sparks and stars through the dark sky and fizzled away into darkness and silence again.

There was a short hush of surprise which was shattered almost immediately by whoops and roars of delight from the crowds. The sign for the festivities had been given. As the crowds began to stream away toward the village a whole cluster of rockets soared into the air with tails like birds of paradise and then exploded into a rainbow of colors which filtered into a disappearing rain of particles of color.

The skeleton of the ox was left gently charring over the still blazing fire. The field, littered with pieces of discarded food, began to clear. Caught in the crowd, trying to remain dignified aloof from it, the Duke of Alfaro's party also made its way toward the lanes which led from the field to the village square.

Cesare, with his officers, followed close in their wake.

Outside the field in the narrow lanes with their crumble-walled cottages and houses and cobbled surfaces, the crush became severe. People pushed, some fell and struggled to their feet shrieking, women were felt by men they couldn't even turn to scold, many a pert buttock was pinched and held, many a masculine loin rubbed and ground impudently against feminine asses as the mob, like a single moving entity, hustled toward the square from which more and yet more rockets were being launched into the still air.

Cesare, who had kept close to the local dignitaries' party, elbowed his way still closer as the mob became less and less controlled. There was a great din of cries and a great strife of falling and pushing and fighting and protesting. Every man for himself, and nobody was very concerned about what his neighbor was doing.

The Duke of Valentinois was slowly separated from his lieutenants, who tried in vain to keep up with him. Shortly he had pushed through to the fringe of the Duke of Alfaro's party which was trying to maintain a semblance of decorum in the crush. Peasants flocking around were trying desperately and often vainly to stop those behind from shoving them into the ladies-in-waiting.

Dorotea was in the midst of the party. Often she looked around until at last she was able to see Cesare. They both knew what they were up to, both accepted that they were working toward each other.

Gradually Dorotea fell back, imperceptibly at first and then more boldly, until she was at the very fringe of her group, all occupied in keeping their own feet, and only a pace or two in front of Cesare. He battled and elbowed a fraction more and he was next to her and had taken her hand, his movement hidden in the crush of bodies. Her fingers clasped and interlaced with his immediately, although she didn't look at him any more.

Gently, but as swiftly as possible, before her disappearance was discovered, he edged her through the crowd toward the side of the line. Nobody noticed them. *Sauve qui peut*.

As they approached the main square, narrow,

arched alleyways gave off from the lane, corridors between rows of large houses. It was into one of these that Cesare eased Dorotea and then quickly through another archway into the deserted gloom of a mansion courtyard. There he pulled her to him and kissed her fiercely on the lips, feeling her response, her lips which softly opened and her hands which moved and dug against his shoulders. He released her a little later and saw her pale face looking up at him in the gloom.

"Who are you?" she whispered.

"The champion wrestler and archer of the Duke of Alfaro's lands," he replied with a chuckle.

"You're no infantryman—you don't look like one, you don't speak like one."

The noise of the crowds, interpolated with the fizz and bang of the rockets and fireworks came to them from a little distance. Within the walls of the empty courtyard it was quiet as if in a glass house. At frequent intervals the flame of a rocket seared the sky, lightly dispersing the gloom surrounding them for a few seconds.

Cesare stepped back from her a little and bowed, a vague shape in the darkness.

"Allow me to present myself, Madame," he said softly. "The Duke of Valentinois."

He heard her sudden intake of breath in the darkness. A short silence followed in which he heard her breathing heavily. Then she came in toward him and he felt her whole body fuse along his own as he put his arms around her.

"One might have known," she whispered. "They say he's the most handsome man in Italy."

He kissed her again, forcing her lips apart,

edging them away from each other with his own. Her tongue darted into his mouth, smooth and slippery and enticing.

"My disguise is not very good if you almost saw through me so easily," he whispered.

"No disguise would hide you," she whispered back. "Even my pompous old host noticed. I think he was afraid of you and certainly envious."

"He obviously desires you."

"Yes—he's an old lecher."

"Then I am a younger lecher."

For answer she laughed softly and kissed him again, running her hands through his hair. Her breath came heavily and he could feel her breasts heaving crazily against his chest. She pulled away from him suddenly, a little wildly.

"Not here," she whispered. "Not now. They'll find I'm missing in no time and search the whole place to find me."

He ran his hands over her breasts, richly draped in her velvet dress, as he spoke. Her body shivered under his touch.

"Where then—when?" he asked.

"I leave tomorrow," she said. "Must you stay here?"

"No, I can take my titles with me."

"We could meet on the road—although it will be difficult to give my retinue the slip. They're sending an armed band of men-at-arms with my ladies-in-waiting."

"I'll kidnap you," he whispered, stroking his hand over her velvet-covered bottom.

"Such a scandal," she chided, not taking him seriously.

"It would be simpler," he said. "Then no blame can be attached to you whatever. You were simply being held for ransom, but managed later to escape."

"But . . ."

"Leave it to me." He kissed her again and she twined her body passionately with his, her tongue searching and probing in a way that made him hot and desperate to have her. He kissed her neck, feeling with the direction of his genitals that perhaps they could take a chance now and find some spot in this courtyard where he could taste her treasure. She was breathing thickly and gasping softly, seeming to come to the same view, for her hand strayed over his body and pressed his buttocks into her loins, while her thighs opened and rubbed against him. But in the midst of their mounting passion there were cries and the sound of footsteps above the dull, distant rumble of the crowd, more incisive. Her name was being called.

Swiftly they drew back into the deeper gloom of the courtyard and, against the lighter patch of gloom which was the arched entrance, saw a band of men with pikes and drawn swords run past.

"They're looking for me. We have no time," she whispered fiercely, as if furious that they had no time now to make love.

He left her and crossed to the archway. Outside all was dark and deserted. The men had passed but they would be back and doubtless there were more. He called to her softly and in a moment she was at his side, her hand on his arm.

"Until tomorrow then," he said. "You can join the crowds quickly now."

"I wish it were now," she said, with a sudden fierce streak of desire. She caught his hand

and put it on her breast. And she kissed him once again, fiercely. He ran his lips over her face: the high, warm brow, the animated, pale blue eyes, the short, straight nose, and he bit at that sexy, jutting underlip which told such an accurate story.

She broke away from him with a little cry.

"Tomorrow," she said and ran off into the gloom.

He followed, slowly, watching her dim figure round the corner. By the time he had reached it, she was swallowed up amidst the stragglers making their way to the fringe of the crowds in the square.

Cesare wandered down to the square where in a roped off space around the pump and an old statue, the fireworks were being exploded. Rockets were still scarring the sky and on the ground a trelliswork of Roman candles, Catherine wheels and other specialities were popping and whirring in profusion and hurtling sparks into the shrieking, joyful crowds. There was no sign of Dorotea, nor yet the Duke of Alfaro's party. Many people were drunk and there were several necking sessions being carried on openly in a way which would have shocked everybody to the core on a day which was more realistic than the present.

Soon the crowds began to waver back to make room for the grotesquely masked figures, many several times life size which marched into the square, followed by great floats and carts with tableaux from which more fireworks were being hurtled into the flame-scratched sky.

Men were swigging back wine from flasks and couples were dancing, alone and in groups.

There was singing, shouting and, doubtless in some dark doorways, there was fucking too.

Cesare began to get into the mood of the crowd. He was disappointed that he'd not managed to possess Dorotea that very night. It had left him hot and frustrated. She had an impish animation with her loveliness, and her obvious desire for him increased his own for her. Now his penis was hot and unsatisfied and his face still flaming from the passion which remained unrequited in his loins. He held out his hand for a flask of wine which was readily passed to him by one of the merrymakers and took a long draught. He joined the group from which he'd received this beneficence and took stock of its members. Among them was an attractive and rather young girl whose cheeks were flushed and whose skirts swished in abandon as she danced and sang. She appeared for the moment to be with nobody and Cesare joined the dancing group next to her.

"You're so beautiful," he whispered to her as they swung around each other in the dance, and her laughing, tipsy eyes laughed up at him and she pouted her mouth as if she wanted to be kissed. A young bud ripe for the plucking, he said to himself as he kissed her lightly on her rosebud lips.

The group raced toward the edge of the crowd for a better view as more floats and carts rumbled into the square. Cesare caught the girl, who was about to run with them and waltzed her into a dance. Laughing and leaning back from his arms, she allowed herself to be danced away from the crowd, until they were almost lost in the gloom at the edge of the square. There Cesare kissed her more ardently and she responded with a similar, but innocent ardor.

"Let's go and salvage the remains of the ox," he suggested.

"But I'm not hungry."

"I am—we can dance all the way and be back in a moment."

She threw back her head and laughed at the thought of dancing through the streets and they moved off with one accord through the gloom of the lane which led to the field where the skeleton of the ox was sagging over the dying fire. On the way they were passed by a group of armed men, who stared at them closely as they passed. You'll find her when you join the throng, Cesare thought with a twinkle. His thoughts roamed for a moment over the face and body of Dorotea. He put his arm around the girl at his side, who was laughing and chattering. A good second best, he thought.

When they reached the field, the fire was a small, flickering spot in a distant point. It was dark and he led her away from the fire. She didn't seem to notice and when, near a clump of small bushes he pulled her around and kissed her again, she closed her eyes and threw back her head. The soft lips on his enveloped him in flame. Her dark hair was lavender-scented. He caught her neck in his hands and crushed his body into her. He stroked her breasts over her dress and drew her down onto the grass in the gloomy shadow of the bushes. She did not resist while he roved over her breasts, but when his hand moved away and traveled up her leg, lifting the hem of her dress and moving up a soft bare thigh, she pulled her face from his.

"No, no," she said.

He ignored her protest, held her tightly and moved his hand right up until he could feel the concave heat of her crotch and his fingertips brushed against a soft down.

"No, no, no," she said softly but desperately. She tried to pull away and closed her thighs over his hand. As she struggled he held her tighter and then his fingers were brushing the soft, hanging folds of her labia. When he dug inside she cried out and began to whimper. She was evidently a virgin. But tonight was revelry night, the night for deflowering, and Cesare was at boiling point from his earlier encounter.

Holding her struggling body he pulled, tugged and tore off her undergarment and stretched her back on the grass. He slithered from his own undergarments and felt the cool night air on his rigid prick.

"No, no, please, no . . ." the girl begged. But the caress of his fingers in her vagina which was moistening rapidly seemed to have subdued her. It was now herself she was fighting as much as him.

Cesare wasted no time. He swung onto her and jabbed his prick at her hole.

"No, no, no—Oooooooooh!"

His penis had coursed into her wet flesh, in pain and excitement. Her mouth screwed up. This was it. This was the point of waiting finally reached on a dark carnival night in a cool field with a strange man. It hurt, but it was exciting and after a while it began to give pleasure. Cesare, thrusting deeper and deeper into her body which quivered like a frightened animal's imagined to himself that it was Dorotea, with whom he looked forward to emulating today's performance on the morrow.

CHAPTER 12

Dorotea had rejoined the Duke of Alfaro's party, explained her absence due to being lost in the crowd and then wandering in curiosity, and had finally left the carnival early. Drunks were already lying around the streets and the Duke and his entourage, who returned to his chateau with her, saw some scenes which the Pope could not officially have approved of.

The Duke, with lovesick, desire-jaundiced eyes seized every opportunity to catch her hand, to press against her, to look down the front of her dress. He seemed to her really like a child. But she could forgive him. If she hadn't come to stay at the chateau she would never have met the Duke of Valentinois, with whom her thoughts were overwhelmed. She wondered how he would execute the daring plan he had decided on for tomorrow. They said he stopped at nothing. That was what thrilled her—the thought of being in the arms of a man who stopped at nothing, to know that even as you felt his organ filling you he was a strange, iron-willed man who stopped at nothing, would take from you whatever he desired and there was nothing you could do about it.

Back in the chateau, she retired to her own suite of rooms, undressed and stood by her window, staring out over the empty grounds to the distant glow of the village. She had been violently frustrated, but now she could wait until tomorrow. But if only he were here with her in this room, if only he could see her from the grounds and find a way in. She might have suggested it . . .

But down in the grounds, hidden among the trees, another figure was watching her windows—the Duke of Alfaro. And when he saw her slim, tight, curvaceous form appear in its fleshly state at her window he nearly died from apoplexy. His gaze became transfixed, his eyes bulged, he hardly breathed during the several minutes that she stood gazing dreamily out over the hill and her body was there for him to see, vaguely, at a distance, but well silhouetted by the lights in her room.

The Duke nearly fainted from desire. His prick felt as if it would burst and he took it out from the robe he was wearing and fondled it, while he watched her. He had to get in the bitch!

* * *

Dorotea lay on her bed, naked and cool, thinking of her night's activity. She pressed her hands down her body. Tomorrow he would be doing that. Tomorrow her body would have no secrets from him. It would be his to do with as he wished. She smiled, her fingers touched her thigh near the lips of her vagina and she turned on her side and lost herself in a sleeping maze of thoughts and images.

* * *

The Duke of Alfaro walked softly through corridors of his castle. He did not creep stealthily in case he met any of the servants, but he walked more quietly and quickly than was usual with him. He still wore his robe under which was nothing but his fat, shaggy body. He had waited outside for some time, hoping that his erection would deflate and not push out the robe in a great protuberance. But his turmoil of sexy thoughts somehow just refused to let it go down, so now he was walking quickly and quietly, hoping he wouldn't meet a soul.

In the pocket of his robe, his clenched hand, against which he could feel the silk-covered, horizontal tower of his ramrod, rested against the cooling metal of a key—a skeleton key, a *passe-partout*, a gateway to heaven and perhaps hell, the key to the suite of rooms that his young, luscious guest was occupying.

The corridors were dark, with an occasional candle at the dark corners. There were old, dusty pictures on the walls and old suits of armor stood, chill and austere, at respectable tilting distance from one another. His feet made no sound on the thick carpet; the slight swishing of his robe and the grating of his excited breath, which he tried to control, were the only sounds.

He reached the door of her suite without seeing anybody, and fitted the key quietly. The first room was a salon. It was doubtful that she would be there. When he'd witnessed her nudity it had been at the large, balcony windows of her bedroom.

The key turned in the lock of the heavy door and his heart thumped furiously and he felt as if the color had drained out of his face. It certainly hadn't drained out of his prick, for his pride stood up stark and stiff still—and tingling with hope eternal.

Inside it was dark, but a vague, diffused light misted through the open archway which connected the salon with the boudoir.

Softly, his heart in his mouth, the Duke closed the door behind him. Just as softly, he locked it and slipped the key back into the pocket of his robe.

For a few seconds he leaned against the door, listening, hearing nothing but the beating of his heart, seeing nothing but the misty light from the next room and the mixed images of her that he carried in his head, the feel of her buttocks and the sight of her uncovered breasts from the torn-off towel, the outline of her firm body from the grounds below.

He tiptoed carefully toward the arch, moving with a nervous skill between the tables, chairs and other objects which sprang up in the twilight to waylay him.

He peered, on tenterhooks, around the edge of the archway. Candlelight was flickering around her huge, four-poster bed and what he saw turned him hot and cold and made his prick give a sudden throb.

She was lying on her side and the vague outline of her showed that she was still utterly naked. He moved in, almost gliding on the carpet, until he stood a few feet from the edge of the bed. She was asleep. Her regular breathing came clearly to him in the still room. Her body was still and vulnerable. The slim shoulders—he was viewing her from behind—curved down into a tight slender waist and then rounded out into voluptuously proportioned hips and buttocks. The flesh was real, alive, would yield when he touched it.

Softly he walked around the bed. His robe had fallen back from his prick and the great tower stood up and out now like a white cannon through an aperture in some battlements.

From the other side he could see her face, with some of the long, fair hair falling over it. Her lips were slightly apart and the lower lip looked ready for eating. Her breasts were not large, but, as he remembered them from his briefest of glimpses before, well-shaped and firm with those pert, pink nipples that looked like lollipops ready for the sucking. Her hips were warmly-fleshed, her thighs, rounded and superb and the hair above her vagina formed a matching triangle with that which swept down to her shoulders.

The Duke was trembling from head to foot. He moved unsteadily back to his former viewpoint, feeling, somehow, safer for the moment behind her. He took off his robe and stood, gross and naked, over her, gloating over her body with his eyes.

Gently he began to fondle and massage his prick, gazing intently all the time at her ass. His gaze tried to see through her buttocks, to feel them through sight. His penis was hot and throbbed furiously in his fingers. He rubbed the skin back and forth, pressing his legs together, pushing sensation through his loins to the aching protuberance which reared over her sleeping form.

His breathing was difficult and he opened his mouth, emitting a gasp into the room. She stirred and he froze—he hardly knew why as he had been willing for his presence to be discovered. She rolled over onto her back and raised one thigh in her sleep. It flopped outwards, revealing the fluff-shrouded mass of flesh around her vagina. Now her breasts stood out, straight and round above her ribs and the flesh of her hips seemed to reach out toward him. He shuffled nearer, with his hand still gently squeezing his knob.

The knob had flamed red and he felt a boiling in his rod as he pulled the foreskin back and forth. His chest was heaving, his eyes roamed over her as if they were physically invading her body.

He moved his other hand down past his massive boom and stroked his balls with his fingertips. He imagined she was stroking them and the tickling sensation in the twin sacs became all the more intense for his imaginings.

I must have her now, he thought intensely. I must have her now—I could be in her with any luck before she realized what was happening.

Strangely, he now felt nervous. His breath seemed to be stifling both his stomach and his chest and he found himself trying to hold his breath. But the turbulence in his loins, reaching up to its zenith in the reddening flower of his passion, was his only *raison d'être* for the moment and he had to have his passion slaked in her body. Nothing less would do.

He moved up still closer so that his knees and thighs touched the coverlet of the bed and he was looking directly down on her prostrate nudity, her sleeping face. That was the face which taunted him. The eyes, of course, were closed and he was deprived of their sudden fluctuation from sphinx to wildcat, but the other features remained to view, the same, voluptuously the same as usual. But she didn't know he was there. He was leaning over her studying those very same features which looked at him with scorn, every detail of which he knew—and she didn't know he was there. Now was the point of crisis. Before now was peace and the sleeping body and features. Beyond now was unknown wakefulness and fighting and . . . who knew? He felt the impulsive importance of this moment on the brink—and then, with a little intake of breath, he fell on her, knocking her other thigh away as he lay between her legs.

* * *

Dorotea was lying in a huge bed with the Duke of Valentinois. He had pulled her close and was stroking her buttocks. She was bathed in a light dew which was the faint sweat of her passion breaking out like a rash all over her body. He was beautiful and warm and she desired him more than she had ever desired anyone or anything. She could feel the warmth of his great weapon of manhood against her hips and she wanted it inside her. But he only went on stroking her buttocks until she was quivering with excitement.

She wanted to show him how much she desired him and she rolled over onto her back and opened her thighs ready for him, inviting him to mount her and fill her with his lust.

But he seemed to hang back and transferred his stroking hand to her aching breast.

When she moved her lips, slightly, and opened her lips to him he moved at last and kneeled over her ready to lower himself and ride her body like a stallion riding a mare, riding, riding in a euphoria of sexuality. His face came down to her and suddenly his body.

But his body was heavier than expected and seemed to be scrabbling, there was confusion and unexpected sensation ... she awoke with a start and a low scream. A face was over hers, its eyes dilated with lust—that of the Duke of Alfaro's and it was his heavy, fat body which covered hers.

For several seconds she didn't know whether this was dream or reality. And in that moment or two in which she lay, petrified, wondering where and who she was, a great, fat prick had thrust roughly into her cunt, finding it moist from her dream, and torn up toward her cervix, while its owner gave a cry of ecstasy.

She began to struggle. She beat him with her fists, lashing his fleshy face. She twisted her legs and writhed her body. She felt his penis drubbing up into her, wider and wider. He was gasping little gasps of pain at her blows, of agonized joy at the tight contraction of his penis in her Dorotea, of the teasing face, of the blue eyes, of the jutting lip, into her firm, slim body.

For several seconds they struggled together. He thrust several strokes into her. But she was stronger than he was, in his fleshy decay. Her firm, athletic body was more capable of tension and thrust than his limp flabbiness and she realized that with a strong effort she could wriggle away from him.

But the Duke's preface of rubbing over her body, his palpitating excitement of getting in her cunt at last, raced him to a record climax.

Even as she gathered her strength, he gave a grating, grinding, heart-shaking groan of a gasp and came in the channel he was spearing.

As she pushed him roughly off her, a stream of viscid liquid streamed after his knob out of her vagina and splayed across her thighs.

"You beast, you beast!" she shouted.

He lay back on the bed, slightly frightened, sorry in many ways that it had been so quick, feeling slightly cheated, feeling that he hadn't really enjoyed her, would remember only with regret the time when he'd snatched at her body only to lose need for it almost immediately.

But she had seized a candelabrum and bashed

it down across his chest. Her eyes were blazing and she looked dangerous.

He rolled off the bed, grabbed his robe, dodged her, winced with the pain of a blow on his shoulder and rushed into the salon and out into the gloomy corridors.

He spent a sleepless, regretful night, wondering if she would complain and wishing he could have had her long and languorously, with her cooperation.

CHAPTER 13

It was on a road through the woods north of Cesena that Cesare waited for Dorotea Caracciolo and her retinue to come on their journey back to Venice.

He waited on his horse in the shadow of a huge tree which blocked him from the view of anyone riding along the narrow road from a southern direction. Around, in the bushes, his half-dozen officers waited with swords drawn, hidden themselves by the trailing, autumn-leafed undergrowth.

The road through the woods was deserted. In the half hour they'd been waiting, nobody had passed. It was unlikely that anyone would.

Cesare felt welling in his breast the daring delight he experienced at being in dangerous action again. That his officers had entered enthusiastically in his plan was as much their sharing of his audacity as their devotion to him. Soon, soon he would be holding the naked body of that lovely, sphinx-eyed girl in his arms. He thought of her substitute of the night before, who had cried at first and then lain passive and groaning and then become animated at approaching orgasm. For a virgin, she'd really been quite a bundle of abandon eventually—and then she'd run off into the darkness after his limp prick had come out of her as if she was ashamed of what had happened and couldn't bear to look him in the face. It wouldn't be long before she took other lovers.

"I hear them, Sire!"

The voice of one of his lieutenants hissed through the light rustle of the breeze on the dry leaves. Cesare's mind became a straining ear to catch the slightest sound. He heard them too, some distance off—the steady thud, thud of approaching hoofs.

"Everybody ready," he called softly.

Whispers echoed through the woods and an answering affirmation came back from his nearest lieutenant.

"They have to think we're a score of men, at least."

"Aye, Sire."

Cesare's horse quivered under him lightly as they waited in a heavy silence, listening to the loudening thud of the hooves until the thud had split up into individual horse-sounds: snorts and jangling of bridles and rustling of dead leaves underfoot. There were voices, too, female voices and male commands to animals. Cesare waited. The sounds spread, seeming to stretch into the forest on either side of him in an eerie echoing. They must have passed the first of his officers. He let them come, judging the moment, holding his quivering horse into the shade of the tree. And then, of a sudden he spurred forward onto the road, arquebus in hand.

There was a startled, astonished pile-up of the leading men-at-arms. Cesare had just a second in which he glimpsed the lady of his desires in the midst of her handmaidens before he shouted immediately:

"Lay down your arms. You're surrounded."

As he shouted these words, there were rustlings in the trees and bushes around the road, everything half hidden in leaves and foliage. The front-quarters of horses eased into view, the extended arms of standing men, there was movement all around, seeming to come in mysterious volume from all sides.

The men-at-arms stared around them fearfully, hands petrified halfway to swords and guns.

"If you try to resist, you'll be shot down on your horses," Cesare cried. "Lay down your arms and you'll not be harmed."

There was still a hesitation and Cesare fired his arquebus into the air: a sign for his men, half hidden in the surrounding bushes, to fire volleys over the heads of the ambushed cortege. Horses shied and nearly threw their riders. The men-at-arms began to throw down their weapons, which thudded softly into the leafmold which covered the road.

"Dismount—and the ladies," Cesare ordered.

He watched them obey him, smiling to himself at Dorotea feigning terror with the rest of her women.

"Three men to secure them," he called. "The rest keep them covered."

Three of his lieutenants, still, like Cesare himself, dressed as peasants, but fully armed, stepped out from the bushes. It was the work of a few minutes to secure the handful of men-at-arms, an even shorter period to tie up the women—all except Dorotea who was left aside.

When all was done, Cesare's men came out of

the surrounding trees—all three of them, leading their horses who had served to indicate greater numbers.

Cesare rode up to Dorotea and commanded her to mount, which she did with every show of reluctance. He cast a last look at the trussed men-at-arms and the ladies. It would be some time before they were discovered or managed to break free. He directed his arquebus at Dorotea, sitting woodenly on her horse beside him.

"You will ride with us," he said in a loud voice, "and if you don't attempt to escape, no harm will come to you."

She made no answer. Her eyes, when she looked at him, twinkled for the briefest of seconds.

Cesare gave a sharp command and he and his band spurred their horses away up the road in the direction of Cesena from which the ambushed party had come. Once out of sight, Dorotea's face lit up and she reached across to clasp his hand at full gallop, Cesare grinned broadly and around them his men were chortling with mirth.

For a mile they rode south and then wheeled abruptly into the forest. They pushed and battled their way for a mile or so and then turned again, toward the north. When, at last, they reached the road to Forli, the trussed party were still trying to shake free of their bonds prior to riding south in pursuit and to raise the alarm.

Some distance from the city which Cesare had captured some time before, they dismounted in the forest. Dorotea retired to a discreet distance. Cesare and his officers changed into their own attire—and when

Dorotea returned she, too, was dressed as a soldier, a young and very attractive soldier, but a soldier nonetheless with her long, blonde hair hidden and her soft, woman's curves disguised.

Thus they rode, a merry band of men, saluted by the guard at the gates of the city, into Forli.

CHAPTER 14

When Cesare turned, having stripped off his clothes, Dorotea was naked. She came toward him with her eyes smoldering and her lips apart. He had time only to glimpse the firm, high breasts, the waist and hips devoid of an ounce of superfluous flesh, the way the thighs tensed as she walked bare-foot across the few feet of boudoir between them, and then she was in his arms, her naked flesh grazing warmly against his, clinging to his like rubber.

His prick rode up between their warm bodies and he felt her hips moving against it, surrounding it hotly with the flesh of her hips and loins.

"Oh, darling," she whispered. And for a fleeting instant her dream came back to her and the memory of her awakening horror. It seemed unbelievable that that beastly old man, after all his vain advances and insinuations, his daring to enter her room and pull a towel from her breasts so that he saw them, his fighting with her and feeling her buttocks, it seemed unbelievable that he should actually have got his prick in her and fucked her for at least a minute. She quivered with outrage at the thought of his effrontery. And that he should have had an orgasm in that time, shooting his load into her reluctant body. That was the most infuriating thing of all. Anyway, she'd caught him a sharp blow or two with the candlestick. He'd have a few bruises to remember — but she wished he didn't have the memory of the feel of her quim to remember as well. It was an insult.

But Cesare was kissing her neck, sucking up the flesh and his hands were roving down her spine, stroking her buttocks, caressing her shoulders, reaching under the buttocks, cupping them and pulling them up and in toward him. This was the man she'd dreamed about and now it was true. She tensed her thighs, sighed a deep sigh of passion and gave herself to their union.

Cesare's fingers seemed to burn as they coursed gently over her flesh, tasting its firmness, its often softness, its roundness, its glossy texture, its warmth and responsive trembling. Her body rubbed and squirmed against his and he dug his fingers deep into her, seizing the flesh in a handful until she squealed and bit his neck.

He lifted her and carried her to the bed.

Light of a watery autumn sun streamed in through a large window which overlooked the rooftops of Forli. They were above and far from all eyes in the citadel where the Countess Sforza-Riario had submitted to him less willingly at first.

Cesare lay her down on the bed and stood over her. He reached down and caught her breasts, easing them up toward him, elongating them with his hands. He knelt beside her and, bending, kissed her fiercely, invaded her sweet mouth with his tongue and bit that sexy lower lip, which in answer enveloped his mouth.

He pulled his mouth suckingly from hers and caught her small, pink nipple between his teeth. He sucked at her breast, drawing as much of the solid, malleable flesh into his mouth as he could. Her nipples hardened in his mouth and she gave a gasp and, taking his hand, put it on the little raised mound of moss-covered flesh at her thigh junction.

Still kneeling, he moved down the bed and raised her thighs, spreading them wide. Her pale, blue eyes watched him with a deep look of concentrated passion.

"Kiss me!" she said.

He looked down at where the raw, pink flesh of her cunt was open and then he slithered down and put his lips to it. She gave a little shriek as she felt his sucking pressure. He began to suck the moist, rain-tasting flesh. He poked his tongue as high as it would go and moved it around against the walls of her vagina. He licked the insides of her hot thighs and found and seized in his lips, the hard, little clitoris.

Dorotea had flung her thighs wide and was wriggling and shrieking with tiny helpless explosions every second. Her hands clenched and unclenched beside her head on the bed and her face, drawn in harrowed passion, swung from side to side with jerky, involuntary movements. Her eyes were closed, her mouth wide open, gasping warm, suffocated breath into the room.

Cesare buried his face between her thighs and put his hands under her buttocks, levering them up.

"Oh, oh, oh, oooooh!"

Her gasping moans assailed his ears, her

moist, warm, slipperiness assailed his mouth, the sweet rain-taste lay on his tongue.

His prick was a long, trembling mass of excited, jostling particles. It was heavy, too heavy, needed to throw off ballast, but when he drew his mouth away, she tried to catch at his head and pleaded desperately.

"Oh, don't stop, please — not now!"

He bent back to her and her loins leapt up to meet him. Her mouth was emitting a long, drawn-out and continuous whine. He could sense her whole body twisting and turning in ecstatic torment. He wanted to get in her, but the fury of her excitement was exciting him even more than if he'd rammed into her at this point.

He heard her gasp, felt her scrabbling on the bed, churning up the covers and then she gave a short, low scream and a sticky heat surrounded him.

She continued to writhe and moan for some time after her climax and he continued to kiss her gently, to bring her back to a tensity of passion.

"Oh, God," she exclaimed at last. "I thought I'd die."

He came away from her loins then, up her body, tracing its light bulges with his lips. He knelt up, astride her, and she reached down and took his rigid, pulsating penis which stuck out horizontally over her breasts.

She put it between her breasts, which she pushed up into a ravine of cleavage and for several seconds he rubbed up and down in the ravine formed by the warm, firm flesh of her teats. He felt a tingling deep in his loins, deep, perhaps, in his bowels and moved forward on her again.

She reached up, her eyes sparkling with depth, and took his organ in both hands. He leaned forward on his hands and she covered the flaming knob with her lips, enveloping it with that sexy lower jut. She took him into her warm, wet mouth and he felt, with streaks of fire, her tongue licking and nuzzling the passionpoint of his knob.

She began to suck as she licked, sucking on the rest of his rigidity, biting gently from time to time. Her eyes watched him, held his, matching his look of furious passion with her own. He held her face with his hands, guiding it, feeling her cheeks hollowing, rhythmically, around the long length of flesh which filled her mouth.

"Harder," he gritted.

He felt her answering response — a greater pressure on his knob, a tighter embrace from her warm lips. He felt his culmination growing in hell-fire in his loins and he wanted to get in her, but couldn't resist the idea of coming into that lovely, sexy mouth, of watching her face hollowing, her eyes recognizing his orgasm even as he came.

He began to rock slightly, flexing his loins forward as she sucked. She had released his prick with her hands and was stroking his buttocks with them. She was breathing heavily, passionately through her flared nostrils and he could feel her hips moving again under him.

Her hands couldn't stay still on him and he felt them, suddenly, drawing lines of loin-convulsing sensation across and around his balls which hung down against her breasts.

He gasped aloud at the new attack and shoved his prick into her mouth so hard that for a moment she fought for breath and nearly choked before reorientating her embrace.

He gasped again, tensing his loins. He could feel himself starting to come, slowly at first in a sort of smoldering ember. The ember grew. He flexed his loins at her hard and held her face, looking into her eyes, which seemed to gasp into his in a strange visual voice.

Inside him the ember burst into a flame and roared from the pit of its sensation along and along . . . he looked deep into her eyes, owning her, subduing her under him, wracked with passion. The fire raced through him, quivered in his penis, trembled at the knob and shattered out of him, as he cried out with the agonizing joy of it.

* * *

Later, after a glass or two of wine, from which his passion flamed again to meet hers, already kindled, they stood at the foot of the bed, embracing fiercely, brokenly.

They were both alive with the desire of at last joining as one. There was no necessity for preliminaries.

Her thighs were open against him as she clung around his neck. Her warm flesh rubbed up on him, catching his penis between the tops of her thighs, so that it reached right through, rubbing against the lips of her vagina.

Cesare caught her under her rump, holding a buttock in each hand, and lifted her off the floor. She put her arms firmly around his neck and brought her legs up on either side of him, hanging around him as he held her.

He moved to a table in one of the corners of the room. He sat her on its edge, reached under her upraised thighs with his hand and guided himself toward her vagina. He needed to bend his knees a little to get down, and when he straightened, his penis rushed in up to its hilt in one long movement.

"Oh-oh-oh-oh!" she cried out in a staccato chatter of gasps.

His knob felt the softness of flesh up at her cervix. The walls of her channel were tight but moistly prepared against the huge expansion of his desire-bloated organ.

Panting, he pulled her right onto the edge of the table and drove up into her with a pressure that came up from his toes and made his abdomen flop against her crotch. His hairs mingled wetly with hers.

She clung, gaspingly, to his neck, her breasts brushing against his chest, her hair swaying across her face, touching his. She bit his neck and moved her trembling lips around his face to fasten them on his, with her searching tongue flopping out in willing surrender into his mouth, keeping her eyes open for a moment and then closing them as his penis crushed up into her so hard that it brought a spasm of pain into the joy.

She groaned in an orgy of passion, her hanging, floating tongue in his mouth was a symbol of the way she gave herself for him to do as he wished, to hurt her, to give her pain, pleasure, ecstasy, to take her body, her life in his hands.

He slid his hands under her buttocks, so that they rested and flowed around his hands. He lifted her in ecstatic fury off the table and walked away around the room, jogging into her, feeling her rise and fall on him, the two of them working together to produce that white-heat which would blaze out and smother them both in the end of everything.

He flung her down on the bed, coming down heavily on top of her and she twisted in masochistic fury under him, swinging her legs up to her shoulders as if she wanted him to pierce her through, right up to her neck.

He straightened up from her, leaning at an angle, pulling her behind off the bed so that her hips were the highest point of her body. He crashed in and in and up and up, tearing her moist flesh with his great rifling cannon.

"Oh, oh, darling!"

She gasped and the gasps became meaningless words and then sometimes crude, filthy words which were pulled out of her in the effort to express what she felt and which couldn't be expressed.

He flopped onto her and bit her neck so hard that she screamed and a little perforation of the white skin exploded and drops of blood oozed through.

Her body was a live animal, active and straining. She opened her eyes one second, looking at him in a smoldering agony and then closed them as if the upthrust of his great prick had forced her to do so from sheer weight of sensation.

Cesare could feel his climax approaching again. It was that much more agonizing the second time. It would be relief to unload his store of sperm. A relief that he didn't want to come because he wanted this agony to go on forever.

"Darling, darling," she screamed. "Now, nearly, now, nearly . . ."

He felt her thighs squirming and wriggling, enclosing his hips in their heat. He felt her little belly brushing hotly against his. She caught his face again and thrust her tongue into his mouth, pushing it out and out as if she wanted to transfer it totally from her own body to his.

He bit it and felt her scream rather than heard it. His prick seemed loaded down with the weight of thunder. The thunder was preparing to burst. The relief was coming.

"Now, yes!" he barked and heard her answering gasps.

The thunder grew into a great, black cloud and suddenly burst so that the liquid, hot rain came thundering down and burst through and up into her belly as she screamed and jackknifed her legs up and down several times.

This was merely the beginning of their night of love.

CHAPTER 15

The winter sun had watered away, black skies had held bruised dominion over the northern plains and spring had come again with a great flowering of oleanders. By the time young men's fancies had led them into woods and dales to suck the nectar of their loved and lusted-after ones, Cesare was sufficiently lord of the northern provinces to be able to declare himself Duke of Romagna and return again to Rome in even greater pomp and glory than before.

But greater campaigns were afoot and it soon filtered to the Vatican, to be followed by official notification from the ambassadors, that by the Treaty of Granada, both France and Spain had come to agreement about the division of a long disputed territory — the Kingdom of

Naples, to which both claimed the right of sovereignty through heritage.

The two claimants, it was revealed, had agreed to undertake the conquest together, sharing the spoils between them. Puglia and Calabria would go to Spain, and Naples and the Abruzzi to Louis.

Pope Alexander immediately declared Federigo of Naples deposed for disobedience to the Church, a charge which was not difficult to fabricate under a number of pretexts.

Cesare, it was decided, should join the French troops, marching through Italy from the north, taking with him a fair proportion of his own troops.

At the same time Gonzalo de Cordoba, the great Spanish soldier, landed a Spanish army in Calabria. Resistance was put up, strong in places, weak in others, but the territory was ravaged and stamped underfoot by the two mighty armies moving inexorably to meet. Within a few weeks they had met at Naples and the days of the House of Aragon were over. Nevertheless, Naples itself put up a stiff resistance and with well-directed cannon fire played such havoc with the lines of the Spaniards who, in enthusiasm to finish the campaign in record time, had permitted themselves to approach too close too soon, that Gonzalo de Cordoba swore a terrible vengeance when the city was taken.

The inevitable breach was made and the waves of the invading armies stormed through. Carnage followed. No quarter was given. The defenders were driven back and back and if they lay down their arms or fled they were slaughtered. This would have been against Cesare's policy. But for once he commanded only a small section of the attack and commands could be issued over his head by the generals of the two main forces, French and Spanish.

Every human being was butchered. The streets of Naples ran with blood as if an animal sacrifice of unheard-of magnitude had been offered for several days running.

But it was with the women of Naples that the invader took the most sadistic vengeance. Women, fleeing, screaming, were seized and raped and massacred. While soldiers ran, searching for victims through the streets, they would pass prostrate huddles of women, their clothes ripped from them by the sword, screaming and weeping, while shaggy soldiers thrust their pricks brutally up into bodies whose thighs they held wide by force.

Gonzalo de Cordoba had some of the most noble families of the city rounded up and saved from the slaughter. He had them taken to the center square of the city where the men were tied so that they couldn't move. He then had the women stripped, surrounded by soldiers wielding whips and forced to dance in front of their menfolk and his army of gawking soldiers to the accompaniment of light lashes around their legs, which grew stronger and stronger and rose around their hips and breasts until many of them fainted and blood had welled out from under their tortured skins.

Cesare, with the situation out of his hands, was indifferent to the suffering. He watched and felt a chill of sensuality course through him as he watched the women pathetically trying to dance, being savagely tickled as soon as they lagged by those stinging lashes. What a variety of breasts and buttocks. And as they fell one by one into a swooning helplessness under the agonized gaze of their helpless husbands and sweethearts, each was seized at the Commander's orders by a rude soldier who proceeded to bury his prick according to his taste, right there on the square in full view. Some of the women remained unconscious throughout the whole proceedings, unaware of the brutality with which they were being shagged or their menfolk's crying fury.

CHAPTER 16

By the time Cesare returned to Rome, richer in money and in French favor, an event of some importance in the Borgia family had taken place: his widowed sister, Lucrezia, had become betrothed to Alfonse d'Este, young son of Duke Ercole of Ferrara. It was a marriage of convenience, although it is probable that the young Alfonse nursed an infatuation for the beautiful Lucrezia.

Into the midst of celebrations, salvoes of artillery, and after dark illuminations, Cesare arrived, crowned with fresh glory from the war, fired still by memories of the spectacle in Naples, desiring the orgasm, coveting his sister.

"Darling, Cesare," she greeted him, when he went to her temporary rooms in the Vatican to invite her down to the supper which was being prepared by the Pope for intimates. "Darling, Cesare," she said, "are you never going to make love to me again? I think you prefer fighting to fucking."

Cesare pulled her to him. He kissed her fiercely on the lips and felt her tongue slide like a snake into his mouth.

"I want you tonight!" he snapped.

"But, darling — I'm married. I have to offer what I have to my new husband. It's his right you know."

She laughed long and merrily and Cesare couldn't help but laugh with her.

"You mean you'd prefer that stripling?"

For answer she sank to her knees, seized his erection which was pushing hard through his clothing and bit it. She got quickly to her feet again and he forced her, panting, back into the room.

"No, Cesare," she said, "not now. I'll come to you tonight — you'll see."

"Do you promise? How can you? Will you leave him on the wedding night to finger his own, unloved cock?"

"He's very young, my sweet, and I think if he's fed a little wine he'll be in no fit state to benefit from the delight he might expect. After all, I don't want to get to bed with him and then find I've only a limp piece of rag trying to squeeze into my vagina."

Cesare laughed. He was delighted with his sister and she still excited him as of old — and he was always certain, absolutely certain of a skillful, satisfying, entrail-tearing fuck with her.

He bent down quickly and lifted her skirt. She wore nothing underneath, which made her feel more natural.

"One kiss until later," he whispered.

"Oh, no, Cesare — you're just trying to excite me!"

But he'd already whipped up her skirt, thrust his head under, pushing aside her thighs and licked his tongue all along the powdered, perfumed folds which hid her sweet tunnel. He felt her thighs rub against his shoulders and pulled the folds aside with the tips of his thumbs. He kissed the moistening flesh hard and heard her gasp.

She broke away from him with a stifled cry.

"Oh, Cesare, stop!"

Kneeling, he grinned.

"I bet you'd love it now," he said.

As he escorted her down the stairway toward the banquet room where they were to dine, she said, softly, looking into his eyes with love: "You are a devil, Cesare, you've made me all wet."

As they descended, she added: "Perhaps he'll go silly with the first glass."

"One can always hope," Cesare answered, smiling.

* * *

But it took more than one glass to put young Alfonse in a stupor. As soon as his glass was half-empty, Lucrezia had it solicitously refilled. The meal progressed; there was music and talk and laughter among the dozen or so guests. There were toasts and good wishes and sly winks from the Pope at his daughter, as if wishing her fun in bed tonight.

Throughout the evening, Cesare's eyes met those of his sister. Sometimes he would nod at her husband's glass to indicate it might be topped up just a shade. Over the dessert, with Lucrezia almost in despair, Alfonse became very talkative — he was usually rather silent — and the sign gave her hope.

Servants carried away the debris of the meal and Alfonse suggested quietly that they retire, but not so quietly that some of the surrounding guests were not forced to suppress grins of amusement to say nothing of more embarrassing indications of envy.

"Oh, but we haven't heard the other orchestra, yet," Lucrezia insisted smoothly. "It's a beautiful orchestra. It will make a fitting goodnight."

Alfonse sat back, slightly disappointed, but prepared to wait for something that he knew was inevitably his.

Lucrezia filled his glass again.

"What excellent wine," she said, and took a sip.

The suggestion produced the desired effect. Alphonse automatically picked up his own glass, sipped it and then emptied it in three long gulps. It was quietly refilled.

As the "other orchestra" began to play — in a manner which hardly justified her description — Alfonse seemed to grow silent. A little later he made a slight effort at conversation with his neighbor, but then his head sank down, he gave a little belch and his eyes glazed over slightly.

Cesare smiled to himself. His clever sister. No difficulty at all.

But Alfonse came drunkenly to. He caught hold of Lucrezia's arm and stood up, lurching a little.

"Well . . . we . . . must . . . retire," he said, slurring each word and waiting for long concentrated pauses.

Those other guests who had heard stood up politely and Lucrezia, so as not to make a scene, found herself obliged to stand up, make her excuses and retire with her drunken husband who hadn't once released his hold on her arm. She was quite taken aback by the sudden reversal of her plan. One minute he'd looked as if he'd have to be carried to bed, the next he'd made a comeback like some punchdrunk fighter who won't go down.

On Cesare the effect was even worse. He saw the image of his night's exhilaration slipping away. No other woman would do. He loved his sister, had more feeling for her than for any other woman, and he had to unite with her tonight.

Thinking furiously, he waited for them to reach the doors of the banquet hall. None of the other guests seemed inclined to leave so early.

Cesare stood up.

"If you'll excuse me father . . ."

"What, my son — we have some saucy dancing to follow. Why, it's not yet midnight."

"I'm sorry father, but I have a bad head. I got a knock in Naples, you know, and they've been recurring, these headaches, ever since."

"My poor boy. We'll have the physician in first thing tomorrow . . ."

"Oh, it's nothing serious, father . . ."

"And you'd better have one of the servants get you something."

The Pope called to an attractive female servant, who had ceased to be a virgin the moment he'd discovered that she was one.

"Carlotta, the Duke needs a brew for his head."

The woman moved off to obey and Cesare took his leave of the guests and followed her. The plan had fallen into his lap if the drink had caught up on Alfonse as much as he thought it should have done by now.

He caught the girl, walking through the corridors, and took her by the arm. She turned toward him, smiling. She was a well-known libertine and Cesare remembered that he'd yet to try her.

He talked to her quietly for a few minutes, explaining that his sister did not want to sleep with her newlywed in his drunken state but could hardly refuse. He outlined a brief plan and slipped an emerald ring into her hand. She held his fingers suggestively and he whispered in her ear that he would like to see her the next day. That seemed to satisfy her more than the ring had, and she followed him as he walked quickly through the various chambers and up the broad steps to Lucrezia's temporary apartment.

At the top of the stairs, Lucrezia was almost supporting Alfonse, whose eyes were half closed, but whose arms were mechanically mauling her while his face nuzzled at hers.

Cesare slowed down and motioned to the servant, Carlotta, who grinned as she moved up. Lucrezia saw them coming and, at a sign from Cesare, pushed open the door to her apartment and moved in, rather awkwardly as Alfonse was trying to kiss her breasts and get his hand up her skirt at the same time.

When Cesare and his companion reached the door, Lucrezia had already maneuvered her part-conscious husband into the bedroom. He had succeeded in getting his hand up her skirt and was rummaging between her thighs as they staggered toward the bed. He pulled her onto the bed as they reached it and her skirt fell up over her hips as she landed beside him. He began to kiss her passionately and she pulled away saying, loudly, to ensure that it got through to him:

"Wait, darling. Let me undress."

He didn't seem to hear. His hand mauled

between her legs, exposing all that was there to the eyes of the two watchers at the door. Lucrezia pulled away from him by main force and he rolled onto his side and lay there muttering to himself, reaching blindly toward her figure which he could probably only vaguely see.

Cesare gave his companion a push and she slipped into the room, pulling off her clothes. As she moved in, Lucrezia moved out.

Brother and sister waited long enough to see the unabashed servant stripped — and very comely, Cesare thought, reserving his true appreciation for the morrow — and settling down to undress Alfonse who slobbered over her naked body. She was hoping he was just conscious enough to get it stiff and stick it in her. She liked the idea of being rammed by young gentry and her hands skillfully teased his prick up to more than life size as she undressed him.

Cesare and his sister made their way quickly to his own apartments. When he had locked the door behind them they both burst into helpless laughter which shook them for several minutes.

"How brilliant, Cesare . . . brilliant!" Lucrezia gasped at last. "But supposing he sobers up?"

"If he does he'll find himself in bed with a maid who'll tell him he dragged her there. He'll be so confused he won't even dare mention it to you. You can say you put him to bed and told the maid to look in later to see if he was all right." He paused. "If he doesn't come to, you'll have time to join him before the morning, and he'll think that he had you before he passed out."

"Brilliant, brilliant — but I'd hate him to

have had a servant girl and think that it was me — a poor level of performance."

"I'll let you know how you compare tomorrow," he said.

"Why you *diablo*, you've got her into your bed for tomorrow night? What about me?"

"You'd better make peace with your Alfonse."

"Cold-hearted brute. You don't care for me one jot."

She came toward him, mock-pouting through her smile and he grabbed her and kissed her as if he wanted to push her mouth through to the back of her head. She opened her mouth under his pressure and, squirming at him, began to undo his doublet.

"I can't wait, darling. God he got me all excited for you with his mauling!"

Cesare stripped rapidly and Lucrezia tore off her astonishingly few garments.

"You should have been a gypsy," he said, and the thought reminded him of another liaison not yet exhausted. Doubtless he would be returning north before very long.

She twisted around for him, moving her limbs in a wild pirouette, showing off the almost exaggerated curves of her highly voluptuous body.

"Do you remember the day you chased me around the pool?" she asked breathlessly, falling into his arms and stroking his penis underneath from base to tip. "What did you think when you saw me running naked, for the first time, in front of you."

Cesare kissed her ear and quivered with the feel of her lovely nakedness against his.

"I thought you had a bottom more beautiful than the moon," he said.

"Oh, darling, how poetic. Is it still?"

She broke away from him and turned her back coquettishly.

He looked down at the bottom. It was perfect, not too much flesh, slightly oval — shaped with the buttocks billowing out, smooth and shiny as a cannon from her tiny waist.

He moved up behind her, so that his prick pressed up along the crack between the buttocks. He put his hand under her armpits and held a bulbous breast in each. She pushed her behind back at him and felt behind her for his prick as she rested her head back against his shoulder.

"So beautiful I could possess that little crevice between them and imagine myself sailing around the moon on a magic carpet."

Lucrezia laughed breathlessly.

"Why not?" she said. "If you do it'll make me so excited by the time you've finished that I'll cut off your penis with my scissors if you can't come up again within half a minute to satisfy me — that is, if I'm not satisfied already."

He pressed hard against her. That tight little posterior hole was just as delightful as the other. It didn't matter which he had first. He pushed her toward the bed and put her hands around behind his back, pushing his buttocks at her as if she were propelling them both along in their movement.

From a table beside his bed she took some pomade with which, in times of peace and pomp, he treated his hair.

"Use a little of that," she said. "It's a long time since I've felt an invasion in that quarter."

She climbed onto the bed and lay on her stomach, holding her thighs together, pressing them into the coverlet, grunting with expectation.

Cesare knelt over her and pulled her buttocks apart as if he were separating the quarters of an orange. Between was that dark, puckered, very bald-looking crack, seeming so tiny that it was impossible to believe his battering-ram could possibly force its way in.

He took the pomade and gently massaged the little hole with it, smearing it around the bald, puckered flesh, gently tickling her tender spot with his fingertips.

Lucrezia wriggled under him so that her buttocks tensed around his fingers and held him in a light grip.

"Oh hurry, darling," she said, her voice coming up, muffled by the coverlet into which she was pressing her face to control her passion.

Her anus was slippery with the pomade and he pushed his index finger at the clinging little hole. It gave without much difficulty and his finger slipped in and was held. His fingertip found soft, loose depths and he waggled his finger around a little and then pushed in another finger.

Lucrezia pressed her hips into the bed, squealing.

"Darling, darling, don't torment me!"

Cesare looked at his prick. It was red and angry looking. He pulled his foreskin right back and smeared a little of the pomade on so that it glistened.

"Spread your legs," he ordered.

Lucrezia, as if she too were hungry and opening her mouth for food, spread her legs in a large, obtuse-angled V, pressing her legs hard and quiveringly into the coverlet. She loosed her buttock-tension and lay there, her mouth open, heart and loins pounding for the stiff entry.

Cesare leveled himself over her, caught his prick in one hand and aimed it as he stretched out on her, feeling at first the gentle brushing of their skins from chest to loins as he positioned himself and then the full, hot weight of flesh against flesh as he lay heavily on her body.

"That's it!" she grated. "Go on darling. I can stand it!"

Cesare pushed down harder, practically pivoting on his vertical stand.

She groaned out a long exclamation which at first was formless and then managed to transform itself into a stifled "Daaarling!"

His penis was pinched and contracted in her deep passage. It felt as if sparks were being squeezed out of it, as if it were being squeezed into little sections, each with its own burning light.

Cesare moaned with the tight excruciating excitement of it and put his arms around and under her, grasping her breasts, slightly flattened against the bed, and began to squeeze and pull them.

Lucrezia uttered a little scream and he felt her undulating under him, her buttocks rising and falling, wriggling and squirming against the hairy flesh of his loins.

The relief he'd felt at shoving his penis at last into the soft receptacle of his sister's body began to fade and its place was taken by a gnawing pressure which was growing agony.

He rose and fell on her with long deep strokes, pushing right up in a tearing invasion of her posterior passage.

His mouth opened of its own accord and his

breath barked out. Under him, muffled in the coverlet he heard Lucrezia's little screams of passion and he strengthened his grip on her breasts which seemed to expand and resist him.

Up and down, in and out he sawed into her, feeling his organ rasp against the warm walls of her fleshy channel. He wanted still more of her and, without coming out of her, he struggled up onto his knees, pulling her up with him so that she was kneeling with her buttocks in an arc towards him, their bodies joined by the single erect bridge.

Her body curved away from him, her head still resting on the coverlet. She arched her back like a stretching cat and rolled her buttocks in all directions in abandon. He caught her buttocks in each hand and pinched up the flesh, holding it in handfuls, squeezing it furiously as he drove in, wanting to hurt her, to communicate to her the ecstasy of pain and delight in which he was plunged.

He rammed his penis in and then waggled his hips around against her stretched, naked buttocks, feeling the warmth of the friction spring up between them.

To Lucrezia it seemed that there was nothing to her body but loins and buttocks. Her loins were afire and her behind was a gaping cavern into which all of Cesare seemed to have plunged. It seemed that all her entrails had been pushed aside to leave only a great empty, palpitating space in which he moved thickly and expanded with more and more fury.

Ramming in, Cesare was caught on a rhythmic tide of movement in which there seemed to be no thought, no mind, only wild, orgiastic movement and loin-tearing sensation. His penis was chafed and burning and seemed to be still growing, thickening in its every particle, stiffening still when it had seemed utterly stiff before.

His gasps came with rhythmic regularity. Every in-stroke pulled breath from his mouth.

He leaned forward, grasping her tiny waist which seemed so fragile under the voluptuous hips that it looked as if it might snap. He held it on either side, gripping it fiercely, revelling in the feel of the tight flesh and the power that he felt in having her body completely at his command. He pressed her waist down against the bed, forcing it to yield. He drew back and rammed into her with shattering force so that her head grazed forward along the coverlet. He drew back again and shattered in again, tearing into her brutally, savagely, hearing her cry out, losing his whole rigid length in her with a single long thrust. As he drove in he pulled her waist toward him so that her round buttocks crushed back to meet his thrust and helped his searing entry.

He varied his stroke, giving short, quick little thrusts in a quick series and then he reverted to long, slow strokes, bringing from her a fresh gasp or groan with every variation of pressure and movement.

"Oh, oh, oh — I'm coming!"

Her wailing moan came up to him and he gritted his teeth in the brutal ecstasy. His fury had produced her orgasm.

He hurried himself, tensing his loins, grinding his inside, with mental and physical aid, feeling the knot of sensation tighten and complicate in his genitals.

He heard her gasp several short, furious emissions of breath. She rammed back at him as if he couldn't penetrate her enough and then she gave out a long, wild wail which slowly choked and faded into a background of groaning whimpers.

Now, now, now, he told himself as he heaved and bucked over her buttocks which still undulated around him.

He gnashed his teeth, feeling the climax upon him. He pushed her waist flat down toward the bed, wanting to destroy her in the sadistic urge which his near orgasm sent quivering and tumulting through his whole body so that even his toes seemed to tingle with it.

He wanted to split her right apart. He couldn't tell what he wanted. He wanted to go further to achieve some end to his thrusting which he had not yet achieved.

Almost crying with the excruciation of sensation, he knew the end was coming up. It twirled and spun in his genitals, growing into a great, inexorable force. And with a great, hot, slippery outrush it spiralled through his depths, raced like a sharp pain along his pounding rod and broke out in a wild mob of scattering sperm which lashed up and around deep inside her.

He collapsed over her and after a while they rolled over and lay exhausted in each other's arms.

"Darling, I don't think dear Alphonse would have been quite capable, somehow," Lucrezia said softly at last.

Cesare smiled and began gently and expertly to caress her breasts.

CHAPTER 17

When some days later Lucrezia Borgia rode north with her young husband it was as if the lucky star of the Borgia family had left with her. Ominous clouds were gathering to change the fortunes which never seemed to have been so high as at this moment with Cesare, Duke of Romagna and the Pope on good terms with Louis and Ferdinand and Isabella of Spain.

Cesare's dreams at this time were centered on the consolidation for himself of a kingdom which would comprise all of central Italy. Vaulting ambition was already beginning to o'erleap itself in his heart. He glimpsed in those dreams of his a conquest even further which would eventually drive both the Spanish and the French from Italy, leaving the whole peninsula in his hands. And then perhaps? Who could say that the glory of the Roman Empire was dead forever . . . ?

At first it seemed that his campaign might succeed. He accomplished what amounted to almost the total subjugation of the Camerino in the space of a very few weeks. But the very fact of his growing power was breeding him more and more enemies — and more and more powerful enemies. Tuscany, Venice and Florence were all worried by the enlarging weight of his mailed fist and agreements were come to between them in preparation for future action. Milan, too, joined the league and rumor had it that the only thing that kept Louis XII himself out of Italy and a containment of the Borgian realm, was that he still needed the Pope's favor in connection with Naples — where the spoils of war were being violently disputed, between the victorious contestants.

Rebellions were provoked among Cesare's mercenaries, by his enemies, for offered reward. He found himself moving hither and yon over Italy crushing first one and then another, growing weary and uncertain in the process.

Although he returned eventually to Rome with a semblance of order in his territories, he knew that powerful Venice was stayed from attacking him only by doubts as to which side the King of France would take in the event of war.

A short time after his return to Rome both Cesare and the Pope fell ill of a mysterious fever which, it was thought, may have been the result of poisoning deliberately designed by their enemies.

The beginnings of their sickness could be traced to a dinner given in the Vatican by the Pope for a number of his cardinals.

So corrupted was the Church from earlier ideals that it was not beyond the bounds of possibility that one of his own ambitious and envious cardinals had contrived to slip some poison into the wine that was drunk and had intended Cesare to be affected also as his temporal power was sufficient to "arrange" the next papacy should his father die.

Father and son both lay for a week between life and death in their rooms in the Vatican. The old man, being of less robust constitution, fought vainly against the inevitable.

Late one evening, with Cesare still tortured by the fever in an adjacent apartment, Pope Alexander — the Cardinal Roderigo that was — feebly summoned his cardinals to his bedside. For a long time they stood in his presence watching his deathlike face, waiting for words which did not come.

When his voice broke through lips which hardly moved, his words seemed to come from some other place than the room in which they stood.

"For years," he murmured — and they

moved softly forward the better to hear — "I have bargained with the devil." He raised his half-closed eyes with an effort to take in the faces of those around his bed and a trace of a smile flickered over his visage.

"A full ... and devilish ... life and I'm not afraid to pay. The devil is not unkind to his disciples ..."

There was a deathly hush in the room. All were aghast, but none dared interrupt this voice coming from the verge of death. There was a flutter-like movement among them as, with a superhuman effort, the old man raised himself up and gazed beyond his bed, but the flutter died into petrification.

"I am coming," he breathed. "I am coming ... it is just ..."

He lay back on his pillow. He was dead.

Those present crossed themselves. Nobody said a word. Each was thinking of his own end, his own life, strayed from the paths of righteousness.

It was only after they'd left the quiet room and were on the broad marble steps which led down, that one whispered to another: "Whom was he talking to? What was just?"

"It was not God in the room with him," the other replied.

Within a few days, the body of Alexander, after exposure on a catafalque in full pontificals in St. Peter's, was removed to the Chapel of Santa Maria delle Febbre.

It was a sweltering day and the poison in the Pope's body aided his obesity in the quick decomposition of his body so that his face had become almost black and looked like some macabre creature from the underworld.

Those who gathered to watch the corpse pass

saw in the blackened, grotesque features the entry of the devil himself into the body.

"That's what happens when you fuck your daughter," declared some peasant bystander, who'd heard the rumors which had sounded all over the kingdom and beyond.

"Then you'd better have your carcass burned as soon as you go," retorted his neighbor.

There was a roar of laughter which seemed to infuriate the first speaker. It was true he had a reputation for initiating his 11-year-old daughter in the rites of love and he was touchy on the point. Rounding on his tormentor he dealt him a lusty blow on the jaw. This brought the intervention of another of the crowd and in no time a battle royal was being waged along the side of the road.

The bearers of the body tried desperately to keep a straight and steady path, but as the crowd swarmed and fought around them, one of them lost his balance and the catafalque, body and bearers found themselves rolling in the dust amidst a mob of flailing legs and arms.

It was the lot of Pope Alexander to be embroiled in violence right to the very coffin.

CHAPTER 18

Cesare recovered slowly, becoming conscious and clear in mind long before he'd regained sufficient physical strength to leave his sickbed.

The northern allies took quick advantage of the absence of both a Pope and a general to lead the Holy Forces. Venice came out in her true colors, sallied across the border and helped to reinstate half the tyrants whom Cesare had driven from the Romagna.

In Rome itself, the powerful Orsini, enemies of the Duke, proved so strong that he was forced to recall a thousand men from the northern provinces for his personal protection in the vulnerable Vatican.

So many of his troops, under treaty obligation, were engaged with Louis of France in checking the Spaniards in Naples that Cesare could do nothing but chafe in his bed and wait for reverse after reverse of his forces, weakened as they were, in Romagna and Camerino.

Meanwhile, in the Vatican, the Sacred College assembled to ask for Holy Inspiration in the election of a new Pope. Whatever divine guidance was expected, due regard was paid by the various factions to letters from Venice and France in which — through the medium of the ambassadors — the cardinals of each of those nationalities were ordered to vote for the favored of the particular power.

Three candidates — any of which would have been hostile to Cesare — appeared, however, in almost equal strength and a compromise had temporarily to be made in the election of someone entirely different — weak and doddering Cardinal Francesco Piccolomini — while the factions canvassed and manipulated to improve their positions *vis-à-vis* one another.

So a feeble, illness-tormented octogenarian became Pius III.

The new Pope was with Cesare, not against him, indicated his displeasure to Venice and issued briefs to the reinstated tyrants commanding their obedience to the Holy See. The Venetians also received a command from France that they desist in their activities under pain of Louis' displeasure. It was the least he could do now that the Borgian power was broken and while he still needed Cesare's troops in Naples and clear passage through Rome.

Cesare, at last able to rise from his bed and buckle on his sword, found Rome so dangerous, with emissaries from the tyrants and even from Venice hidden in the city with orders to kill him, that he had to pass from the Vatican to the Castle of San' Angelo by the way of a secret underground passage connecting them.

There he summoned his captains, planned to withdraw some of his men from the banners of the King of France and prepared to attempt the arduous task of reestablishing his power and his dukedoms.

Even while plans were under way, a further blow shattered the Duke's hopes. Pius III, for whom excitement of succeeding to high office had, perhaps, proved too much, died suddenly overnight. And with his death came a fresh wave of attacks in the north. It seemed that even the voice of France — tied up as the French were in Naples — had little weight in checking the violence which lost Cesare city after city of his old territories.

* * *

The strongest candidate for the Papacy was a life-long enemy of the Borgias, Cardinal della Rovere. This was the man whom Roderigo Borgia had defeated in the Conclave of 1492 and kept out of the coveted throne for 12 years. This was the man who for a number of years had nursed his hatred under a mask of friendship and flattery toward the Pope and Cesare Borgia.

Cardinal della Rovere's election was certain but for one thing, the possible non-support of the Spanish cardinals with whom Cesare wielded considerable influence. A bargain was struck: for the votes of these Spanish cardinals, della Rovere would confirm Cesare in his office of Gonfalonier and Captain-General and support and preserve his title to Romagna.

Cesare felt the ground of his influence with the Spanish cardinals and then agreed to these terms. The election of the longest-standing enemy of the House of Borgia was ensured. For once, and fatally, Cesare's political brain had allowed him to go astray.

Giuliano della Rovere took the name of Julius II at his election and a few days later issued briefs to the Romagna towns that Cesare was to be obeyed. But insurrection and invasion continued in the north and Cesare prepared to go himself into the Romagna and raise a fresh army from loyal subjects in the once liberated cities.

The new Pope asked that Tuscany and the enemy city of Florence should grant Cesare a safe conduct through the territory he would have to cross, but intimated in private dispatches that he quite understood the disturbances in the north were against Cesare Borgia and not against the Church. With this indication of the turn of events were likely to take, no safe conduct was forthcoming.

Out of patience, Cesare asked for the escort of the Pontifical navy by sea to Genoa from which point he would travel into the Romagna via Ferrara. The Pope acquiesced and Cesare set out.

While Cesare was still at sea, news came that the Venetians had captured Faenza and were massing powerful armies in the Duke's lands. Pope Julius came out into the open at last and sent a message to Cesare suggesting that he surrendered the pontifical fiefs into the Pope's hands in an effort to bring law and order into the Romagna.

Cesare, smelling a rat at last, refused and was immediately arrested by the captain of the navy on the Pope's orders.

Julius broke his agreement blatantly and appointed a bishop as new governor of Cesare's old territories. As it was against Cesare that the enemy was moving, he speciously held the only way to bring peace was for the territories to come directly into his own hands under the Church.

Cesare was brought back to Rome and virtually held a prisoner in the Vatican while the war in the north, in spite of the Pope's argument, continued.

While, Cesare, stripped of his titles, property and power, was being treated with an outward show of friendliness in the Vatican, news came of the resounding victory of Gonzalo de Cordoba in Naples. French power was smashed south of Rome. Ferdinand and Isabella, became monarchs of Naples. Spanish influence with the Pope rose like a sudden heat wave.

Not wishing to make a wrong move which could endanger his position, Julius allowed Cesare to depart by sea to the north where he was to enter France. It amounted virtually to deportation.

But, not far out from Ostia, Cesare, with his few loyal men, had his ship turned about and made full sail for Naples to seek asylum in the Spanish camp where he was assured of a friendly welcome.

There, he found other members of the Borgia family, rallying around Gonzalo de Cordoba in an attempt to escape the antagonism of the Pope, and he was made very welcome by the Great Captain with whose troops he had fought in the original quelling of Naples.

Encouraged by the success in the south, Spain was, in fact, considering an invasion of Tuscany — which was allied to France — and then Milan. It was confidently hoped to drive all French power and influence out of the peninsula which for so long had been dominated by a Spanish-born Pope; Cesare was such an obvious choice to lead an expedition into country that he knew well and which bordered areas where he still had friends, that he was chosen a few days after his arrival to lead the Spanish troops north.

This choice gave Cesare fresh hope for his dreams. With the peninsula subjugated to Spain he saw himself in the role of pro-consul, wielding a complete power, divorced from the distant Spanish Crown. But it was not to be.

Nothing could go right for the Borgias after so many years of everything dropping into their laps.

A few days before he was due to depart at the head of a sizeable army, Cesare was arrested by the order of Gonzalo de Cordoba himself.

In the wings of action, diplomatic exchanges had been passing from Julius to the Spanish monarchs and back. The Pope in these exchanges had complained bitterly and with skill of Cesare's refusal to hand the Romagna to the Church in spite, he alleged, of the desires of the local populace, and of the Borgia's designs on an all-powerful state which he would try to expand againt Spanish and French influence, coveting for himself the lordship of all territory south of the Alps.

So successfully did he plead his cause — which, indeed, was not without a basis of fact in its latter hypotheses — that Ferdinand and Isabella took fright. They had heard distant echoes of the determination and ability to succeed with his projected plans of Cesare Borgia and they had no desire to risk a future colony by placing its formation in the hands of a ruthless man who would use their power for his own ends.

Word was sent to Gonzalo de Cordoba and — reluctantly — he complied with the order from his monarchs. Cesare was held in close confinement.

In vain did his friends and his sister Lucrezia write to the new Gonfalonier of the Church to exert his influence with the Pope in securing Cesare's release; the very ardor of their pleas seemed to frighten Julius into renewing his persecution of Cesare's name.

All his former officers were rounded up — some of them fortifying towns they still held in his name and giving bitter resistance — and brought to Rome where they were tortured in an effort to make them sign statements as to the selfish aims of their former chief.

In August of 1504, Cesare Borgia was once again on the high seas. But the bright Mediterranean sun and the loveliness of the azure sea afforded him little joy. He was bound for a Spanish dungeon in the fortress of Medina del Campo where his power would have no hope of revival and his dreams of glory fade into memories of what used to be.

CHAPTER 19

Lucrezia was riding south on what, so she had assured her husband, was a sentimental journey to see her father's grave and visit the places of her youth. In fact, she had come to plead and use every means at her disposal to persuade the Pope to use his influence in securing her brother's release from the Spanish prison in which he was languishing, and from which an occasional letter arrived telling her of his boredom and depression although he was not treated unkindly.

Lucrezia had little to offer. But one trump still remained with her — the undecaying beauty of her flesh. Della Rovere was accounted just as much a libertine as his predecessors and Lucrezia in a moment of sarcastic humor had declared that to have been the source of gratification for three Popes should open the gates of heaven for her without fail.

She traveled with a small retinue of ladies-in-waiting and a posse of men-at-arms. Her passing occasioned no apprehension in territories which once would have regarded her as a potential spy. Her brother was being forgotten. Some people were no longer sure whether he was dead or alive. Talk was centered rather on the possibility of Spanish invasion, which, since Cesare's departure, had come to nothing so far.

Lucrezia and her party were received with mock cordiality by Julius and accommodated in the Vatican for a short stay. Della Rovere could guess why the beautiful Borgia had come and he was interested to see what her pleading and encouragement would be.

Over a luncheon which the two of them had

alone in the Pope's private quarters, Lucrezia had broached the subject.

"My dear lady," the Pope said, thinking at the same time what an exquisite creature she was and wondering just how true were all the stories he'd heard, "your brother is a remarkable man, but remarkableness alone is not enough to allow a man pardon for misdeeds."

"But what did he do? Didn't he recapture for the Holy See lands that had long been lost?"

"He dreamed himself another Caesar, dear lady, but Caesars depend not only on personal qualities. They depend upon propitious circumstances at the right time. The world has, perhaps, become more complicated than in the days of Republic and Empire. Too many powers are equal, so much more depends on compromise, alliance, knowing when to change allies and how to maneuver a man out of favor with his superiors."

"A cynical outlook."

"One that your brother practiced well enough in his day, but failed to maintain to the bitter end."

"But if he were permitted to return to Rome, Capua — anywhere — and undertook to take no part in political or military life. What would you say to that?"

"I would say, my lady, that a man's word is a reed which will bend and bend and eventually snap."

"Do you think me beautiful?"

The Pope was startled by this change of flow in the conversation. But he replied with a smile which contained a hint of lechery.

"Your beauty is well-known, madam, and likewise your accomplishment."

He placed an impudent emphasis on the final

word and his eyes moved down to her neck and the low bodice which revealed the rising swell of her breasts.

Lucrezia's heart beat rapidly. This thought of giving herself to a lifelong enemy, of having his prick gouge her where her dear father's and beloved Cesare's had been before, was a bitter pill. But she had nothing else to offer.

"My accomplishment is admirable," she said brazenly, "but it demands that return be made."

"I see. If I don't mistake you, you are offering to be my mistress at the price of your brother's freedom — as far as my persuasion can achieve it."

Julius' penis had moved and staggered up at the thought. This would be sweet vengeance, indeed. The old man dead, the son in prison and now the daughter to lie under him while he made her a harlot, punishing her body with his bludgeon to push home the subservience of the Borgia family to his will in the most sadistically dominating manner. And why need he keep his word. She had no way of enforcing it. She was completely at his mercy. She had to take him at his word.

"Your brother would be unable to resist trying to avenge your family's honor," he hedged, feeling for how serious her proposal was.

Her hand came under the table at which they sat and rested on his thigh, a warm, foreign pressure, harbinger of things to come.

"He shall never know," she said.

His eyes moved over her. The whiteness of her soft skin at the half-bulge of her breasts was a spur. It was so little of that beautiful body to see and it made the hidden remainder superbly exciting.

He leaned forward and kissed the white, soft

patch and Lucrezia closed her eyes to hide her shame. She felt his lips glide over the revealed bulge and his fingers pull her dress away at its top so that he could look down the front. The man was a piggish brute.

But while her thoughts were those of hatred, her actions belied them and her hand moved up his thigh and pulled at the hard core of flesh she could feel under his robes. The Pope drew back his head and looked at her. She opened her eyes and smiled, forcing her look to be one of invitation.

Julius was suddenly hot with desire. To know that this famous beauty would be his, all naked in a bed, her whole body at his disposal. It was too much for a man like him to resist — particularly as he was not bound to make any return.

"I agree to your terms," he said.

She took her hand off his erect penis and he felt naked and filled with passion.

"How shall I know you will keep your word?"

"I will draft out the letter and send it off immediately."

"Very well."

Lucrezia was well aware of the probability of trickery, but her bargain was a long shot. She had to take a chance if anything was to be done for her brother.

Julius, now, could hardly keep his hands off her and as they stood up he took her in his arms and pulled her to him. He crushed his lips hungrily on hers and she fought down her anger and opened her lips so that she could flick her tongue into his mouth.

She drew back as his hand began to fumble with her body.

"Later," she said.

He laughed fiercely and rang a bell for his servants.

Lucrezia watched while the letter was written. When it was powdered and signed, she took it in her hands and read it with a glow of hope. It explained that due to new information which had come to light, Cesare Borgia was, in fact, no longer considered guilty of the motives which had previously been ascribed to him. It asked, on behalf of the Pope, that he be returned to Rome as soon as possible as his services were needed.

The letter was sealed, a courier summoned and then dispatched to Ostia that the document might leave on the next ship setting sail for Spain. He had hardly left the Vatican when he was intercepted and the letter taken from him to be burnt to ashes within minutes.

Lucrezia, all unaware of the promptness of the treachery, feeling that there was a good chance of Cesare's rejoining her within the next month or so prepared to fulfill her side of the bargain.

The Pope excused himself for a few minutes to give her time to undress. While she stripped herself of her few garments, bitter and almost tearful at preparing to be ignominiously used by the oldest enemy of her family, the Pope was inviting one of his nearest cardinals, Cardinal Rimini, to secrete himself in the papal rooms and witness all that followed. For so overjoyed and proud was the Pope that the beautiful, luscious daughter of his old enemy was to open her legs in subjection to him that he could not keep it to himself. Only by having a witness could he be sure that he would be believed if ever he told the story. The thought of a voyeur—and how that would further humiliate Lucrezia—added to his own lecherous expectation of enjoyment.

So by the time Julius returned to his bedroom, where Lucrezia lay on the bed, naked, not looking at him, Cardinal Rimini had slipped into the papal apartment and was peering through the crack of an open door at the beautiful and unexpected sight.

"So this is the luscious Lucrezia Borgia," Julius said, with a slight break in his voice as he saw her curved nudity. He flicked his tongue over dry lips. Her buttocks and breasts were the most superb he'd seen in his life, full and juicy but with a firmness which indicated a power in the act and a luster which made them look as smooth as he was to find they felt. Her shoulders were slim, her waist tiny, which accentuated the voluptuous quality of her rotundities. Her thighs were soft and full, with muscles hidden under the surface which could work like a Trojan when her body was afire.

"A bargain well made," he added, with theatrical hypocrisy.

Lucrezia turned her eyes toward him as he stripped off his robes. He had an ugly narrow body, with a rough, pockmarked skin. His prick which pointed out at her like a cannon seemed out of proportion to the rest of his body. It looked wicked and capable of producing pain and desecration.

"How do you find that?" he asked, taking it in his hand and holding it toward her. Obviously he'd been told by other conquests that he had a prick second to none.

"I have seen its equals," Lucrezia lied with a haughty irritation.

"Never its superior, however," he chuckled.

He came toward the bed and the sight of his

prick almost frightened her. Belonging to a desired friend she would have regarded it with a trembling anticipation. It promised a brutal and therefore ecstatic penetration. But, belonging as it did to an enemy, she felt it had the power to humiliate and destroy her.

The Pope stretched out on the bed beside her and his hands trembled as they began to feel her body. She shivered with repressed antipathy as she felt his hated hands foraging her breasts and buttocks, stroking her thighs. She hated him more than ever now that the moment had come and she saw in his eyes as he bent and ravaged her lips, a gleam of triumph mingled with his passion.

She felt no answering passion. His body, his face, the whole hostile idea of his position repelled her. He was the master. She had sold herself to him. He was not lost and reveling in his passion, he was owning her—with passion —but cruelly, knowing that she could not escape him, had no option but to submit to what he demanded from her body.

"Ah, I want you, I want you," he whispered hoarsely, as if the very sound of the words increased the power he felt over her.

"You're mine, mine. Lucrezia Borgia, you're mine!"

She uttered a little cry at the wanton ring in his words and the cry was muffled in her groan as, with a quick movement he mounted her and thrust into her dry vagina.

The dryness, unresponsiveness of her flesh tore at his prick, drawing a hoarse cry from his lips.

"Oh, oh, you beauty—you slave!" he shouted, his voice broken with ecstatic fury.

Lucrezia, pain shooting between her thighs,

winced at his words. She had never been taken thus. She was virtually being raped. She hated the man who was joined in one flesh with her.

Her passage was so dry that his penis scraped and drubbed it so that it seemed to her he must be drawing blood. She relaxed. It was too painful not to, and gradually her channel moistened a little and his progress became easier and with it her comfort greater.

Julius was determined to be brutal. Watching the old man die and going to the devil, breaking Cesare's power and getting him imprisoned were not made of the same physical revenge as this—this flesh-to-flesh punishment and chastisement of the living body.

He saw the disgust and self-hatred in her face and the hatred of himself and it increased his appetite for savagery so that he crashed his prick into her with all the force of his loins, so that their crotches met in a smack which was bruising and made her cry out.

He pushed her thighs out and up so that they were waving at first out over the bed and then crushed back against her shoulders. She was doubled up under him, twisted and pain-racked, with her naked toes against the sides of his hips and the whole pressure of his upraised body meeting hers at the out-curved point of his loins, culminating in the stiff tree of organ that rammed into her with increasing force and vigor.

Forgotten, out in the next room, with his fine view of the proceedings, Cardinal Rimini was beside himself. He had never in his wildest dreams hoped to see even the breast of such a woman as Lucrezia Borgia. And now to be seeing all—and to be seeing it in operation. It was too much for a man to bear.

On the bed, Lucrezia felt as if she were suffocating under the narrow, bony body of her invader. His prick, digging to its full depth in her, seemed to be splitting her passage, to be tearing away layers of it in a painful, sickening, widening process.

He was mouthing oaths and wild expressions of his power over her. He called her names, harlot names and spat words like "fuck" and "cunt" at her as if they would physically hurt her.

Hurt and seared with pain, Lucrezia moved her head from side to side, biting her lips. His words humiliated her and in conjunction with having her legs cramped and defenseless as she lay naked on her back under him and felt his penis filling her loins with a persistent, drubbing, dominating rhythm, the humiliation was overwhelming.

His hands pulled and twisted her breasts as he undulated on her. He made them into weird shapes and she cried out with protest at the pain and tried to wriggle free. But she seemed to be pinned to the bed as with a spear by his enormous fleshy weapon. Her body was being ransacked, torn and turned inside out for the savage pleasure of an old enemy who had her at his mercy.

She opened her eyes and saw his eyes on her face, taking in her fear and horror. His eyes were mad with lust and triumph and his mouth twisted into an ugly gash of sadism from which burst roaring explosions of passion as he speared her.

Lucrezia closed her eyes again to keep the sight of him away from her, but its image followed her eyes, creeping under the closed lids, making a picture in the darkness, which the physical touch of his rapacious taking of her body seemed to hold in position no matter how she tried to thrust it out.

She heard him growing frantic with excitement and her crotch and lower buttocks were aching where his loins around that protruding sword rammed at them. There was pain and aching and hatred all contained in a melting pot which was her vagina.

And suddenly there was something else. Her head had been caught by hot hands and, while Julius still drummed into her with frenzy, a hot, pliable-feeling penis was wormed into her mouth which opened in astonishment.

The excitement of watching had become too much for Cardinal Rimini. The soothing touch of his own hand on his prick was not soothing enough. He needed something cooler, something more foreign, some part of the luscious fruit of a woman on the bed to coax his juices from him.

For several minutes he had stood, trembling, fondling his organ in the doorway in full view of their unseeing eyes. He had gone through fear and desire in quick succession, alternately several times, until he could stand it no more. He would risk the Pope's displeasure. The woman was obviously in no position to resist.

With a guilty, scuffling movement, he had rushed to the bedside, seized her face and thrust himself into her mouth.

His eyes took in the Pope as he did so and the Pope nodded and he said through his gasps: "Take care of him Lucrezia, or I'll recall the letter."

Infamy, infamy. Lucrezia felt a tear roll from her eye. She was helpless and chastened. To be doing this against her will and with these men who had brought about her brother's downfall. The tears were rage and humiliation, with the rage suppressed of necessity.

She began to work. The sooner it was over the better.

On top of her still, the Pope had slipped his hands under her buttocks, raising them slightly off the bed and was squeezing them so hard that it made her cry out. He was gasping and groaning in a wild excresence of sound and his loins were not only pummelling at her but undergoing contortions in every direction as well.

The object in her mouth had bloated until she could hardly breathe. She bit it with a sudden supreme fury at what was being forced on her and the bite brought a wild, wavering cry from the lips of Cardinal Rimini.

Lucrezia, still struggling for breath, looked up at the Pope. Her pelvis was numb with its buffeting and her quim was a raging area of pain. She saw his head go back and then come forward sharply so that his eyes could look at her. The eyes dilated and he emitted a shrill gasp as he came into the pain that he'd caused her. There was savage conquest in his eyes and the thought that this man's sperm was a great lake in her belly was the final humiliation.

CHAPTER 20

"Mate!" said Cesare, as he moved his knight, exposing the clear path between his castle and his opponent's king. Count Benavente sighed and then smiled.

"I begin to understand why your enemies

find you such a redoubtable opponent," he said. "May I never be among them."

"Come, your mind wasn't on the play."

Count Benavente, who had been a frequent visitor to Cesare's confinement quarters these last few weeks, pushed back his chair from the table and stood up, looking not at Cesare but at the chessboard. He walked away after a second or two and stared out of the narrow window to the flat, green land a hundred or more feet below. Cesare watched him without speaking.

"I was thinking," the Count said, "of the matter we mentioned a few days ago."

Cesare glanced quickly at the door and then back at the Count.

"It's too well guarded," he said quietly. "You'd need an army."

"For once I believe I'm right and you're wrong," the Count continued. "But of course I know the place and the people in a way you couldn't possibly."

Cesare didn't answer. It was clear the Count had been mulling over some plan. Best let him speak. He liked the Count, who was a good, upright man and one of the most powerful lords in this part of Spain. He was aware, too, that in some way he fascinated the man, who had lost no opportunity of visiting, talking to and playing chess with him once their acquaintanceship had been made.

"I think, in fact..." At this point the Count, too, turned and glanced at the heavy wooden door which was closed. "I think you could be away from here within a few days."

Cesare quickened with interest. This sounded like something concrete. If he could get out of this fortress he'd start immediately to find ways and means of getting back to Italy for the reconquest of his realms — and then death to anyone who tried to stop him. He had many accounts to settle.

The Count played idly with a pawn, his brow creased in concentration. When he looked up at Cesare, his eyes were intent with purpose.

"I have bribed the guard two nights from now," he said softly, "and we have the help of one of the governor's servants. At two in the morning a rope will be lowered from the battlements. It will pass your window . . . "

The Count took several quick steps across the room and studied the window.

"Yes . . ." he said. "There's just room for you to squeeze through — but you must be careful. You will climb down the rope — preceded by the servant who will make sure that everything is safe — and my men will be waiting above the castle ditch."

Cesare got up slowly, his eyes shining. He moved over to the Count and took his hand, pressing it in both his own. The Count returned the pressure with a smile.

"Some men were meant to be hermits," he said, "but not you."

"But the risk to you . . ."

"Little enough and worth the trouble. My men will escort you at all speed to Santander. I will provide you with money and you should be able to get a boat immediately to France." He smiled wanly: "My only regret is that I shall be deprived of your play and your conversation—but we shall meet again."

"I hope I shall live to repay you," Cesare said.

"Oh, come, it's a small enough thing. Any man with blood would do such for another were it in his power. But . . . " he became practical again, "it must be done with no noise for only the two guards on the western battlements are in our pay."

He shook Cesare's hand again.

"My dear Duke, I must take my leave. I'll come again on the day to assure you that everything is unchanged."

When the heavy door with its fastenings had grated shut and been bolted behind the Count, Cesare sat down at the chessboard. How long had he been here? He'd lost count of the months. He'd had odd contacts with the outside world beyond the Spanish frontier. His sister Lucrezia had written saying that she had pleaded with the Pope and that Julius had sent off a letter of reprieve. Whatever had happened, Cesare had not been released. He wondered what machinations had gone on to account for Lucrezia's certainty and then the lack of results. Certainly to get even with the Pope and then with Gonzalo de Cordoba would be two of his most desired objectives. He would offer himself to Louis. At the head of a French army, he'd soon have the whole peninsula falling over itself to make terms with him.

Smiling, he lifted a knight from the board and with it, triumphantly took a bishop.

CHAPTER 21

Through the narrow embrasure was the free, sleeping, peaceful world. The stars were out. It was a clear, moonlit night, which was a pity.

Beside Cesare was the Governor's servant, a small man, with quick intelligent eyes who kept his gaze fixed on the oblong of light.

"There!" he said suddenly.

Cesare felt a needling in his stomach as he saw the thick rope snake down across the window, swing away out of sight for a second and then float back again to be grabbed by the man at his side.

Quickly he helped his companion up onto the still of the embrasure. The man squeezed the top part of his body through and looked back.

"Better wait until I'm off, Sire," he whispered. "It would be wise not to put too much weight on the rope."

"Yes, yes. Off you go!" Cesare said quickly.

He watched while the man took the strain on his arms and pulled himself through the opening. He swung out high over the ground and the rope swayed away from the sheer wall of the battlements and then back, grazing him along its stone surface.

In what seemed like agonizingly slow time he began to go down the rope hand under hand, his feet twisted around it, helping to take the strain.

Cesare climbed onto the sill and knelt precariously, peering out. Down below he could see the servant descending, growing smaller, just the top of his head a vague black mass. He looked down to the distant ground. He couldn't see Benavente's men but he had no doubt they'd be there, waiting in the shadows and that above the guards were watching, cursing at the time it took for the prisoner to escape, risking their skins a little more with every second that passed.

He shifted his cramped position on the sill. Hurry man, hurry! He could see the black dot, but it was impossible to tell now whether it was going down or had stopped. At any rate the man was still on the rope, holding him back from launching himself in the void.

Cesare strained his eyes into the moonlit darkness. It was gloomy in the shadow of the walls, which cut off the moon. What was the matter with the man? His head was still there, a tiny, indistinct point far down, surely not far from the ground. He seemed not to be moving.

And then the point moved and even from his height Cesare heard the thud. A groan rose on the still air and vaguely he saw shadows moving in a flurry down in the deep, empty ditch.

The fool, the idiot! What had he done—got tangled with the rope? There was another groan, sounding like thunder in the motionless night.

Cesare caught the rope which swung in loosely towards him. He heard challenging shouts from somewhere down near the gates of the fortress and cursed. What a bungling farce! He could have spat with rage, but he kept his head, swinging out from the embrasure and back against the rough wall as he began to let hand under hand and slide his feet with the rope between them.

He felt the chafing on his hands, but speed was essential, he had not time to lower himself in correct, comfortable fashion.

Lights were flashing a way off on the ground and he slid faster. Up above there were shouts on the battlements too. The bribed guards could not pretend to be blind for so long without risking their necks.

Down, down with a blank face of wall, a turmoil in his stomach, a long drop to the ditch and noise and light growing off on his right.

"Hurry!" He heard the single, sharp shout

from below and slid so rapidly that he could feel the skin being torn on his hands.

And then another cry—of warning.

"The rope is short—take care!"

Cesare glanced down into the gloom which had cleared sufficiently to enable him to see several of Benavente's men, with the Count at the head of them, and to see the dangling end of the rope some fifteen feet short of the ground. Along in the ditch he saw some of the men trying to lift the servant, who was still groaning audibly.

He swarmed down the last few feet of rope, measured the dangerous distance to the ground and jumped—just as the rope was cut from above. It came hurtling down on top of him, heavy and painful. But he landed with nothing more than a shaking and probably a bruised arm and knee as he fell sideways.

With furious haste he was pulled from the ditch by Benavente's men as shouts from the castle barked out close by.

From further along the ditch one of the men called.

"He seems to have both legs broken—it's difficult to move him."

Cesare, slightly winded, his ears singing, was pulled onto a horse as cries of recognition sounded from the corner of the wall down which he had crawled. A small crowd of guards were racing toward the group. Behind them was commotion and sounds of horses clattering over the lowered drawbridge.

The Count thrust a sword into Cesare's hand.

"Take that my friend—you'll have to use it yet."

He called back to his men in the ditch.

"Leave him!"

There was no hope of escape with an injured man. And it was important that the Count was not recognized.

They could see the light of the moon glinting on the pikes and swords of their pursuers as they wheeled and set their horses at a gallop away from the fortress. There was a crash of gunshot from the castle turrets and then they were outdistancing the guards who faded back into anonymous shadows, calling and shouting to the horsemen who were yelling for direction.

Cesare's head cleared as they streamed through the night air, setting up a wind from their rapid motion through its stillness. He could feel the irritating pains in his arm and leg, but they were worth nothing compared with the exhilarating vigor he felt in freedom.

They rode at all speed until there was neither sight nor sound of any pursuit.

"A narrow success," the Count called against the wind as he galloped beside Cesare.

"A little spice to give it perfection," Cesare called back, laughing into the wind.

CHAPTER 22

"I tell you, you can name your price," Cesare said.

The ship's master with whom he spoke turned a steady searching gaze on him. There was no compromise in his hard eyes.

"I tell you that my route is not to France—and I know of nobody else who has such a direction."

He stared hard at Cesare.

"Besides, from what you sound there's danger in it—and I'll not risk my ship for any money."

"As you wish," Cesare sighed. "The loss is yours."

He bade the captain goodnight and left the tavern.

Throughout the small town, the Count's men were plying all and sundry with similar questions. Meeting at pre-determined times in an auberge down near the seashore they discussed their latest lack of success. All efforts so far had been in vain. Nobody was able or willing to take the risk of going off his route with a man who was obviously in some way an enemy of the State.

The Count himself had taken his leave of the party earlier, to return to his domain, leaving several of his men to aid Cesare in Santander. He had not anticipated such difficulty as the party was now encountering.

Meeting for the umpteenth time to quaff ale in the little inn within sound of the waves breaking on the shore, Cesare and the Count's men were glum with failure.

"We'll have a last attempt," Cesare said at last, downing his liquor and rising. "If it fails then there's one thing left—I'll have to cross the frontier into Navarre."

"You run more risk on land than on sea."

"I run more risk still stuck here without hope of escape."

They began, for the last time, to scour the bars and inns of the town, cutting it into sections, working methodically.

It was in a little tavern where everyone seemed to be slightly the worse for drink, that Cesare got what sounded like a hopeful tip. He had sat himself in a corner to take stock of those in the place, which was alive with noise and the clatter of tankards.

An old seadog, talkative with wine, flopped down on the bench beside him.

"I say that we're the freest of 'em all," he said fiercely, not looking at Cesare, but apparently speaking to him as there was nobody else very near.

"If we don' like our wives we go on a long trip, if we do we go on a short 'un. We got fresh air and good pay an' all the world to see. What more?"

He turned to Cesare, beetling his thick brows, as if he expected argument. His eyes within their crinkled, sunburned lids were bright blue and ringed with little red veins and the yellow wash of age and liquor. His tankard sagged in his hand and there was a beer stain on his old black neckerchief.

"Quite right. Let me fill 'em up on it," Cesare said, taking the tankard from his hand and calling to the skivvy who hopped around and tripped over sprawling feet.

"You'm a stranger. New face around here."

It was a question and the man suddenly seemed soberer than first appearance would have suggested.

"Yes, looking for a boat to take me to France."

"To France?"

The old man gazed reflectively as their filled tankards were set down on the rough table in front of them. He raised his, glanced over Cesare's clothes which were well-to-do although a disguise.

"Your health, sir."

"And yours—and to the free life."

"Aye. You'll get no boat going to France at this time."

"I can pay well. It would be a good bargain."

The old man looked at him again, with his eyes narrowed slightly.

"You'm very anxious to get there."

"A matter of urgent business," Cesare snapped. He was irritated at the man's irrelevant interest in his activities.

"Could be done, I suppose . . . could be done . . ."

"What can you tell me?" Cesare demanded. "It's very urgent."

The old man considered, glancing around the tavern with eyes that seemed to have awakened completely from the half-stupor of liquor.

"Don't know as I ought," he said. "Don't sound legal to me—what you're up to."

"I'll thank you to keep your opinions to yourself," Cesare snapped. "I'll make it worth your while to give me any useful information."

"How worth."

Cesare opened a pouch on his belt and threw some gold pieces on the table. The man's eyes glistened and he stared, fascinated, at the money. He put out his hand to pick them up and Cesare's hand closed on his wrist with a force which made him start.

"Not before you tell me what you have to say."

The man stared at him. He was beginning to wonder with whom he was dealing. There was an authority about the stranger which, even in this familiar seaman's bar where every strong arm would be with him, made his spirit yield.

"All right. Take them off the table."

Cesare grinned and swept the pieces off the table and onto the wooden bench between them.

"She's a ship-owner's widow," the seaman explained. "Lives just on the outskirts o' the town. They say she likes a 'andsome man though she's nothin' to look at 'erself. There was some young duke came through here three year ago with a price on 'is head. 'E went and offered isself to her for work on one of 'er ships and she told him he could 'ave a job if he was nice to 'er." The old man laughed coarsely. "Least thats 'ow the tale goes. Ain't nothin' can 'appen in a place like this without folks get to know about it afore long."

"Where can this woman be found?"

But the old man had warmed to the lechery of his story.

"They do say she's real frustrated—her husband been dead for six year and none as she thinks are suitable as'll have 'er. They do say . . . " he grinned lasciviously . . . "as she likes a little tickle with a rope afore she has 'er cranny stuffed."

He guffawed suddenly in a tone which made the nearest people turn towards him and then grin before resuming their own conversation.

"But o' course if you was goin' to pay, anyway, you probably wouldn' 'ave to pander to 'er every whim."

"Where can this woman be found—enough of your prattle!"

The seaman sobered down although his eyes were still alight with mirth at his humor. He picked up the golden pieces and slipped them quickly into a pocket as if he were afraid to be seen looking at them.

"For another such, I'll show ye."

"Right, but quick about it."

They left the inn and ambled at a pace which exasperated Cesare, through the narrow streets near the seashore. At last the man pointed out a large house on the corner of a narrow street, with a porch and steps over which shone a lantern.

"There—an' I hope you'm feelin fit and 'earty."

Cesare caught him by the arm and held it with a grip which made the old man wince.

"Not a word about this to anyone," he said, knowing that his words were probably useless. "I have men here and if you start shouting this around it'll be the worse for you."

There was real startled fear in the old man's eyes.

"Aye, aye, sir," he said. "I wouldn' want 'em to know as I'd got rich, anyway."

He ambled off into the darkness and Cesare knocked at the door of the big house. Shortly Cesare was being ushered by one of what seemed to be many servants into the presence of the mistress of the house.

After he had explained his business, the woman relapsed into thought, toying with a cushion. He judged her to be about sixty or a little under. She had a commanding face and had probably once been quite beautiful. But now she had grown stout and flabby and the skin hung on her fingers like plain rings.

After a while she looked up at him, lightly studying his face and figure.

"It is a risky thing you're asking," she said.

"I'm offering a good price."

"But I'm not poor. I'm not in great need of money so your price isn't all that interesting to me."

So the town gossip was true. How impossible these small towns were. He decided to make things easy for her.

"But what else can I offer, my dear madam?"

She smiled and stood up. She began to move slowly around the lighted room as if thinking. She stopped in front of a painting, small painting above a grate where a log fire was burning low. He watched her, her stout bottom and belly rustling in her skirts.

"This is a picture of my husband," she said, staring at it.

Cesare moved across the room and stood beside her and just a little behind.

"A good-looking man."

"Yes, he had many virtues and I miss him—particularly in bed."

Cesare smiled. So she was going to brazen it. She didn't look at him. She had crossed the bounds of decorum and was waiting with bated breath to see how he reacted.

"I'm sure the loss is more his."

"Ah, you mustn't say such blasphemy," she said—but quite disarmed at his reply.

She moved away again, leaving him standing beside the portrait. When she turned, her eyes dropped to his loins and then rose to meet his.

"I long for people to take his place—just for a while," she said in a tone which, Cesare was surprised to find, made him feel rather sorry for her.

"Madam, there can be few could resist such an open-hearted admission from such a fine woman as yourself."

"Oh tush!" But she smiled again and moved toward him. "A beautiful person like yourself has no need of elderly women but . . . " she hesitated . . . "that is my price."

"My dear lady you overestimate me. You offer me delight and disparage yourself at the same time."

337

She was pleased with his gallantry even if she hardly believed it. She came toward him and put her hands on his shoulders, her head against his breast as he pressed her body into his.

That it should come to this, Cesare thought with a sardonic humor. But bargainers can't be choosers.

"My husband was so good because he knew my quirks," she said softly, rubbing her loins gently against his, so that in spite of his reservations he found his prick responding.

"Your quirks—you like to be excited in some —abnormal—manner?"

Gallantly he helped her, saving her embarrassment. Besides he was in a hurry.

"Yes—he used to whip me. But I no longer have the whip and, besides, now that I'm a little older, I prefer the more intimate touch of the hand and then perhaps a few strokes from a cane I keep in my boudoir."

Better get it going, Cesare decided. He pushed his hips back at hers and tried to get his hands around her big buttocks. She looked up at him with her mouth open and he lowered his face onto hers as if going into a dungeon. Her skin was rather dry under her powder but she had kept herself well and he was surprised at the keenness of passion with which she responded.

"I'll send the servants to their quarters," she whispered.

She disappeared for several minutes and when she was once again in the doorway, he saw she was dressed in a silk gown which hid her stout flabbiness and gave a certain silken luster to her appearance.

She beckoned and he followed. She led him up a flight of stairs and into a tasteful boudoir with a large bed to one side on which was a long, whippy cane.

"Will you undress?" she pleaded.

He began to slip out of his clothes and she watched as if she would eat his body. When he stood in front of her, naked and with his upstanding penis rearing toward her, he could hear the rustle of the gown where she was trembling. She stared at his body in admiration and desire.

"So young—so strong," she whispered.

She came over to him, opened her gown and enclosed them both in it, crushing against him. He could feel the sag of her breasts, low down on his chest and the bush of hair around her cunt. The fat thighs were hot and met his like bastions.

"Kiss me—and then beat me until I scream," she said fiercely.

He kissed her and she held his prick, squeezing it gently so that he felt the blood running into and expanding it. He was surprisingly excited. It occurred to him that she'd be the oldest woman he'd ever fucked.

She dragged him to the bed, pushed him down, flung off her gown and threw herself face down, sinking into its soft depth. For a moment he gazed at the fat, flabby buttocks which quivered like jelly, so fleshy were they. He glimpsed her breasts, large and hanging down toward her waist. There were rolls of fat at her waist and lines across her thighs. He could see the fringe of a tuft of black hair protruding between her buttocks.

Well, she should have her money's worth. He'd make fine play with that fat, soft body.

He knelt beside her on the bed, holding her down in the small of the back with one hand.

He brought his other sharply down across her buttocks, feeling it sink, stingingly into the flesh, leaving a red and white mark as he lifted it again. She winced and muffled her gasp in the bed. Her buttocks quivered with that jelly-like helplessness and she winced with her whole body.

He raised his hand again and smacked it down in the wake of the first blow. Again she smothered her gasp in the sheets. Again and again he brought down his hand, until she was writhing and squirming and her buttocks were fiery red. Sometimes he stopped, thinking from her stifled scream that she'd had enough, but then she'd raised her smarting bottom up toward him to indicate that she needed yet more.

When her rump was glowing in a single smoldering flush, he took hold of the cane, swished it once in the air and then brought it down with half-force across her backside. It made a single deeper weal across the blush of her puddings. She cried out, made as if to escape, and then pushed her loins hard into the bed, remaining where she was.

Cesare held her firmly with his left hand and brought the cane down with all his force. This time she shrieked with pain and the weal came up immediately, bruised and angry-looking. Three more times, holding her fast as she squirmed and struggled and screamed with the pain, he lashed the flickering stick down across her fat behind and then she cried out in a loud voice.

"Screw me now! Stuff me up, quickly—oh now!"

He pulled her up onto her knees and slipped between them. His prick was stretching and in excitement, invigorated by the thrashing he'd subjected her to. He eased back, directed his organ and surged forward into her, pushing the walls of her vagina aside like earth under a pick.

She quivered and screamed. And he caught those tender buttocks in his hands and began to punish her with his prick, ramming in and in with strong, rough thrusts which jerked her forward on her face every time he reached the extremity of her passage.

She cried out again and again and at last she was laughing and sobbing with joy at the same time. He wondered through his teeth-gritting labor how long it was since she'd had a young man's prick up her cranny.

Every time he jabbed it in a long, breath-sucking stroke, the friction of his loins against her fat pink behind set off her buttocks wobbling furiously. He separated them in rolls of fat and plunged his fingers between their great curves. He pulled on the tuft of black hair he found, making her shriek with ecstacy and skewer her unsupple body against him.

He reached right under her with his other hand and felt through the sticky juices which were beginning to flow. Her clitoris was as hard as a nut, and big, too. He pinched it, hurting her and then held her fat wobbling belly in handfuls, feeling it heave and jump under the emotional and physical turmoil through which she was passing.

"Oh, oh," he heard her cry. "I can't . . . can't bear . . . it."

He slashed her buttocks with his hands, making them roll and squirm and drubbed her harder and harder, pulling his lips back from his teeth in the bone-splitting fury of it.

He could hardly feel anything now, just a

light slippery stroke as he thrust in and up. Only at the very end was there sharp sensation for him. But she was racing to a climax. A climax, it seemed, such as could hardly be imagined.

He had difficulty in holding her upright on the bed. She seemed to have lost all control, was emitting lost, soul-rending cries, which made him realize why she'd dismissed the servants, and was swaying and pitching on the end of his penis like a wild young horse.

Of a sudden she shrieked out:

"Oh, love, love—uuuuuuuugh!"

And her body seemed to petrify in a tense pushing orgasm and even Cesare could feel the added warmth surround his prick. Having controlled himself to some extent to the point where he was waiting for her to be satisfied, he now let himself go and within seconds was discharging his venom into her wide, vanquished quim and subsiding over her gross behind, which gradually lost its quiver as she calmed.

* * *

On the way to the tavern with one of the woman's servants who carried a message from her to the master of one of her ships, Cesare was waylaid by one of the Count's men.

"Quick, Sire, off the road."

The man took hold of him by the arm and dragged him into a doorway while the servant stood uncertainly, watching them in astonishment.

"What's up?" Cesare demanded. "Quick man—I've got a boat."

"Too late, Sire. Someone's talked out and the King's men are scouring the town. They have the port under close surveillance. It would be impossible to get through."

Cesare cursed furiously. He could hardly believe in such shocking luck.

"I'd like to get my hands on that old dog!" he snarled.

"Sire, our horses have been brought to a stable a little way from here. The men are waiting. Your only chance is to ride for the frontier as you foresaw."

Cesare lost no further time with his fury. He dismissed the servant, telling him to say to his mistress that circumstances had arisen which made the passage unnecessary but that he considered himself, taking everything into account, not to be at such a great loss.

He smiled grimly as they ran through the streets toward the stables. The experience had been more amusing than he'd expected and she'd practically abased herself before him on his departure, even offering him a permanent pension if he'd stay in the region and visit her no more than once a fortnight. He had been forced to explain the urgency of his leaving this part of the world.

In the stables the horses were ready, champing at the bit, and they made no secret of their departure as they clattered full pelt through the streets toward the open country. For once it was more haste, more speed.

CHAPTER 23

So it was to Navarre that Cesare managed at last to escape from Spain, to the court of his brother-in-law, King Jean. His arrival threw the kingdom into confusion and as far off as the Vatican, hearts were quaking at news of his escape.

He was given asylum and every attention and wrote to the King of France offering his services in any capacity which would provide him with an army in the service of Louis.

After some weeks he received the cool communication that as he had for a period joined the camp of Gonzalo de Cordoba he could no longer be considered a friend of France. Just that and no more. A bitter pill, which retarded, it seemed, indefinitely his hopes of reconquest of his former territories in Italy.

Cesare champed and chafed and wrote to friends and his sister to seek intelligence of the situation in his homeland. He wanted action and instead he had to remain, tucked away in Navarre eating fruit and drinking wine all day long while he listened to interminable lute-playing.

It was at this time that trouble grew in the teacup of Navarre, a small storm in which Cesare would have taken not the slightest interest had accident of circumstance not held him in the country at the time—a gratuitous, irrelevant involvement which, it seemed, by some prank of destiny, making a mockery of man's aims and ambitions, was to cost him all.

The country was suddenly torn by opposite factions which had long been snarling at each other. The Beaumontes, principal of these factions, refused to be brought to heel and surrender to the King. Into Cesare's lap fell the offer of the Captain-Generalcy of Navarre with a force of 10,000 men. He was to lay siege to the main Beaumontese fortress of Viana and make the name of the King absolute throughout his realms.

Seeing in this, the possibility of an ally and material assistance at some later date, Cesare agreed and led the army into its siege position.

The fortress was strong, but its provisions were running low. It stood fair to be starved to surrender in a short time.

But Beaumont, who gave his name to his faction, conceived the risky and daring plan of creeping through the enemy lines at night and getting supplies from a nearby, friendly town.

The attempt—a complete surprise to the besiegers—would have been completely successful had not a party of reinforcements coming up to join Cesare's army bumped into the retreating Beaumontese with the first light of dawn preparing to break through.

The alarm was given, and Cesare, who had been unable to sleep, was one of the first in pursuit, leaving his men to follow the obvious trail of the Beaumontese through the hillocks surrounding the fortress.

He was full of fury at the trick. This would mean weeks more for the siege and he could not be involved in the petty disturbances of a petty kingdom for that long. Such troubles, as he rode in pursuit, unaware of his start on the men of his own army, blinded him to the risk one could run equally in petty kingdoms.

At a turn in the track he was ambushed by a score of the Beaumontese who, seeing a lone rider well ahead of the main body of the pursuit and being so near safety themselves, had turned back for the sake of the kill.

Cesare was surrounded, realized for the first time that the pursuit party of his army was not yet even in earshot and tried to break free from the encircling horses. But he was hemmed in and although he dispatched several of the enemy he was dragged from his horse at last and there on the road near the lonely fortress of Viana in Navarre in a cause which was not his own and of no real interest to him, Cesare Borgia was cut down under a rain of blows.

The thunder of the hooves of the pursuit came into earshot as those of the retreat died away and Cesare lay dying beside the road, stood over by his horse.

His army was dismayed and Navarre stricken by the gratuitous death of this man who had been such a fine leader in his day. There were few, even among his enemies, as the news raged over the border and into the surrounding countries, who did not feel a pang of regret that he should have met such a strange end.

There were many who said that God had finally decided that this creature of his creation who had murdered and schemed and raped and dallied with incest, had done enough; that he had made him lose his reason just at the moment when there had been no cause for him to risk his life.

Of Lucrezia no more was heard after her brother's death. It was rumored that she was so stricken with grief that she never again left the walls of her quarters in her husband's palace. Others again insisted that she was seen no more simply because she continued to indulge in practices for which she needed the secrecy of a screen from the public eyes.

Centuries later, it was said, Italian mothers would occasionally use the names of Cesare and Lucrezia or Roderigo Borgia to frighten their naughty children and send them scurrying, subdued, to bed.

THE END

LUSTS OF THE BORGIAS

POSTSCRIPT

POSTSCRIPT

Throughout history, humanity has given birth to many monsters. From Caligula to Hitler the names roll off the tongue and doubtless there were many before and others yet to come.

But the world has never known, and probably never will, an evil quite so peculiar as that synonymous with the name, Borgia.

True, the mores of 15th-century Italy—or the many separate states which then made up the peninsula—were what is sometimes euphemistically described as "robust," but the excesses of licentiousness, treachery and murder perpetrated by this notorious family are heightened beyond parallel by the fact that one of their number reigned supreme over the Roman Catholic world while such depravity was indulged to the full. As Pope Alexander VI, Roderigo de Borja not only condoned the rape, murder and incest committed by his progeny, but joined them in the airing of their infamous appetites.

Roderigo, in fact, already had a number of children by a Roman girl, Vannozza dei Cattanei, when he was elected Pope. Two of them, Cesare and Lucrezia, both of outstanding looks and intelligence, were, with the Pope, responsible for the family reputation.

Cesare, idealized by Machiavelli in his book, *Il Principe*, murdered his brother to improve his position in the Church and was himself a cardinal before he stood down to take an army on a mission to subdue a large part of the peninsula to the overlordship of the Holy See. He is described by one historian as "handsome, brave, talented, a brilliant soldier and a just and able administrator," but we also know him as a man of cruelty, avarice and sexual predatoriness, who would stop at nothing to satisfy these appetites. Like his father, he gloated over his lovely sister and there is little reason to doubt that he enjoyed her charms to the full, sharing her in this respect with Roderigo. So pronounced was his incestuous passion that he was responsible for the murder of one of Lucrezia's three husbands, the Duke of Bisceglie.

Lucrezia herself was a born seductress, who enjoyed the game of ensnaring men, even to the point of alluring her own son, and was only too willing to give them outlet for their lust to ensure the achievement of her purpose.

There are many apologists for the Borgias, but the wealth of evidence concerning their sinister and all-embracing corruption is overwhelming. Theirs is a fascinating story whose details beg to be laid bare in an attempt to understand the full motivation of their actions and the depths of perversion to which they jointly sank.

When I first read a book on the Borgias as a 17-year-old schoolboy in the sedate provincialism of the English West Country where I spent my adolescence, I was unaware that the notorious family differed only in degree from so much of society. To someone raised in a moral atmosphere of Victorian dimensions, the idea of sex used not only to gratify appetite, but as a currency to gain ends, was exotic in the extreme.

It was not until I became a journalist, working at first in those same provincial backwaters, that I discovered the barely-disguised libidos running abrasively through the most apparently placid areas. In the courts I heard tales of Borgia quality, from the tenements to high society; local politics and cultural life were rife with this subcutaneous ferment.

At the age of 23, I uprooted myself and went to Paris to write and—perhaps partly through that process—to find some meaning in things. What, in fact, I found was more Borgia evidence everywhere. While working for the expatriate literary magazine, *Merlin*, writing for the Olympia Press and teaching English to classes of air personnel at Orly Airport, I viewed at first hand the naked use of sex to gain other than sensual satisfaction: writers sleeping with publishers to ensure they were published; publishers going to bed with writers to secure their next novel; impecunious artists getting sexually involved with heiresses to acquire funds for their creative activities; wives of airline pilots trying to seduce the English teacher as a guarantee of language tuition.

After four and a half years of this—with periods in Spain and Italy, where the predatory youth emulate their infamous forebears for gain from rich tourists—I returned to England to a job in Government publicity. In those Civil Service corridors of power, too, I found the phallus reigning supreme: career ladies sleeping with their directors for promotion; sexual jockeying for advantage; nepotism; above it all a well publicized case of a middle-aged woman colleague allured into an affair by an Eastern European diplomat and, in no time, providing him with confidential and secret papers as security against the loss of his prowess in bed.

All this we come to accept as part of the pattern of "ordinary" life. To each protagonist his activities seem completely understandable and even inevitable expressions of personality produced by pressures of environment, both material and mental. Doubtless the Borgias would have felt the same way about their own excesses. For the question of evil is relative. It has many levels and it is in all of us. Like Eichmann, we seldom recognize or accept it for what it is.

The Borgias do not stand alone, extreme though their story may be. They are a monument to the world today—and a warning.

Marcus van Heller
London, July 1967

Adam & Eve

CHAPTER ONE

The lawyer sat on his desk, gently swinging one leg. He spoke in a slow American drawl, with no trace left of an Italian accent, measuring his words, carrying in them the weight of a weary, resigned philosophy...

"There are times when you want to spread an alarm, but nothing has happened. I knew, I knew then and there—I could have finished the whole story that afternoon..." His voice droned on relentlessly... "It wasn't as though there was a mystery to unravel. I could see every step coming, step after step, like a dark figure walking down a hall toward a certain door..." The voice went on speaking out into the dark auditorium from its spotlit aura on the stage. It was dead quiet in the theatre. You would have heard a piece of confetti drop.

Sitting right up in the gallery, which they called the dress circle though it was really only a backward extension of it, the girl sat hunched forward with her arms on the gold-painted handrail. Her buttocks ached a little from sitting for so long on the thin velvet of the seat without moving, but she kept absolutely still so as not to miss a word, the least nuance. The lights went out on Alfieri, the lawyer, and rose on the Sicilian slum apartment near Brooklyn Bridge with Beatrice and

Catherine clearing the table. The girl reached down into her lap with a long, slender, well manicured hand and drew the little pair of opera glasses up to her eyes. She trained them on Beatrice. This was her goddess, Lady Celia Duncan, the finest actress in Britain. She moved them over the girl, Catherine, otherwise Greta Plowman, who was good, very good but not in quite the same category, and so on to Eddie Carbone, Sir George Duncan, the other half of the husband and wife team. He was superb. He gave her a little, sharp thrill in her stomach just to listen to his voice. But it was with Celia Duncan that she identified herself. She could not, after all, change her sex, but she could have Celia Duncan's place one day.

The voices came up to her from the stage, Eddie's, Beatrice's, Catherine's Rodolpho's, Marco's and she absorbed them with her whole being, living their glories with them, feeling their occasional flatness, while the gripping story of consuming possessive passion unfolded itself with the unyielding quality of Greek tragedy. She was aware of nothing else, nobody else at all in the dark theatre around her which now breathed and rustled sometimes, like an animal twitching in its sleep.

She kept the opera glasses clamped to her eyes, ranging them from one to another, her own face tightening in sympathy with theirs, smiling with theirs, frowning with theirs, her breathing faster with theirs, slower with theirs. She watched, her entrails twisted tight like a wrung-out sheet while Marco raised the chair, straining smoothly above his head, and looked down at Eddie with that glint of menace. And she went on staring as the curtain fell and then the safety curtain followed it down and the lights went up all around.

"I can see those adverts without a magnifying glass."

The girl sighed, smiled and turned to her companion.

"Aren't they wonderful," she said.

"They're pretty hot."

He was a handsome boy of about nineteen, a year older than her. He wore a turtle-necked sweater and a pair of smart, tight, Italian trousers. His long, thin face with its rather prominent nose over finely delineated lips carried with it a suggestion of superiority over men of more common clay. His long, dark eyes, which at first glance looked liquid and soft, deepened into a hint of ruthlessness the longer you looked at them.

"Let's have a drink," he said.

"Can we afford it?"

"Of course not. Let's go."

"Just a minute, Adam."

The girl looked around the theatre with a smile of sheer pleasure. It was crowded with people, many now pushing along the aisles towards the bars. It had an air of opulence about its red and gilt and, from the flamboyant gold carving around the boxes and the magnificent cascading chandelier, you could have imagined yourself back in the days of Nell Gwynne and a rowdier audience. The girl could just see the front rows of the stalls, the fur coats and jewellery; all those fat women doing the right social thing, only just heard of Arthur Miller because even they could hardly have missed the name.

She stood up and began to edge along the aisle, followed by the boy. Her name was Eve Patten. It was rather odd that their names should be Adam and Eve and, although they laughed about it, they were both rather embarrassed when people found out and made jokes. She was a secretary, and a very efficient one, in a provincial town in the middle of the south of England. She was a secretary to everyone else, but to herself she was a great actress. Even though amateur productions had been her only outlet so far, she was a great actress. There was really no other point to her life, so that if in appearance she never became one, she was just nothing else in her own mind. She was like the writer who carries the developing book around in his mind year after year after year, going through the motions of jobs, social contacts, empty conversations, but never being anything else but a writer, even though he might never write the book. But all she needed, like everyone, was a start. For this she had not only enthusiasm, a certain amount of talent, but beauty as well. She had been the beauty queen of her city two years running since she left school. "You ought to be in films with your looks," people told her, and that had strengthened her belief that there was a great public waiting for a great actress. She was tall, almost as tall as her companion, with a well developed body and eye-catching legs. Her hair was the colour of champagne, her blue eyes had a slightly luminous quality like the sun on a very blue sea; and her delicate, youthful skin was firmly set over fine bones which had a trace of the oriental in their small, hard prominence.

She was smartly, fashionably dressed; indeed both she and her companion might easily have been taken for two smart young aristocrats from Mayfair.

The bar was crowded, but Adam pushed his way through leaving the girl studying the programme near the door, the focus of attention for several pairs of male eyes who undressed her systematically, imagined that body warmly cushioning theirs in a bed to match her own elegance.

She exhausted the programme and let the images of the play flood back into her head. "A View from the Bridge" was one of the most moving plays she'd seen for some time, although she and Adam had been making this trip to London at weekends for more than a year. Oh for a chance to get in! She thought of Mr. Grampion, the one theatrical agent who hadn't told her: "Not a hope, Miss, all the theatres are booked for a year or more, all the casts set; and in any case looks aren't enough these days, you've got to have talent, experience, masses of experience, and the right moment to help you." Mr. Grampion had said instead: "I might be able to do something for you, but you'll have to sleep with me first." Just like that. No frills, no beating about the bush. They weren't necessary. The market was all his. Mr. Grampion was middle-aged and ugly. The thought would have horrified her even if she hadn't been a virgin. But that had been months and months ago and now she was used to the repeated offer as she made the weary regular round, and nothing else, absolutely nothing, had come up. But she was still frightened. She couldn't even allow herself to start to picture the actual event: the room, the bed, the getting undressed, the seeing him undressed, the contact between the sheets, the... Ugh!

The back of Adam's head came into her conscious thoughts as he leaned over the bar, taking up the glasses. With Adam it could happen. Oh, she had nothing against it, but real opportunities were rare and also something told her, some instinctive sixth sense, that his attitude would change towards her immediately their relationship changed in that way. They'd got very close to it, of course, foolish though she knew it was to play with fire and hope not to get burnt. But always she read something in his eyes, something in that ruthlessness that was suddenly there so naked that she wondered why she didn't see it all the time. And that pulled her up. It wasn't any corny woman magazine trash about

"They don't respect you once they've had you," it was just a particular understanding of an individual character —and she knew her Adam. Because he was very much like her.

He came weaving back towards her, a bottle of tonic and a gin in one hand, a glass of brown ale in the other. She smiled and raised an eyebrow.

"A beer would have done, Adam. We won't have the fare to get to Aunt Beatie's if you throw it around like that."

He grinned.

"I won a sweepstake at the office," he said. "Shilling in, twenty out—have another."

Adam worked for the biggest firm of solicitors in their town. He was one of the clerks. Both he and Eve were misfits, which was almost certainly why they kept each other's company. Adam was a fine painter, at least a lot of local people thought he was a fine painter, including Mr. Grant, his art master at school and now his tutor at the evening classes to which he went for the sake of the cheaper paint and canvases. But if it was difficult to get on the stage, it was even more difficult to get an exhibition. Local ones weren't worth having and London—well. While she made the round of the agents, Adam made the round of the galleries, pleading, cajoling, looking at the work on view, frequently wondering exactly what it had that his hadn't. Like Eve, he had one overwhelming disadvantage. He didn't know anyone. Not one of the right people. Not even one of the off-right people. Not a soul who mattered, except for his art master who, in spite of a more cosmopolitan history, had for years been buried away in the provincial town which was now his whole, quiet life.

The couple stood in the bar, sipping their drinks, talking about the play. Adam was particularly impressed with the scenery, which combined two views in one by which you could see the interior of the apartment on the left hand and the dockside, simply and vividly evoked with a black silhouette of scaffolding, on the right.

"As a matter of fact, I wouldn't mind doing a bit of stage designing," he said. "But it's not worth much, unless you have a big name."

The bell went for the second act. The interval was, as usual, much too short to enable you to have a drink in comfort. They tipped back their glasses and pushed back up the stairs to the dress-circle-cum-gallery, with the lights already going dim.

During the second act the girl sat breathless on the edge of her not very comfortable seat, letting the play swamp her, the words subdue her to a state of trance... Alfieri: "You won't have a friend in the world, Eddie! Even those who understand you will turn against you..." Catherine: "I'm gonna get married, Eddie. So if you wanna come, the wedding be on Saturday... " Beatrice: "She loves him, Eddie. Why don't you give her a good word?"... the Immigration Officers... the seizure of the illegal immigrants... the fight... Eddie's death. And Alfieri at the end: "Most of the time we settle for half and I like it better. But the truth is holy, and even as I know how wrong he was, and his death useless, I tremble, for I confess that something perversely pure calls to me from his memory—not purely good—but himself purely..." She repeated to herself in her mind the words which seemed to have meaning for her... "not purely good, but himself purely." The curtain came down. These was a long moment's pause and then a rapture of applause. The applause thrilled her like blood coursing through her veins, setting all her flesh a-tingle, making her head suddenly hot. She pictured the applause as being for herself, saw her own figure on the brightly lit stage as Lady Celia and Sir George joined hands and moved forward together away from the rest of the cast to a sudden increase in the volume of applause. And then Lady Celia drew back and Sir George stepped forward a couple of paces alone to another lift in the acclamation. Eve clapped until her hands stung. Of course it should be the other way round to please her, with Lady Celia alone on the stage, but of course Eddie Carbone was the major character in the play. The curtain fell, rose, fell and rose again until finally it came down with that air of finality which quelled even the most ardent fans. The clapping petered out and the audience was making for the exits, a swell of animated chatter and shuffling feet rising through the auditorium like hot air.

Eve glanced at Adam and they stood up and began to move towards the steps of the aisle. She looked at the people, tightly packed, brushing their way out, but without seeing them. She had made a decision. It was the last sight of Eddie dying in the arms of Beatrice. It had called to her like a saint, or a devil, calling to men to follow him. She needed to be on that stage. It was more than life, more than disgust for Mr. Grampion. She would sleep with him and he would get her a part. That was how the beginning would be. And then if necessary she would sleep with him again or with anyone else who could push her on. She glanced back at Adam's handsome face and he looked at her quizzically. She would have liked it to be Adam, the first time. But one had to work these things out or one never got anywhere. She thought of all the girls back at the office, their total lack of ambition, except to own a house or a vacuum sweeper and to keep their boyfriends so that they married them with the biggest show of wedding they could manage, together with spotty, featureless photographs in the local papers. Not one of them used any real charm to get a more interesting life. She sometimes wondered if they thought of their boyfriends in any different way from their dream of a refrigerator. And sometimes, when one of them slept with the boy, giving way to pressure, how surprised she was when his ardour cooled. It was a game, after all, and you had to play it.

CHAPTER TWO

Eve hated the long, long tube journey out to her aunt's house in the suburbs. It was one of those typically semi-detached doll's houses with tiny rooms and a neat garden, three up and two down as regards the rooms. Everything was spotless, for her aunt cleaned and cleaned until you were almost afraid to put one foot in front of another in case you stepped on something you shouldn't or knocked something over. The area was the sort that working class people strove for when they wanted to better themselves, neat, green, uniform, fairly "good" and characterless as a tailor's dummy. Her aunt had devoted her whole life to getting it, dragging her husband along with her. Everything else had been sacrificed; no effort to develop taste, brain, enjoyment of life, nothing. Now her aunt suffered from the enormous sense of inadequacy, lightly covered with a veneer of snobbery, which all such people who have made material betterment their god are prey to.

Eve knew that her aunt regarded her with a mixture of adoration and disapproval. Adoration for her appearance and general presence, which blinded people to her origins, adoration too for her ambition and determination to succeed. Disapproval of her desire to succeed in such an uncertain, unknown, weird world as that of the stage rather than stick at her good job in the office. She didn't really approve of Adam either. She didn't understand what he was talking about most of the time and she felt, quite correctly, that he disliked her and looked down on her values.

"If I lived in London, I wouldn't dream of living out so far," she said, as the train swayed through the dark tunnel. "Might just as well live at home."

"Doesn't make any difference to your aunt," Adam said. "The metropolis hasn't got anything to offer her. She doesn't want theatre, restaurants, art galleries, museums, the colour of people. As long as she can make an occasional trip in to the sales so that she can imagine she's getting something for next to nothing, she's happy."

"You sound like the appreciative guest should," Eve said.

"You know I'd just as soon sleep on the Embankment."

Eve shivered.

"Give me a warm bed every time," she said. "Even if it does mean playing the hypocrite to get it."

The train thundered on and they fell into silence. She glanced slyly at his face. Their relationship had rather peculiar ups and downs, due to her refusal to sleep with him. Now was one of the downs when they were sort of polite and he sounded cynical and bitter. Tomorrow, or in an hour, it would be quite different.

Her thoughts went back to the last tender episode. After dusk in a field on the outskirts of the town. Her heart missed a beat at the thought of it. They had lain in the dark shadow of a bus and she'd been able to feel in his pants the hard bulge which confessed his desire. Their kissing had reached a level of extreme sexuality, to the point where it no longer compensated for the real thing. She remembered his hand on her breasts, over the brassiere, the way she'd made no attempt to stop him undoing the catch, thinking that would be all right, the tender tingling of his fingers over the hot, bare flesh of her breast, the way he pinched her nipple suddenly, making her squeal and pant so that she hadn't stopped his hand as it stole up her leg with one smooth, unhesitating movement and went straight under the thin strip of her briefs to the moist lips of her vagina. Her mouth went dry now to think of how near they'd come. She'd been almost beside herself as he massaged her clitoris and reached his fingers deep into the hot passage between her legs. He'd tried to take off her briefs, the night air had been cold on her completely bared thighs. But she'd made a huge effort and stopped him. They'd argued, threatened, pleaded and finally he'd got up in disgust and lit a cigarette. They'd both sat smoking silently in the darkness. She pretending she was merely frightened, rather than admit that she wouldn't risk losing him. He bitterly reproaching her, showing her the packet of Durex, which would make it safe. She had said nothing was 100 per cent safe. So they had remained with their passions cooling and the uncomfortable wetness between her legs growing colder and colder, until bad temper had worn itself out and he'd seen her home and left. He hadn't yet recovered from that refusal.

She stole another glance at his handsome, slightly bitter profile. What a handsome couple we make, she suddenly thought.

They reached the distant suburb and caught the last bus for the short journey to her aunt's house. Everything was in darkness. All these joyless people had gone to bed ages ago, to bed from one day which was just like the next. Everything they did was just like the thing they'd done before and would do again next time. I wouldn't be my aunt for ten thousand pounds, she thought—a hundred thousand.

Aunt Beatie let them in, kissed her, shook hands with Adam. She was pleased and nervous, as she always was when she had to organise anything, such as a late supper for two people. She pottered about the kitchen while they made themselves at home. Uncle Den had gone to bed.

"How was the play, dear?"

"Wonderful, auntie."

"What did you say it was?"

"*A View from the Bridge*—Arthur Miller."

"Arthur Miller. Oh yes, dear, that would be good. He's been on television. I forget what it was called—all about a commercial traveller who treated his wife badly."

Eve sighed and Adam grinned at her maliciously.

The aunt asked no more questions about the play. She'd made all the conversation on that subject of which she was capable. While she prepared their rather unimaginative cold salad with cups of tea, she talked about the sales and what she'd bought—all useless things she'd wear once and never again. She also talked about some of her friends whom Adam and Eve hardly knew and she talked about the weather. She would have liked to mention something harmless about the Aldermaston March, whose stupidity, as she thought it, fascinated her in some perverse way. But she was vaguely afraid there might be some subtlety about it and its motives that she didn't understand and either

Adam or Eve—particularly Adam—might make her feel an utter imbecile with her ignorance. She was, of course, after starting out as a Socialist and getting where she had with the help of Socialism, an out and out Tory. One of those Tories who knows nothing about Europe, Africa, the H-Bomb, housing policies, exports and imports or anything like that. But who feels in her bones that the Socialists might take her refrigerator away and give it to a slum family, or build a road across her back garden without a by-your-leave, one of those, in fact, who sees about three inches high.

Eve washed up afterwards to show willing, and the aunt indicated their beds—clean sheets, everything clinical. Eve in the back bedroom, Adam in the boxroom. They all said goodnight.

Eve undressed slowly, studying herself in the mirror. No superfluous flesh, creamy smooth skin, taut, high breasts and gentle, sloped shoulders. She mouthed a few lines from the play, bringing tears to her eyes with her silent passion. She didn't put on her pyjamas. Instead she pulled back the curtains and looked out into the neat, tidy, moonlit garden. Oh for a blade of grass out of place, she thought. Why doesn't aunt realise this garden and this house don't reflect life at all and that's what makes them so artificial. But then, aunt didn't realise her life was artificial either, so how could she? She thought of Mr. Grampion. It was to him her thoughts kept coming, even though she tried to think of other things. She smoothed her hands over her body and shuddered. Even though the thought of him doing that had no reality, she shuddered. She sat on the clean coverlet of the bed and looked down at the soft, silky hair at the V of her loins. To imagine him putting his thing up inside there was just impossible. She went suddenly hot—a strange mixture of revulsion and desire.

Her door opened gently and she swung round. Adam slid into the moonlit room, wearing only his tight, Y-front pants.

"Adam!" she hissed. "You must be mad!"

He came over towards her with his slim, muscular body which the moon turned silver, and the heavy sag in the front of his pants and the big protuberance pointing at her through the cloth.

"Adam," she said again with soft intensity. "Auntie'll hear you. You mustn't stay."

But he came at her and pulled her up into his arms, naked as she was and kissed her with fury, splaying her lips out so that she automatically splurged her tongue into his mouth. She felt frightened and hollow in the pit of her stomach and she fell back under his pressure so that they were both stretched out on top of the bed. His hands began to rake her body, smoothing over the swell of the breasts. He bit her nipple and she checked with difficulty the cry that came into her throat.

"No Adam, no!" she whispered furiously, scenting the danger.

But his hand roamed at large, over ribs and belly, stroked the soft pubic hair so that she itched between her legs and squirmed away. But his hand came after her and splayed the lips of her vagina apart as his lips had hers. She gasped, unable to choke the sound. She squirmed on his fingers.

"Adam, Adam," she whispered into his face, "this is madness. Not here, not here!"

He slipped out of his pants. She heard him grunt at his own nakedness. She felt the huge, hot throbbing of his penis against her hip. His fingers raped her passage, delving deeper and deeper. Her neck arched and she moved her face from side to side, gritting her teeth with the word "No" concertina-ing in her head.

Adam took her hand and placed it on his prick. She let it rest there. It was enormous. She'd never have realised they were so big. Instinctively she began to stroke it and then to massage it, rubbing the skin back and forth. She remembered what a fast friend of hers had once told her and felt down for his balls. Their hairiness and texture surprised her. She'd heard how vulnerable they were and stroked them gently, holding them in her palm. Adam was grinding his teeth and grunting between breaths. She felt a light moisture cold on her thigh. She wondered if he'd come, but his prick was still as stiff as a ramrod. That must be the lubricant they talked about.

"Eve, Eve—I want you, I must, must, must...!" he whispered frenziedly.

"No Adam, no!"

She must let him, she told herself through her longing. But she couldn't stop him if he really tried. She was losing the fight with herself.

"Eve, Eve!"

He rolled on top of her suddenly.

"No Adam, no."

She jacknifed her legs down and felt his penis caught, hard and long between her thighs. She pressed her thighs together. Adam moaned and and panted, fighting to lift his penis up and into her quim. She resisted desperately, feeling his prick coming nearer, jerking and thrusting between her legs.

Suddenly Adam let out a hoarse cry. She felt his prick expand and contract against the sensitive flesh of her thighs. He gasped and gasped and gasped again. She felt hot fluid running all over her thighs, dripping down between them.

Adam collapsed on her body, panting, almost sobbing.

She stroked his head. My god, she thought, what a racket. And as if prompted by her thought, there was movement on the landing outside and her aunt's voice cried out anxiously.

"Are you all right, dear?"

Eve went rigid.

"Quick, under the bed in case she comes in," she whispered.

Adam slid reluctantly off her and disappeared.

Eve tried to still her heavy breathing and called out.

"I'm all right, aunty, what's up?"

"I thought I heard you call out?"

"Just a cough, aunt."

"Would you like some cough mixture, dear? There's some in the bathroom. Shall I get it for you?"

"No, no, aunty. It's nothing at all. Just got something in my throat. I'm all right, really."

All right then, dear. Goodnight."

"Goodnight."

Eve waited until she heard her aunt's door close and then she got off the bed and switched on the light. Adam was lying on the rug. He looked exhausted and hadn't bothered to hide under the bed. In any case, he'd left his pants on the coverlet and, worse than that, there was a great trail of heavy, glue-coloured sperm all across the clean, peach coverlet.

Eve pushed back her hair from her face. All her nerves were a-jangle. She went to Adam and caught his shoulder. He kneeled up and she pulled him to her and kissed him. They held each other for a minute or two.

"We'd better clean up," she whispered then.

She slipped out of his arms, found her handkerchief and wiped her legs. She began to wipe the coverlet, but, although the sperm came off, it left a thick, greasy mark which was clearly going to show.

"Good god," she said. "Aunt will never get over this."

"It's all right," Adam said, behind her. "She'll never guess in a million years what it is."

She looked round at his sardonically grinning face. She looked at the whole of him, standing there in the full light with his deflated penis dripping moisture down onto her aunt's clean rug. She grinned back and began to laugh. They both began to laugh. It became almost uncontrollable. She could tell now that this was one of the ups.

CHAPTER THREE

Eve saw Adam off at Waterloo the next morning. He had to go back to their home town because his art master particularly wanted him to meet some old friend who had some influence in the art world and might be able to help him. Mr. Grant had been rather vague about the person, but very insistent on them meeting. No chance of help could ever be turned down.

Eve, in the meantime, would continue to see agents in the hope of getting something. This, at least was her story.

They kissed *au revoir* on the train steps in the great, dim cavern of the station, with steam gushing and whistles blowing and people scurrying to and fro shouting their farewells, calling for porters.

"I wish I didn't have to go back," Adam said. "Perhaps we could finish what we started."

"I thought we did," Eve said. "Anyway we certainly finished Aunt Beatie's coverlet. It was stiff as a board this morning. I made the bed and left it. Perhaps she'll think I had a celestial visitation."

"She'll be envious," Adam said.

The whistle blew, the green flag was waved, the last door slammed and the train strained slowly away out of the station. Eve went back through the barrier and caught a bus over Waterloo Bridge to the West End.

In a little street in Soho, near the film offices, she walked past a narrow doorway with a bronze tablet at its side. The tablet said: J. Grampion Ltd., Theatrical Agent. Eve walked past the doorway half a dozen times. Finally she went into a bar, ignoring the stares of the clientele, bought herself a gin with her meagre resources, knocked it back straight and went out again without looking at anyone. The liquor warmed her inside. It didn't amount to much, but it was a help.

She went up the stairs from the doorway. There was no carpet, they were covered with rubber pads. At the top of the stairs was a landing, dark and gloomy, and half way along a sign hanging over a door said "Enquiries." She went along to the door, stood still outside for twenty seconds fighting to control her breath, her fast-beating heart, and then went in.

An automatic bell jangled and the well-known secretary looked up from her typewriter. She was a supercilious young woman, rather plain, but making the best of herself. She had extraordinarily large breasts. Eve had sometimes wondered how many inches over 40 they were. She had also wondered if, to keep her job, she had to lie on her back for Mr. Grampion once in a while. With breasts like that, she could be able to keep him at arm's length in emergency.

The secretary raised her eyebrows and said in an ultra-refined voice, whose vowel sounds you'd never find in a dictionary: "Mr. Grampion's rawthah busy. Caaan you wait?"

"All right," Eve said.

The girl motioned her to the familiar and admittedly comfortable leather chair. She made no effort to communicate with her employer, which irritated Eve, feeling as she did that the waiting was as often due to the secretary's whim as to Grampion's pressure of work.

After about five minutes the secretary picked up a phone extension and said into it.

"Miss Patten to see you, Mr. Grampion. Are you busy or shall I tell her to come in?"

She listened, replaced the receiver and resumed her typing without looking at Eve. Eve sighed. There was no point in getting hot under the collar when you wanted something. This she knew from bitter experience. You had to wait until the power was in your own hands.

After another five minutes, the secretary looked up as if she was surprised to see the client still patiently waiting.

"Mr. Grampion will see you now," she said.

"Thaaank you so much," Eve said, unable to resist the mimicry.

The secretary looked at her sharply and Eve knocked on the frosted glass of the inner door and went in.

John Grampion was sitting behind a broad, baize-topped table, making a few notes with a handsome pen. There was always an air of make-believe about his work. He was a fat, heavy man of about 50 with fish eyes that looked as if they couldn't stand to hear another word from you. He had a small, slightly turned up nose and thin, hard lips over a full, fleshy chin. He dressed well and spoke well, but with a certain rather coarse suaveness which theatrical agents are either born with or acquire. His office was sumptuous compared with the secretary's. It was fitted with a dove-grey carpet and decorated in white and grey with small touches of blue. There were a couple of elegant modern chairs and an elegant modern sideboard along a wall. The other wall was a window which looked out, rather surprisingly, on a charming little courtyard.

"Well, well, Miss Patten. How are you?" he asked, looking at her with eyes which were devoid of any generosity but chock-full of sensuality and lust.

"I'm fine, Mr. Grampion, thank you. I just came to see if you have anything you can throw my way."

Grampion drew out a card index from a small cabinet perched on one side of his desk. He flicked through the card index till he found her name. On the card he had a few details about her. They were not very encouraging. No experience to speak of at all. Also scrawled on the card in pencil were the words "Might eventually" which referred to matters other than theatrical.

He turned to a similar cabinet on the other side of his desk and made a show of looking through another card index. He closed the cabinet and looked up.

"Nothing suitable, I'm afraid, Miss Patten," he said, staring insolently at her legs.

Eve had sat at his invitation on one of the chairs opposite the desk. As he looked at her legs she deliberately hitched up her skirt half an inch. She didn't know how to broach the subject.

Grampion raised his eyes slowly up her legs and body to her face and gave her a long searching look.

"Let me see, when did you last come?" he asked.

"About a month ago," she said.

"And on that occasion I had nothing."

"I don't know. Only on certain conditions."

Grampion smiled lewdly. He wasn't the slightest embarrassed. He was enjoying himself, sensing that he had fresh prey.

"And have you changed you mind, by any chance?"

Eve hesitated. It was still not too late to refuse. She

blushed slowly.

"Yes," she said, looking at his desk.

"Well, well. How very, very nice."

Grampion rose from the desk. There was real lustful delight in his fish eyes. He could hardly take in yet that this beautiful chicken had finally come to roost in his nest. He was very tired of Miss Jones, his secretary, in spite of those enormous mouthfuls of breast of hers and it was some time since he'd had an offer such as this. He went to the sideboard and opened it.

"Let's have a drink, my dear. Your name is Eve, I understand, and mine is John. What will you have?"

Eve fought back her truculence. Might as well make it all as easy as possible. She wondered where he wanted to do it. On the fitted carpet? Not with his secretary next door and this big window, surely.

"I'll have a gin and tonic," she said. "A double gin."

"A triple, by all means, if you'd like it," Grampion said, smiling delightedly. "A little more than you fancy does you good, I always say."

He poured an enormous gin and added a little tonic. He poured a large Scotch for himself, added a drop of water and walked across to Eve. He handed her the drink and stood looking down at her. He made no attempt to touch her.

"Chin-chin," he said.

Eve didn't answer. She took a long, deep, spine-tingling swig of the drink. It seared through her, easing her tensions almost immediately. What did it matter? she asked herself. What did it matter? You ate things you didn't like. Visited places you didn't like. Put up with cuts and sores. Nothing was really unbearable any more than anyone was indispensable.

Grampion's eyes ranged over her, gloating over her body. He licked his thin lips and touched her neck with his fingers. She sat stockstill, looking at her drink. He took his fingers away and said: "Well, my dear Eve. I shall be through in half an hour. I suggest you go and have a coffee at the Expresso two corners up. Have anything you like there. I'll pick you up there in half an hour."

"What about a part?" she said. "What can you do for me?"

He smiled smoothly.

"Well, as always in this profession, there are certain changes that can be made in the recommendations," he said. "There's this new play coming on at the Criterion in two months' time. I've already suggested someone for one of the parts that I think you could fill just as well. It's not the lead, of course. Can't expect that straight away. But it's a meaty small part with good lines, good entrances, good exits—a chance to make a real impression if you grab it. I'll start to work on it right away."

"What's the play?" she asked.

"It's this new one by William Inge. He's fed up with New York. Told me so himself when I was over there a little while ago. Wants to try London. I can give you full details later and of the part. Leave everything to me."

Eve left his office and walked past the secretary, who glanced at her suspiciously.

"Don't bother to show me out," Eve said. "I can tell by the look of you how overworked and underpaid you are, poor thing."

The secretary's mouth sagged and Eve closed the door behind her with a grim little smile and went down the stairs to find the coffee bar. She hoped they had plenty of delicious and expensive sandwiches to put on Grampion's account.

CHAPTER FOUR

Eve leaned back in the big Oldsmobile. Trust him to have a big, flashy American car. But at least he wasn't mean with his money once he'd got what he wanted. She'd made a pig of herself over the sandwiches at the coffee bar but he hadn't batted an eyelid at the bill and had promptly whisked her off to an elegant bar for drinks. He was in the best of spirits. He was even faintly amusing. If only he hadn't been such a greasy character and had such greasy looks, she would have found the thought of the forthcoming ordeal easier to bear.

Now they were flashing out to his flat at Maida Vale. The area where the expensive prostitutes lived. She felt quite high, but instead of making her gay it had depressed her.

Grampion chattered: gossip, theatrical gossip all the time, dropping names, spending money in words like water. She found herself wondering if he really knew all these people as well as he pretended, or did he get it all from the newspaper and cinema magazine diaries.

They raced up the Edgeware Road, beating the lights at every hundred yards until they came to the smooth stretch of sumptuous flats which heralded the golden mile of Maida Vale. Here Grampion turned off with a screech of brakes, shot up a side street, down another, as if he couldn't wait to get his pants off and pulled up in front of a small block of stone and brick flats with big glass doors leading into quite an elegant hall.

Grampion parked the car and led her in. It was clear that he made more money than his office indicated. They went up in the lift, cramped together. But although he gloated over her, he still didn't touch her, as if he were savouring the moment to come, not prepared to spoil it with preliminaries which might be abortive.

On the third floor they got out and walked along the carpeted passage to a door at the end of it. Grampion let them in with a key and Eve walked into what was virtually a one-room flat. One room, elegant and comfortable, in which Grampion slept on a divan at night, lazed on it during the day. Off the tiny entrance which led into this room were a tiny kitchen and a rather larger bathroom. It was all shining and clean, obviously serviced.

"A small place but mine own," Grampion said. "Very expensive, very useful and convenient. Take off your coat."

She took off her coat obediently and he took it and hung it in a concealed cupboard in the entrance hall. He looked at her in her elegant tight-fitting black dress which showed off her champagne coloured hair and blue eyes so well. He licked his lips and the delight had gone out of his eyes leaving only an urgent lust which made his whole face even uglier.

Eve walked before him right into the little room. He came up behind her and put his hand on her buttocks. She stopped.

"Beautiful," he murmured. "You are beautiful." He ran his hand over her bottom and then up over her breasts, still standing behind her. She could hear the wheeze of his breathing. She felt nothing at all. And then he moved away again and said: "Well, let's have one for the bed, as you might say."

She shuddered then, a little shiver of revulsion which started at her toes and ran right up to her scalp. It would be on that divan. There was no mystery any longer. No sheltering vagueness. It would be there that he would do things to her, with his grossness and his ugliness. She looked out of the small window to the front courtyard as if to escape into the sun and the fresh air. When she turned back, he had brim-full glasses of drink and was holding one out to her.

"You certainly like your liquor," she said, almost disgustedly, though she had no objection to liquor at all.

"It always improves my performance," he said with a leer. "And with such a beautiful girl, I particularly want to be in top form."

He knocked back a large part of the drink and then he began to take off his clothes. Eve watched him, half fascinated, as if his undressing had nothing to do with her at all.

"Shall I do it for you?" he asked, looking at her dress.

"I can manage very well, thank you," she said.

She undid the buttons of her dress at the back, wriggled it off her shoulders, down over her hips and stepped out of it. She felt Grampion's eyes devouring her but she didn't look at him. She pulled her slip over her head, picked up both garments and draped them over a chair. She felt suddenly extremely naked. She also felt a little dizzy from the drink. She glanced at Grampion. He was naked, taking off his socks. His body was as huge and gross as his face; his yellow flesh sagged and perspired so that she could see it glistening across the room. His penis jutted out under the overhang of his belly, surrounded by a jet black fuzz of hair. It reminded her of a cannon poking from a thicket under an overhanging cliff. She giggled hysterically and then shuddered violently. The thought of his fat body on hers revolted her. The thought...! She couldn't go through with it. She felt quite clearly now to the depths of her being that she couldn't go through with it.

Grampion had stood up and turned towards her. His mouth was open, his fish eyes popped, he gazed wildly at her long legs in the sheer nylon stoockings, the stretch of chalk white thigh above, the pert breasts which made smooth hillocks, above the cup-shaped brassiere, the chalk white midriff, the long strength of the hips. His look appalled her and she said, gasping: "I made a mistake, Mr. Grampion. I can't do it!"

"But my dear—your part."

He came towards her. His eyes held no humanity— lust, cruel and unyielding, shone in them like an unforgiving headlight which permitted no shelter.

"Your future... your future...," he murmured. And his body towered over her, his fish eyes shone into her face, absorbing it.

"No, no, Mr. Grampion. I mean it. I can't do it. I'm leaving now. It doesn't matter about the part. I don't want it."

His arms enveloped her and his face covered her and his lips engulfed her, wetly, voraciously, sucking her own mouth into his like a vacuum cleaner. She began to struggle. She was so dizzy she could hardly stand up, kept feeling she was falling. He held her tight. She couldn't tell whether he was so strong or she was so weak. His tongue was in her mouth like a great wet fish, exploring, brushing wetly all around the inside. She was overwhelmed with his smell of sweat and perfume, and his great amorphous body flowed around her, bulging here, receding there, inescapable.

"No, no, no," she insisted. "Let me go. How dare you!"

She struggled furiously but he moved her with him across the room as if they were one body, seeming to flow with her struggles so that she seemed to have nothing definite to fight against. She felt a great, frenzied fear in her belly and her body and limbs began to tremble uncontrollably. Te dizziness was worse, the room was going round.

She found she was parallel with the ceiling. It couldn't be true. The ceiling was coming down to meet her and the fish eyes joined it, like spotlights coming at her in a dark theatre. She struggled vaguely, turned her face away. There was a great weight on her and her clothes were being removed as if by some inevitable, mechanical process... And the great, crushing amorphous body was emitting all sorts of noises which fused together in a great thunder which seemed to split her eardrums until she was sure that it was in fact the ceiling that was crashing down on her head; and then, between her legs, whose existence she'd forgotten, there was a sudden deep, thrusting entry as if a red-hot pole had been shoved into her body. She screamed and jerked away, but it followed her and the mouth came back on hers, eating at her lips and her tongue and the red-hot poker came in and in, drubbing into her cunt so that it seemed on fire and her whole lower body seemed to be split apart and tears ran down her cheeks and she began to sob and the room went round and round and finally she passed right out.

Eve came to, much later. She wasn't sure how much later, but it was beginning to get dark. She was aware that her breasts were being stroked and that there was a great hot weight of flesh along her back. She was lying on her side. She was on a divan with a blanket over her. She was naked except for her torn stockings. She was in a strange room. Her head was aching. Her vagina was aching—and sore—and it felt as if a solid block of something was inside it, but there was nothing. Gradually it began to come back to her. Without stirring she dropped her eyes to the fat, fleshy hand which moved over her breasts, disarranging the blanket. It had happened. It was over. She'd had it. She was no longer one of the vast legion of virgins. Well and truly not, by the fury of the inflamed fire between her legs. It didn't seem to matter now. It seemed rather unimportant. All that fear. It was all in the mind before the event, like most things. Except it would have been better for it to have happened with someone she liked, like Adam, instead of this coarse slug. The only thing was to think of the reward: a part. Even that seemed rather remote at the moment, however. She felt terribly thirsty. She spoke to the room ahead of her.

"I'd like a glass of water."

The hand ran down her belly and the fingers traced a line over her hip to rest on the hollow of her buttock. There was a great heaving movement. Grampion slithered off the divan and it rose up an inch or two carrying her up with it.

"Certainly, my dear," his voice said. "For the sake of your tight little fanny you shall have one."

He came into view from the foot of the divan. She watched his plump buttocks shake as he walked to the sideboard. His intimate penetration of her had no reality. It was impossible to believe it.

"A hair of the dog is better," he said.

"I want a long drink. I'm parched."

"Hair of the dog's still better."

She watched him pour a little drop of gin into a tumbler. He took two bottles of tonic, the split size, and drowned the gin with them. He handed her the tumbler and she drank greedily, leaning over the edge of the divan. He climbed over her and lay down behind her again. She ignored his heavy heat, thinking—almost without thinking—how differently one viewed these things once they'd happened.

The tonic was wonderful, braced her and the gin in it warmed her stomach. She felt his body snuggle closer. He had a big erection; she could feel it against the cleavage of her bottom.

"You have smoother skin than any other woman I've known," he said.

"Thanks," she said flatly.

"You're the first virgin I've ever had," he said thoughtfully, as if he were flicking back through a car index, checking that he hadn't made a mistake.

"Thanks again. What makes you think I was?"

"You were wild until you passed out. It was like holy murder."

He said the words with gleeful pleasure. It was clear he'd enjoyed every moment of the assault.

She said nothing. She simply lay there, her mind almost a blank, a blank into whose corners occasionally flickered the thought of her standing on a stage somewhere, the thought of Aunt Beatie and the sperm on the coverlet, of Adam, of her mother and father.

"What time is it?" she asked.

She felt his pulsing rod of flesh press against her buttocks and he placed his hands on her waist, drawing her bottom at his loins.

"Quite early," he said.

"I must be going. I have to go home."

"Plenty of trains," he said. "If not I'll run you down."

She relaxed. That took the pressure off anyway. Might as well get all she could for what she'd given.

His body pressed very close to her and his lips took a nibble from the nape of her neck to her shoulder. She lay still, uncooperative, and felt is hand ooze between her thighs where the buttocks joined them. It no longer shocked her to have him exploring her nudity in this way. It didn't please her either, but it didn't shock her in any way at all. His fingers caressed the lips of her vagina and finally entered and stroked the walls of the passage. She felt a little wet down there and contracted her bowels in spite of herself. She supposed you couldn't help getting a slight kick out of it even if the partner was obnoxious. His rigid penis oozed between her thighs after his fingers and prodded for the opening in her pelvis.

"I'm too sore," she said. "Leave me alone."

"Now, now," he said unctuously, pretending to be only joking, but reminding her of his power, "you want that part, don't you."

Her mind froze and she gritted her teeth in a spasm of anger. He could hold this over her for anything and for ever until she got the part. But the spasm passed.

Now the chunky knob of his prick had found the inflamed ring of moist flesh. She groaned as it moved into her, but he ignored her discomfiture. At the moment of entry, he seemed to lose himself in a torrent of passion. His breath came up from his belly in raking gasps and he skewered furiously and completely into her so that she cried out and tried to pull away.

"You're hurting me!" she gasped.

But he held her fast, with a hand curving round each hip so that the fingers pressed hard into the firm, elastic flesh of her abdomen. He moved into her like a series

of ripples of water, growing ever larger. She gasped and
squirmed, caught like a stuck pig on the end of a lance.
His thighs were hairy and hot along the undersides
of hers and the hairs of his loins brushed her behind. He
pummelled into her with force. He seemed to fill the
whole of her belly, up to her breasts. Sometimes he hurt
her in some unaccountable way, with a sudden extra
sharp point of pain. At other moments it seemed as if
he was exploding in her like gunpowder, spreading wide
parts of her that had always been hidden and closed.
Behind her in the bed he was like a tempestuous sea,
tossing and whirling and thundering and battering
against her ass.

"My god," she heard him yell and his fingers dug
deeply into her belly, making her squeal. She felt an
extra pressure against her hips and his fingers began to
pull and guide her over onto her knees, levering himself
up behind her. She let herself be led, although she felt
extremely undignified and, somehow, completely abased
before him as if she were some old-world slave bowing
before her master while he took her almost anonymously.

Now he slithered close between her widespread thighs,
pushing them apart even more with his knees and he
squirmed his prick right up, and deep, up to the very
hilt, into her quim. Now that she was spread out he
seemed to invade her even deeper, splitting her body
in two, forcing gasp after gasp from her panting mouth.
Her back began to ache from the pressure of his hands
around her waist, bending her waist down so that her
rump soared up towards his face. She felt totally naked
to her soul. Her loins tingled and clamped, a thousand
red hot bars inside battering one against the other,
sending out a million sparks throughout her body from
the molten nucleus of her vagina. His flesh buffetted
her buttocks with bruising force. She heard him give

little whining screams. She thought, My god, he's not using anything, but she herself was on fire and unable to complain, only to cough out a gathering storm of passion. He squirmed and skewered, bringing a cry from her throat with every in-thrust. He seemed to be getting bigger and bigger and going higher and higher towards her very throat. Her breasts heaved and danced. She found herself swaying a dance with her behind on the stem of his prick, like some windblown flower. She was sore as hell but afire with a great building pressure, too, a liquid screeching pressure in her loins which was growing to a pinpoint of agony. She couldn't think of anything but the enormous, agonisingly sweet buildup inside her. This was it. This was it. Somehow she'd never thought it would really happen to her. The buildup grew into a great, expanding bubble which was swelling up her inside to several times its real size. She screamed and screamed again, loud and shrill, and the bubble burst and it seemed like blood rushing from her loins in a torrent, hot and wet, and she screamed again with the tears of fright and ecstasy and relief running down her cheeks.

She began to calm a little. She was trembling all over and her stomach was quaking as if she'd just missed being run over by an express train—and still he was stuffing his penis up into her cunt with fury, wheezing between his teeth and practically hurling her off the divan with every harsh forward thrust. Now her forgotten soreness began to reassert itself. Her vagina felt scoured as if someone had used a potato peeler on its lining. She gritted her teeth, wondering how long she could stand it, and then she heard him muttering to himself, a muttering which grew into a waterfall of moaning, groaning agony, rose to a gasping howl and exploded into a barking shout. She felt nothing in her quim except that his thrusts slowed to great solid, slow heaves and she knew he was coming right up inside her with dangerous, child-giving sperm and she thought, "My god, that's twice today. Suppose I have a child," and then he fell forward on her with a groan and such a mountain of weight that she collapsed under him. He lay on her for some time, gasping, and then she said: "Why didn't you use something. Suppose I have a child?"

"It's all right," he said. "I'm sterile as a clinic. We could do this for years."

After a few minutes more, she protested and he rolled off her. She slithered off the bed and went into the bathroom. She cleaned herself up, spread her hands over her aching loins, put on a dressing gown she found on a hook on the door and went back into the room where he was still lying fat and naked and sated on the divan.

"Tell me about the play and the part," she said. "And then you can drive me home."

She found she did not feel very well disposed towards him. Though it now seemed as if they'd known each other for years.

"The part?"

"Yes, the part in the Inge play?"

"Oh, yes."

He leered at her. "Well it's not absolutely certain the play's going on, of course. Things are very uncertain in the theatre world, you know."

She saw it all in a flash of understanding that hit her like a thunderbolt. But she refused to believe it immediately. It was impossible that, if it was the way it seemed, that it wouldn't have occurred to her before. So it couldn't be. Thus her reasoning went.

"How uncertain?" she asked. "And why didn't you say that before?"

"Can't tell," he said. "Trouble with the managements."

"What's the play called? What's it about?" It seemed incredible to her now that she hadn't asked these simple questions before. Why hadn't she got something in writing? That was elementary.

"I don't remember the name off hand," he said. "It's one of these domestic drama-cum-psychological-tracts, you know."

"Well, what's the part for me?"

"Young wife, doesn't get on well with her husband."

"What's her name?"

She saw him hesitate and he saw her see him. He grinned.

"You ask too many questions," he said. "I told you the play might not go on at all. Wait and see what happens."

She flew at him then. Giving vent to all the rage that had been building up inside her. He had her, used her body with his hateful, lustful filthy desires—for nothing. NOTHING! She knew with intuitive certainty that there was no play, no part. It was all a figment of his imagination. And she allowed herself to be stripped and screwed, paraded naked in front of him, bent over in front of him, screwed until she hurt —for nothing! Nothing but his vile pleasure!

Her nails ripped his face. Her hand lashed across his eyes. He was taken aback and made no move for a moment to defend himself. He put up his hand and she seized and bit it, deep, catching the immediate taste of blood. He cried out in pain and rolled away across the divan and off, falling onto the floor. Some older girl's tale came to her and she lashed out with her bare foot at the limp balls which hung to the floor under his thick, heavy penis. He jerked away just in time and her foot caught him up the behind instead, so that he cried out again and jackknifed forward, with his hand to his buttocks. He scrambled to his feet as she leapt at him again. He took two swipes across his startled face and his nose suddenly began to bleed. His fish eyes went cold, as if they had gone out. He seized her arm and threw her onto the divan. She realized how very much stronger than her he was, but her blood was up and she sprang at him as he came at her, spitting and snarling. Her nails tore red welts across his fat chest and then he'd flattened her. His weight knocked the breath out of her body. She bit the hand again which roughly swung her over onto her stomach. He slapped the back of her head with stunning force, wheezing between his teeth with the effort. He tore up the dressing gown, exposing her slim naked body with the tiny waist and beautiful round buttocks. He knelt heavily on her flawless back and began to lash her bottom with his hand with all his strength. She struggled, but she could only writhe her hips under the fury of the stinging blows which fell thick and fast across the smooth orbs of flesh, now on her buttocks, now on her thighs.

"You beast, beast, beast!" she gasped. But now he seemed like some highly efficient piece of machinery, belting her with the flat of his large hand with a force that made her rump begin to sting, to feel raw as a skinned beetroot. Her struggles weakened. She was exhausted. Tears of tired rage welled in her eyes. After a while the blows ceased and then he quickly tied her hands with the cord of the gown. She struggled again furiously. No, it couldn't be true. One person couldn't inflict such shameful indignity on another. But her hands were tied fast.

He pulled her back across the edge of the divan so that her hips rested on the edge, her legs trailing down to the floor. He pushed her thighs wide apart once again. She began to sob as he pushed his rod into her cunt yet again, half standing, half lying across her bent bottom. As his hot, fleshy staff drubbed up and up into her flayed passage, he gave a sexy, mirthless, gasping chuckle, which mingled with her sobs and then lost itself in a continuous pant of lust.

CHAPTER FIVE

"I just love these little English country towns—so very picturesque. But how anyone could want to live in them for ever and ever, I just can't begin to understand. Give me a bit of life—and people are life, interesting people, vital, creative people. They carry life with them and infuse it in the people they meet. All these others are dead, just as this quaint, charming, mediaeval town is dead. You can only look at it, beautifully embalmed, like a corpse in a New York funeral parlour and think how lovely it is and how unutterably, unshakeably and irredeemably dead. I'm sorry, Joseph. I know you live here and all that. But I remember when you had other ideas. And if you're not careful, you'll grow into a stuffed dummy just like this place."

Mrs. Gracie Goldenbaum was talking with all the confidence bred of great wealth and great reputation as a personality. The reputation was not unearned. And although the few people in the lunch-time bar in the market town could hardly be expected to agree with the opinions she was at no pains to hide or keep to her own very small group, they did at least find her, as a person, entertaining. It wasn't often you got anyone quite so obviously fearless and outspoken and colourfully sophisticated as Mrs. Goldenbaum, twice divorced, once from the great surrealist painter Simon Earpit, once from that talented writer Pieter Hansohl and many times separated from many famous liaisons in addition. She herself was a well known patroness of the arts, but not everyone trusted her judgment and nowadays she hadn't quite so much money to give quite so many parties and keep her name in the Press. She could help painters enormously, as she always had done, but she no longer had the power to make or break them.

Joseph Grant, the art master, smiled self-effacingly at her tirade. She was incapable of offending him. He'd always adored her, from the time he'd first met her at Raoul Dufy's studio many years ago—and she liked him well enough or she wouldn't have broken her journey from New York to Paris to see him.

"People like you never get older, Gracie," he said. "But people like me do and we have to take it quietly."

"Anybody who lives in a morgue will grow old with the morgue," she said. "You don't really know what's good for you, Joseph. You only think you do. You don't realise how short life is. You really have to fill the unforgiving minute unless you're going to sit in a rocking chair full of regrets for the last ten years."

She glanced at Adam.

"You listen to what I say, young man. Handsome boy like you shouldn't come under the influence of an old fuddy-duddy like Joseph. He might be a good teacher of painting, but when it comes to Life with a capital L, he's as out of his depth as a cocktail in a sewer. What did you say your name was?"

"Adam Blythe."

"Adam. That's a good name for a start. You can't go right with a name like that so you'll be all right."

Her eyes lingered on him.

"Well let's have another and then we'll take a look at these paintings of yours."

Adam drank his Scotch. He didn't normally touch it; couldn't afford it, but she'd insisted. He was quite fascinated by her. She was no oil painting, he told himself with a grin. But she was very well preserved and her exuberance and that hint of ever-present sensuality gave her rather piquant Jewish looks a quality of elan which many younger women would have envied. She was thin, too, which was a help to a Jew and, rather unusual—quite sinewy. And she was beautifully dressed in a thoughtless sort of way, without any jewellery at all. He wondered if she'd like his paintings. After all she'd not only studied, but had lived with and loved with some of the most famous artists of the century. Must make it rather difficult for her to adjust herself to new talents. Though he had heard tell that she supported a number of young artists of all nationalities and that the price of their work on the world's market had risen sharply due to her patronage. But one never knew how much credence to give to these stories. Such exaggerated tales grew up around all these celebrated people, particularly if they gained a reputation for never bothering to contradict anything that was said about them. Fancy old Grant knowing her like this. He'd had to look again at the old boy. What sort of wild oats had he sown in that long-lost youth?

They left the old pub and took a taxi at her insistence for the half mile to the evening class studio. Studio! A school classroom with a few easels and other gear in it. There wasn't much of Adam's work here, really. Most of it was at home in the empty attic room he used. Sitting in the taxi, he suddenly thought of Eve and wondered if she was having any luck with the agents. She'd be interested to hear about this old girl.

Mr. Grant let them into the school and led the way to the art room.

"So this is what you've come to, Joseph," she said, looking round at the desks and the meagre equipment.

"This is what I've risen to," he said. "Giving the joy of knowledge to others."

"Nonsense," she said, continuing the feud. "It's still a truism that you can't teach painting. Anyone interested can pick up the technique, as far as you can teach him, by himself with a concentrated effort. What's happened to that individuality of yours. That's all that counts in this line—and many others."

"Perhaps I should get the next plane to Paris," he said, grinning. Adam had never seen him so relaxed, nor yet so flippant.

"Perhaps! Perhaps!" She appealed to Adam. "Don't you ever give up, like this shining example. He should never have left. That's his story."

"Come on, now, Gracie," Joseph Grant said. "I was never really that good. Where was my individual voice? Some of us are meant to help along those more talented."

"How many individual voices have you known that found their special vocal cords from the beginning?" she asked. "Some people start with them, others find them at thirty, others at fifty, some much later. When you don't find them is when you give up."

"Don't keep on, you'll depress me."

Grace Goldenbaum glanced at him quickly, saw the smile and smiled back with warmth.

"Well, where are these paintings?" she asked.

Adam went to a cupboard and slid back the door. He took out three canvases. He turned them round and stood them up against the wall. They were surprising

for a young painter only because one didn't expect to
find such thoroughly talented and mature work stuck
away in the evening classes of a local institute in the
English provinces. Although in England, of course,
that's where it usually is and where it usually wastes its
fragrance on the desert air.

They were surrealist, which Mrs. Goldenbaum hadn't
expected—as a matter of fact she hadn't expected very
much at all. She had to put up with approaches like
this all the time, but not often from an old friend like
Joe Grant. They were well composed, electrifying in
their choice of object juxtaposition, subtle in their colour
blends and containing a mystic hint of other worlds.

Grace Goldenbaum stared at them for a minute or
two without speaking. Mr. Grant smiled quietly to
himself. Adam looked at them with a critical eye, quite
forgetting that other people were looking, too.

"Hmmm." Gracie Goldenbaum was impressed. She
stared a bit longer and then she said: "There's a bit of
Simon in them. Do you like my old flame?"

"Yes," Adam admitted reluctantly. "But they're not
so gloomy as his; the colours are more interesting and
half the time he was only kidding around anyway."

Mrs. Goldenbaum looked slowly round at him with
wide, amused eyes.

"Well dig that," she said. "The painter speaks."

She laughed delightedly and went closer for a detailed
inspection.

"You're quite right, as it happens," she said. "A
gloomier man never lived. That's why I left him. He
used to sit for hours gazing at a Camembert. He hated
Camembert for some reason—delicious cheese—and then
all of sudden he'd pound it to a pulp with a wine bottle.
There was a lot of hate in that man. There was something he felt in himself that he could never quite get

to and that made him mean and moody. Sometimes he produced a fake work out of spite."

"Why don't you write your memoirs, Grace?" Joseph Grant asked. "You'd make a fortune." He laughed then at what he'd said. Imagine her needing a fortune.

"I am," she said. "First draft, eleventh chapter. I've already got a publisher."

Joseph Grant whistled in admiration.

"You make me feel older and more washed out with every word you say," he said.

"I'll dedicate it to you," she said. "Or did I promise that to Ernest Hemingway? I'll dedicate it to you anyway." She smiled another warm smile and bent down to look at the paintings.

"Well, these are good," she said, reluctantly, after a while. "Are there any more?"

"Not here," Adam said. "I have a whole heap at home."

She gave him a long, steady look. It was a different look from any she'd given him so far. She said: "Bring them round to my hotel tonight at seven. We'll have a drink and discuss what's to be done."

Grace Goldenbaum was one of those celebrities who is immediately impressed by the potentiality for celebrity in someone else. She could look at someone one minute and think: that's a good-looking person and forget it. Told that that person was so-and-so, the painter, or so-and-so, the Earl of Whatsit, she would look again and see them differently, in terms of people that were worth knowing, making an effort for, etcetera. That was how she'd looked at Adam after seeing his paintings. Suddenly he was no longer a handsome young provincial who could live and die in this "hamlet" as far as she was concerned. Suddenly he was a famous artist in embryo, another protégé, lover, lifelong addition to the legend of Grace Goldenbaum. Creative people, lords and ladies, how she loved them!

She and Joseph Grant, who had begged her to stay at his home but was not surprised at her unabated insistence on complete independence—"It means I can be generous to my friends from the heart, without feeling I owe it to them,"—watched Adam leave the school.

"He has real brilliance," she said. "What does he do apart from paint?"

"Clerking," he said. "He's one of the world's outsiders. Intelligent, quite well read, never attempted to get anything better."

"Good for him," she said. "But he mustn't waste *any* of his time on a whippersnapping job like that. I'll have to see what I can do."

CHAPTER SIX

Adam viewed his appointment at seven with mixed feelings. He didn't feel too much at ease in big hotels —and this was the only really big one in the town. And he wasn't quite sure what was expected of him. There had been something in her look...

Anyway, she'd been impressed with his work. There was no doubt about that.

Walking to the hotel, carrying a dozen of his paintings awkwardly, he glanced down at himself. Well, he'd made a bit of an effort. She should consider herself honoured. Suit for once: the new smart Italian blue, no turnups, 17-inch hem, short jacket, small bow-tie. His mother couldn't and never would understand it all. These enthusiasms for some things, unconcern about others, unexpected meetings and so on. This was what made life worth living: the unexpected boost waiting round the corner.

He went into the hotel. It wasn't so grand, really. Just a good county hotel with a few people in livery. He asked for Mrs. Goldenbaum. She'd taken one of the two suites. All the others were simply rooms, some with private bathrooms, others without.

Adam took the lift up three floors and stepped out into a short passage with a carpet which curled over his shoe welts. He followed the directions he'd been given at the desk and walked to door 22. There was a bright little highly polished knocker in the shape of a knight of King Arthur's Court. Of course the hotel was called King Arthur's Court.

He knocked solidly and after a pause the door opened.

"Hello," she said. "You're dead on time. I like people to be punctual. Everybody but me, that is."

He followed her into the suite. She was quite an eyeful. She was dressed in a simple black cocktail dress, with three rows of diamonds around her bronzed neck. Her stockings were so sheer that they shone like quartz and her black crocodile-skin shoes were long in the toe and dainty. She had a couple of Indian bangles around her right wrist which obviously had more sentimental than material value.

She led the way through the first room into another which looked almost exactly the same. The motif was rose—various shades—cool and warm from the middle rose of the carpet to the deep ruby of the velvet curtains and the deep red of the lampshades with their soft yellowish-pink tassels. The only other colours were pink rosewood and an odd bit of chrome. The effect was pretty good. Adam had had no idea there was quite such luxury in the town. From the outside one would have said untidy oak fireplaces and pebbled windows.

She took his canvases from him without looking at them and placed them against a rose-coloured wall.

"Time for them," she said. "What's yours? Scotch?"

"Champagne," he said, surprising himself. "If you have any."

She stared at him and smiled slowly.

"Sure there's champagne," she said. "I like a man who knows his own mind."

She produced a champagne bucket, glittering with ice, the bottle steamed over, enticing. She pulled the cork expertly and poured them both a large glassful. The champagne was cool and the bubbles ran up and down in it. Adam looked at it for some seconds before he raised the glass towards her. He didn't feel nervous at all. He felt a beginning of power. He felt good, as if he had finally found the world he belonged in.

She settled herself in a large, modern velvet armchair, far from the dim wall lights, and indicated another for him opposite her. It occurred to him that she'd already been knocking it back—Scotch, probably. Her cheeks were slightly flushed. In the rose light she looked positively alluring.

"Well, well," she said. "Tell me what you think. Tell me about yourself."

Adam was rather taken aback. What did he think? What was there to say about himself? But before he could answer, she said: "No, I can see you're not ready. You can tell me later. How often do you drink champagne? Do you really prefer it to Scotch?"

"It makes me lightheaded," he said. "I automatically associate it with Paris. Scotch just remains me of the local pubs and maybe a London theatre bar."

"You don't drink champagne much then?"

"Can't afford it."

"Don't make much money?"

"What do you think—I'm a solicitor's clerk."

"And hate it?"

"Naturally."

"Why not try something else?"

"Gives me a lot of spare time. Doesn't make any demands on my mind at all. Most other work would, I imagine."

"That's the way," she said. "Let's kill this bottle and have another."

They drank. He looked at the room; she looked at him.

"Would you like to see the paintings?" he asked after a bit.

"Later," she said. "I don't really need to. You have it all right."

He flushed with pleasure, felt himself flush and found the flush didn't go. He looked at the champagne. His glass was a third full. The bottle was empty.

But why, he suddenly thought, did she ask me round here if she'd already decided that my paintings were okay? He looked up at her and she smiled at him and held his eyes. Cleopatra looked at him, a Queen inviting, summoning. The flush enveloped him like a flame from the Inferno. He didn't have to think about why, looking at her. It was all clear and inevitable.

She brought another bucket of champagne and some cocktail biscuits. He began to feel quite lightheaded. He looked around the room again. This was riches. He had a quick flash of feeling about it, a real sense of glamour as if he belonged in this world as a rightful owner of it with its champagne, money, comfort, luxury, promise of the pleasures of the flesh, with way beyond it like something coming out of the mists fast cars and aeroplanes and blue seas and yachts and hot sun and long iced brandies by the palms near the beach. She carried this with her, he realised. He was so unlike Joseph Grant. Movement meant life for him: new places, new people, a new blind.

"Have you got a girl friend?" she asked suddenly. The yellow liquid cascaded from the bottle and splashed and bubbled in his glass.

"Nobody special," he said. He couldn't admit anchors in the world around him.

"Well in that case there'll be nobody to get jealous if we have a little dance, eh?"

She switched on a radiogram. He wondered if it really went with the hotel or whether it went with her. After a second, soft dance music, lush music, began to pervade the room. It was old fashioned in a way, but perfect of its type—Glen Miller in fact. He stood up and she came into his arms. She was surprisingly light and graceful and she glued her hips to his, swivelling them slightly as they turned so that she managed to massage his penis in a manner so subtle and expert that she must have been learning it since she was fifteen. He had an erection in no time and there was no hiding the fact, no need to. She put her hand round the back of his neck and stroked his hair. He put his cheek against her hair, thinking: This is working out like a woman's magazine story except for the sex.

"You're such a handsome boy," she said softly. "You'll have the world, your own world, at your feet once you get out of this rut."

"I'm nineteen," he said, "and feel much older."

"Nineteen," she said, smiling into his neck. "Youth, youth, youth, where is thy fling? Have you had many girls?"

"Had?"

"Been to bed with many?"

"Not many."

He realised suddenly that she was quivering. She moved her thighs against his loins.

"I can tell you want to go to bed with me," she said.

He didn't know what to say, dropped his hand down on her moving buttocks.

She slipped her hand down from his back between them, began to play with his penis.

"Let's take our clothes off," she said.

A little thrill squirmed through him. This rich, unfamiliar woman from worlds he'd only dreamed of—what was she saying?"

He glanced at the door.

"It's all right," she said. "It's locked—nobody will come in."

She unbuttoned his flies as they danced, to encourage him. She took both his hands and placed them on her rump, so that he was holding one of her buttocks in each hand. They were as finely-shaped and sinewy as he'd expected. Her body was very warm against him and she raised her face to his as she found his penis under the leg of his pants. He gasped at the cool pressure. He inclined his head and kissed her. She smelt of some faint jasmine perfume. Her lips gave in like a soft cushion and her tongue came into his mouth like a little darting eel. She crushed the length of her body against his and undulated furiously against him before pulling away.

She pulled off her dress. She wasn't wearing very much underneath, must have been prepared.

Adam, feeling rather self-conscious with his erection cleaving the air in front of this stranger, began to take off his clothes. He watched her undress to the last stitch. She had a well-kept body, sagging a little here and there but well dieted and highly tanned. It was the tan that gave it a sort of lustre, made it twice as good looking as it would otherwise have been. Her breasts were slightly thin and long; they swung a little from side to side as she came towards him. The muscles in her thighs rippled slightly and the bones of her hips just showed through, two tiny embossments at each side of the tuft of black hair below her navel.

He pulled off his socks and met her. It was very warm in the room but their flesh met like a touch of icewater. They both began to breathe fast. Adam thought: I dare not think about it, or it'll amaze me so much I'll just faint away into a dreaming sleep.

She ran her hands searchingly down over his body, pressing all the hollows, exploring, learning it all. She got his prick between her thighs as they swayed together to the music, and let it rest, jiggling lightly against the moist lips between her legs.

Adam ran his hands down her back. He could feel the articulated line of her backbone, suddenly blossoming out into those neat, sinewy buttocks. There was a lot of muscular strength in her body. He wondered how those strong thighs would grip.

"You beautiful, beautiful boy." she whispered. She kissed him again, writhing her hips against him. She dug her fingernails into his shoulders. He gripped her buttocks, pulling them towards him, rubbing his prick between the strong thighs.

"My god," she said. "I want you now! Put it in—quick!"

She dragged him with her to a divan and fell back, pulling him over on her in an expert manner that made him think, in passing, of a certain judo throw. Her fingers came down and guided his aching penis at her cunt. She was moaning into his face, her eyes closed, her hips grinding.

Adam entered her with a rush. He had the thought as he did that she was old enough to be his mother, but this simply added a perverse fascination to the whole thing.

His prick rode up in her, tightly at first, hurting along its whole, hard flesh—and then more easily. She let out a short howl, like an animal. He thrust right up into her so that their pelvic flesh bruised and bumped together.

She strained back under him, arching her loins up at his, lifting them both up off the divan for seconds at a time. She moaned incessantly and scratched all round her at the divan until the coverlet was screwed up in a ragdoll mess under them. She bit his lips, turned her face convulsively away, came back and bit his lips again, over and over.

"Put your fingers in my ass," she coughed.

He reached under her between the buttocks as he stroked rhythmically into her juicy quim. He spread them apart, felt the sweating down, found the puckered ring and thrust a finger in. She gave another gasp and screwed her behind back at his hand. He moved his finger around in her asshole. It was soft and fleshy. He felt his nail catch the flesh and she moaned and jerked and then came back again offering her rump for further exploration.

Adam's loins were coiled up like a spring. His penis felt monstrous, as if it were growing away from him in its own separate existence, increasing in size all the time like some fairytale beanstalk, a fairytale prick that would grow and grow and would spear her right through and come out of her mouth and go on searching around the room and out of the window. It expanded and contracted, throbbing painfully.

She held him tightly in the strong thighs, clamping them round his hips, slackening them, clamping them again.

She murmured obscenities in his face. Her own face began to turn a deep, furious colour, her neck strained back, her fingernails raked great weals across his back and shoulders.

"I'm coming," she rasped. The first time it was almost a matter-of-fact statement. And then she began to repeat it at lessening intervals until the words all ran together in a scream. She pulled back her thighs, presenting him with a stretched and widely open cavern of pink at the core of her body. Her legs squirmed up over his shoulders. She thrust her loins at him with bruising force. Her mouth opened, tried to close, couldn't, her eyes glazed, her nostrils flared. She gave a sudden thin unearthly whine and screwed herself onto his prick and held herself there while her loins worked up and down. And then she expelled her breath as if she were a diver suddenly coming to the surface at the end of her tether. She collapsed under him and went limp, only her body shaking and quivering like an animal in its death throes.

Adam felt a little apprehensive, even through his own mounting passion. He was afraid he'd injured her in some way. But after a few moments of simply lying still, moaning quietly, limply permitting him to go on sawing into her quim, she seemed to revive.

She looked at him with a long, purring look like a satisfied cat. She closed her eyes and uttered a cosy exclamation as he dug into her a little further.

"That was something," she murmured.

She gave another exclamation. She held his panting mouth with hers.

"Honey," she said, releasing his lips. "Like a damn virginal fool I've packed my pessary in a trunk that's on the high seas to Le Havre—and I'm not quite so old that I can afford not to have it. It's not fair on you, I know. But I'll do my best. Turn over."

Adam allowed hemself to be turned over on his back, coming out of her with a faint plop. His penis reached yearningly up to the ceiling. He didn't see what difference it made if he screwed her one way or the other, but he let her move him around.

She leaned over him, stroking the stiff rod, first with one hand and then with both. She brought her mouth down to it and enclosed the glans in a moist warm pressure. The very thought of what she was doing as much as the actual feeling gave Adam a sharp kick, like an injection. She held his prick with one hand, lying on his loins, while she began to suck his prick, steadily, rhythmically. Up and down and with a twisting motion of her tongue at the point of each stroke.

He tensed his loins. The sight of the action made it all the more exciting. She began to suck a little harder, sometimes giving him a little bite, or scraping his bone of thick flesh with her teeth. His penis was white under the scraping suck and bright purple at its tip.

She released his jack with her hand and put both hands under his ass, holding his buttocks while she rammed her mouth down on his penis. His prick disappeared right down her. He wondered that it didn't choke her, but she was clearly a specialist.

Her tongue, with that final swiping lick, was making the glans vibrate and pulse as if it were a beacon flashing out a code into the darkness. He stiffened his hips, crossing his legs, pressing his ankles together. He felt the movement growing in his balls, as if he wanted to piss but couldn't. He watched her face working over his abdomen, her lips being pulled out grotesquely, clinging to his staff, sucking it voraciously. He pushed his loins up at her face, arching the lower part of his body from hips to toes. His mouth worked in a sweet agony. His throat was dry. His penis felt like a huge, top-heavy tree trunk. It was a tree trunk that was being felled, growing heavier and heavier until it would suddenly fall down, down... He gasped. But what would she do when he came? He couldn't think about it. Because the moment was nearly here. It was growing, growing. Strangled noises forced their way up from his lungs through the tortured passage of his gullet. There wasn't far to go. He was coming, now, now. He writhed his hips, furiously. He seemed to be standing on his head. He saw as in a wild roundabout her face working, the lips sucking, his penis soaring, his body straining, the lights, the rose, the red, the pink, a whirl. NOW! NOW! He let out a long, high-pitched cry. He felt the needle-thin stream of sperm rush from his balls along the tube at a great, unstemmable rate. She went on sucking furiously as his load shot into her mouth and his hands sought convulsively for her head and pushed it hard at his prick...

Gradually his penis deflated in her mouth but she went on gently nibbling it, sucking every last ounce of his sperm. He gave a great sigh and flopped back, exhausted. She lay for some time with her head against his belly and then she slithered up his body and kissed him on the mouth.

"Come on, sonny," she said. "Let's eat. I have a very special meal ordered. Just get dressed and I'll ring down for them to bring it up."

Adam began to dress. He heard her on the internal telephone asking for the food to be brought up and for this wine and that wine to go with it.

"This," he said to himself softly, "is the life—the only life for me."

CHAPTER SEVEN

"And so she promised to write to me from Paris," Adam said. "She's coming back to London in a week or two and she says she'll fix something up. She has a lot of friends who run galleries."

"Do you think she will?" Eve asked. "Or is she just one of those people who promise these things and then forget all about them?"

Adam formed a picture of the previous evening's bacchanalia. That was an aspect of the affair he had not described to Eve. Mrs. Goldenbaum would want another but once he was within reach, he was sure. She had suggested he might like to come to Paris with her, but that would have presented him with too many problems and he'd regretfully declined.

"I think she's reliable if she really likes someone's paintings," he said.

"This is marvellous then, Adam," Eve said. It may be *the* break. Perhaps in a year's time you'll be famous."

"Not so fast," he chuckled. But the thought was in his own mind all the time.

He sipped his half pint of bitter with a mental grimace, remembering the champagne, the fine wines of the night before. Back to normal for the moment. Eve had a half of bitter, too. She seemed to Adam to be rather depressed today and she looked as if she'd had a late night. No luck with the agents, that was the trouble. It put a year on you every time you tried them.

"I can't stand this one-eyed town, anyway," he said suddenly. "Something had to happen soon."

Eve nodded sadly.

"Well I've decided I must have another try at the repertory here," she said. "They all say it's because I've got no experience."

"I thought old Rushton was difficult."

"I'll just have to persuade him. Maybe he'll watch me do a part."

Eve said one thing, thought another. Rushton, the manager of the local repertory, was another Grampion, a lesser one. He, too, badly wanted to sleep with her. They were all the same. It was the only key to the door. So she'd sleep with him. That was her decision. It would be easy now, after Grampion. But this time she'd make absolutely certain that she got something out of it, and that wouldn't be difficult. Grampion was a married man. He would be scared as hell once he'd let himself in for it.

Poor Adam, she thought. He'd have a fit if he knew what I'd done, what I'm going to do. But it all seemed remote from Adam. It was, after all, business.

"I have the feeling that things will begin to change soon," she said. "They couldn't be much worse."

"I think they will," Adam said, thinking of himself. "There's so much worth having in the world. All you've got to do is make up your mind and then get it."

"We haven't been very clever about it up till now, I think," she said.

He glanced at her curiously, wondering if she'd read his thoughts, but she was thinking about the stage.

"Well to hell," he said. "To hell with this bloody bitter. Let's both have a Scotch for the sake of things to come."

CHAPTER EIGHT

Eve stood on the opposite side of the narrow main street of the town and studied the front of the local theatre. It was an old-fashioned stone building with ornate pillars framing the foyer on either side and the word "Playhouse" flamboyantly painted on a yellow board which filled the broad gable of the roof. The lights were on in the foyer, revealing several glass cases containing photographs of past productions by the repertory company. The box office was empty. They would soon be coming out, the show over, the audience racing to wolf a last drink before England's barbaric licensing laws decreed that drinking must stop for the night, unless one wanted to cart bottles home.

The nicely-designed advertisement placard on the front of the narrow theatre building showed that the company were playing "Blithe Spirit." They seldom attempted anything more ambitious. But this wasn't because they lacked ambition. It was simple economics. The theatre was small, rent was high, houses were about 70 per cent, which was good but hardly enough to keep body and soul together. A local television company gave a grant of a few hundred pounds, the Arts Council gave a few hundred more, the "enlightened" local council gave a hundred—which was a hundred more than most local councils gave—and a small but energetic supporters' club gave another few hundred raised from donations, whist drives and a big annual bazaar, regularly opened by some second-rate television star. So one had to be sure of at least that 70 per cent house. And the only way was to present harmless, superficially entertaining, safe plays. This dictum could, on occasion, be confounded. But it was a risk, always a risk and if the actors were to eat they couldn't afford to take risks more than two or at the most three times a year.

These thoughts went through Eve's head as she waited for the curtain and for the audience to stream out into the street. It wouldn't be much. In fact she wasn't interested in the parts she could or couldn't get in this little hole. The main thing was to get in and to get to know people.

Up the side of the theatre ran a small passage in which were two dustbins and a couple of bicycles. At the end of that passage was the stage door and beyond it the two dressing rooms: one male, one female, and the room which served as an office for the manager. There was also a small and completely inadequate toilet with a broken chain and no lid to the seat. None of it was a dream come true and Eve's thoughts went far beyond it. Many actors and actresses passed their lives in repertory, moving from one to another throughout the provinces, sometimes spending a couple of years in one place, never getting a bigger chance, celebrities only in the local small town—and not even very celebrated there, if one considered the small proportion of any given population which went to the theatre more than three times in their lives.

An attendant appeared in the foyer and clipped back the doors leading to the auditorium. There was a confused sound of people from inside and then the first couples began to emerge, developing into a crush of people, filling the foyer and, as always, hardly moving, aimlessly blocking the path of those yet to come out.

Eve waited until the crowd thinned a little and then she saw Rushton appear in the foyer, a tall man with a sneering, foxy face dressed in a grey tweed suit. He smiled, nodded, sometimes bowed. He thought himself a real personage.

Eve wandered over to the foyer and climbed up the four stone steps. Rushton saw her, smiled warily and turned back to someone who was trying to engage him in conversation. Eve wandered from panel to panel of the photographs which she already knew so well. She knew most of the company already. She was, after all, quite well known in amateur theatrical circles in the town and the standard was pretty high.

The crowd got thinner and thinner until finally Rushton was left with only Brigadier Jankers and Mrs. Jankers, towers of strength in the supporters' club. They knew what they liked. A good play: beginning, middle and end, with plenty of laughs preferably. None of this bolshie-angry stuff and none of this Tennessee Williams psychological muck. Real people weren't like that. Real people like them, like Brigadier Jankers and Mrs. Jankers and woe betide anyone who deviated from their honest, decent norm. Sub-norm, some people would have said. But those were the sort of people the Brigadier would have put under lock and key, or given a good spell in the Pioneers to make them understand what life was about—so they didn't worry him.

"You don't get them the calibre of Coward these days," he was saying. "All plays about nothing these days— filth and Communism (it was surprising he made any distinction) and people shouting about nothing. Rattigan's all right of course, but as for these other fools—I could write a better play myself."

"You should, Brigadier, you should," Rushton said smoothly. He was able to say things with complete ambiguity. Whichever side you were on it sounded as if he was on yours.

"Hah. Yes. Hah. Will one of these days. Surprise the old town," the Brigadier said. "Well, keep up the good work..."

Rushton bowed and said goodnight. He turned to Eve and looked at her without speaking.

"Sounds as if you might get a good play sometime," Eve said. She was completely familiar with Rushton because he was the sort of character she saw right through and felt a mild contempt for.

He smiled and put his tongue in the side of his mouth to make a bulge.

"What can I do for you?" he said. "Decided to give yourself to me body and soul?"

"Body only," she said. "You wouldn't know what to do with a soul if you had one."

He stared at her. He laughed nervously and came towards her. His reaction was different from Grampion's. He didn't really believe her.

"And you, in return, have to take me into the rep and give me a good part in the first play you haven't cast fort yet," she said. "Which I suppose means the week after next."

He continued to stare at her and then he gulped. She saw his Adam's apple move up and down.

"Come back to the office," he said. "You'd better not be fooling."

"I'm not fooling," she said.

She saw the desire in his eyes. His chest was heaving rapidly under his suit jacket. His mind started turning the situation to the auditorium and peered through to where an attendant was walking along the rows of seats looking for lost property.

"Perhaps we'd better not go to the office," he said. "I'll get my car."

"No," she said. "We'll go to the office first. I want something in writing."

"In writing?"

"Yes, I don't trust people very much."

She saw his mind groping over what this meant.

"But how can I trust you?" he asked.

She came up close to him. She pressed her hips against him. "You just can," she said.

He broke away from her, flushing.

"Careful," he said. "Careful, for god's sake."

She smiled to herself. Once he'd fucked her he'd be completely in her power. Strange that he didn't realise that. Or perhaps he did, but his desire was just too much for him.

"Come on then," he said.

He led the way through the auditorium, up the steps onto the stage, off at the wings and round the back to the office. There was a subdued chatting from the dressing rooms. He took her into the office, but didn't lock the door, after a moment's deliberation.

"All right," he said. He sat down behind the shabby desk, pretending to be businesslike for the sake of possible interruptions. He motioned her to a chair opposite.

"So what do you want," he said. "I'll have to take you on as assistant stage manager—you know, making the tea—or it'll look suspicious. But the week after next I can give you a part. We're doing *Flowering Cherry*. You can have the part of the daughter. It's not a bad one for a start. How about it?"

She reflected. Now, she really felt quite excited. The part wasn't a large one, but it wasn't a small one either. And the play was good. Robert Bolt was now respectable enough for them to put on his plays without too much risk.

"All right," she said. "Suits me."

He pulled out a form contract and added a proviso about "Flowering Cherry." He let her read it and then he signed it and she signed it. His eyes ranged all over her while she signed. He'd admired her looks for years. But he'd never really imagined...

"So where do you want payment?" she asked, matter-of-factly. She felt as if she were simply exchanging one commodity for another. He licked his lips. She could see his brain grappling with the possibilities. He'd probably have suggested a weekend if he hadn't been afraid of her changing her mind. He wanted her now, but he couldn't think where.

"We'll go for a drive," he said. "It's too dangerous here."

"All right," she said.

He got up and she stood up. He came round the desk and caught hold of her. He kissed her and she responded coolly. He rubbed his palms over her breasts under her coat. He was sweating at the temples. He turned away from her abruptly and brushed back his hair nervously.

What a seducer, she thought. If his wife so much as telephoned now, he'd have a blue fit.

"All right," he said aimlessly. "Right."

He opened the door gently.

"Let them all go and I'll lock up," he said. "I'll pick you up on the corner by the Crown."

She grinned at the way she was becoming a street corner clandestine. She felt cool and clear headed. At least she was really getting *something* out of this. It gave her a sense of achievement.

She left the theatre and stood for a few minutes on the street corner, looking back at the theatre. She saw a group of the cast leave and set off in the opposite direction. And then the front of house girls came out and walked towards her. She turned into the doorway of a shop and studied the objects in the window: beds, appropriately enough. The girls passed, chattering, and she stepped out from the doorway and watched them go. Everything would be shortly closing up in the town. Last drinks were being called. Then there would only be the two expresso bars, the transport cafe and the two decent restaurants that stayed open until 11.30. There would be the bus queues and the emptying cinemas and the lonely policemen on their beats, a few passengers from the late night train from Waterloo.

Rushton's black Ford Consul came gently down the street. He pulled over to the corner beyond her. That was so that he could see down the other street, in case anyone was coming.

She crossed the road and he snapped open the door. She got in and he leapt away from the kerb and headed through the side streets of the town towards the open country.

"Where are we going?" she asked.

"We'll just have to find a quiet spot," he said. "I can't take you home. There's nowhere else to go."

She sat back in the car, letting the darkness race by outside like a wild dream. This, she felt, was the first real step. How ridiculous of her not to have taken it before.

"What made you decide to... to," Rushton couldn't think how to put it and ended lamely.

"To let you screw me?" She suddenly felt much more experienced, much stronger, than him.

He broke the brief silence with a laugh.

"The soul of delicacy," he said.

"Let's call a spade a spade," she said.

They drove fast and far. He kept slowing at every likely-looking layby, but he was clearly scared. Police cars passed occasionally, people out for a drive. Someone might recognise him. Scandal!

After a while she said: "Are we going to the Continent?"

He titered and then said: "Why, do you want it that badly?"

She was about to make a suitable retort when it occurred to her that she might badly overplay her hardboiled exterior. And in fact, she didn't feel quite so hardboiled now. Shortly he would find somewhere to pull in and then she'd be forced to go through all those intimate things with him. It was embarrassing if she allowed her imagination to dwell on it; it made her stomach flutter.

He turned up a little lane eventually, with the comment: "We'll see where this goes."

It didn't go anywhere to judge by fifteen minutes driving, just meandered through wood and meadow and eventually he pulled in by a five-barred gate, leaving just room for the unexpected vehicle to pass. The engine went dead and he turned off the headlights, leaving them in darkness with the moon-silvered field around them. He turned towards her and she turned her face at his. His breath had a hot, winy smell as his mouth closed on hers. He held her face in his hands and ran his lips all over it and then his tongue.

"You lovely creature," he kept repeating.

And then his hands started moving all over her inside the coat, weighing her breasts, gripping her buttocks, pinching her waist and smoothing her back. He undid the buttons of her blouse, breathing asthmatically through his nose. He felt her breasts with trembling hands. She melted in a little shiver. He tried clumsily to undo the brassiere, lost patience and pulled the cups off the breasts, which poked suddenly and cheekily out below. His legs moved around on the car seat. One hand went away and she sensed rather than saw it fumbling with his trouser buttons.

"Hold that," he said tensely after a second.

He took her hand and moved it over onto his lap. Her fingers encountered the upstanding sticky flesh, sticky with lubricant from his passion. She held it limply for a moment and then she began to stroke and caress it mechanically. She felt now almost in a state of shock. Her sangfroid had deserted her. Was it really happening all over again?

His hands came back onto the flushed bulbs of her breasts. He stroked them at first tenderly, so that the pores of the skin seemed to open to his fingers, and then more roughly as he began to push his loins in time with her caressing hand. He kissed her again, hard and wetly and then he buried his face in her clothes and she felt his lips sucking at her breasts, pulling at the skin all over the pears, as if, indeed, they were ripe fruit. He hurt her a couple of times but she gritted her teeth and bore the pain. It was beginning to unsettle her. She found herself moving her buttocks on the seat; she felt heat between her legs and under her armpits.

Then she felt his hand on her leg. He stroked the stockinged calf, digging his fingers into it, then holding it lightly as if he wanted fully to get the feel of it. And then his hand started to move away, up the warm stockinged leg to her knee. He fondled the underside of her knee for a moment and then went on, advancing slowly, without opposition, up the thigh until he reached the point where the silk covering ceded to soft, filmy flesh. He caught his breath and moved on. His prick was jumping in her hand, jerking with a life of its own and his loins were heaving like a chest after great physical effort.

He came to the frill of her briefs, murmured her name, jiggled towards her and went on into the wet crevice. She gave a little gasp and flattened her crutch against the seat, holding his hand trapped, unable to move. He jiffled his fingers around in the wet little pit until she relaxed. He pushed his fingers further up her quim and now she leaned her torso backwards and thrust her loins forward towards him, releasing his prick.

Breathing in a sort of broken morse code, he pulled at her girdle, somehow getting it undone; he pulled the briefs off her legs and she kicked her shoes into the front of the car.

"Let me take my skirt off," she said. "I'll get creased."

She slipped out of the garment while he wriggled out of his trousers and pants. And then he came back at her, groping for her loins, running his hands all over them as if he wanted to savour every millimetre. She felt quite hot and lustful now and she reached under his shirt and stroked his testicles and pinched his prick with tiny nibbling pressures.

"Let's get out," he suggested hoarsely. "There's not room in here."

Without waiting for her answer he knelt up and reached over the seat for his coat in the back. She drew her sharp fingernails down the underside of his stiff penis and then opened the car door. She stepped out onto the cool tarmac, wearing only her blouse and her stockings with the girdle hanging down. She stood uncertainly in the lane looking along it into the darkness and then he followed her in his shirt and socks with his penis reaching out like a boom and protruding from under the hem.

"The field," he said.

The field was cut off by the gate and a six-foot hedge. It meant climbing over the gate. She felt her embarrassment now. It meant presenting him with her bare rump as she got over. He put a hand on her buttocks.

"Come on," he said, "quickly."

She put a foot on the bottom bar and climbed up. He gave her behind a lustful slap and then shoved his index finger inside her as she swung one leg over. She jumped down to the grass on the other side. It was damp to her stockinged feet. I'll get pneumonia, she thought.

Rushton followed her and she watched his balls swing like a kilt as he levered himself over the top, his penis sticking out above them like a long, searching, dangerous cannon.

He led the way along the back of the hedge, just a few yards, and then he arranged his coat, grabbed her by the waist and practically forced her down onto it. He was in a hurry to get inside her now and he dropped down on her as she lay down, surging into her with a gasp almost before her back had touched the ground. His thrust almost took her breath away. She felt wet, hot and vulnerable with that space between her legs. She really felt she wanted it inside her. If he'd left her now she would have gone mad.

But such thought of leaving was far from his mind. He was scrabbling and shoving to get farther and farther inside her, as if to ram up into her and pierce her womb were his only desire.

His hips danced against her upturned buttocks. She pulled her thighs high under him and bit her lip. This was different from before. Was this familiarity breeding know-how and desire? His thighs were hot on the undersides of hers. She could smell the wetness of the grass around them and see the moon, sleek and bright in the sky. The strange, airy openness of it all added to her sense of being completely free, a child of nature to do exactly as she pleased.

Their grunts and moans mingled together like smoke and steam and their bodies writhed like one with two heads, four arms and four legs. Once she thought: If anybody passed now and stopped, we just wouldn't hear them. And would it matter?

She felt his flexing thrust become suddenly furious, as if he were going to shoot a load of semen into her and then he suddenly relaxed, pulling himself up with an effort. He came out of her and she felt acute disappointment. So much so that she caught hold of his penis and tried to pull it back into her.

"What's up, for god's sake?" she whispered.

"I haven't got any contraceptives on me," he gasped. "I nearly came."

She hadn't even been able to think of it. She grimaced to herself. But now that he was out of her she cooled a little. She was really very stupid taking these risks, she realised. But she was astonished that he was concerned. And then she realised. He could hardly deny paternity—

at least not without going through the courts. Imagine the scandal, the inconvenience.

She reached down and massaged his prick. It was wet with her own juices.

"Why haven't you got any contraceptives?" she said in mock annoyance.

"It's not every day I get this sort of offer," he said.

"Well," she said, "what are we going to do?"

He rubbed up against her. He bit her nipples and rolled his loins on her until she hissed with fresh desire.

"Turn over," he whispered. "I'll make love to you in your bottom."

She was sufficiently roused with passion not to consider his proposal as complete lunacy or to be wholly disgusted. She had heard that people did this sort of thing. It avoided kids. She remembered it had even come out in connection with the homosexual part of the Wolfenden Report that 15 per cent of married couples in Britain made love sometimes that way to avoid pregnancy. It was supposed to be quite exciting for the woman; something to do with a gland there was inside. But surely very painful.

"I don't know," she said. "I don't know..." She couldn't think what to say. And it was getting colder and she was aware of the dampness of the field around them.

He stroked the inside of her thigh right up to the wet opening of her cunt.

"You agreed to let me make love to you," he said. "You're lucky I just didn't go straight on and get you knocked up."

"That wouldn't have suited you either," she said, and then gave a sharp grunt as his fingers found her clitoris. He lowered his head to her body and ran it down her belly. He nibbled the soft protuberance of flesh just under the navel, gathering it into his mouth in a thin roll. He moved on down and licked her thighs. And then he found the fleshy tunnel and thrust his tongue into it. She gave a gasp and then another as his lips closed on the hard little clitoris. She strained her hips up at his mouth, arching her back and gritting her teeth. She had an enormous desire to come into his mouth. She revolved her hips in a grinding, circular motion with a push at his lips every time the motion reached the six o'clock position.

"Don't stop," she pleaded. "Don't stop!"

And at that he bit her clitoris, making her scream. She felt as if the walls of her womb were peeling off. All of a sudden all her inside was crumbling away like a house falling in.

"Go on!" she panted. "Go on!"

And then there was a rushing in her ears and she choked and the house fell right in with a great resounding and echoing crash and she screamed at the sweet, intolerable delight of it and wanted it to go on for ever and never stop.

When it was over and she lay gasping and slowly recovering, he turned her over. She didn't resist. Her will power seemed to have been drained out of her with the orgasm. He kissed her smooth, oval buttocks and bits them with sharp little nips. He drew them apart with his hands and licked the crevice between them. She felt the stain on her asshole as he pulled the skin around it. She felt obscenely naked with him hovering above the deep red little hole, but it didn't matter any longer. Nothing seemed to matter; there was no embarrassment.

She felt his finger probing the little puckered inlet.

"Spread your legs," he ordered.

She spread her legs out, so far that the toes of her stockinged feet touched the grass on either side of the coat. His finger prodded. She winced and strained at it and suddenly it had entered. It didn't hurt very much at all; it was rather pleasant.

He moved it around in her rectum, expanding the anus. He began to saw it in and out in preparation for what was to follow. She wriggled her hips. She felt she wanted to fart, but couldn't.

After a time he dug another finger into the hole and this time it hurt her, enormously, and she bounced away. But he came after her, pinning her down with one hand in the small of her back. She felt like a mounted insect. The finger stayed in her anus, still for a time and then it began to intrude and move with the other one. She wriggled more. Once she'd got used to the extra pressure, it wasn't too bad. In fact she felt subjugated in a way that appealed to her deeply in some unexpected and, to her, rather mysterious manner.

She could feel him deliberately stretching her asshole. It hurt quite a bit every time he made a sharp, sudden movement of his fingers, but now she wanted him to get in her and do the thing properly.

"Do it," she called, turning her head to one side so that he looked down on her flushed face with the hair strewn over it. "Screw me there."

He pulled his fingers out of her. They seemed to come out reluctantly, the rubbery skin of the anus clinging to them until they came out with a sucking noise.

She felt his hot body come down on hers and stretch out along its length. She shivered with anticipation. Then he changed his mind and kneeled up between her thighs.

"Kneel up," he said.

Obediently she kneeled up, presenting him with the stretched moons of her buttocks, bending away before him as she had in front of Grampion.

She felt his hands close on the tops of her thighs, gripping them tighly. And then one hand went away and pushed her arms between her legs so that she could reach his balls. She held them and stroked them for a second and then he said: "Place it for me."

She took hold of his penis. It felt enormous. It was really much bigger than two fingers. She strained outwards and placed the blunt cudgel at the opening of her backside. She felt it prodding and working against her anus. It was going to be much too big. She suddenly felt that with certainty. Now the tip of it had found the comparatively tight aperture and was worming its way into it. It was all right, all right... and then suddenly she felt as if a tree trunk were trying to burst into her body.

She pulled away, but he held her tight and persisted.

"Oh no, no!" It hurts!" she cried.

But he ignored her pleas. He held her now in a bear hug and just pushed and pushed.

"It's too big! It won't ever go in!" she screamed.

She couldn't escape from him. His thighs thrust her thighs forward; his arms held her hips back at his. She was helpless.

"Push back!" he yelled.

She could hardly think. Every way was pain and more pain. She pushed back and opened her ass, as if by deliberate effort, that final centimetre. It was like flicking a plaster off a wound: the quicker the better. His penis surged right into her rectum, solid and very painful, but now better because there was no more to go.

"Oh, oh, oh!" she gasped.

It was like having her asshole shored up with huge

supports, like a mine that would collapse if they were moved.

Now gasping and crooning with delight he began to saw rhythmically and without the slightest mercy deep up into the soft confines of her back passage.

Gradually the pain eased a little, though it was still a mixture of hurful discomfort and stimulation. She felt strangely wet between her buttocks and also strangely ashamed. She had never expected to be sodomised and there seemed something not quite decent about it, something rather debasing. But every time these thoughts crept into her head, they were hurled right out again by a skin-splitting thrust which jolted her forward and made her squirm back onto the rod which was meting out the punishment. She began to feel a masochistic joy. The pain was weirdly pleasurable. She began to move backwards to meet the forward thrust of his loins. She began to undulate her body and move her buttocks in tiny circles. She even began to feel quite excited through the pain and she reached under her and scratched his swinging balls gently, turning her face sideways just so that he could see the effect he was having on her.

Kneeling above her, Rushton watched the reddish skin of the little round hole draw back with his prick, clutching it as if it didn't want him to come out. At first the pressure on his cock had been almost too much to bear, but now it was just tight and exhilarating. The sort of squeeze that promised to pull the sperm right out of his tube like a dozen razor blades at every thrust.

He watched his white, furious penis disappear right up her ass with every stroke. It went right in so that not a half inch of it showed and then it moved about in that tight, resistant passage with the knob straining out as if it were going to burst like a boil.

There was a speck of shit on the rough edge of her anus where his rod entered it and the skin against his prick already looked inflamed.

His balls ached and his penis danced with a thousand hot sparks every time he surged into her, and she herself was moaning and adding to his pleasure by the movement of her bottom and the hollowing of her back. He watched her face as his lips drew back from his teeth. Her beautiful face was flushed crimson in the moonlight, dark in the moonlight, and her shoulders shook in time with the fishlike opening and closing of her full mouth. Her long, blonde hair fell over her face and flopped around her neck as she squirmed. She was completely his. A slave, submitting to him. He could do with her anything he liked and he did, digging his penis into her ass and leaving it there, hearing her groan while he simply joggled his loins and moved it gently around in her channel like a probing, hard-bodied snake.

"Oh, yes," she breathed. "Go on!"

He drew it out to the glans and then plunged it right in again in one long, slow stroke. His prick was tingling, his balls alive. He could come now whenever he chose and he wanted to feel that rush of sperm into her ass; that would be the ultimate submission.

He began to rub rapidly into her, hard and fast, battering her quivering buttocks with his hips. He gripped her waist hard with his fingers, squeezing the spare flesh into odd shapes. His mouth opened and wouldn't close again. His breath whirled out of it in long, broken gasps, like that of a man rowing. He stared at her slender body as he spread the thighs wide and pulled her buttocks apart even more with his hands. He wanted to skewer her like a carcase, split her body wide open. His prick was huge and heavy, loaded with weight as if it had ripened in the last seconds.

"My god!" he groaned. "My god!"

His shirt got in his way and he tore at it convulsively with sharp, jerky movements, like a puppet. His fingers scratched her buttocks hard, grabbing the flesh in handfuls. He touched her anus with his fingers, feeling the heat of friction where his cock drubbed in. She was murmuring incoherently and turning her face from side to side on the blanket of his coat. He pulled her back onto his staff like fitting a boot. His prick was swollen and bloated like a body three days in water. It was like a balloon, a balloon full of intensity. He gasped, choked out her name, gasped again, gave a last spine-chilling ramrod thrust and shattered his sperm in wave after wave into the depths of her behind. It seemed as if his scrotum had never been emptied before. He groaned and almost cried with excruciating delight...

Some minutes later he got up from his kneeling position against her backside. He wiped his penis on the grass. The field and the moon and the nearby lane and the car all swam back into the picture. He glanced at his watch. God, they'd been a long time!

"Better go," he said.

The girl straightened up as if she'd been asleep.

"That hurt," she said accusingly.

They stood up and went to the car. They both felt ridiculous standing nearly naked in the lane. They dressed quickly and he turned the car with some difficulty and they headed back to the town.

"You can start when you like," he said, after a while.

"I'll have to give a week's notice," she said.

They drove on in silence. Her bottom ached now. Her back passage was sore as hell.

"I'll make sure I get my money's worth for this," she told herself. And she gave a little wintery smile in the darkness.

CHAPTER NINE

"But it's so dangerous," Rushton said. "Don't you understand how dangerous it is?"

"It may seem dangerous to you, but to me it's just something I'm not going to miss—not for anything."

"What do you mean—not going to miss. It depends on me if I take you."

"If you don't take me, you know what I told you I'd do."

"I don't believe it. You wouldn't be such a bitch. And in any case it would affect you too."

Eve smiled at Rushton. She didn't have to press her point. He knew she had the whip hand.

It was midweek, lunchtime. He had driven her 30 miles to a distant town so that they wouldn't be seen having lunch together. Later he would drive her back and drop her on the bus route and then they'd meet later at the theatre where she was having a big local success in *Flowering Cherry*. Their attitude in company together was of friendly banter and comparative indifference. They played their parts well. So well, in fact, that nobody seemed to have guessed that her sudden entry into the ranks of the repertory was more than persistent soliciting on her part and an eventual recognition of her quite apparent talent. The public took to her looks; the company found her a good but inexperienced actress. She was unlikely, they felt, to reach higher levels.

Rushton was infatuated with her, she could tell. But he was annoyed with himself for being so. Half the time he was pleading, half the time bullying. Very, very occasionally she let him drive her out into the field and enjoy a repeat performance of the tender delights her charms could give him. Very occasionally. In fact, every time he gave evidence of being so exasperated that she feared he might try to kick her out rather than put up with the torment. She enjoyed sex with him occasionally, but most of the time she was aloof. She used him as she needed him. And now she needed him to take her to the London party he'd been boasting about for some days. It was a party being given by a repertory company on the ringe of Central London. They were one of the best reps in the country; members were always being taken into West End productions. They got a bigger grant from the Arts Council than most and they even had a special dispensation from the Gulbenkian Foundation—the only repertory in the country for this distinction. Of course, they were no better off materially than most repertory companies—worse than many. They produced in a converted church hall which held an audience of about 150 people on hard canvas chairs, the canvas stretched over tubular frames. There was no bar, and coffee in the interval behind the petition at the back of the auditorium just seemed to emphasise how very cold it always was in the theatre. But they were very good, and they had this reputation.

The party was being given in honour of their twentieth anniversary and they'd invited a few friends from the provinces. Rushton had been manager there before moving to the greater material comfort of his present post. No actors of any great note were going to be at the party, but at least one famous drama critic and a couple of the new young playwrights had promised to turn up. This had been enough for Eve to determine that she was going to be there. The environment of London was enough to raise her blood pressure; to be in theatrical circles there, even if they weren't the highest, was like a shot of cocaine.

But Rushton had been difficult. Some of them knew him up there. They didn't know his wife but they might think it strange. She might bump into one of them some day. Who could tell?

She had cut right through his arguments. She was going and that was all and if he didn't agree, then his wife would begin to hear things she shouldn't. He'd fought a desperate losing battle, as much against himself as against her, as in many ways he wanted her to come— and there was a chance they might be able to spend the night together. This thought gave him goose flesh. He wanted to see just how many times he was still capable of performing the act in the same night; he wanted to have her naked against him in the cosy, long-lasting warmth of a bed, away in a strange hotel where nobody knew them and there could be no fear at all of discovery, no anxieties. But he was a little frightened of her determination. Her self-possession often disturbed him. He would have liked her to be madly in love with him, prostrate at his feet. He'd had one or two affairs since his marriage, but they'd been with older women, married women. And they'd either been more lukewarm than this or he'd been in command of the situation. This time, although he never dared admit it to himself in so many words, she had all the power in the world to hurt him. And although he hid this from her frantically, it often seemed that she knew it and, worse, that she didn't give a damn. He was seldom allowed to intrude in her private life. He knew she had a boy friend, but she wouldn't even say if the boy friend had an inkling about him. He was both jealous and helpless. The only time he could pretend he dominated was when he had her moaning under him. Then he gritted his teeth and really gave it her, imagining he was hurting her, paying her back for her rebellion. But alas, the moment passed, and he saw that she'd enjoyed her own sexual fulfilment in a little whirl of passion which had nothing to do with him personally. It was as if he were the slave serving his powerful mistress and then being banished to the stables.

He tinkled his spoon nervously in his empty coffee cup. He looked up at her, thanking heaven that he had these moments when, at least, she was with him alone and forced to direct her attention on him, even if it was only to dismay and menace him.

"All right," he said, slowly. "I'll have to say I met you in town and brought you along. It'll look bloody suspicious, but nobody'll be able to prove otherwise. And then we need never mention it unless something totally unexpected happens to throw it in our faces."

"That's right. It's simple, really."

She smiled across the table at him and put her hand on his. The gesture made him feel better. He looked forward to the Saturday, to the long time alone with her, to the possible night. The party itself became meaningless.

CHAPTER TEN

Somewhere in the background Lottie Lenya was singing snatches from the *Threepenny Opera* in German, but the wonderful voice was almost drowned in the hum of conversation, the movement from bottle to bottle, the clink of glasses, the coming and going throughout the house. They had arrived when the party was well under way. They'd had several drinks on a tour of London bars to brace her for the ordeal of meeting the sort of people she'd never really met before outside the small circle of the home town rep. She felt slightly high and gazed around the house in delight. It belonged to the chairman of the directors of the company which owned the theatre—a Sir Hugh Cassidy-Cox, who had once written his own play which the company had dutifully performed, and who liked to think of himself, old bachelor as he was, belonging to the young, creative set, being a regular bohemian. Nobody could say he lacked generosity.

He was fixing drinks for several people now—for those who preferred not to help themselves. A round, chubby man with grizzled grey hair and crinkled, sharp eyes, he listened to everyone's conversation at once, chuckling and agreeing and making suggestions and then suddenly coming out with something so reactionary that nobody could even take him seriously. Except that he was serious, for he'd never allowed his interest in the theatre to rid him of any of his prejudices, which were all of the most solid Victorian variety. But he had to be tolerated or the theatre might fall around the ears of the actors. So they drank and were merry and turned away from him when they wanted serious conversation.

Eve accepted a drink from someone and looked around the room into which they'd come. They'd entered through a little courtyard from the street and come straight through French windows into a delightful room with modern furniture and paintings and a stairway running up one side of it to the floor above. There was a huge log fire in a very large grate and the cigarette smoke was thick. Someone wandered in from a room on the right carrying two more bottles of Scotch and dragging a crate of beer. Low voices came down from the stairs where all was in darkness.

Rushton was cut off from her and she was left contemplating a couple of paintings for a moment. Nobody was ready to jump up from established conversation and comfort to make a beeline for the attractive girl who'd just arrived. That would have been a little too corny.

She caught snatches of conversation:

"I thought your answer to Noel Coward was very good; really that man is a supreme idiot." ... "So is your new play going to be more or less a sequel to 'The Voice of the Herd'?" ... "I just dislike playing those roles where everything's laid on for you. Look at O'Toole as Private Bamforth—very good, of course, but he couldn't do more than act out a rigid type, the barrack room lawyer. Give me a more subtle part every time." ... "Oh, there's money in television all right and there's no need to move over full time." ... "Yes, Sir Michael invited me to the first night. He told me to go backstage afterwards; some sort of party..."

She felt a thrill of longing and apprehension. She glanced surreptitiously at the speakers. She began to place them. That would be Edwin Fryer, who was making such a name for himself with his Royal Court plays. And that would be James Harrod, the famous drama critic. How young he was, and handsome! And he'd already travelled over half the world for his newspaper and been invited as guest critic to half a dozen publications in other parts of the world. And that face she'd seen in character parts in films. And they all looked so vital, as if they were all going somewhere, not just stagnating and slowly dying in a little provincial slough.

"I'd like you to meet Eve Patten..."

She turned from the paintings. Rushton was approaching with a big, bearded man in a check shirt with a hairy chest visible at the open front. Here we go, she thought. This is the beginning of Eve Patten's bid for stardom.

Two hours and many gins later she found herself sitting in a corner with the famous drama critic. At first she hadn't heard a word he'd said just out of dazzlement at the proximity of a celebrity, but now she was listening and doing her best to keep up with him, feeling very young and inexperienced, but trying hard not to show it. It didn't seem to worry him, anyway. He was content to talk to a willing and, indeed, fascinated listener.

More people had come and there was dancing going on in what seemed like the far reaches of the room. Actually it was a few feet away, but drink had lent distance to everything. Sometimes she glanced up to see who was looking and noticed the figures swaying thickly together, licentiously many of them—there was a lot of undisguised mauling going on—or squatting on the floor, on divans, clustered in groups around chairs, dozing, chattering, drinking, nibbling food. Rushton was deep in conversation with the bearded man, having made full circle and come back to him. But not so deep that he failed to cast a possessive eye in Eve's direction every five minutes.

It hadn't taken Eve long to realise that, in spite of the greater fame of the two playwrights present, the drama critic was the man with far and away the most influence. He knew the most people; his opinion was law for a great many.

"Of course," James Harrod was saying, "all these plays suffer badly in translation. You find that even in such obvious things as the titles. I mean 'Huis Clos'— 'Vicious Circle' ... 'In Camera', no, neither; the words are untranslatable as an identical concept and you find exactly this point on the more serious level of values and attitude. It's difficult for so many of us to accept that purity of Anouilh's. It crosses the Channel badly. It has nothing to do with morality, but with keeping one's own nature strong and clear, preserving it in a pure state..."

His voice went on, a beautiful voice which roamed among the words so easily and fluently. She had the feeling that she could ask him about absolutely anything and he'd be able to give her a long and detailed answer without any hesitation at all. She toyed with funny questions in her mind—"Tell me about West Highland Terriers"—so that she nearly giggled at her own thoughts. Being a good drama critic must involve so much more knowledge and powers of analysis than ever a playwright needed, she realised.

She looked up at him and his eyes devoured hers as he talked. His voice went on ranging over his thesis, but she could tell that he was looking at her too as a woman. She let her skirt move up her thigh a little and his eyes flicked away to the leg and back again to her face without there being a break in his words.

They drank their liquor and he went on talking while she listened.

"...you ought to meet some of these people," he said. "I'm sure you'd find them interesting—and you can never know too many people when you're trying to create opportunities for yourself."

Her ears went back. This was the sort of language she understood immediately.

"I should like that very much," she said. Her hand brushed his arm as she put down her glass, apparently accidentally. She looked into his eyes and repeated:

"Yes, I really would like that."

He seemed about to say something more when Rushton came over. Rushton beamed at him and got a lukewarm response, but, not put off, he joined in the conversation with them for a few minutes before he was pulled away by somebody else. The critic began to discourse about another topic. The chance had been lost.

After a time he put down his glass.

"Call of the wild," he said. "Don't go away."

He stood up, stretched and climbed up the stairs to the storey above. She let Rushton see her sitting alone, smiled at him, waited for him to return to his conversation and then stood up. She edged round the fringe of the body of dancers, noting on the way that one girl had both hands down inside the waist of her husband's trousers, and began to climb the stairs.

Several rooms led off a landing at the top. She heard the obvious gasps of lovemaking coming from a couple. Another had the door open and beyond its darkness she saw a thin streak of light coming from under a door. That must be the bathroom. She peered into the dark room. There was a bed in the corner and a couple were smooching on it. They paid no attention to her.

She waited in the light of the landing until she heard the cistern being flushed in the bathroom. The door opened throwing a flood of light across the intervening room and the critic came out. She moved forward and he saw her.

"The call of the wild is strong tonight," she said, moving towards him.

The ambiguous words were an invitation and he accepted without hesitation. He turned the light out in the bathroom and pulled her into the shadow. He kissed her, enveloping half her face in his mouth and straining her body to his until she was almost breathless.

"Let's make love," he whispered, as he ran his lips over her willing face. His hands felt her body all over. He grabbed her by the buttocks and pulled her hips at his as he bent her backwards.

He drew her towards the bed and then he saw the couple already in occupation.

"Fuck!" he said.

She resisted then, very gently.

"I'm with someone," she said.

He didn't seem to hear.

"Let's go back to my place, baby," he said, reaching out to hold her breasts.

"I'm with someone," she insisted. "I can't possibly."

She kissed him, putting her tongue in his mouth and rubbing her hips against his.

"Why don't you take me to one of the parties where I can meet some people," she said. "We can have a ball afterwards."

She sensed him hesitate. He wasn't short of attractive women. But, of course, she was new. If he'd had her now that would have been the end of it. She understood that only too well, sure as she was that he hadn't even the vaguest idea of her name.

She put her hand on his buttocks and that seemed to decide it for him.

"All right," he said. "Give me a ring."

He thought better of that.

"No let's make it a date. There's a party next week with Sir George and Lady Celia Duncan. Call me Tuesday lunch time and we'll fix it."

He gave her a card with his name, address and telephone number. He didn't ask where she came from. She supposed he thought she lived in London.

"My name is Eve," she said. "Eve Patten. I haven't got a card—you'll have to remember."

"Eve Patten," he repeated.

She sensed him smile in the darkness.

"That's a good name," he said. "Well Eve, bring your apples with you next time. A basket load."

She let the back of her hand rest against his prick, as if by accident. She could feel its hardness. He pressed against her, gave her a fierce French kiss and then walked away to the landing.

Eve went into the bathroom and looked at herself in the mirror. She made up her lips and meditated, trying to keep as calm as possible. As long as he didn't forget or change his mind, things were working out wonderfully. She looked at her body in the full-length mirror. It was serving her very well at the moment. She left the bathroom and went downstairs. James Harrod was talking to another group of people across the room and she made no effort to approach him.

She joined Rushton, who looked at her, smiling, pleased that she came to him as if it was the natural thing to do. Perhaps, he thought, she was finally succumbing to him. He'd put the finishing touches to her tender submission in the hotel bed tonight, that he would. He grinned, with the Scotch inside him. All was right with the world.

CHAPTER ELEVEN

Adam read and re-read the letter. It was written on blue notepaper that had the appearance of cloth. It ended with kisses. He studied the envelope with the attractive French stamp—a view of a beauty spot instead of the unimaginative, interminable head of the English stamps. The stamp conjured up the city: Paris with all the glamour attaching to the name. He saw a dream city and he saw Mrs. Goldenbaum—a dream woman— from it. And now, good as her word, she was plucking him from the ugly pettiness of this little town and pulling him up there with her in the world of dreams. The invitation was for next week. He was to come to the Dorchester where she would be staying and he could stay in her suite with her for the weekend. They were to meet Leon Dalmain, one of the most influential gallery owners, at a party on the Saturday night. There would be an art critic or two and even a painter or two as well. All this she mentioned in brief. The letter was mostly about what they would do in her suite at the Dorchester, in the bedroom, in the bed. She told him what a wonderful fuck he'd given her, how she was looking forward to licking his prick again, how she wanted him to do this and that to her.

He smiled to himself. A pleasure, he thought. At your service, Ma'am, as long and as often as you like, always provided you help me up that ladder.

Adam put the letter down on the table beside his bed. He'd received it a couple of days ago and the big problem seemed to be how to explain his being away to Eve. He'd finally decided simply to pass Mrs. Goldenbaum off as a man. To his surprise, Eve had made no difficulty at all. She had almost seemed relieved that he wasn't going to see her at the weekend, said something about an awful lot of work she had to do for the next repertory production. They hadn't been seeing quite as much of each other lately. Of course, now that she had this particular job with no set hours, she was often caught up in rehearsal, or in simply learning her part, or in some activity of the theatre. They'd been out a couple of times in the last week or so. She seemed a little tired, a fact he put down to the great amount of work she was doing. He'd tried hard, after the night at her aunt's, to get her to let him screw her, but she just wouldn't quite give in, although she did toss him off now, not seeming to mind that his semen went all over her stockings or her skirt as they lay together in some field. He couldn't really understand why she wouldn't let him have her. It seemed like some strange sort of virginal pride which contrasted strangely with her broad-minded attitude to most things. She pretended to be afraid of the consequences, but she wouldn't let him do it even right after her period, using a contraceptive. His desire for her increased the more she refused him. He'd seen her naked, he'd caressed her body, her quim, done everything, in fact, but the ultimate. He wanted to have her pinioned under him, to hear her gasping reaction to his screwing. He was well aware that if he didn't have the outlet of

Mrs. Goldenbaum, he'd probably have raped Eve by now; it wasn't fair of her to tease him in this way.

His mind lingered on Mrs. Goldenbaum, on her nudity and what they would do together. It was a voluptuously pleasant thought and the images in his memory seemed hardly possible, now. He knew nothing about her. He didn't even know her Christian name... and yet that had happened between them.

He dozed off, slowly, picturing screwing Mrs. Goldenbaum, and in his dream she gradually became Eve.

CHAPTER TWELVE

The wall lights were low, giving a dark, velvet splendour to the room. At intervals the wall was adorned with old Flemish paintings, illuminated by a tiny strip of fluorescent light below each. Little bronze statuettes and a couple of marble busts had their places in the corners. The wallpaper was dark red and the curtains were leaf green. The heavy atmosphere of decadence just came off.

This room led into another through a Spanish archway and that room too was heavy and splendid like an over-ripe fruit. Where this one was red and green, the other was just blue. And beyond it was another in yellow. It was strangely impressive and Eve was impressed.

She was impressed, too, by the people who thronged these rooms, knocking back Scotch and champagne as if it was tea. She could only think that they glittered. They exuded a rich glitter—with their clothes, their jewels and their manners. They were not of the world she knew. They were money, money and more money, not ostentatiously but in a way that just quietly acknowledged itself, without shouting, but without shame.

This was the home of the Earl of Haverford and the people at the party were drawn from the top rung of the Arts and the top rung of the people who patronised them. Most of the people were much older than Eve and she felt a sense of inadequacy against them. Things that had taken her a long time to acquire—such as a slight familiarity with Chekhov, Ibsen, Strindberg and so on—they had grown up with, absorbing into the bloodstream every nuance not only of the world's theatre, but the world's literature and art together with a personal acquaintance with the currents of politics and current affairs and banking and motor cars and travel and... everything was known to them. Impossible to see how they could have learned so much in the years at their disposal. She would have thought there were limits to how much one would absorb in a given time. They had another thing in common. These who were not actually artists themselves in one field or another had a respect for those that were which transcended any admiration of knowledge and learning for its own sake. It was only the recognition of this that made her able to stay there and face this galaxy of concentrated experience.

"Ah—there's Sir George," James Harrod said. "Let's go and have a word with him."

Eve followed his glance and her heart jumped. Sir George Duncan in person—and that would mean that Lady Celia was somewhere near. He looked shorter than he did on the stage, and older. His face was a little overpowering with that large nose and those deep-set eyes with their heavy brows. Her heart fluttered as they moved through the drinking, chatting crowd towards him.

He saw them coming and smiled at James Harrod.
"Hello Jim. How's the novel coming on?"

"Frightened of it. Can't bear to think that when it finally gets down on the paper it won't amount to anything."

"Always run it as a serial in the *Daily Express* if it's no good."

James Harrod chuckled.

"There are some things even I won't do," he said.

Sir George looked expectantly at Eve. In fact he looked at her very expectantly so that she felt herself flush.

Harrod introduced them and Sir George seemed to stroke her hand as they shook them.

"What are you doing here with such a bunch of old fogies?" he asked.

"Old fogies!" Her words were an eloquent answer to his question.

"Well perhaps we have our points, eh James?" Sir George said.

He looked at Eve appraisingly. To her astonishment she saw he was stripping her with his eyes. For some reason it was the last thing she had expected. It reduced him to an easy, familiar level.

"You certainly *do* have your points," she heard herself saying. "When I see you and Lady Celia in *A View from the Bridge* I feel like giving up trying."

"Ah, flattery, flattery," said Sir George. "I'm never too old or famous to love it. So you're in the business, eh?"

Eve told him what she did and all the time she talked his eyes studied her, dropping to the prominent points of her breasts, measuring the slim waist, ranging over her features as if he were sizing her up for a portrait. She found this very personal interest highly exciting.

"Ah yes," he said. "I know the company. There are better ones, if you'll forgive my saying so, but of course there are so many of us, sadly so many of us." He grinned at Harrod. "There must be more people wanting to get on the stage even than there are others wanting to be drama critics, eh James?"

"Not quite," Harrod said. "There's a waiting list of ten thousand for my funeral. It becomes embarrassing with so many people enthusiastic for your ruin. Worse than being Prime Minister."

"What's the answer then, Jim. Wine, women or opium?"

"Whatever comes to hand," Harrod said, glancing obliquely at Eve. She had the feeling that they both wanted to take her off and debauch her.

A small, rather heavily made up woman joined them. She exuded an animal magnetism like perfume. Lady Celia! Eve felt that her system would never recover form the jolts of excitement it was getting today.

"Hello darling," she said to Sir George with a hint of sarcasm. "Searching out the talent?"

Eve smiled nervously, not knowing quite what to make of this approach.

"Finding it, my dear," Sir George retorted smoothly.

Lady Celia gave Eve a long, cool, soul-searching glance. She had the most flaming dark eyes Eve had ever seen. Eve felt that her innermost thoughts were revealed to this woman. She sensed that there was absolutely no point in trying to ingratiate oneself with her. She was the sort of person who liked very few people and made no bones about everyone knowing it.

"Has my husband made any indecent suggestions to you yet?" she asked.

James Harrod came to the rescue.

"He was waiting for you to arrive, Ce, so as not to have any advantage."

"It would be the first time he'd ever played it straight," she said, without humour.

The burning eyes roamed over Eve. There was no direct hostility in them, simply a cold, analytical penetration. Eve felt extremely uncomfortable. She didn't pretend to understand the turn the conversation had taken. Nobody remembered or bothered to introduce her to Lady Celia. Introductions had been bypassed.

"You're an actress, are you?" Lady Celia asked. "You have the look."

"In a small way," Eve said.

"Don't be modest, dear. It isn't becoming."

"I'm not concerned about being becoming," Eve heard herself say.

"Oh you should, dear. It's the only saving grace."

"I think treating other people like human beings is the only saving grace."

Harrod grinned. Sir George looked at his wife in amusement.

"How old fashioned, my dear," Lady Celia said, her eyes unyielding.

"Not at all," Harrod interrupted. "It all depends on how we think human beings should be treated. It leaves the question wide open for personal idiosyncracies."

Sir George chuckled.

"A good answer then, eh my dear?" he said to his wife. "I think we should invite her to the anniversary party, don't you?"

"By all means," Lady Celia said sweetly.

"Two hundredth performance of the show," Sir George said to Eve. "A little gathering *chez nous*. Will you come?"

"I'd love to," Eve said.

This seemed hardly to be the world of reality. This was the stuff that dreams were made of. And yet... she had the impression they expected something from her.

"Right," Sir George said. "The more the merrier. Jim here will tell you how to get there—next Sunday. We prefer the Sabbath for these dos."

Eve was making quick calculations. She could just about spare the fare. It would mean more excuses to Adam and Rushton, but that was a small matter. As it was Sunday she wouldn't have to pretend to fall ill as she had today to get the evening off.

"What's lined up for the future," James Harrod was asking them.

Eve hardly listened. She watched their lips moving, saw their eyes flicker back over her, but she didn't really take in any of the words. All you had to do was to move in the right circles. That was all there was to it. Amazing!

After a time they excused themselves and moved on and Harrod went to get them some more drinks.

"Want to have a look at the place?" he asked. "You know the flat across the landing belongs too."

They walked through the plush and gilt rooms, helping themselves to canapes on the way. She was enthusiastic about the Duncans.

"Oh they have some strange sides," Harrod said.

"How? What do you mean?"

"You'll find out."

He refused to discuss them further, but led her instead across the thick-carpetted landing from which the broad thick-carpetted stairways ran away to one side of the lift and into the suite of rooms beyond the open door opposite.

There were few people in this section of the flat, but there were trays of glasses and bottles everywhere and they helped themselves liberally. Some of the rooms were in darkness and it was through the big wooden doors of one of them that Harrod led her. He closed the door behind them and pulled her to him, breathing hard.

"Where are we?" she asked softly. "Somebody will come."

"It will only be me," he grinned. "This is one of the bedrooms. I know this place like the palm of my hand."

"But won't anybody come in?"

"Only for a screw. If they find it's occupied they'll leave. In any case they won't be able to see who we are."

He took her glass and she heard him put them down somewhere, though she could hardly see anything in the darkness.

He came back to her and his lips came moistly down on hers, drawing them into his mouth and then crushing them back against her teeth. She felt his teeth against hers and then his tongue probing between them.

"My god," he said. "I want you badly."

He pushed her back, gently, kissing her neck, and lowered her onto a bed.

"My dress," she whispered. "It'll be ruined."

"Take it off," he whispered back.

She took it off. She was trembling with excitement. The strangeness of the surroundings, the drink, the fact that someone might come and that that someone might even be Sir George or Lady Celia, those Olympian figures, thrilled and frightened her to the very core. She felt a thrilling desire to be naked, completely naked, on the silk coverlet she could now feel against her bare thighs and shoulders. She undid her brassiere. She heard rustlings in the darkness. He was undressing, too.

She undid her girdle, took off her briefs and kicked off her shoes. She lay back voluptuously on the silk coverlet, feeling like a royal favourite of centuries gone by. She felt her breasts tenderly with her own hands, and the soft firmness of her belly and thighs.

"What luxury," she whispered.

Harrod came down on her then, panting. The moment his flesh touched hers she quivered with sensual delight and he gritted out between his teeth: "My god, I'm going to fuck you as you've never been fucked before."

"Please, please," she whispered.

Their mouths locked together and she rubbed against him, stroking his hard cock with her slim fingers, drawing her nails gently over his testicles. He gasped a couple of times and his prick jerked up of its own volition away from her pursuing fingers.

His mouth moved on voraciously over her neck and shoulders and down to her hard, erect-nippled breasts. He sucked the nipples, bringing gasps of mixed pleasure and pain from her with his hard little bites. And then his mouth moved on away and he slid down her body. His lips were on her ribs, below the breasts, on her belly. His tongue explored her navel, briefly and moved away following the line of down straight down to the sudden protrusion of pubic hair. He slid his hands under her buttocks and lifted them slightly. She felt his tongue on her thighs. Her loins were a whirlpool. And suddenly his tongue had shot into her cunt, like a darting lizard, sending a sharp, quivering spasm up her spine.

"Oh, wonderful, wonderful," she breathed.

He licked and sucked, drawing the clitoris up to its full erect state, using lips and teeth and a fluid tongue. She wanted him inside her. She wanted her quim to be turned inside out and drubbed with his prick.

She pulled his hair gently, her eyes closed in ecstasy.

"Get inside me," she breathed. "Fuck me; fuck me to death."

The drink was making her slightly dizzy. The effect added to the illusion that she was just a personified quim, aching and longing. Nothing mattered in the world but sex. At this moment, nothing else mattered. Not the theatre, not Sir George, not fame, not riches. Only this lovely, swirling, exultantly dizzying nucleus of pleasure in her cunt which throbbed and pulsated under his attack.

He slithered up her, forcing her thighs wide. She was wet and wide open to him. Her cunt was like a redhot tunnel waiting for an ice-cold penis to come stinging in.

And it came, suddenly, smoothly, superbly, shatteringly. It came in at the beginning and soared right through to the end, bringing one long scream of ecstasy from her open mouth. And it began to move around inside her and in and out, never stopping, always probing, seeming to go farther all the time, as if it was eating at her heart.

She pinned back her legs, wriggling her buttocks on the slippery luxury of the silken coverlet. She was a mass of exquisite moisture between her thighs. Her loins blazed at her mind as if to overpower all thought, all being except themselves. She was vaguely aware of his hands running over her like flames, of his lips, of the hot friction of his body as he squirmed and swarmed against her.

She saw the flash of light as the door opened and somebody came in but she paid no attention and nor did he. Nothing mattered but this blaze of soul-raking passion which had caught them as if they were boiling together in a cauldron. He filled her, filled her utterly like a lost piece of herself. If only this could go on for ever, she could live and be happy for ever, wanting nothing else in this world.

She gasped out words at him between her streams of panting breath.

"Screw me, darling! Screw me for ever!... Wonderful, wonderful... Oh, up, up, up... Come high in me, darling..."

She panted and writhed. She heard his wailing breath. His penis was a huge, unrelenting animal, snuffling and hurtling into her, making her tingle from the tips of her toes to the back of her skull. It was a dream, a heavenly nightmare. To have such exquisite happiness in one's own power all the time, within one's own body, was unthinkably glorious. She was a goddess and he was a god—the goddess of cunt and the god of prick in a heavenly fuck. She screamed and gasped, on and on endlessly...

CHAPTER THIRTEEN

Adam was already high in the taxi which took them from the Dorchester to the party where he was to meet the kings of the art world. London was a glittering world of yellow lights shining on the leaves of trees in Park Lane, of commissionaires in brown and yellow, of stars high in a bright sky, of bits of blue and yellow neon and the flood of light from shopwindows; a glorious, warm and gold and silver fairyland.

They had just been locked in her suite for four hours. God, she'd made him work and now he was pleasantly exhausted. He'd had her in every position they could both think of. They'd rolled over and over on the bed in passion, over and over on the floor, spilling the bottles of champagne she'd ordered in the suite. They rubbed their naked bodies together, every separate inch of hers against every separate inch of his. He'd bent her over chairs, stood her on her head, rolled her in a ball. Had he done it? Or had she done it? He wasn't sure of anything now. They had just had an orgy. A real, wild orgy, dripping and groaning and slapping and scratching and clinging and thrusting and coming all over the place.

And then they had collapsed, lying side by side on a ruined bed, naked, just touching at the hips, in a sleep of the dead, from which they had been roused by the telephone call she'd asked to be made to let them know when it was nine o'clock.

"You're a lovely, handsome boy," she told him. And she kissed him tenderly on the tip of his hanging penis, gave his buttocks a gentle slap and said they must get ready to leave for the party.

They'd had a shower together, drunk a hair of the dog, dressed, and now they were cruising through the mystery of the metropolis with relaxed, surfeited bodies and minds.

He really began to like her. He'd certainly learned a lot from her. There was nothing the woman didn't know about sex. Once she'd sucked him off with a mouthful of hot water, without swallowing the water, a feat that he thought was near impossible and certainly one which had an excruciatingly gorgeous effect.

"I don't think his wife will be there," she said, as the taxi sped through the cool, elegant streets. "Which is a pity in a way, because she'd fall for you and influence him on your behalf. But on the other hand if you paid her any attention I'd be jealous, so perhaps it's just as well. Perhaps I'll offer him a quick go in return for your exhibition."

"How could you find the energy?" he asked with a lazy grin.

"Truth to tell I don't think I could," she said. "For the first time in my life I don't think I could. Now there's a compliment for you."

She pressed his hand.

"Don't you go wandering off with any other women, or I shan't help you at all," she warned. "I want another session in the morning when we'll be so full of wine that it'll be bursting our glands with sexuality."

Adam smiled. What a pity, he thought, that Eve couldn't know about this amazing double life of luxury he was leading. How envious she would be of the Dorchester and Park Lane and rich parties and millionaires. Perhaps once he'd won fame and riches he'd be able to buy her the role she wanted.

They reached the block of luxury flats where the party would now be well in progress. He paid the taxi with some of the money she'd given him ("It looks better if you pay") and they took the lift up to the fourth floor where a doorman was guarding the open doors which formed separate parts of the flat on each side of the landing.

"I hope the old bastard's turned up," she said softly as a servant took their coats.

They went through the entrance hall into the first of the rooms. It was dimly lit and the dark red walls gave off an air of decadent splendour.

Adam noticed the old paintings around the wall immediately. Old masterpieces, worth a fortune, which brought a whistle of admiration from his lips.

The place was thronged with guests and the drink and canapes looked like a royal wedding. The carpet was so thick it was like walking on a mattress to cross it.

The party was very well under way. In fact nobody appeared to notice their arrival; the time for formal reception had long since passed.

"Grab yourself a drink," Mrs. Goldenbaum said, "and we'll find Leon."

They pushed through the room, to an accompaniment of nods and smiles from various groups, until they reached the buffet. Adam looked in awe at the massive array of bottles and the huge variety of canapes: smoked salmon on toast, little Greek meat balls, miniature baclavas that turned out not to be baclavas at all, but to have meat in them.

"He's Greek—as you can see," Mrs. Goldenbaum said, referring to the host.

With their glasses filled with the best champagne—"Better not mix it too much," she'd warned—they moved back into the room searching for Leon Dalmain, the gallery owner.

They found him in the next room, standing alone, studying a visiting card which someone had just given him.

"Gracie, my dear—I didn't think you'd really get back from Paris, you know. Whoever wants to."

"There speaks a man who's never had permanent quarters there," Mrs. Goldenbaum said. "It's always nice to have a break, Leon. Makes the return so more tasty."

"I suppose you're right, darling. I must get myself a little place there some time. But I'll have to sell the house in Malaga to be able to afford it."

"You poor man."

Gracie Goldenbaum smiled solicitously and turned to Adam.

"I'd like you to meet a friend of mine—a very talented friend," she said, giving Adam a look which said that she regarded him as having more talents than one. Introductions were made and Mrs. Goldenbaum, after a little general conversation, launched herself on the object of the meeting to such good purpose than within half an hour Leon Dalmain, who respected her opinion, invited Adam to produce some paintings for him to see. Mrs. Goldenbaum invited him round to the Dorchester next day. With her usual optimistic gusto she'd seen to it that Adam had some of his work ready to view.

Leon Dalmain accepted with a grin. He turned to Adam.

"Well young man, when Grace Goldenbaum roots for someone so completely, I can only assume that he must have really enormous talent." He, too, placed an ambiguous emphasis on the word and smiled at Mrs. Goldenbaum.

"His talent," she assured him, "is prodigious."

They moved on through the party. Adam had a couple of short but memorable conversations with two artists of international stature. And, with the courage of drink, disagreed firmly with the opinion of an eminent art critic on the qualities of Berthe Morisot.

He and Grace Goldenbaum separated for periods, but she never left him long at any critical time, such as when his group might include an attractive woman, old and experienced enough to seduce him away.

Adam hardly noticed how often his glass was brimful of champagne. If the level dropped more than an inch somebody usually refilled it for him. On the few occasions that he managed to drink it down, another glass was always handy. The cumulative effect began to tell on him. His eyes grew heavy and his head a little dizzy.

"I have to lie down for a bit," he told her quietly as they met in a tour of the room. "I should hate to be sick all over this beautiful carpet."

"I must just wait and see Arthur Bryant," she said. "He's been promising for years to get a Chagall from Lord Edwards for me, but the noble lord hasn't been induced to part with it yet... Why don't you lie down in one of the bedrooms across the landing and I'll come and find you in half an hour."

"Yes," he agreed. "Best thing; I'll do that."

"Don't have any more drink," she said. "And don't get up to mischief. If any sex-starved old ladies come and tickle your secret weapon, just warn them I'll drop an atom bomb where it hurts most."

She led him to the door and showed him the open rooms across the landing.

"Don't worry about anything," she said. "They're quite bohemian in this establishment. You'll probably find some of the beds already occupied—just curl up at their feet."

Adam walked out onto the landing and into the rooms opposite. The first was illuminated, but rather more dimly than those from which he'd come. There were a few couples chatting quietly. It seemed the room in which business deals were furthered on the side, or perhaps a job was offered from one to another, or perhaps clandestine liaisons were worked out.

Adam hardly looked at them. He blundered through the room into the doorway of another in which there was no light except the path cut by the glow from the first. He opened a door at the end. The next room was not a bedroom. He considered curling up on the floor, but desire for greater comfort drove him on through another door which he opened and then closed after him as the trace of light, filtering through from way back, showed him that this was what he sought.

With a sigh of relief he stumbled to the bed whose vague outline he'd seen and rolled onto it, a blissful smile covering his face as he felt the soft give and the cool silk of the coverlet under him. The fact of lying down, relaxed, cleared his mind a little. It had been clouded by pure nervousness that he was going to find nowhere to be alone and in the comfortable dark.

A continuous noise filtered through to him. It was very close. He closed his eyes, opened them again and

strained to see into the darkness, gave up, thinking
What the hell does it matter? and rolled over onto his
back.

With both ears now clear, he heard the sound more
distinctly, a soft, but penetrating gasping on two levels,
one high, one low. He kept absolutely still, his flesh
creeping.

He listened to the gasping. It was somebody. It was
somebody in pain. He lay motionless, holding his breath,
wondering what he should do. And then he heard a
female murmur, a sound of quiet exclamations and then
a male obscenity. He relaxed and laughed convulsively
inside. It was a couple making love. My god, he
thought, they must be really at it not to have noticed
me come in, not to have cared.

They were very close, presumably on an adjacent bed.
He could make out the rustling of the bedclothes. He
even imagined he could hear the friction of their labour-
ing bodies. And the gasps and moans rose and fell in
the quiet room.

He began to grow quite excited. He wished he could
see them. Were they naked? Or did she simply have
her dress up over her thighs and was he simply thrusting
out through his open flies?

The girl's voice was giving little shrieks. My god, he
thought, what a shag she sounds like. He imagined
her young. The gasps sounded young and the murmur,
so passionate, of the voice sounded young. That's what
I really need, he thought, a beautiful young girl rather
than this elderly sex maniac I'm stuck with. He thought
of Eve and his heart and loins filled with longing. He
found he had an erection and his hand moved down to
his loins and fondled it.

Now he heard the girl murmuring words, words
broken and swallowed and spat with her passion, so that

he thought he would die if he didn't have a girl like that.

"Darling... deep, deep... hard... oh wonderful..."

He listened with aching, strained ears for every nuance and it suddenly seemed to him that there was something familiar about the voice, but he dismissed the idea.

He almost dozed off to the verbal accompaniment of their passion. It would fill his ears and swamp him, that pleasure and pain that came from them. And then he would come back to full consciousness with a start and stare over into the darkness, aware that he could probably reach out, lean a bit and touch their bodies.

He heard the bed creaking and groaning under their furious movement. He could hardly distinguish their groans and explosions of breath.

He heard the girl's voice say: "I'm coming... coming..." and then croon off into a weird little wail as she choked and spluttered.

Adam's body was tense, his throat parched and a furious aching desire expanded his lungs to breaking point. He considered going to find Grace Goldenbaum and dragging her in here with him to get relief from his pent-up sexuality, but he couldn't tear himself away from the fascinating eavesdropping for a minute.

He heard the girl sigh deeply and then give occasional cries as if of surprise or pain when, presumably, her partner shoved his prick a little deeper than before.

Now the man's cry was growing and he began to mutter commands to the girl to excite himself as his orgasm approached.

"Spread them wider... open... open... I'll split your belly..."

Adam heard these oaths with a flushed and haunted desire. His curiosity about them was overwhelming.

How he envied them their fury, the man the enthusiasm of the girl who was his cushion.

Adam's prick was standing up on end, bursting through his pants, or trying to. It felt hot and razor sharp inside with feeling. He felt that shortly he might come in his trousers.

He listened to the humping fury of the man, belabouring the now satisfied girl. He pictured him pushing her legs up to her shoulders to get farther in. He heard her responding squeals begin to jerk from her lips once more. He felt he wouldn't be able to bear the male climax; it would be too much torture for his own aching body.

But when it finally came, he lay quiet, his eyes wide, his limbs aching with the tension in which he'd held them.

Gasp after gasp after gasp came from the unseen lips in wave after passionate wave until it seemed to him that the man must be a reservoir of sperm. And then it finally simmered away and there was a final, luxurious gasp and then silence except for a strong panting and little post-act moans from the girl.

They lay still for a long time with only an occasional murmur and Adam, listening for anything there was to hear, finally began to grow drowsy again and almost forget they were there.

In fact he did doze off, but he became alert again with the rustling of the nearby bedclothes. He listened to a fresh murmuring and then the girl gave another voluptuous intake of breath and cried "Oh darling!"

They were at it again. That hadn't taken long. He felt again there was something familiar about the voice, but he couldn't imagine what it could possibly be.

The male voice whispered: "Who taught you to make love like that?"

The answer was a gasp and an exclamation of: "Oh, do that again; it's beautiful!"

A wild thought flashed through Adam's mind. It flushed him in a quick, nervous spasm. He lay with all his senses alert. But he couldn't take in the idea. It was ridiculous. He listened to the gulps and groans and occasional sucking noises of their lovemaking and grinned nervously to himself for having such a ridiculous idea. He wished he could relate his thought to Eve. It would fill her with mirth if he could isolate the fact that he thought he'd come across her making love with a stranger in a dark bedroom, from admission of his own activities.

His penis, which had deflated, began to elongate again. He had to find relief somehow.

The girl's voice said, broken by little gasps: "This is so wonderful—nobody's done it to me so marvellously before."

Adam froze. It *was* Eve! While his mind denied the possibility, his instincts told him there could be no doubt. That was her voice, broken and racked with the passion of being dominated and fucked by some strange man. It *couldn't* be. There were millions of voices like that. No, there weren't; there was only one and there was no doubt about it. He was having hallucinations—probably asleep. His thoughts see-sawed and leapfrogged and fell one against the other in utter confusion. There was only one way to find out. But it was just *too* ridiculous. Why, Eve was at home, learning her next role. And in any case Eve wouldn't fuck. And in any case... The arguments against what his ears had told him were overwhelming.

He relaxed uncomfortably. In any case the girl had spoken like a whore. He relaxed a little more. Impossible!

Their sobs and heart-rending, genital-rending, animal noises, had continued unabated, unconcerned for the drama they had awakened in the unknown listener's mind.

"Yes, yes," the man's voice grunted, "stick your finger up me..."

"Let me put my legs over your shoulders," the girl groaned.

Adam turned cold. He rolled off the bed, shaking, and fumbled around the walls. His head throbbed. He couldn't find one—and all the time their intertwining sounds of sex went on. He reached frantically around the floor, found a wire and followed it with his hands.

It led to a lamp on a small table. He switched it on and turned in the sudden glare to the noise of the coupling. His jaw clamped and something in his head blazed as if a glinting spear had slashed through it.

Eve's startled face turned towards him and a man's face looked over in bewilderment. She was naked, utterly naked, spreadeagled under him with her thighs pulled back at a sharp angle. Even in the split second before he moved towards them, Adam saw the way the man's rigid cock disappeared into the crack between her thighs, so that only a tiny little stretch of it was showing, wet and glistening.

Eve was too horrified to speak. But then she yelled as Adam launched himself at them.

James Harrod scrambled out of her and met Adam's drunken rush with a desperate straight right, which made his head spin but didn't stop his momentum.

The three of them sprawled on the bed in a flail of arms and legs and heaving bodies. Adam lashed out at Eve's face, but his hand only caught her juicy rump as she slithered away. Harrod caught him round the neck and they fell together, rolling over and over on the floor.

Adam kicked out and felt his shoe crash into flesh, a fist hit him on the side of the face and he lashed back, feeling a nose splay. He followed that up, rising to his feet with another blow which caught Harrod on the neck. Harrod, also rising, fell backward and his foot caught Adam in the groin.

Adam rolled over backwards. His head hit something sharp and hard and the world dissolved in a dizzying, light-streaked blackness.

CHAPTER FOURTEEN

In Adam's dream, he was visiting a brothel. He went up the stairs and entered a room where the prize prostitute awaited him on a bed. She was Eve. She had Eve's face and Eve's body, but she was a stranger to him. She didn't recognise him, only confronted him with a look which was half quizzical, half voluptuous. There was a remoteness under the invitation in her eyes. The communication was aloof, under the pretence of interest. It was like being in a big city that you felt you should know and yet you found no friends in it, no doors open to you, no friendliness, nothing with which you could feel at home.

The scene changed and now he was looking down through the window at the same Eve. She looked passionate now, as if she were lost in a green, tropical, orchid world of ecstasy that was beyond him, that he had never dreamed of in his weirdest dreams. She was a thousand years old and he was in his adolescence. She was a thousand years old and she had the body of a beautiful girl and she lay on a bed and men came to her. He tried to move but it was impossible. He was embedded in concrete. He tried to turn his eyes away, but they would not turn, to close them, but they would not close. And he watched the men come to her through mists which accentuated their strangeness. They were nobody he knew. He could not believe in them. Except when their naked bodies flowed over and settled onto Eve and they began that dance of love in which she languidly joined. He watched the langour change to a ferocity that belonged to the jungle with wild animals that roamed and spat and lashed out with inch-long claws and drew back their lips on sabre teeth.

He saw the men drift away and others come. He saw the hundred and one things that happened between them. There was nothing they didn't do to one another. And at the end of each Eve smiled and stretched out like a satisfied cat and her eyes opened and looked up at him with that strange, remote, hard, indifferent look that saw in him only some accomplice spirit.

He cried out and tried to struggle. He wanted to smash the face that smiled up at him with that disgusting mixture of innocence and craft. But he couldn't move. He couldn't move a muscle of his body except his jaws.

Without being able to see, he suddenly realised that, in fact, he had no body; there was nothing to him below the face in which all hatred was concentrated. He was a statue, nothing but a statue. He was ceasing to exist... ceasing to exist... and all the while the face below stared up at him with an awful, knowing grin.

He awoke, crying out and sweating and frightened and empty deep inside.

Mrs. Goldenbaum was sitting beside the bed in the Dorchester suite, the picture of concern. She was holding a glass of water and she had a soft sponge in her other hand.

"Easy... easy..." she said. "You're all right, my sweetheart."

He came back to normal fairly quickly, gazing around in surprise.

"What happened?" he asked, knowing that something strange had taken place. "What happened?"

"Relax, relax, my silly boy," she said gently. "Next time your champagne is going to be severely rationed so that you don't get into any silly fights with drama critics over the way Ibsen should be played."

CHAPTER FIFTEEN

It was a dark night with a high breeze which sent the clouds scudding across the moon from blackness to sudden washes of smoky white. The trees and bushes on the stretch of Common stood out like old black gallows with bodies flapping and swaying from them, lit up every few minutes by the sudden appearance of the moon and then plunged again into a darkness which reduced them to ghoulish outlines towering above the heath.

Eve glanced around her apprehensively as she crossed the waste. She had been relying on Rushton giving her a lift to within a short distance of her home, but his wife had arrived unexpectedly at the theatre after the performance and she had had to make the journey across the stretch of Common alone. She didn't know quite what she was apprehensive about—it was true of course that there were so many assaults on girls and young women and even elderly women by rape-rob-and-run sex maniacs. But there was no history of that sort of thing on this Common. After all, the area was a good-class one where that sort of thing didn't happen. Everyone was too well balanced. She tittered to herself at the thought. Nonetheless... and she sobered up... there was always a first time, and there was something very eerie about this particular night.

She forced herself to think about pleasant things to take her mind off her surroundings and she pictured the coming Sunday when she was going to visit Lord and Lady Duncan at their country home. She went over in her mind the way to get there. Harrod had given her full details. He had another engagement.

She thought of Harrod and that took her mind back to the shattering scene in which Adam had discovered them at the party. To think of it now made her blood run cold. She just hadn't seen Adam since. He'd made no attempt to contact her nor she him. It was finished between them, of course; impossible after that. In any case, her mind was on the future, which glittered with a glamour in which Adam had no place. She found herself trying very hard to convince herself that this was so. But somewhere deep down inside her she felt the shadowy presence of a great aching regret. Adam. Adam. She whispered his name to herself.

She had no idea what had happened to him. She had run into another dark room to dress while they fought. There, drama within drama—and she smiled to herself at how incredible it all was—she had had to fight off the lecherous hands of some elderly man who'd said he was the Count of Mons. He'd caught her naked, she'd run right into him. And what a struggle that had been, with his leathery hand mauling all over her, until the stinging fury of her nails had finally convinced him that he'd better lay off. And then Harrod, fully dressed, had come to find her and then they'd bumped into that sinewy Jewish woman as they looked back into the bedroom and she'd shouted at them: What had they done to Adam, who was lying unconscious on the floor? Harrod had told her that calm story about a disagreement they'd had about producing Ibsen and the ensuing fight. Adam was all right, just banged his head a bit.

Then they'd left, with the woman fussing towards Adam behind them. Eve had felt torn between her desire to get away and her desire to see that Adam was really all right. There had really been nothing for it. She had gone home with Harrod and they'd made love and love again throughout the night, until in the morning they were sick of the sight of each other. No, that was an exaggeration, she told herself. But for comparative strangers they'd had rather a lot of extreme intimacy all in one lump. She'd promised to ring him after the Duncan's party. There were several books he said she ought to read, but she hadn't wanted to take them away with her that morning.

Life was getting rather complicated, she told herself. Excuses to her mother, to her aunt, to Adam, to Rushton. There was no end to it.

She gave a start. There was a movement near her. Her heart began to thump furiously and she stared into the darkness, increasing her pace. She could see nobody. It must have been a movement of the wind in the shrubbery. She quickened her pace. The quicker she was off the Common and under the lights of the lane where she lived, the better she'd be pleased.

She sensed the movement again. It was something more than the breeze. It contained a menace which was difficult to define. But she was still not sure if it was the ever-lurking menace of her own imagination.

Again it happened. There was somebody following her, moving alongside her, half screened by the bushes. Her heart leapt up into her mouth. She glanced around. The lights of the town behind her were distant, those of the built up area ahead not yet in view. She refused to run. Never let them see you're afraid. In any case, she told herself desperately, it may be someone exercising his dog.

And then a figure sprang through the bushes towards her. She opened her mouth, but was too paralysed with fright to scream. And then she saw it was Adam.

"Adam, my god!" she burst out. "What a fright you gave me."

But she was still frightened. Why had he stalked her across the waste like this? Why this spot for a confrontation—the first since the night of the party?

He came towards her without speaking. She stood her ground, the backs of her knees sweating.

"Adam," she said, "I was going to ring you."

The words sounded pathetically hollow and false, like a feeble, crooked arm raised to fend off a blow.

He stopped close to her and looked at her. His face was contorted and his eyes looked bloodshot and more ruthless than she'd seen them. He smelt of drink, but there was something terribly sober about him.

"Adam," she said. "Come home and have a coffee. I wanted to see you."

Still he didn't speak, just stood gazing at her face with a hard, snarling expression, as if he hated her to the very marrow.

"Why don't you speak?" she cried sharply. And then coaxingly: "Let's got home and have a talk. Mother will have gone to bed."

"You vile bitch!"

He spat the words so fiercely she imagined them hurtling wetly into her face. And then he stepped forward and caught her by the shoulders, holding his face within an inch or two of hers.

"How many others have fucked you?" he snarled.

"You virgin! You pure, frightened creature! What had you got against me, you filthy rotten bitch. You whore, whore, whore!"

He pulled her to him and slammed his mouth on hers. But there was such a hostile savagery in his manner even of the kiss, that she pulled away from him instinctively, frightened. He slapped her then, his face hard and vicious. The blow lashed across her face, so hard that it knocked her sideways. She was so frightened that she hardly felt it and she turned to run.

He caught her before she'd taken two steps and twisted her round. His second slap caught her higher up on the side of the head, jolting her neck.

"No Adam, please... don't be silly... we can talk..."

He hit her again so that her face stung cold with the blow. He caught her by the neck. She struggled, fighting and pleading at the same time. They fell to the ground and he sat astride her, lashing her face from side to side until she was almost insensible and hardly knew whether she was on the way to dying. He began to tear at her clothes wildly, ripping and tearing them off her. She tried to get up but he knocked her back. She struggled with him, vaguely aware she was in her underclothes and then that her stockings were round her ankles and that her brassiere straps had broken and that he had ripped her knickers away.

"Adam, Adam," she managed to sob. "Have mercy... you'll kill me."

But all the time he didn't speak. He slashed her breasts with his hands. He pulled a whippy stick from the bushes at his hands and lashed her across the belly with it so that she writhed away in pain and rolled over onto her smarting stomach. He pinioned her and whipped her buttocks, her back, her thighs, with the thin, swishing cane. And then he rolled her over and, in the midst of the pain, she found her legs forced brutally apart and his prick pushed nastily into her unready quim.

She began to cry, completely breaking down, but, firmly inserted in her, he began to fuck her savagely, intending to hurt, scraping his penis along the walls of her vagina, bending her thighs back to her shoulders, coming right out of her and then thrusting right up to the cervix in a thunderous jab so that she choked with the sudden agony and humiliation.

"Adam, no... not like this... no, no... it hurts Adam..."

But he ignored her, panting, snarling into her face, twisting her body like a rubber shape so that he could fill the increasing breadth of her hole. He seemed to go so high up in her that at the zenith of every stroke a little pain stabbed her loins as if he were breaking into some delicate inner tube.

"It's just another fuck," he snarled, breaking silence at last. "Just another shag like the scores you've had already."

"It's not true Adam... oh, Adam, stop..." she pleaded, hardly knowing what she was saying.

His hand smashed across her mouth, bruising the lips and he dug his fingers cruelly hard into her breasts. She wanted to faint, but couldn't, aware all the time that he was forcing her into a back-aching position and that his every thrust was a physical semi-sweet agony, a mental horror because of the hate that drove it. This, in the wild confusion of her thoughts, she realised, was rape. She'd always thought it couldn't hurt really, but she'd never understood the hate that made it unbearable.

He began to go wild with passion and disgust at the same time. He twisted her body, worried it like a wild bull as he fucked. She felt the wet grass and the branches and the heat of the lashes and the cold blear of her tears. His hands pinched and pummelled her and she twisted unavailingly away from them. She saw his face above her a great mask of hatred, as his cock filled her finally like a stake that was impaling her slowly to death and then his face crumpled into a snarling, mouthing mess as he shot all the venom of his pent-up loathing into her quim...

He got up and left her soon afterwards with the weary, disgusted words: "You're just a cunt and a whore —and you'll be treated like a whore. I hope you choke with it!"

And then he had gone.

Eve lay exactly where he'd left her for some minutes. Not caring if anybody came by, her legs wide apart with the raw crevice open and her lashed body naked to the passing moon. If anyone else had sprung out and begun to screw her she wouldn't have bothered to resist. This was the lowest ebb—guilt, disgust, humiliation, misery and a sense of powerlessness which sprang from her complete inability to fight him off when it had really come to the underlying law of the jungle— strongest to survive. Except that she was still alive, after all. She pulled her limbs achingly together. There was mud and moss on her nude body and marks on her breasts and her belly. She winced at a dozen pains all over her and her passage felt so bruised and shaken that it seemed it must be coming to pieces.

She sat for further minutes, gently touching the weals on her breasts. She felt no anger against Adam yet; she was still a little dazed by it all.

She reached around for her bedraggled clothing. She hung the brassiere over her shoulders and put the torn briefs in the pocket of her coat which was screwed up beside her. She pulled her laddered stockings up her legs, noticing how cold her flesh was now, and then she put on her skirt and then the jumper. She forced herself to be composed. She stood up. Her body was shaken and her limbs trembled slightly as if she'd been on a blind the night before and felt very fragile. Standing there, crumpled, painful and disheveled, she felt the loneliness of herself well up inside her. A girl raped and beaten on a heath, with nobody to defend her. It was cold and sordid.

She began to walk awkwardly towards home, wiping her face with a handkerchief and combing her hair. Under the first lights she came to she made up her face, covering the bruise on her lips and blinking against the red rims of her eyes. She brushed herself down and prepared to sneak in quietly so as not to wake her mother. By the morning she'd be all right. A good rest without thinking was what she needed. To go out like a felled ox.

And, she reminded herself, with a surge of anger against the world, tomorrow she'd make Rushton buy her some new clothes.

CHAPTER SIXTEEN

Several of Adam's pictures were lined against the wall opposite. He and Leon Dalmain stood surveying them in the latter's Hampstead flat. Dalmain was being strangely non-committal, although it was obvious he was interested. There seemed no reason why he shouldn't have given a definite answer the week before at Mrs. Goldenbaum's suite in the Morchester.

"Hmmm," he said, rubbing his nose, thoughtfully. "Of course, nobody does anything for nothing these days you know," and added, "And they never did, come to think of it."

Adam didn't answer, not knowing what he was expected to say.

"Well, let's go back and have a drink with the family," Dalmain said.

Adam didn't mind that at all. Dalmain and his wife —a charming, gentle woman of about 50—had two quite beautiful daughters of 17 and 18. These two, Emily and Catherine, were dark, long-haired beauties, giving off a strange, rather voluptuous atmosphere of the Victorian beauties of old prints—full flowing curves, a rather secretive, withdrawn manner which was oddly suggestive of passion waiting for an opportunity to burst from them like sudden perspiration.

The family seemed to hang together as a group; the girls did not get on with their own activities. They indulged in strange pastimes, like combing their mother's hair and curling at their father's feet as he sat and talked, listening and smiling at Adam. There was something not quite normal about them but they were certainly handsome and that was enough for Adam to enjoy their presence.

He and Leon Dalmain wandered back into the room where they all were now and they all stopped what they were doing to smile and concentrate their attention on the newcomers.

"I think we'll have another drink, Joanna," he said to his wife. "Not the usual, the special one."

His wife smiled.

"Yes dear."

She disappeared and came back with a decanter filled with a reddish brown liquid, which she placed on a sideboard, and then arranged glasses.

"This is a specially potent drink," Leon Dalmain said. "Goes to the head and to the genitals with equal potency."

Adam was startled by his expression, but nobody else gave a hint of recognition, so he smiled politely. He'd already had a Scotch and felt in the mood for more.

"What is it?" he asked.

"Ah, that is a family secret," Dalmain told him, putting a slight emphasis on the word "family."

"Well give me some idea," Adam insisted.

"Well," Dalmain said. "It has many of the drinks you've heard of and some you haven't." And that was all he would say.

Joanna Dalmain poured five tumblers half full and handed them round. Adam was surprised to see that both the girls were permitted to quaff this supposedly potent drink which was, according to their father, a powerful aphrodisiac.

Dalmain raised his glass.

"Here's to quick stiff pricks and cannibal cunts," he said.

Adam stared at him in amazement, turning brick-red.

The others solemnly raised their glasses with murmurs of approval and took long draughts.

Purely to hide his embarrassment, Adam buried his face in his glass, taking a long, long swig. The liquid was firewater. It seemed to turn his whole body pink as if he'd broken out in a rash. It burned his throat too, a strange-tasting mixture with a nondescript parentage. He thought perhaps Scotch was the dominating ingredient, but then it seemed it might be vodka, or perhaps some strange rough wine or cider. But there were hints of other flavours he couldn't account for at all.

The effect was very quick. He felt different within twenty seconds and by the time he'd stopped thinking about the taste, he felt strangely light-headed, as if he were likely to take off to the ceiling.

"Good, eh?" Dalmain said, eyeing him curiously.

"What *is* it?" Adam insisted, feeling the effect creeping all over him, stronger every second. He looked around at the others. They were all watching him, the daughters with their lips slightly parted and gleaming desireful smiles on their faces. The wife slowly put her hand down on her thigh, watching him, and began to rub it gently as if it itched.

"Let us call it a witches' brew," Dalmain said. "A brew for Walpurgis night."

He held the bottle towards Adam and Adam, as if it were beyond his control, held out his glass and had it refilled. Dalmain smiled approvingly. He refilled the others' glasses and they all raised them together.

"Here's to fuck," Dalmain announced.

"And to suck," Emily said.

"To fucking in the ass," Catherine declared.

"To our guest," Joanna Dalmain toasted, with a meaningful stare at Adam.

They all looked at Adam, who no longer felt embarrassed. It was hilarious, he thought: these charming Victorian daughters, this gentle mother, this eminent father. And it was oddly exhilarating, as if all inhibitions were slipping away.

"To Walpurgis brew that makes all things possible," he said.

They all laughed and the daughters gave little claps in delight.

"I can see you catch on fast," Dalmain said.

They were all high. He refilled the glasses.

"We," he announced to Adam, "are members of the British Society of Witches. We worship the devil, we love so-called vice. Sex, in particular orgy, is our favourite pastime. You may have read of our procedure in one of the national Sunday newspapers—a mass-circulation organ for the masses Its particular gimmick is to give sex and 'vice' to its public under the guise of moralistic condemnation—a sickening newspaper, with cynical, nauseating young men working on it. One of their number got on to one of our newer members—a shorthand typist from Hendon, as a matter of fact—and she spilled the beans to him as if quite unaware of the furore she might create. He managed to get himself to one of our little festivals—a branch of us, that is—nobody well known fortunately—and watched our rites, which are pagan dances in the nude, minor beatings with switches and copulation. He was, apparently, so sickened by this spectacle that he wrote a slushy-mushy article about 'evil men and women' and 'vile rituals' which I'm told increased that week's circulation by rather more than half a million. He did not of course produce this masterpiece of cant and hypocrisy before he'd joined in for long enough to taste the delights of shagging our most voluptuous member and tried to date another in his room for a week later—telling her, if you please, to bring a pessary if she had one as he couldn't stand using contraceptives. The world is made of hypocrisy, of course; morality built on subconscious envy. Seduce a virtuous woman and you'll find she changes her view about ostracising fornicators. Screw her in the anus and you'll see she ceases to regard it as a vile habit indulged in by perverts. Make her suck you off and she'll no longer regard that as a disgusting aberration of Continental whores, und so weiter, und so weiter..."

Dalmain paused for breath, while Adam listened, fascinated not only by the words, but by the significance of this spiel. He looked at the daughters, glowing and alight with desire and he began to understand what was in store for him and it filled him with an ecstasy in glorious Technicolor. The daughters wriggled a little on their buttocks as if the words had began to make them feel too sexy to keep still. Adam knocked back the rest of his brew.

"Better take it easy," Dalmain said. "It's against the rules to pass out... As I was saying, we have these rites which we indulge in at varying times all over the country. There are many branches and sometimes one will exchange all its women with those of another branch to add a little zest. Joanna here has been screwed and sodomised by several hundreds I suppose in our time as witches. My daughters, however, are novices, not virgins, not in any of their passages, but novices, you understand. There are things they still don't know, pricks that could still frighten them... Now every so often we are expected to make a convert, doesn't matter which sex. Now, to come to the point, your painting is very good. Left to its own devices it might still make you famous—or it might never find the light of day other than that which filters through your studio window. Exhibited by me, however, it might not make you famous overnight—or it might—but, in any case it wall pass your name around and will certainly ensure some good purchases on the spot. Only the best people come to exhibitions in my gallery, the best, the richest and so on. From them, the fashion in painters radiates downwards..."

He filled Adam's glass a third full and gave a drop more to each of his family. Joanna Dalmain had now pulled her knees up under her chin with her feet on her chair. Adam could see the whole of the undersides of her thighs and her hairy quim, as he was obviously intended to since she wore no knickers and simply smiled at him when she saw his eyes drop down to the spot between her buttocks. He remained gazing at it in fascination while Dalmain went on talking.

"...so I have a bargain to make with you. I'll exhibit your work, if you'll exhibit yourself and join with us in the devil's rites from now on. Become, in short, a witch."

What an offer, Adam thought. Seldom had such an unnecessary bargain been struck. He would have paid thém all he possessed to get at either of those daughters, or the mother for that matter. In fact, he could see how excited she was from the moisture on her pelvis and she was certainly no crone.

"I accept with pleasure," he said.

"Good," Dalmain said. "Right, everyone. Walpurgis night!"

They all stood up and begain to take off their clothes. Adam watched them. The mother was stripped first. She had been wearing nothing under her skirt and jumper. He pictured the "hundreds of men who'd screwed and sodomised" her as he looked at her strong, full, generous body and her smile, which was like an open cunt beckoning to him.

He tore his gaze away and looked at the daughters. They too disrobed rapidly. A quick striptease in which first one and then another part of their lovely, soft young bodies were uncovered. Finally naked, they twirled joyously in front of his gaze. Adam felt likely to have an orgasm down his trouser leg. Their youthful bodies were firmly curved with full breasts hard as large cooking apples, nicely rounded bellies like a Renoir painting and dimpled spheres of buttocks which looked soft as down. Their pubic hair was slight and silky and their little mounds jutted from between their moon-white thighs.

"Come on," Dalmain said. "This is a mixed party."

He was in the act of peeling off his underpants. Adam stared at him, too, fascinated. He had an unexpectedly bulky, muscular body covered in black hair which began at his chest and ran halfway down his thighs with his penis sticking out like a great lighthouse in a rough sea from the middle. One of his daughters, Emily, played with the tip of his prick absently while she watched Adam with a smile.

They were all looking at him, waiting for him to join them. Adam knocked back the last of the devil's potion, feeling it rage like hell-fire through his innards, and began to strip.

The air on his skin hit him like a douche of cold water. His prick was hot and moist with sweat, all his genital area was sweating profusely. He threw his clothes over a chair. Joanna, the wife, came over to him, smiling deeply. She didn't touch his prick. She poked her index finger up his ass, squirming it in to the first and then to the second knuckle joint. Adam was astonished at the extremely erotic effect this had on him. She moved her finger around in his bum and he let his mouth fall on the pointed nipples which reached out at him.

"That's enough," Dalmain shouted. "First things first. We must have order."

Mrs. Dalmain took her finger out of Adam's rectum. He contracted his ass over its tip, loath to let it escape, and then she gave his penis a gentle stroke and smiled at him as if to say they had plenty of time.

They formed in a circle and, on a sign from Dalmain, began to dance round one behind the other in a strange weaving dance that was half South American, half Indian. Moving behind Catherine, the elder of the two daughters, Adam felt his prick straining out to reach her. Her rump rotated provocatively, each buttock moving separately, hollowing into a dimple, rounding out again like a bubble. Her slim shoulders shook in a ripple which shivered down her smooth, tight-skinned back and ended at her nipped-in waist. He saw the muscles in her thighs, long and slender, protruding in long, fascinating ridges and then disappearing. His prick rode up almost against his belly, almost vertical with his desire. Beyond her he saw the younger one, Catherine, looking just that little, softer and more vulnerable. He had a profile view of her cheeky, upturned breasts and the s-shape in which her bottom stuck out behind her, waving like a little, fleshy signal to come right in. Dalmain led them, with his ramrod out like a buffer to clear the way of any obstruction, and Joanna Dalmain brought up the rear, occasionally letting her fingers wisp over Adam's buttocks or tickle very gently down his back.

Adam swayed his hips like the rest of them and undulated his buttocks. The very movement made him feel all the more sexy. His penis, with the foreskin tight back, stood out like a red-hot torch with its end burning with a strange pink light.

They all followed Dalmain, the drink in them goading them on to greater excesses of movement. Catherine began to lunge her ass backwards and downwards in sudden squatting movements and to jump flat-footed like an African warrior. Adam wanted to throw himself on her and feel that warm, beautifully-moulded density of flesh against him, but he controlled himself, maintaining the pattern which they were evidently to follow.

Without pausing in his body movements, Dalmain brought the party to a mark-time while he pulled a series of switches out of an old chest against one wall. They were like the heads of witches' broomsticks, except that instead of being made of rough twigs, they were composed of a thin, willowy, synthetic substance. Dalmain tossed them back, one each, and led off on the dance again.

Adam didn't know quite what to do with his switch until he suddenly felt a soft, many-fingered, titillating blow across his behind. It stung just a little, just enough to jerk his erection up in a quick arc. And then it came again, jerking him up once again as if he'd had a sudden injection in his cock.

He saw the same thing happening in front of him so he gave Catherine a good swish across the buttocks, delighted at the sexy way she squirmed in response. He began to lash her with the switch, across, between, over, under her buttocks, while they all weaved and swayed and squirmed their way around the room like a quintet of blind, wriggling worms.

Suddenly Dalmain gave a shout, whereupon Emily turned her back quickly to him, touched her toes, spread her legs apart, reached behind her with her hands and pulled apart her buttocks like a stage curtain, displaying a sweet little anus which stretched open like a fish's mouth as they watched and had obviously been well used. Dalmain waited until she was in position and then made a rush at her, ramming his prick straight home at the same time as he grabbed her hips to prevent her from falling over. He began to sodomise her hard and fast while she continued a strange, swaying dance from her hips, as if her torso had nothing to do with the part of her he was having.

Adam watched in an agony of discomfort and unsatisfied desire. They all watched for long enough to bring them to a state of sexual constriction even more intense than they'd felt during the dance, and then Catherine turned towards him, dropped to her knees and began to suck him with her full lips and hot, little mouth with its cool, glossy tongue. Joanna Dalmain came up behind them and guided them over to a divan. She pushed Adam down on it on his side and Catherine, who hadn't once released his throbbing rod, dropped down beside it, sucking. Joanna Dalmain then knelt over in front of his head beside the divan with her back towards him and pushed her wide-open cunt at his face. Adam took the cue and began to suck the soft, wet flesh of her vaginal lips. At the same time, Emily, still with her father bumming her like mad, moved over behind the divan and pushed two fingers up Adam's ass and began to saw away like a homosexual who'd abstained for forty days and nights.

They were a knot of wriggled, gasping bodies, a many-headed, many-legged, many armed monster with five voracious sexual organs.

Adam licked and bit the lips of Joanna Dalmain's quim, pushing his tongue up the crevice which she pushed down hard at his face. His mouth and nose and even his eyes were lost in a morass of glutinous flesh beyond which a body heaved and a mouth gasped encouragement. Catherine meanwhile sucked and pulled with moaning enjoyment at his raw, expanding cock. Behind him his ears were filled with the bellow of Dalmain's thunderous passion as he sodomised his daughter. And this sensation came vicariously to Adam through her twisting fingers, like a searching prick in his ass, enlarging his anus and giving him a little quiver of feeling in that vulnerable aperture.

He heard Dalmain come first in a great soul-rending cry and he must have barraged his prick so far up his daughter's hole that she gave a squeal of pain and pulled her fingers out of Adam's ass in a convulsive flick of her hand.

As if this were her cue, Catherine suddenly stopped sucking Adam's penis, pushed him over on his back and leapt astride him. She poised herself above his stiff tower and then, with a sharp lunge and a wild dervish howl, plunged her loins down on him so that she rode down his prick, enclosing it in the soft channel of her cunt like a dark tunnel with an express train racing through it. She let out another howl and began to dance and heave her hips about on his belly, screwing and squirming and gnashing her teeth.

Joanna Dalmain, who had been left in the cold, bent over her ass presented to Adam's profile, sprang into action and leapt astride his face to begin the grinding of her vagina in his mouth all over again.

As Catherine's tight quim rubbed up and down, up and down on Adam's weapon and he became more and more excited, so he sucked and bit more voraciously at Joanna's quim, until it seemed to have spread and enveloped him like a rubber mask and he was biting at the walls of her vagina and thrusting his tongue far up towards her soft cervix.

She grew more and more wild and whirling above him, squashing his face so that he could hardly breathe, falling away from him at times in her passion. Her breathing became a soft whistling whine of breath which rose to a level he could hardly hear. And then she sprang away from him with a rigid convulsion of her body and then squashed back, letting out a groaning exclamation as a flood of liquid seemed to cover his face, and he finished her off with a last swiping flourish of his tongue.

She slithered off him and fell in a limp heap on the floor. Catherine continued to slide up and down, tightly and sweetly and wonderfully on his prick, and now Emily leapt in to take her mother's place.

As he sucked her and she started to give fluttering little shouts, Adam felt his pulsating rod swelling up. Catherine was crying out to him: "Come, come, come!"

He tensed his limbs, pushing his hips up at her as she descended along his hard, fleshy length. He could feel the movement in his bowels, such sweet, unbearable movement. "Now, now!" Catherine yelled, her firm, young body shaking like a leaf as her own orgasm reached the point where it was about to flow over. Adam thrust up, gasping into the quim over his mouth. He felt his swollen prick tremble, hesitate, heard Catherine's shout of "Aaaaaaah!" and then he bit hard into Emily's nether lips and held on like a bulldog while he shot his load of sperm up into the sweet, youthful belly of his host's daughter.

He went on sucking as Catherine rolled off him, until he heard Emily crying out for him to stop but not wanting him to. He clutched her taut, impudent breasts and squeezed, and then he squeezed her soft, young buttocks, crushing them viciously like soft flowers he wanted to destroy. He poked a finger up her rectum and jiggled it around inside the soft, rubbery depths. Suddenly she screamed and jerked away; she rolled off the divan onto the floor beside her mother. She lay there using her legs as if she was cycling for a couple of seconds and then she shot them out straight and rigid and jack-knifed her body three times before she fell back in a state of abandon, her thighs wide apart, her eyes closed.

Adam relaxed and then he felt himself being pushed over onto his side, and where various fingers had already made the opening larger, he felt Dalmain's prick prodding in. He thought of resistance.

Dalmain whispered: "Just an interlude while you and they regain your breath ready for the next bout."

What the hell, Adam thought. It's all for the good of Art. And he pulled his legs up to make it easier and grunted with pain and excitement as Dalmain's prick went right up his bottom and began to bugger him for all it was worth.

CHAPTER SEVENTEEN

"...How tender 'tis to love the babe that milks me—
I would, while it was smiling in my face, have plucked
my nipple from his boneless gums, and dash'd the brains
out had I so sworn as you have done to do this."

Eve was no longer Eve. She was Lady Macbeth. To
herself she was Lady Macbeth and her performance was
achieving some effect on the Duncans, though that
might have been because it was late and everyone had
drunk a lot.

Sir George Duncan said: "If we should fail?" And
in the line as he said it there was all of Macbeth's anguish.

"We fail! But screw your courage to the sticking
place and we'll fail not. When Duncan is asleep..."

This had been the suggestion of the Duncans, .partly
because Lady Celia had wanted to reduce Eve to a
nonentity. But her performance was surprising them,
having the very reverse effect. They let her go on, the
two of them, while the rest of the party sat around in
appreciative silence.

"All right," Sir George said, at last. "That'll do.
You've made your point. You want to get on in the
theatre and if talent has anything to do with it you
should, my dear."

Eve smiled and somebody turned on the record-player and they all got up and began to dance. Lady Celia stared at Eve with eyes that still contained an ultimate hostility although it appeared she was trying to be friendly. She was rather drunk and her eyes burned more than ever and bored right through Eve's skull to her brain. Sir George went off to find another bottle, leaving them alone. Eve, too, was rather drunk, otherwise she would have been more reticent to read Lady Macbeth in front of such great theatre stars. In her present state and, with increasing familiarity, she no longer felt the awe of them she had at the first meeting. Everybody seemed to be the same underneath. They all wanted something from other people and if you could give it you got on with them, if you couldn't they ignored you.

She wasn't sure what her position was. She remembered something Harrod had said about them being a strange couple. She looked around the room to take her thoughts off insoluble mysteries. It was a banqueting hall. The place was a veritable mansion in its own ground to the southwest of London. The courtyard when she'd arrived on foot, having come from the station, was crammed with cars and champagne, and Scotch had been flowing inside. It seemed that these people lived on champagne and Scotch and canapes. And here, as always, they had the run of the house. People disappeared onto the terraces, into the upper rooms, into the grounds. There seemed to be a tacit understanding that anything went. The Duncan mansion was exactly the way she had always imagined a baronial castle. Wide stairway from the entrance hall leading to landing which led off at both sides to a series of rooms. The banqueting hall opened off the entrance hall to one side of the stairs and the kitchens were somewhere through other rooms at the other side. Everywhere there was oak panelling and parquet flooring with rich red carpets and hangings at strategic points and chandeliers descending in glinting cascades of glass from the ceilings. The champagne was drunk from silver goblets as a change from the usual glasses and the canapes were piled on silver salvers. There were other dishes, too, of salads with various meats and fishes. And there were cigarettes everywhere in little wooden pots.

It had been eight o'clock when Eve arrived. It was now two in the morning and, as far as she could tell, nobody at all of the forty or so guests had left—or even looked like leaving. Sir George had invited her to stay the night, adding that he would show her to her room later.

Eve came out of her reverie to find Lady Celia moving over towards her.

"Would you like to come upstairs?" she asked. "There's something I'd like to show you."

There was something in Lady Celia's manner that Eve didn't trust, some underlying urgency which belied the casual nature of her words...

"What is it?" Eve asked.

"Wait and see," Lady Celia said. "I don't suppose you've seen one before."

Eve followed her from the banqueting hall. There was something about those burning eyes that both fascinated and repelled her; the strength of the woman's personality was overwhelming.

They went out and up the broad stairs and along the interior balcony to a door at the end. Lady Celia unlocked the door, let them in and then locked it behind them. Eve watched her, half tipsily, feeling that she had walked into a trap and should make some protest, but quite unable to do so.

The room was a rose-coloured bedroom—a boudoir. It was too full of Lady Celia's things for it possibly to have anything to do with Sir George. There was a smell of incense rather than perfume and the room was in some indefinable way rather unfeminine. It was dominated by a huge fourposter bed of the really old-fashioned kind, with a curtain you could close all the way round it. There were the usual wardrobes and dressing tables and big French windows opening out onto a balcony. There were also a surprising number of mirrors all around the room, including a couple of loose ones leaning against the wall in a corner.

Lady Celia went to the windows and drew heavy, red curtains across. She turned back to Eve and studied her, every inch of her.

"You're a very lovely girl," she said.

Eve stared at her, embarrassed, not knowing what to say.

"I can help you get into a West End production," she said. "If you're willing to do something for me, that is."

"A West End production?"

"A West End production. It goes without saying that I have a great deal of influence—and you have beauty and talent. That is a formidable combination for success on the stage."

"It would be wonderful if you could help me," Eve said. She was torn between a stomach-chilling delight and a nervous apprehension caused solely by the avidity of those eyes devouring her.

Lady Celia came close to her, the blazing eyes penetrating deep at a foot's range. Eve felt quite unnerved and had to fight down a creeping desire to run to the door and batter on it for help.

The woman's hand reached out and touched Eve's cheek, while the eyes held her as if she were under hypnosis. She stood stockstill while the fingers ran down to her lips and moved gently along them and then over her chin to the long, smooth neck. She shivered.

"A very lovely girl," Lady Celia said, as if to herself. "Do you go to bed with many men?" she asked.

Eve was almost afraid to answer.

"Not *many*," she said finally.

"You're much too good for them," Lady Celia said. "Men don't appreciate anything."

Eve stayed rooted to the spot as the eyes came nearer and the fingers dropped to her breast. She felt as if she were being strangled, but quite unable to resist. Was this the way rabbits felt as the weasel approached? She caught the smell of champagne from Lady Celia's breath and felt the pressure of her dress very slightly against her own. She found she couldn't move as the face came close to hers, as if this was what she wanted. The lips, Lady Celia's lips, closed down on hers, gently at first, so that she could feel the full, sharply delinated imprint, and then more furiously. Eve felt her own lips, rigid at first, slowly relax under the pressure and then, as the tongue clove into her mouth, she gave way completely and let the body follow it up, rubbing hard against her, with loins undulating.

"My lovely girl," Lady Celia breathed. "I will help you, if you will help me."

Eve didn't answer, simply put her own tongue out against the tongue that invaded her mouth.

Lady Celia's hands caressed her breasts with a woman's knowledge, and ran down her sides and her back, while their bodies locked together. After a bit she broke away, gasping, her eyes still dominating, leaping almost from her head. She moved away to a wardrobe, opened it, rummaged behind a pile of clothes folded in a heap on its floor and produced a strange instrument, strange, but immediately recognisable. Eve looked at it in fascination. She had a very queer feeling in the pit of her stomach. The intimate touch of another woman on her had excited and revolted her in almost equal proportions, the combined effect of the two emotions leaving her bereft of any power to act.

The instrument was a solid rubber length in the shape of a male organ. Attached to it were two empty rubber testicles and the base of the imitation penis had a leather strap long enough to stretch round a pair of hips attached to it. Another strap ran from the testicles to fit between a pair of thighs and join the first strap at the back where they were buckled together.

Lady Celia brought the object out and fondled it, looking at Eve with a deep, sexy expression.

"I want to do this to you and then have you do it to me," she said.

Eve simply stared at the instrument and Lady Celia came over to her and led her towards the bed.

"Let's take off our clothes," she said.

Eve felt dazed, not really knowing what to do. Her upbringing had never accepted this sort of thing. But Lady Celia had promised to help her and also... like the man who takes his first shot of heroin, she found something horridly fascinating about it.

Lady Celia began to strip with hands that shook. She was naked in two minutes flat, standing watching Eve, her slim, firm, slightly muscular body quivering with anticipation.

Eve fumbled with a zip fastener. Her fingers trembled. Lady Celia, her naked body exuding a warmth which Eve could feel before she reached her, came over and began to undress her with gentle, expert fingers.

Eve closed her eyes. She began to tremble all over at the strange forbiddenness of the situation. The alien

fingers crept over her like spiders, undoing intimate
buttons, brushing against normally hidden areas of flesh,
slowly, relentlessly peeling her covering to the point
where all resistance would be quite hopeless.

"My beauty, my beauty," Lady Celia whispered.

She stood back and looked over Eve's nude body. Her
cheeks burned with a furious lustre and her eyes were
now like black gems. Eve stood like a statue, the air
cool on her nakedness, the points of her breasts hard, a
painful constriction in her chest and loins.

Lady Celia came close to her, rubbed her own naked
body against Eve's so that the nipples of their breasts
met and the breasts of the one crushed those of the other.
Lady Celia's thighs twined around Eve's and her muff of
pubic hair brushed warmly against that of Eve's. She
felt Eve's buttocks and pulled them apart to caress the
tight anus with her finger and then she dropped on her
knees and began to shower kisses on the thighs and then
on the triangle of raised flesh between them and then,
inching the legs apart, on the soft, moistening flesh
between the thighs. A huge shudder ran down Eve's
spine and petered out somewhere amongst her toes as
Lady Celia's unyielding lips closed on her clitoris. She
felt quite out of her depth, and yet the sexual stimulation
was enormous, with that additional chill that a real sense
of indulging in something sinful always gives.

Lady Celia pushed her back towards the bed and she
fell over backwards onto it, sinking into it as if it were
a haystack.

Lady Celia followed, pulling Eve's thighs up against
her shoulders, burying her face in Eve's quim, licking
and sucking like a maniac.

Eve was quite inarticulate with still conflicting
emotions when Lady Celia suddenly left her. Eve opened
her eyes and saw her hostess take the instrument and

disappear into an adjoining room. She heard a tap running and then Lady Celia reappeared. She was wearing the false genitals, the cock standing out long and stiff from her triangle of hair, the balls hanging down between her thighs. But now the balls, too, were bloated.

"Hot water," Lady Celia said. "Half a gallon to empty into your pretty little cunt. No man could ever do that for you."

Eve lay still, with her thighs apart, her heart beating so loudly she felt something would burst inside her, her belly heaving as if she were already being screwed to the very core.

Lady Celia flowed down onto the bed, her body half covering Eve's, her ruthless hands explored again and her lips plucked at the nipples at the breasts, at any part of the expanse of flesh which was offered her.

"My lovely, lovely darling," Lady Celia whispered and her eyes were hard and ruthless in her passion. "I'm going to screw you as no man ever has or could. I want to see you squirm and cry out in helpless passion."

The tension in Eve's body was unbearable. Still something inside her had refused to relax.

"Open your legs wide, sweetheart, I'm coming in now," Lady Celia whispered.

Mechanically, quivering like a frightened horse, Eve opened her thighs wider. Lady Celia's body came over onto hers. She felt the woman arranging her hips between the obtuse angle formed by the two thighs. She closed her eyes, held her breath and waited, knowing that this was the point of final surrender.

The rubber prick slid into her cunt and went up and up and up without quarter, drawing a long expulsion of breath from Eve's tormented lungs.

"O dear god, dear god," she cried and, for some reason, tears came into her eyes.

Lady Celia sank into her, breathing fiercely. She began to work her hips like an Amazon. Her hands oozed all over Eve like a dozen snakes, searching and entering and pulling apart and digging to allow her no part of herself that was still her own. The cock was enormously long and thick. When Lady Celia thrust in the last half inch, Eve jerked in pain. But there was no escape now, and she didn't want it anyway. Lady Celia held her in a vice-like grip, pressing down on her with all the weight of her slim, muscular body, gripping now her shoulders, now her waist, now her buttocks with fingers like whipcord.

It was like being impaled on a stake. Thrust after thrust shot up into Eve's helpless loins to explode in a spark of pain at each apex. Eve began to thresh about. Her body had gone now into the relaxed realms of complete acceptance. Her loins were a mass of consuming flame and her breasts were painful as if they, too, wanted to burst and be free.

"You beauty, beauty!" Lady Celia kept muttering. And every time she said it she gritted her teeth and gave an extra twist to the in-thrust or swooped down and bit Eve's lips until blood flowed from them.

"You're mine, mine, mine," Lady Celia murmured and her fingers gripped Eve's shoulders until they bruised, or her buttocks until she squealed for them to be released. And all the time she made rushing sallies into Eve's cunt with the prick which stood up straight and never-yielding as a ramrod, tearing straight up to the cervix and tickling it apart with every stroke.

Eve began to respond wildly to the screwing. She'd never been fucked like this before. The organ was so huge. It was like handing over one's soul. She would have done anything, promised anything for the rhythmic penetration to continue. Had it stopped she felt she would have died. In fact, that became her great fear: that Lady Celia might tire.

"Don't stop," she breathed. "Don't ever stop or I shall die." And her own hands dug into the feminine shoulders which wriggled against her, and moved down the splendid, firm, sinewy back of the leading lady of the English stage who had turned out to be the leading Liz as well.

Eve's climax was fast coming. The determined rhythm, the consistent stroke and the hugeness of the tool brought her quickly up to fever pitch.

"Come my darling creature, come!" Lady Celia urged and she quickened up the rhythm like a rowing crew raising the rate of the stroke.

"Oh, it's beautiful, beautiful," Eve shrieked. Between her thighs was one mass of sweet, wet sensitivity which grew more and more sharp in its sensitivity with every second, reaching up to a pinpoint of needle-sharp feeling, until suddenly from this pinpoint would explode and tumble an incredible weight of aching feeling.

Lady Celia's eyes filled her vision. They were slit in a ruthless joy of possession and of power.

"There and there and there," she grunted as she rammed the artificial cock deep into Eve's belly.

"I can't stand it," Eve screamed. "It's too much... too much..." Her voice died in a strangled mixture of sob and sigh and then broke out again in a high-pitched scream as her passion overflowed all bounds and swept through her loins like a jet fighter racing towards the sun and suddenly exploding in a puff of smoke against the great molten disc.

And as she came, Lady Celia squeezed the mock balls between her thighs and the hot fluid rushed through a narrow tube in the centre of the penis and spurted into Eve's vagina like a tidal wave...

A little later, Lady Cella strapped the contraption onto Eve's loins, arranged one of the spare mirrors at the head of the bed, turned sideways to it, knelt on all fours and had Eve screw her from behind for three-quarters of an hour, while—as long as she could keep her head still—she watched Eve's movement in the glass.

It was only after the last ounce of energy had been drawn out of them and they lay exhausted, their bodies lightly touching, that a piece of the ceiling opened like a trapdoor and Sir George peered through.

"Wonderful," he said. "I've lived through every second of it."

CHAPTER EIGHTEEN

The gallery was crowded with a colourful array of people. It was a large one in Bond Street—an extra large one on two floors. Dalmain had done him so proud, Adam thought, he'd had difficulty finding enough paintings to fill the exhibition space. Now they were all tastefully arranged on a white background with plenty of space for each so that the viewers could really concentrate on each separately.

Dalmain, himself, had marked up the prices—and what prices he'd decided to mark up! Adam had been horrified and then flattered and then he'd come to realise how necessary it was to price so high if you wanted to impress the majority of the people who might buy.

Dalmain had told him: "You must realise the power of publicity—and that includes self-publicity. It's one of the wonders of the modern world that you only have to paint a picture and then go and stand on your head for an hour with it outside Piccadilly underground station and people will gather, you'll be written up in the popular press, interviewed—perhaps satirically, but it doesn't matter—by at least one of the quality papers and you'll sell your painting and create the market for more so that someone has to give you an exhibition. This principle, in various ways and to varying degrees applies to almost anything: witness the beatniks, the angry young men, etcetera. That they may have talent is beside the point. Many people have talent tenfold but only get across to a small audience because they don't stand on their heads, so to speak.

"Now, about the prices of your paintings. If they're put on in my gallery *and* outrageous prices are charged, that in itself is publicity. You'll see, my dear Adam, that tomorrow some newspaper is going to draw attention to the ridiculous prices being charged for an unknown painter. Another will follow by agreeing and expressing surprise that these prices are charged for paintings exhibited in my gallery and viewed by this very select bunch of viewers. What is the idea, they will ask? And the fact that they are asking will create a mystery, a public one, which will interest more and more people until nobody can afford not to know anything about your paintings. It is a very simple matter, dear boy. All you need is a sense of humour in the very real sense. Remember that this whole aspect has nothing to do with art as far as you are concerned; it has to do with what people are prepared to pay for the notorious, the hugely publicised. You will see."

Adam listened to all this in fascination. And he watched the viewers in fascination. They were, of course, all people who could afford these inflated prices if they so chose. His paintings impressed. They were good, after all. Many people were introduced to him, but the selling ball started rolling after he'd met the nymphomaniac wife of a shipowner, an elegant cosmopolitan woman of uncertain nationality.

She held his hand rather long, said she thought he had enormous talent, but she wasn't sure whether to buy because she liked to know the sort of ideas an artist had before she decided whether or not to support him. Adam was confused by this, but encouraged by a big wink from Dalmain.

Would he care, she asked, to have dinner with her on her husband's yacht off the Isle of Wight next weekend—say Friday. Her husband would unfortunately not be there, but that would mean they could get to know each other even better. Her gorgeous, longing eyes looked right through his mind to his genitals and Adam said he would be delighted, and they made the date.

"Good," the shipowner's wife said. "Well, to show that I think your talent is very considerable, quite apart from your views, I think I'll take the five red and blue compositions with the seagulls and guitars along the end of the upper gallery."

She took a chequebook from the little crocodile skin handbag and wrote out a cheque. Adam could hardly control his breathing. It was fabulous—he was on the way to being a rich man. Several people watched this rapid transaction and the word flew round the galleries. Mrs. Goldenbaum appeared from nowhere and showed some solicitousness about Adam, wondering what exactly had taken place betwen him and the other woman. Then, not to be outdone, she ordered another five. And the ball really started rolling. Within an hour, every painting in the gallery had been sold and Dalmain was on the telephone to a number of newspapers to tell them the news.

Within another hour, Adam had been interviewed by a number of reporters—different people with different functions from the art critics.

By the time everyone had left, including Mrs. Goldenbaum, whom Adam was to meet later at the Dorchester,

Dalmain was smiling with amused triumph at how completely his words had been borne out and he and Adam toasted themselves in a special old brandy for a change.

Adam felt enormously grateful to Dalmain.

"When I see her at the weekend," he said, "I'll make her into a witch. Then you'll be able to have a go to."

CHAPTER NINETEEN

Eve studied the newspapers with increasing admiration. She was spending another weekend with Sir George and Lady Celia. Lady Celia had a bad cold coming on, which might turn out to be influenza. Even her lovemaking had been rather laboured due to her difficulty in breathing, but she'd performed with her usual gusto and Eve was rather sore in her rectum.

She sat on her bottom now in a garden chair, tensing her buttocks to ease the discomfort and learning all about Adam's success. After seeing the Daily Dandy, she'd ordered all the others available at the village shop. It was remarkable. As she read the reports it was difficult to realise that Adam had become a national figure overnight. His total sale had reaped an amazing financial return and the critics, whilst hardly reacting in the bowled-over manner of the buyers, were treating his work with considerable respect, particularly in view of his youth. There were paragraphs about him in all the gossip columns, mentions of him at fashionable parties, one or two searching interviews about his likes and dislikes, humble origins, single-mindedness. Eve could hardly take it all in. In spite of the way he'd treated her during their last meeting on the Common, she felt she wanted to telephone him and offer her congratulations. But one thing stopped her from doing this—her own lack of success. She felt it would seem that she was wanting to make up to him purely because of his triumph, and in spite of her machinations on her own behalf, she did not consider Adam a fit subject to kow-tow to.

She saw his handsome face, full and profile, in a dozen newspapers. He had got there first, but she would follow. She put down the papers on the wicker table and leaned back in the cool spring air. She would follow all right. She reflected on the past few weeks. Everyone was eating out of her hand. Rushton gave her the best roles and nonetheless allowed her to stand down from them any evening she liked as long as she gave him a couple of days' notice. He'd accepted that she now had her own contacts in London and that she was furthering her career. He had no choice if he still wanted to exercise his longing prick on her occasionally—and that he did.

Lady Celia, in the meantime, could hardly see enough of her. She was extremely possessive and sometimes so savage in lovemaking that Eve was half frightened that she might suddenly produce a knife and use it instead of the makebelieve penis. Sir George had continued to watch them through the one-way glass in the ceiling; it had been an open secret. It appeared that in the normal act he was impotent, but that he could achieve an orgasm jacking off while he watched two women screwing in that way—particularly if they were women with whom he had intimate relations in the spiritual sense.

His impotency had fascinated Eve—and presented her with a challenge. She'd got into the habit of wandering around their house dressed only in a bathrobe and this she had sometimes left open in Sir George's presence, sometimes slipped off completely when alone in a room and knowing he was likely to come in. The net result was that one evening when Lady Celia gone to pay a short visit to friends in the nearby town, he'd come across Eve displaying her pretty little ass provocatively and decided to try to overcome his affliction. He'd grabbed her and fucked her hard, bending her over the back of an easy chair. He'd worked himself up, but failed to pass that seemingly impenetrable barrier. He'd come so near, however, that it had given him hope. From then on he'd watched and waited for opportunities until, finally, with Lady Celia's absence again in the nearby town, he'd pinned Eve down on the very bed where she and his wife had earlier rampaged. He'd arranged the mirrors all around, had her suck him for half an hour and then shoved his penis first in her quim for another half hour and then in her ass for a final effort.

Eve had been so sore and aching in her vagina and her back passage that she'd been on the point, having come several times herself during his efforts, of asking him to give over, when his breath had started mounting again in a furious spiral of sound. She'd revived her flagging interest and screwed her bum hard and cooperatively back onto his fat skewer. She'd heard his breathing grow to the volume of a baby hurricane, heard him cry: "No, it's not possible, not possible!"

She'd thundered her soft behind back at his loins, then, shouting: "Yes it is, it is—you can!".

So they had seemed to battle for several minutes. Her energy and determination against his disbelief and built-in anticipation of failure. Until, all at once, he'd begun to choke as if he were really going to be sick and then he'd come so hard that she'd felt the solid heat of it fill her like a lake flooding through a dam to the dried up valley below.

Afterwards they'd lain for a long time on the bed together while he marveled at what had happened and talked to her about his long history of failure. They had decided that no hint of what had happened should by given to Lady Celia. Although she didn't mind her husband watching her own indulgence, his dallying with her girl would hardly be tolerated.

From then on the psychological barrier was smashed. Sir George was able to come every time he screwed Eve and he had come to depend upon her for his sexual-emotional neeeds to the exclusion of all else.

So while Lady Celia was working to get Eve a meaty part in a new West End production, due on in some months' time, Sir George, under Eve's direction, began to work in a completely different channel. He began to encourage his wife in all sort of subtle ways to get influenza: walking on wet grass after an all-night blind, going out into chilly air from great heat without adequate clothing. The slightest hints and suggestions—a mere indication that he thought she was being unnecessarily fussy in wanting to put on a shawl, or to dry her hair after washing it before they went for a drive.

The plan had worked. Lady Celia was in the foothills of influenza now. If it worsened, she would be unable to continue with her role in *A View from the Bridge,* which was having a long run. In that case an understudy would have to be brought in. Sir George had already seen to that. He was making it worth the understudy's while financially, plus the promise of a good part in a forthcoming production, to have her old mother in the Shetlands fall ill just about the time of his wife's affliction. He was then going to bring all pressure to bear to get Eve, who had been rehearsing the role for some time under his secret tutoring, into the part.

What was the harm? Eve had asked during his

initial doubts. Lady Celia would recover after a week or a fortnight. By then Eve would have made or failed to make a bigger impact by reason of the inevitable comparison with Lady Celia than she'd ever have made in a new play, and the normal understudy would have lost nothing tangible and gained a great deal materially.

"It's the best present you could possibly give me," she'd told Sir George, who so frequently expressed his desire to buy her a castle in thanks for the new pleasures she'd opened up for him.

Lady Celia came out into the grounds now and wandered over to Eve. It was Eve, now, who felt the more powerful; more powerful than both of them put together.

"Darling, I really feel quite sick," Lady Celia said, without bothering to sit down. "In fact, I must go to bed with some hot rum and milk and a hot water bottle. You will stay until tomorrow so that I can see you, won't you? Perhaps I'll feel better then."

Eve knew what that suggestion meant. At the moment, Lady Celia felt *hors de combat*.

"Yes dear," she said. "Of course I will. You go to bed and I'll make your rum and hot milk myself. Then I'll have a game of snap with George until bedtime."

"Sweetie," Lady Celia said. She leaned down to kiss Eve, but thought better of it and straightened.

"I don't want you to get my cold," she explained.

523

CHAPTER TWENTY

There was a moment's electric silence behind the curtain as it swung down in its peculiar progression of little jerks to cut the audience off from the stage.

Eve glanced nervously at Sir George—Eddie Carbone, rather—and he smiled at her and raised a thumb. And then the applause broke out and the curtain began to go up again.

The cast moved forward into a line across the stage and the applause came at them in great waves of sound and seemed to lift them off their feet. It was tremendous. The actors' and actresses' eyes were alight with recognition. There seemed to have been a new spirit in the play tonight after the way it had settled into a standard of high consistency over the past months. They had felt it—and they had felt the response coming from the audience, that sense of the audience being right with them on their side—not only with the applause at the intervals, but during the whole production.

Various members of the cast stepped forward for their own separate ovations. And then Sir George stepped forward and the ovation lifted to a crescendo. And then he, with a gallant gesture—contrived long before the evening—stretched back his hand to the courageous understudy who had stepped into that impossible breach.

Eve moved forward and the crescendo became a crescendo of crescendos, if such a thing were possible. Shouts of "Bravo" rang out through the building. The clapping became that strange, humming ovation which includes feet and the human voice as well as the hands.

Sir George stepped back suddenly, leaving Eve in the centre of the stage in front of the smiling cast. The action was an effective one, accentuating still more the role she had played and his view of the honour she deserved. An opinion thus given could not be ignored and the applause went on and on with the curtain going up and down until there seemed a hint almost of hopefulness in the way it flopped to the boards. The lights went up but still the applause continued and it was only the first bars of the national anthem which quelled the fervour to a reluctant but respectful silence.

The cast gathered around Eve as the anthem died and the audience began to file out of the theatre with much chattering and scraping of feet.

"You were wonderful, Eve," Sir George said quietly in a voice suitably restrained for the public nature of the occasion.

"And so say all of us," piped up the various voices.

"A party," Sir George cried. "A party to celebrate—a late supper with champagne!"

There were cheers all around and they hurried off to remove their makeup.

Eve stood on the empty stage with Sir George. There was a little fire of satisfaction inside her and an indefinable sadness that now the hurdle was past. She looked up at her companion.

"How do you think everyone'll like it?" she asked, "honestly?"

"They'll rave," he told her. "Don't give it another thought. My reputation is staked on it."

CHAPTER TWENTY-ONE

Adam lounged on a foam mattress on the deck of the handsome yacht with the newspapers spread in front of him in untidy profusion.

Celeste Manzoni, the shipowner's wife, came up from the companion hatch wearing a white bikini which covered very little of her elegant proportions. She was a superb bronze. Her skin shone like a polished shield. She looked for Adam through her dark glasses, saw him and came strolling over. Even when she walked her hips seemed to quiver with sexual desire.

Adam looked up and watched her approach. He just hoped her husband stayed away a little longer. The night of tossing and heaving on the narrow bunk in her berth, with the silent, silky sea showing through the porthole, had been unutterable bliss. Her body had been warm as the sun, her clinging quim as cool and caressing as the tepid water of the sea. She had been insatiable. If it hadn't been for the lazy day they'd spent yesterday, he would not have felt so fresh today.

She settled down beside him. The small crew had been sent ashore for the weekend and they were alone. She ran her long, slim hand down his back and smiled.

"How does it feel to be suddenly so famous and the lover of one of the richest women in the world—" she asked.

"The latter makes the former seem superfluous," Adam said.

She smiled, happily, at his flattery and ran her hand over his chest.

"For that," she said, "I'll only allow you an hour's rest instead of two."

Adam laughed and kissed her hand.

She glanced at the newspapers.

"Who is this girl they're making such a fuss of?" she asked.

"A new stage star," Adam said, casually. "Taken the world by storm."

"How wonderful to have real artistic talent," Celeste Manzoni said, "instead of being just a spectator on the sidelines like me."

"Nonsense," Adam said. "You have superb talent in the greatest art in the world."

She broke into a peal of laughter and pulled him over so that his head was cushioned between her breasts. She removed the brassiere so that his face lay against her bare breasts.

"Let me know if you see a helicopter," she said.

Adam closed his eyes, letting the sun seep into them, hot and relaxing through the eyelids. She reached round him and picked up one of the newspapers.

"Good heavens," she said. "They say she's better in the role than Lady Celia Duncan!"

"I know," Adam said. "Unbelievable isn't it?"

His mind went back to the few short months ago when he and Eve has sat in the gods looking down from a height on the play in which she was now proving so successful. A height and a distance seemingly unbridgeable. And now... what a way they had come.

"I wonder who she is," Celeste mused. "I've never heard of her before and I thought I knew everybody, those arriving as well as those arrived."

"She was in some provincial rep," Adam said. "Got to know the right people, I expect."

She looked down at him curiously.

"You sound rather cynical for one so young," she said.

"Do you think it's not true. How else would she suddenly get such a part?"

"You must be right," she agreed. "How fascinating. I think I must invite her to a party."

Adam fell silent. He hadn't seen Eve for a long time. Her image recurred in his brain every so often and when, as today, he heard mention of her, he felt a pang of nostalgia and guilt. The guilt was for the beating he'd given her. In the calm following the act, he'd begun to feel that it was really not his business to commit violence on her just because she'd allowed one or two men to have her in what he now saw was the furtherance of her career. After all, he'd done just that himself, hadn't he? What irked him always was the fact that she had consistently refused him so that eventually the only way he'd been able to make love to her was to take her by force.

"Penny for them?"

He looked along at Celeste's rounded brown limbs which stretched out at right angles to his own prostrate body. He tried to recall the details of Eve's body, but could only remember the vague salient features.

"I was wondering who else you'd have, if you had a party," he said. "I'd feel jealous if you had too many Counts and Cabinet Ministers trying to make you."

"They wouldn't stand a chance," she said, looking glowingly down at him. "Not the Prime Minister nor the Duke of Edinburgh, nor the Shah of Persia. They're old men—and they're not artists."

"Shall I paint your portrait?" Adam asked, stroking her leg.

"You might make me ugly."

"No, I would paint you with me making love to you. You would be doubly beautiful then."

"How would we pose."

"Like this," Adam said.

He twisted round and pushed her back on the mattress, coming down on top of her.

His hands caressed her bare breasts.

"But how will you paint it?" she gasped.

"From memory."

She pressed her body hard against his.

"Hurry, darling," she pleaded. "Screw me quickly. My portrait will be the most passionate that's ever been painted."

A few minutes later as he threaded into her loins like a needle running through soft cloth, Adam felt that with every thrust which brought a grimace of feeling from her he was moulding her picture like a sculptor his clay.

CHAPTER TWENTY-TWO

Far out on the horizon dark and white specks passed with smudges of smoke above them blemishing the light blue of the sky. The sea was flecked white and in the distance appeared to be glazed and calm, though closer to the boat there were small waves. It was a wonderful balmy day which might almost have been transported from the Mediterranean had it not been for the slight freshness in the air and the comparatively muted colours.

A rowing boat scudded out from the shore where, far off, thousands of people were lying on the beaches getting sun-tanned, dropping sandwich papers, playing with children, buying ice creams, riding donkeys...

"Here comes another lot," Celeste said, leaning over the boat-rail beside Adam. "I wonder if our famous actress will be aboard?"

"I wonder?" Adam was preoccupied.

The deck was already littered with people arrived for the party. The lounge below was also full of them and the chink of ice tinkled above the conversation.

"She agreed to."

Would she come, Adam wondered, if she knew he were there? Would she know he might be? Probably. The gossip hounds would provide her with plenty of sources. He thought bitterly, yet again, of those insinuating columns in which names were linked, as if innocently, but with all the suggestion in the world. His name had been linked with that of Celeste by a variety of verbal formulae used in these interfering gutter columns: "Exceptionally frequent visitor of late aboard the..." "Seen often these past weeks in the company of..." And so on. The penalty of being famous; what you ate became famous too, and how many times you said good morning between breakfast and lunch, and whom you had a cup of coffee with, and naturally whom you were sleeping with. The implications had been so clear that Grace Goldenbaum had written to Adam from Paris asking him what he thought he was up to and Celeste's husband had cabled from a business conference in New York. Things had been smoothed over, of course. One defence to that sort of intrusion is that many of the famous come to learn that the suggestions amount to absolutely nothing except unutterable tastelessness and inhumanity on the part of those who make them. Except that, naturally, sometimes the insinuations are one hundred per cent correct. The best thing, as always, was to carry on as before, never allowing the limelight to force you into separation or hiding, with its implication of guilt, and this is what Celeste and Adam had done, thus continuing an affair of great sexual satisfaction to both of them.

"That looks like her pictures—the girl sitting in the stern."

Celeste sounded quite excited, and Adam, knowing exactly who and what Eve was felt a surge of astonishment that this social queen could be in the slightest moved by somebody so ordinary.

But then was Eve ordinary? In the sense that attracted Celeste, he realised, she wasn't. Apart from her talent

—and here was someone who could actually do something—the very fact that she'd gained the position she had indicated certain qualities of character which, obviously, could be fascinating to strangers. She was like him. They both had an elemental quality of toughness that these rich socialites lacked.

Yes, it was Eve all right: that champagne hair blown out in the breeze, that firm elegance with that suggestion of the oriental, so elusive one wasn't really sure it was there at all. She was wearing dark glasses and looking towards the boat. It seemed to Adam she was staring straight at him.

"I'm going down to get a drink," he said.

"Don't you want to meet our new star?"

"Later."

He went down the steps of the companion way, smiled at a beautiful girl sitting on the floor, who stretched out her long brown legs in silent invitation and smiled sleepily back.

He poured himself a large Scotch and soda and walked back to the companion way. He climbed up the steps and sat on one near the top. He heard the scraping noises of the rowing boat alongside and listened hard but could hear nothing beyond the anonymous hum of conversation which enveloped the yacht like an aura.

But then he heard Celeste's voice leading the way along towards the companion way.

"...yes, you need gallons... and I suppose you have to look after your voice very carefully, anyway."

And then Eve's voice.

"I never think about that. I just like champagne, really chilled, and with a hot day to go with it."

They came nearer and, although he wanted to move away so that he wouldn't be bothered, he found himself continuing to sit on the steps waiting for them to virtually fall over him.

"Here we are," Celeste said, appearing against the rectangle of sky above. "I'll lead the way."

She saw Adam.

"Oh there you are, Adam. I'd like you to meet Eve Patten."

She turned back, making the introductions.

Eve stopped a couple of steps above Adam and looked at him with the blank discs of glass.

"How do you do," she said.

"How do you do," Adam replied.

Eve looked lovely to him. He recalled her features with a sense of physical shock now that she stood before him. She was a little more carefully made up than she used to be, a little more elegantly dressed and there was an even greater air of confidence about her bearing. The contrast between her air of calm self-possession, awareness of her own beauty at this moment and the sweating, flailing, sobbing figure he'd raped some months ago was strangely moving to both heart and loins.

"Did you say champagne?" he asked.

"We'll all have some," Celeste said.

Adam left them chatting and went through the lounge deck to the bar, exchanging a brief, pick-me-up smile with the girl on the floor. The barman poured the champagne and gave him a tray.

"So you've been one of these absolutely single-minded people," Celeste was saying, when he got back to them. "Adam is another. I do admire you so. It's the only way to achieve anything."

"We seem to have achieved success more or less at the same moment," Eve said, looking at Adam.

He couldn't tell what her thoughts might be behind the vizor of those dark glasses.

"I still have some way to go," Adam said.

"We both have, haven't we?"

"Well, here's to the end of the road, whatever it might be," Celeste said. She looked from one to the other curiously as if something in their demeanour was not quite normal.

A white-coated steward came down the steps and approached them.

"Telephone call for you, Madame," he said.

Celeste checked a grimace, which Adam was intended to see.

"That'll be my husband," she said. She looked at him. "Perhaps you'll look after Miss Patten while I'm away. Shan't be long."

She disappeared up the companion way, leaving the two of them together, silent and embarrassed.

"Is your champagne chill enough?" Adam asked after a moment.

Eve began to giggle, suddenly in tiny, half stifled bursts. Adam stared at her for a moment and then he too began to laugh.

"Have you forgiven me?" he asked, when they managed to calm down.

"Forgiven you? Of course," Eve said. "I deserved it after the way I treated you." She paused. "And anyway, it wasn't so bad," she added, smiling behind the glasses.

"I hated you," he said. "I could still get pangs thinking about all that I didn't know."

"You don't still hate me?"

"Too much to think about."

She laughed.

"She's very beautiful, isn't she," she said.

535

"Who—Celeste? Yes, I suppose she is."

"Are the stories true?"

"What stories?"

She chucked her tongue.

"Don't worry, Adam," she said, "I wouldn't tell a soul."

"Nor would I," he said.

She laughed.

"How's the painting?" she asked.

"Pretty good. I've got exhibitions in Paris, Rome and New York, one after the other, through to the winter and I'm already making thousands. But I'm not working as hard as I used to."

"Wine, women and painting don't go together?"

"How about you? How do you find wine, men and acting?"

"Well, I'm working as hard as ever. The discipline's imposed from outside, of course. I've had a lot of offers for the future, including an enormous one from J. Arthur Rank."

"We'll be millionaires before we're thirty," Adam said.

"Have you missed me?" Eve asked, ignoring his statement.

"As much as you've missed me," Adam said.

"You've missed me a lot, then?"

"All right."

"Can I have another glass of champagne?" she asked. "I feel more like it than I have for months."

CHAPTER TWENTY-THREE

The water was warm, but cooling to the body after the sun's heat. The boat had receded to a miniature reproduction of itself and the water seemed deep and alien so far out in the bay.

Adam and Eve swam in leisurely towards the outer sea, a few feet apart. Their brown arms and bodies glistened in the sparkling water and could be seen palely under the surface. They had left the boat in a state of embalmment, bronzed bodies stretched out in the sun all over the place, with every cabin and berth occupied. Celeste had had to go ashore to follow out some instruction of her husband. She had left reluctantly, wanting as she had to spend the afternoon in bed with Adam. However, the necessity for some sort of discretion had swayed her not to insist on his accompanying her.

So he and Eve—she in the briefest of bikinis which revealed more than they concealed—and he in a tiny pair of trunks which were more like a g-string—had taken the opportunity to drift away from the madding crowd.

"How beautiful it is," Eve said, floating over on her stomach and gazing back at the shore line.

"There are more beautiful places," Adam said.

"No, I mean the life—all those riches, the way you're outside the rest of the world."

"Allied with our creative urges, those riches could provide the ideal existence," Adam said. "But they're not that much good to her."

"What a pity that the right combinations never fit together."

"We'll get there," Adam said.

They had been swimming towards a buoy, huge and gaunt and rather rusty, bobbing gently on the slight swell. Eve reached it and caught hold of one of the several handgrips.

Adam swam up beside her and his hand touched her shoulder as he too reached out for a grip. She turned and looked at him, her finely-chiseled features catching a golden glint from the sun.

"I wish," she said, "that our first time hadn't been in such awful, angry circumstances."

He leaned over and kissed her and they slammed together under the water, splashing gently as their bodies moved in contact. Her tongue came out and into his mouth, smooth as a little sea fish.

"It was your fault that they weren't," he said.

"I know... I know."

Her hand ran down and over his almost naked buttocks and then crossed his hip lightly to caress the large bulk of his genitals under the tiny triangle of silk.

"There were things I had to do to get where I am," she said.

The gentle touch of her hand, like a probing octupus, filled him with all the old longings for her that had never been consumated except in violence and anger. He didn't care about the past. He wanted her body.

"I know," he said. "We're the same, as I said."

He ran his free hand down her back. It was strong and supple with a hint of gooseflesh from the coolness of the water. He stroked her buttocks, wet and silky and rounded tight under the little bikini. He brought his hand up around her body and stroked the taut volume of her left breast, simultaneously feeling the large part which was naked, the smaller part which was covered by the flimsy brassiere. He kissed her again and saw the deep desire that made her limbs fight against the water towards him. She had his prick up hard now and was squeezing it between her thumb and the tips of her fingers.

"Can we do it here?" she asked, looking out over the water.

Adam surveyed the horizon: the boat in the far distance, others beyond it nearer to the crowded shore. It was so far away; they could have been in the middle of an ocean. True someone might race out in a speed-boat but that merely added spice.

"If you're not afraid," he said. "Think of the scandal if the gossip columns got to know about it."

"I can't think of that," she said. "I just want you inside me."

"I never imagined anything like this," Adam said, with a trace of irony.

"It should be like this," she said. "Strange and free like this."

Her fingers wormed inside his tight triangle of silk to touch the rigid flesh. Adam reached down, awkwardly under the water, unzipped the side, kicked the tiny garment off and hung it over one of the iron handgrips. Eve's hand immediately fastened on his organ like a clam. The gentle weight of the sea on his loins accentuated the clean, exhilarating feeling of nakedness and Adam reached down to her loins and slid the tight little bikini over the rotundity of her buttocks so that she could wriggle it down her legs, kick it off her feet, catch it and hang it with his. Adam didn't bother to take off the brassiere. He pushed it up, without undoing it so that her breasts shot out underneath like a nose through a raised visor.

He could see her lower body floating muzzily white and free below the surface, with the feet kicking gently against the water. Her body was distorted slightly by the sea and he ran his hand down over it to savour its half remembered contours.

"How can we do it?" she asked. "Hurry, I'm dying."

Adam drifted around her, holding her shoulder for support. When he was behind her, with the front of his body pressed against her bare back, he pushed her legs up with his knees so that they formed a horizontal V against the buoy as if she were sitting with her legs apart on the water. Her feet, pressed against the buoy, kept her steady as she held the handgrip with both hands.

Adam reached around her and held the handgrip, too, with each of his hands. And then he let his body float upwards between her legs so that she seemed to be sitting on his lap. The water made him buoyant, held him up against her, and he released the handgrip with his right hand and felt down between her back-sagging buttocks, inching his fingers forward until he found the lips of her vagina, washed strangely dry and cool by the sea. He held his prick and guided it up to these lips. And then as he felt the contact, he pulled her hips down with his one free hand and burst in with a flexing of his hips.

He heard her groan and his penis seemed to him to be quite apart from the cool expanse of the rest of his body which the sea cushioned and washed gently.

His feet, too, found a purchase on the buoy which began to sway ponderously and he began to jerk into her quim with an expert rippling motion of his hips alone.

The water rose and fell around them, but his prick filled her cunt completely and inside there was a soft, clinging warmth which contrasted with the coolness of the rest of their bodies and the chill of the buoy.

Eve began to sag back onto his stiff tower, countering his upthrust and, for brief periods, he found he could let go of the handhold and cling onto her body, grasping the breasts or the belly in luscious handfuls as he shagged her.

He could hear her moaning above the lapping of the waves and the drone of an airplane far above them in the cloudless sky. It was almost as if he were making love to the sea, smooth and voluptuously penetrable and moaning gently under the attack.

"Oh, Adam," she murmured. "It's so good, so wonderful."

He worked his penis higher up into her passage, like a corkscrew in the cork of a wine bottle. His organ was getting hotter and hotter in ever greater contrast to the endless coolness all round them.

He held the handgrip tight and rammed his loins up at the underside of her thighs and buttocks, bringing shrieks from her with every sharp, furious entry. The water around them was churned up a little in a distinct white foam which drifted away from them like scum and gradually disintegrated.

She wriggled her cunt around on the length of his penis, tensing her long, beautiful thighs, gasping out his name. And for seconds at a time he stopped pistoning and just left his bloated, hot, excited cock right up as far as it would go, letting her squirm around on it, bringing pinpricks and waves of shock from it as he contracted his loins.

Adam found that he could lie back in the water, holding onto her breasts, his face just clear of the surface, and let her saw up and down on him, doing all the work and crying with delight at having all the sensation in her own control.

But when he felt the steam rising inside him, bubbling to the boil inside his loins, he clawed up her back again and began to thrust furiously and savagely into her belly, producing a cry of mingled pain and pleasure from her with every brutal stroke.

When she came, the sea went mad around them as if a ship had foundered and wrecked itself and her voice spun across the surface of the bay in a weird siren's cry which broke and sobbed itself into eventual silence.

Adam continued to rub into her with mounting heat and need. His prick was the size of ten and he relied on her completely to keep him up, releasing the handgrip and clasping her belly to pull her hard back onto his staff.

The sensation in his prick grew to the unbearable pressure of a boil being squeezed to bursting point. At the last moment, he thought, this is the great painter screwing the great actress, proving the Colonel's Lady and Judy O'Grady... and then the boil burst with a shattering like the end of the world and his face crumpled and wrinkled in a thousand pressures and his breath was knocked out of him and he fucked his sperm into her quim, pumping it in and in as if from an endless well.

The water held them up and cooled them, helping them to recover with its cleansing, deathless quality.

"As good as a douche," Eve remarked, later, as she wriggled into her bikini.

They began the long swim back to the yacht with lazy, gentle strokes, like a return to a forgotten but unavoidable world.

"Now that we've made up, perhaps we could see more of each other," Eve said.

Adam reflected, his arms slowly cleaving the water like tired oars.

"I dare say," he said... and then more enthusiastically: "We could have a real ball for a weekend once every few months."

"Why so parsimonious with your time?" she asked.

Adam glanced sideways at her as they edged together through the great expanse of the bay.

"You know we can never go back together," he said, "not for a long time anyway."

"Yes," she said thoughtfully. "I do."

"Because," he continued, "we've both got to the crest of the wave by operating like hell... and you have to go on operating to stay there. You'll still have to sleep with people and so will I. There will still be parties and affairs and everything until we decide to call quits and then it won't matter anymore."

"Yes," she said. "It's true. The crest is a lonely place and you can only stay on it by being prepared to sacrifice everything to it. Have we both learned that?"

"We both have, I think," Adam said.

Ahead of them the yacht loomed near and several figures lined the rail to watch them come in. There was no privacy any more.

Adam smiled at her as they swam.

"But we must have plenty of swims in future," he said.

"Yes," she said. "That will be nice. And some day, when I get giddy from being on the crest and you get giddy, maybe we'll meet quietly in the trough—and then we'll have a long, long ball."

THE END